About th

Ste Sharp studied Evolutionary Biology at Sheffield University and is the lead singer/guitarist of indie band Atlas, so considers himself a rock-'n'-roll scientist at heart. When he's not writing fantastical adventures, Ste wrestles computers and lives in Suffolk with his wife and two sons.

Survival Machines

Ste Sharp

unbound

This edition first published in 2021

Unbound
TC Group, Level 1, Devonshire House, One Mayfair Place, London, W1J
8AJ
www.unbound.com

ISBN (eBook): 978-1-78965-128-7
ISBN (Paperback): 978-1-78965-127-0

Cover design by Mecob

Printed and bound in Great Britain by Clays Ltd, Elcograf S.p.A.

For Mum. Thank you for sharing your love of reading and for your support.

Super Patrons

Diane Adams
Lynette Allison
Martin Banham
Tracy Banham
Nick Breeze
Tom Chapman
Jamie Chipperfield
Joanne Colman-Bown
Dave Cottrell
Simon Dell
Luke Gormley (Jeez)
Abigail Gormley (Monkey)
John Greene
Mike Griffiths
Matt Holmes
Alison Hunt
Michael Hunt
Chris, Natasha & Libby Knowles
David & Chris Knowles
Rob MacAndrew
Joy May

Tim May
Olivia and Zac O'Leary
Sheryll Osbiston
Casey Pearce
Paul Riley
Cath Sharp
Harry Sharp
Oscar Sharp
Roger Sidwell
Andrew Smith
Annette Smith
Steve Smith
Daniel Spencer
Rupal Sumaria
Danny Ward
Jay Ward
Vanessa Ward
Mark Winborn
Mandy Wultsch

Chapter 1

John Greene stared at the pitch-black sky and realised how much he'd missed the stars.

Thousands of brilliant pinpricks dotted the sky in constellations he didn't recognise, a cascade of diamonds, sparkling yellow and white. He didn't get to see them often when he was home in Whitechapel but, out in the trenches, in the middle of what had been a French field, John had spent many a night staring up in wonder.

John looked around him. As soon as the sun had disappeared behind the horizon, the eclectic group of soldiers had set up camp not far from the silver gates. Peronicus-Rax had told them it got far colder out here than in the dome, and John felt bone-weary after their day of battle, yet the sights of this new world kept him and his compatriots awake. John listened to the crackling campfires burning what firewood they'd carried with them, and to his friends' conversations.

'The large ones have to be planets,' Crossley said, lying with his head resting on a bag.

'Or small moons?' someone replied.

'Look at that one,' Althorn said, pointing to a speeding star which crossed their view in seconds.

'Make a wish,' Crossley replied.

John thought about Joe and Rosie, but Delta-Six spoke, cutting his reverie short.

'That was no shooting star.'

'What are they then?' Crossley asked, without his usual tone of sarcasm.

'Satellites, most likely,' Delta-Six replied.

'Or interstellar craft,' came the deep voice of a Lutamek.

John turned as a huge silhouette moved close, glinting in the firelight. He recognised Ten-ten, the Lutamek science officer.

'We are triangulating our position using known star points,' it said to Delta-Six, who nodded. 'We were given information from the human soldier, Li, but require any further information you hold.'

'Of course,' Delta-Six replied and walked off with Ten-ten. 'I have detail on our home star and the nearest stars. Are you using pulsars to fix points of reference?'

'Still sounds crazy to me,' Crossley said and coughed twice before shaking his head. 'We could be anywhere.'

'Who knows what we have yet to discover?' Althorn added.

John returned his gaze to the sky and let the conversations flow over him again. Some of the speeding stars were moving across the heavens in a bizarre way: some zigzagged; others zipped and paused. Beyond lay a blurred swathe of tiny, distant stars, and John couldn't help but wonder about the theories he'd heard as to where this land actually was. Were they still on Earth, in some distant future perhaps? Or were they on another planet? Was it a planet in their system or somewhere much further away? And if the latter was the case, which star out there was their Sun? Their home star, with planet Earth circling it, still covered with the scars of war.

The thought would have been enough to unsettle the old John, but he'd seen a lot in the last few weeks that had hardened his thoughts. He'd witnessed enough to turn a man insane, he thought. It was a surprise none of the other soldiers here had become crazed; back in the trenches it had seemed someone went doolally every week.

Maybe it was just a matter of time?

The flashbacks were coming less often now, but echoes of John's Great War still came back to him. The war to end all wars. John huffed and remembered what Li had said about his son, Joe. He'd gone on to fight too, in Crossley's war.

But Joe was dead and there was no way back home.

John pushed the thought away and focussed on the men, women and alien soldiers surrounding him, most of whom he was proud to call his friends. Althorn looked wiser with his eyepatch and deep hood. Lavalle was with Euryleia. Samas and several Lutamek stood with Jakan-tar, the leader of the cat-like Sorean. And in the distance he could just make out the silhouettes of the equine tocka and Gal-qadan's cavalrymen.

'That reminds me,' John leaned up and said to Althorn.

'What is it?' The Celt looked over.

John pulled the straps tight across his chest, fixing his gun-arm in place, and stood up. 'I need to see how Mata is.'

'Good idea,' Crossley replied. 'Tell him to wake up soon or we'll turn him to firewood.'

John smiled and beelined for the huge tub the Lutamek had created for Mata. Back in the dome, they'd filled the barrel with precious drinking water, scooped up his dry, broken body and plunged him in. On the battlefield he'd been second to none so nobody was going to complain.

John took the last few steps tentatively, as though creeping up on a sleeping child, and peered into the still water. A soft orange light emanated from within, giving shape to what John recognised as the gnarled bulk of bark, thorn and twisted vine: all that remained of the immense plant-creature Mata had become. It was still twice the size of John though.

'Heal soon, Mata,' he said, tapping the barrel's side and wishing he knew some of the Maori's true words. 'You'll be amazed when you see this place.'

John looked out across the dark plain which sloped away from their vantage point near the dome and tried to remember what detail he'd seen before the sun had gone down. There were scores of domes, identical to theirs, way off in the distance, each emitting a faint green light. The ground between the domes was dusty, like the battle plain they had crossed, but there were no obelisks like the ones that had greeted them at every stage inside the dome.

One object held John's attention though. He hadn't seen it when they had first left the dome, but its silhouette stood tall and clear behind the many domes and seemed to be lit up from below: a tall, pointed tower.

'John.' Lavalle's voice pulled John out of his thoughts. 'John, come over.' The knight beckoned him back to the fires.

'See you in the morning.' John patted Mata's barrel and strode to where the whole army of nearly 200 soldiers were convening.

'Okay,' Delta-Six started, 'so we've pooled our data and we have found our location.'

A murmur ran round the crowd, a mix of hopeful cheers and mumbled questions.

'Where are we then?' Crossley shouted out.

Delta-Six held a hand up. 'I'll get to that... because although it's important to know *where*... we have also worked out *when* we are.'

Looking around at the human faces, which all stared at Delta-Six with a mixture of hope and worry, John had the tingling feeling they were about to have their dreams dashed.

Just as his own dreams had been destroyed when Li had told him that his son, Joe, had died in old age, in what was now distant history.

'So what year is it then?' Crossley asked.

'One step at a time,' Delta-Six said. 'Many of us come from different time periods, so I don't want the reality of our situation to come as a shock.' He paused and stared from soldier to soldier. 'Look, I'm probably the last human taken from Earth, and I'm finding it hard to accept the calculated date, so…'

Samas stepped forward and spoke. 'Li explained how much time had passed between my life and hers. The cities I lived in had turned to dust by her time. Our songs had been forgotten, and our treasured gifts to loved ones were either buried under sand or hidden in museum boxes. My time has passed. How many years is irrelevant.'

A few murmurs backed Samas up, and John saw their leader was growing into his new role.

A silence fell and the red-striped Lutamek leader, Nine-five, stepped forward and projected a laser image hovering above their heads. All eyes rose to the swirling mass of what looked to John like smoke, with drifts reaching out in curved arms, a flat, spinning mass of dust with a bulge at its centre.

'This is our galaxy,' Delta-Six said, walking around the image as he spoke. 'Immense regions of dust, gas and over 200 *billion* stars spiralling around the galactic centre, which is most likely home to a supermassive black hole.'

'Scientific studies,' Nine-five cut in, 'indicate there is a 97.8 per cent chance of the central mass and associated gravitational pull belonging to a black-hole phenomenon.'

Delta-Six raised an eyebrow as he waited for the behemoth robot to finish before continuing. 'We believe we are currently here.'

One of the tiny stars towards the centre of the swirling mass grew brighter and turned orange.

'Which is approximately 13,000 light years from the galactic centre.' Delta-Six looked around. 'The human home planet, Earth, is positioned here, 25,000 light years from the centre.'

A second star, closer to the outer edge, lit up and glowed blue.

'So the humans among us have been brought roughly halfway towards the centre of the galaxy.'

John breathed in deeply and heard similar gasps around him. Some soldiers sat down and others walked away.

They were on a different world alright. John had assumed so, but there had always been a flicker of hope that they were at least close to home.

Nine-five added, 'The Lutamek home system is located here.' A star relatively close to Earth lit up green. 'And the Sorean home world is located here.' Another star turned yellow.

John looked to Jakan-tar, standing at the front of the huddle of warriors, and felt like he saw the Sorean in its true alien form for the first time.

'They're not far apart,' Althorn said.

'Yeah, we're practically neighbours,' Delta-Six replied, 'but each star is over 200 light years apart.'

John frowned, trying to work out what that meant. He looked to Crossley, but the American looked equally confused, so he had to ask, 'So... it would take 200 years to travel from Earth to the Sorean world?'

'Yes,' Delta-Six replied, 'if you were able to travel at the speed of light, which is impossible.'

'So, say you could travel at half that speed,' Crossley looked at John as he explained, 'it would take twice as long, right?'

John nodded. That was several lifetimes.

'Four hundred years,' Euryleia said. 'But how is such a thing possible? How could we survive for that long?'

'It's irrelevant,' Nine-five said. 'What matters is how long it took to get here. To this world.'

'The distance from our home stars to here is approximately 12,000 light years,' Delta-Six said.

The whole group seemed to shrink under the weight of the number.

'So at half the speed of light – if that's even possible – it would have taken 24,000 years for us to get here.'

'That can't be right,' Lavalle said, shaking his head.

'So, let me get this right,' Crossley said with his hands on his hips. 'We're in the year 24,000?'

'No,' John said and felt his head start to spin.

When he'd seen the Roman wall in London as a boy, and read about the Roman Empire, John had struggled to accept the number of centuries which had passed between its construction and his time. After talking to Li, he'd accepted that London must have changed since his parents and Joe lived there. A few hundred years would mean some changes, obviously, but John knew there would be buildings he would recognise and the curve of the river... but after thousands of years, what would have become of the city John had grown up in?

'This is irrelevant,' Ten-ten spoke. 'We shall accurately quantify our current date by correlating current star ages against our historical records.'

'I agree,' Delta-Six replied. 'But the laws of physics can't be bent.'

'But what if there was another way to get here?' Crossley asked. 'A quicker route?'

'Like a tunnel cuts through a mountain,' Althorn added and Crossley nodded.

'There's nothing to show anything like that exists,' said Delta-Six.

John watched Jakan-tar step forward to study the galactic map.

'Many generations ago, a mechanical life form found a path to our world which was on no map,' the Sorean leader said. 'When we defeated them, information from their craft showed they came from here.' Jakan-tar pointed a furred claw at a star system four times further away from his home world than the Lutamek or human stars. 'We used their technology, and revenge missions were sent to find their home world and destroy it, but none returned.'

'So we *could* have travelled faster,' Samas said.

'Technology may exist to reach nearer to light speed, but the rules of physics are fixed,' Delta-Six replied, clearly getting flustered.

'There is some speculation on spatial anomalies,' Ten-ten said, 'which are capable of connecting distant regions of the galaxy.'

'Speculation. And, if they exist, I presume you must travel to these anomalies,' Delta-Six replied.

'Agreed,' Ten-ten replied. 'None have been located near known star systems.'

'Which means,' Delta-Six replied, 'even at light speed, with the time to accelerate and decelerate, it would still take years to travel to these anomalies and then travel here.' Delta-Six looked around the group. 'The point is we aren't going home.'

John felt his shoulders drop and tightened his gun-arm.

It took a few silent moments before Jakan-tar spoke. 'What about the other species we met in the dome? Where are they from?'

Delta-Six shrugged. 'To work out where each one comes

from, we need detailed information on the stars visible from their home world, and we don't have that.'

'The Lutamek might have it,' John said.

'We have added all relevant information from our databanks,' Nine-five replied.

'Well, what about him then,' Crossley pointed to Peronicus-Rax, who stood at the back of the crowd near Gal-qadan and his crew, 'and the giant armadillos, do you know where they come from?'

'The location of Peronicus-Rax's home world has been narrowed down to one of these five,' Nine-five replied, and five stars in the vicinity of the other highlighted stars pulsed twice. 'The brothers, Das and Pod, do not possess that level of data. But,' the Lutamek leader raised a hand to stop any further questions, 'we theorise that all species passing through our dome are from the same region.'

He paused to let the idea sink in.

'So each dome is full of species from the same part of the galaxy?' Samas asked.

'It's highly likely,' Delta-Six replied.

John turned to peer through the crowd at the vast landscape where the distant domes emitted a faint light.

'Going by what we've seen of the process at work here,' Delta-Six continued, 'there's a high level of organisation, so sectioning up the galaxy to create harvest zones would make sense.'

'Harvest zones?' Euryleia asked with a look of horror. 'You think we have been reared and brought here like some prize pig?'

More questions came and voices rose as Delta-Six tried to calm them all. John looked at Althorn and realised this must have been how he felt when he read the first obelisk. Delta-Six was trying to give some answers, but each one opened up more questions.

'We could get a better fix on our date if we used pulsars, but our Earth date is irrelevant.'

John expected Althorn or Samas to step forward and quieten the group but it was Lavalle who made the move, still wearing his night-black armour.

'Quieten down,' his deep voice cut through the voices. 'We have a great deal to understand,' he looked up at the huge shape of the dome which blocked out a quarter of the sky, 'and how we got here is just the start, but – just as when we were inside the dome – we need to fix our priorities and I say we need rest, shelter, water and food.'

'Typical quartermaster,' Crossley joked and was met with a schoolteacher glare from Lavalle.

'We intend to form a plan of action,' Nine-five replied.

'Meaning the leaders will discuss our next steps?' Lavalle asked.

John could see the knight was still smarting from being ousted from the hierarchy after the Black Sword revelation. Lavalle's last kill might have been an execution, not a battle-kill, but that didn't mean he was a bad leader.

'I will discuss potential next steps with Jakan-tar,' Nine-five said, 'and Samas.'

'And Delta-Six too, no doubt?' Crossley said. 'Who – no offence, big man – turned up at our battle in the last minute to book his passage through the gates, while Lavalle here,' he gestured, 'led his tocka to defend the ford and spearheaded the cavalry attacks.'

Lavalle looked as surprised as John by Crossley's defence.

'And me,' a gruff voice shouted from the back.

Gal-qadan rode his tall tocka through the crowd. 'I deserve my place on this army council,' he said.

'If the council grows any bigger, we may as well have an open forum,' Delta-Six said. 'We need Peronicus-Rax and the brothers to guide us as well.'

'So be it,' Nine-five said. 'The humans constitute the largest portion of the army but can have no more than four representatives. Now, we have other matters to discuss, including...'

Crossley turned to John and whispered in his ear, 'It's all a bit suspicious if you ask me.'

'What?'

'The Lutamek needed our help to get out of the dome, and now they let us have more people on the council? They didn't put up much of a fight, did they?'

'But that's what you argued for,' John said.

Crossley shrugged. 'But what else is going on here, eh?' He nodded to the carts full of large metal spheres. 'I mean, what are they? Bombs? What if the Lutamek have their own agenda?'

John didn't know how to reply. There might have been plenty to distrust in the dome – the creatures, the shape-shifters and the Brakari – but surely the alliance with the Lutamek and Sorean had become stronger after their victory? John stared out across the huge vista and realised how small they really were.

'We need each other,' John said, but Crossley wasn't listening.

Nine-five was projecting a new hologram, this time of a deep-red ball of flame.

'We didn't have long to take readings,' Delta-Six said, 'but some of Ten-ten's images back up our theory that this world is orbiting a strange type of sun.'

'How strange?' Lavalle asked.

'It's a rare star,' Delta-Six said. 'And not one noted for harbouring habitable planets.'

'A red-dwarf star,' Nine-five added.

'Is that why we had so little light in the dome?' Crossley asked.

'No,' Nine-five replied, 'the shell inhibited certain light waves.'

'And the clouds?' Lavalle asked.

Delta-Six replied. 'My guess is the clouds were camouflaging the structure of the dome.'

'But why was the sky green?' Jakan-tar asked.

'That's easy,' Crossley said with a laugh. 'With all that moisture in there it has to be algae on the glass of the dome, right?'

'Yes,' Nine-five said, 'even a constructed environment of such complexity had weaknesses. As for the star – we will observe it tomorrow and report our findings.'

'And then what?' John asked.

'Then,' Nine-five replied, 'we will prepare for a journey to the location most likely to hold the answers to our questions.'

'Where?' John asked, along with many others.

Nine-five's huge arm swung up and pointed towards the cluster of domes.

John peered between the warriors and saw the glowing needle of the tower.

Chapter 2

When morning came, the red sun warmed the worn sole of John's right boot. The rays crept up his dusty trousers, across the coat he had wrapped around his body and up to his eyes, which tightened before blinking and opening.

He sat up and rubbed the sleep out of his eyes.

'Ow… dammit!'

It wasn't the first time he had poked himself in the eye with the muzzle of his gun-arm. He rested it on his lap and rubbed his face with his good hand. It was going to take more time to get used to the changes, he thought as he uncovered his metal arm to warm it up in the sun. It always moved better when warmer.

John scanned his companions and wondered how they were getting on with their new skills, or if any new ones had appeared? Back in the dome there hadn't been any new 'mutations', as Nine-five had called them, by the time they fought the Brakari. But that didn't mean the existing changes had stopped. John could have sworn his gun was still changing, becoming more rounded, more arm-like.

A silhouette moved across his view as a Lutamek patrol walked by; guards of varying sizes and species had been on watch throughout the night, wary of what might be on the prowl in this new world outside the dome. John's eyes drifted to the almost-endless view beyond the camp, where the distant domes glittered like dew-covered eggs. The sharp, white tower was clear too in the daylight, poking up behind a cluster of domes. What was it? he wondered. It was the total opposite of the broad domes and somehow reminded him of the first obelisk on the hill in the dome.

John listened to the snuffles of the tocka and growls of the Sorean as the soldiers slowly roused from their sleep. He watched the stars fade as the orange–blue sky slowly painted out the black night. Several moving stars caught his attention, some in clusters. Were these the satellites Delta-Six had mentioned or could they really be spaceships from other worlds?

'Good morning, John Greene,' a voice spoke softly.

Althorn pulled his hood back.

'Morning, Althorn,' John replied and made a conscious effort not to stare at the Celt's eyepatch.

'A great view, isn't it?'

John raised his eyebrows as he replied. 'A lot to take in, if I'm honest. Have you explored far?'

Althorn shook his head and sat next to John. 'Not yet. I need to build my strength up and, like you,' he gestured at John's robotic leg, 'I need to adjust to my changes.'

A sound by the storage containers behind him made John turn, but he saw nothing move.

'I think the weather here will be drier than in the dome,' Althorn said.

'Well, no mud sounds good to me!' John replied, and gave Althorn a smile, remembering the earthen walls of the trenches, the rat holes and the body parts floating in puddles. 'What are we going to do for water though? And food?' His stomach growled at the thought.

'This land is barren,' Althorn said. 'There may be roots we can dig up and desert animals to catch, but little else.' He shook his head slowly. 'Not enough to feed an army.'

John searched for landmarks in the space between their vantage point and the nearest domes, but could see none. He heard the strange bubbling sound again, but ignored it. 'What I don't understand,' he said eventually, 'is where everyone else is?'

'Who?'

'The victorious soldiers. Like the ones who beat the Brakari first time round. Did they just walk off into the desert, or did whoever brought us here take them away? There aren't any clues... no obelisks or signs. Not even any rubbish.'

'Tell me about it.' Crossley joined the conversation as he sat up and brushed the dust from his hair. 'That's exactly the sort of question we should be asking Peronicus-Rax and those... armadillos. They've been out here before, right?'

'But they went back into the dome,' Althorn said.

'Yeah, about that – anyone ask them why?' Crossley asked.

John shrugged and looked over to where the gurgling sound had started up again.

'I'll have a talk with Samas,' Crossley said, 'and make sure he asks the right questions.'

John stood up and walked through the stirring soldiers to the pile of crates, following the bubbling sound, with Althorn and Crossley beside him. Althorn pointed to the right, so John lowered his gun and stepped to the left. He could hear a deep noise that sounded like a voice mixed with the popping sound. Then he saw the broad barrel with two feet sticking out, each with wiry roots on their soles.

'Mata!' John rushed forward.

'Is he stuck?' Althorn asked.

John shook his head and remembered the awesome, Brakari-shell-crushing war machine Mata had become during the battle. That mass of bark, vines and spines should have no trouble with this barrel.

John listened carefully and whispered, 'I think he's asleep.'

'Sounds like snoring to me!' Crossley said. 'But are you man enough to wake him up?'

'Err... no, I won't give it a go.' John remembered Mata's face when he'd accidentally woke him up on their first morning in the dome.

Althorn peered into the barrel. 'There's only a finger of water left.'

'Which we don't want to waste,' Crossley said.

'I know who we need!' John said and rushed off.

Two minutes later, he returned with Two-eight-four, the Lutamek he had saved from the Brakari and who had given John metal from his body for his false leg.

'We just need to pick him out,' John said, pointing at Mata's feet.

'Maybe set a force field,' Crossley suggested. 'He's grumpy when he wakes up.'

Two-eight-four gave a nod but remained silent, as was his way, as he reached down to pluck Mata out of the barrel. His giant metal hand wrapped around the Maori's thick ankles and John stepped back as the warrior was raised out, water dripping off him. Despite the armoured bark and needle-sharp spines which covered his arms and back, Mata looked more human again. His face had returned to normal, John noticed as Mata snuffled twice and stretched, pushing an array of vines out of his branch-like elbows and twig fingertips. Then he opened his weary eyes.

'John,' he said and frowned, 'you can fly now?'

16

John smiled and turned his head round. 'No, my friend, you're upside down!'

'Oh.' A flash of embarrassment crossed Mata's face.

He sent out two thick vines from his wrists to the ground and Two-eight-four released his ankles, letting Mata deftly cartwheel to the ground, back onto his feet.

'Ah!' He stretched again and faced the rising sun. 'That feels better,' he said with a grin.

John watched Mata take in his surroundings: the distant domes; the desert; their dome.

'Tane-Mahuta!' he said and gave it a long, hard stare. Eventually, he turned to John with a broad smile. 'So we won then?'

'Yep!' John replied.

'Couldn't have done it without you, friend,' Crossley said but stayed a few feet away.

'You fought well,' Althorn added.

Mata gave a nonchalant twist of the head and started picking through the boxes next to his barrel. 'I had fun, but things got a little out of hand towards the end… I needed to go defensive.'

'But you survived,' John said, picturing Mata when they had found him: a broad, charred stump of thick bark.

'Thanks to this new…' Mata gestured at the bark across his chest and shrugged. 'Li called it an adaptation, am I right?'

'A mutation,' Two-eight-four said.

'But a mutation would be random,' Crossley said, folding his arms and facing the robot. 'What happened to us was useful – well, kinda useful – every time. That's not random.'

Mata was busy searching through the boxes, so Crossley turned to John.

'Your gun was useful, right? And your speed, Althorn?'

'Yes, but the root cause wasn't speed, was it?' Althorn looked at Two-eight-four. 'At least that was what Ten-ten told us.'

'I was not present when our species met,' Two-eight-four replied.

'No,' John said, picturing Two-eight-four when he had first seen him as a Brakari slave, 'nor was I.'

'Well,' Crossley said, 'your friend, Ten-ten? He... Ten-ten is a he, right?'

Two-eight-four bleeped and whirred for a second then said, 'We Lutamek have no gender.'

'Oh, that sucks,' Crossley replied. 'Anyway, Ten-ten told us about our adaptations. I had two... my sinuses got bigger and my vocal cords lengthened. So I can create sonic waves high enough to go through solid matter and, wait for it... *feel* the responding waves in my sinus cavity.' He looked from soldier to soldier, waiting for a reaction. 'How can that be chance? Two mutations leading to one ability!'

'They are still mutations,' Two-eight-four replied.

'And you're an expert on these changes, I'm guessing, right?' Crossley's cheeks had reddened.

'No,' Two-eight-four replied in its monotone voice, 'but I have access to the shared Lutamek info-base and know that the RNA, DNA and mitochondrial DNA within your cells have mutated on hundreds of occasions, two of which were coercive manipulations: once during your lifetime; and once during the time of an ancient ancestor.'

Crossley shook his head. 'What does that even mean?' He looked to John for answers but he just raised his eyebrows. It was all way over his head.

'You talk of new skills?' Another soldier, intrigued by the conversation, had walked over to join in. John remembered seeing him fight with Kastor but wasn't sure they'd talked. 'Yet I have no new skill,' he said.

'You are Osayimwese?' Two-eight-four asked.

The tall, dark warrior nodded.

'I have no record of you possessing any mutated genes, but I can check again if you wish?' Two-eight-four asked.

'No.' Osayimwese raised a hand. 'Thank you. I am happy without.' He glanced at John's gun-arm and gave him a sympathetic look.

'Your change might not be physical though,' John said. 'Just look at Mihran and what he could do.'

Osayimwese nodded but was clearly distracted by Mata, who had found what he was looking for and was now noisily tucking into a box of dried deer meat.

'Hey, don't eat all the rations!' Crossley shouted and took a step forward.

Mata stopped eating and glared at him with wide eyes.

Crossley stepped back. 'Okay, but, why're you eating meat anyway? You're a plant, right?'

Mata shook his head and carried on chewing.

Althorn walked over and took a strip of meat for himself.

'But what if we had lots of changes?' John asked, horrified at the thought.

'It is possible,' Two-eight-four said, 'that one genetic mutation can manifest itself in a host of different ways.'

Althorn rubbed his beard and said, 'Or one change can be used in different ways? My fast metabolism,' he gave the jerky in his hand a look, 'means I can move at incredible speed… but also means I can digest poisons quicker.'

'Good point,' Crossley said. 'Hey, Two-eight-four, have you guys had any mutations? I mean, you're mostly metal but what about your fleshy bits?'

'Yes, we have witnessed numerous new traits,' Two-eight-four replied and started to walk away, 'but evolution doesn't truly manifest itself until the offspring carry the changes to the next generation.'

'Right,' Crossley said and looked at the others, 'like that's gonna happen round here any time soon!'

Samas flexed the fingers on his shield hand as he marched with the army, noting the earthy colour where the clay cast had absorbed into his skin. Snaps and crunches as each knuckle clicked into place told of the power he now held in his fist.

He relaxed his hand, sighed and took in the men and women he now commanded as they walked in the morning sun, keeping the immense dome on their left. In a central column, Lutamek soldiers pulled the carts carrying the injured and their meagre rations, flanked by the bulk of the Sorean army bounding along on the dome side and the human soldiers stomping on the other. A low cloud of dust ebbed away behind them, flowing away from the dome.

These were good soldiers, Samas thought, who deserved a strong leader. His eyes moved from face to face, wishing Li was still here to share her knowledge and help him understand the new world he found himself in. He caught a glimpse of Nine-five walking amongst the Lutamek, and for a second he missed Mihran's presence too.

Samas thought back to his previous army, the men who'd followed him at Issus and the children who had played at the rear of the army. What had happened to them? he wondered. Had Alexander's army taken them prisoner? Had they been killed or assimilated into the new empire Li had told him about?

'Samas!' Jakan-tar shouted. 'Time to talk.'

'I'll be right there,' Samas called back and tightened his sword belt.

He'd never wanted to be one of the high-born leaders, detached and arrogant, coolly making decisions which cost other men their lives, yet here he was, an equal with the leaders of each species. The pit of his stomach tensed when he thought about it – having that level of power didn't feel right. He was good at making life-or-death decisions in the blink of an eye, but that was instinct. These meetings were different: they were long and protracted ordeals where every leader gave their thoughts and decisions were made through consensus. Samas huffed, realising he couldn't change how he felt – he would just have to approach the meeting as though he were going into battle.

'Samas.' Nine-five welcomed him as he joined the ever-increasing group of decision-makers who walked at the head of the army: Nine-five; Jakan-tar; Peronicus-Rax; the brothers, Das and Pod; and Lavalle and Gal-qadan riding a tocka on either flank.

'No need for the armour, human,' one of the huge, armadillo-like brothers said with a chuckle.

'You never know in this land,' Samas replied. 'Isn't that right, Jakan-tar?' Samas threw a small stone at the short Sorean and smiled when it triggered his green shield.

Good to see the shields working again, he thought.

'And if I did that to you,' Samas said to Nine-five, 'I expect the stone would be vaporised in less than a second?'

'Along with your arm, no doubt,' the other brother said with a smile.

Samas shook his head. 'Not this arm, my friend.' He bent down and tapped the dusty ground with his forefinger, creating an inch-wide crack.

'Enough of this,' Peronicus-Rax's deep voice made Samas flinch. 'We have wasted enough time. When do we travel to the tower?' He gestured at the distant shaft of white set in the myriad shining semicircular domes off their right flank.

'When we're ready,' Nine-five replied.

Samas felt the tension rising so asked, 'Isn't Delta-Six joining us?'

'He's with my scouts,' Nine-five said.

'Well, let's hope they find water,' Samas said and pointed a thumb at the horde behind them, 'because we'll need it.'

Jakan-tar said, 'And we'll need adequate resources if we're to travel across this desert.'

'As I explained before,' Peronicus-Rax said, 'we must search for the Ascent if we are to find out why we are here.'

Nine-five looked at Peronicus-Rax and said, 'Yet you give us little information. We Lutamek need little sustenance, so are prepared to make the journey, but we believe more information can be found here, near our dome.'

'I gave you a bio-sample,' Peronicus-Rax said.

'Yes,' Nine-five replied, 'and it was most useful. I can confirm our theory is upheld – our five species' replicating-protein synthesis methods hold high levels of similarity.'

Samas struggled to understand what the Lutamek was talking about, so he stayed silent, nodded and let one of the other leaders ask the questions.

'Also, and possibly more surprising, we found matching strings of genetic information in all five samples.'

'So we're related?' Jakan-tar asked.

'No,' Nine-five replied, 'each string of code manifests itself with differing functional purpose in each species, but we calculate each version of the string did not evolve naturally.'

'Which means?' One of the brothers asked.

'The information was added manually... possibly through viral activity,' Ten-ten said.

Peronicus-Rax didn't look surprised, Samas thought.

'Interstellar viral communities are not rare,' the large, one-eyed soldier said. 'If our home worlds are within the same portion of the galaxy, it's highly likely an ancestral virus would be found on all of our worlds.'

'Yes,' Nine-five replied, 'but the natural level of mutation in each species suggests it was added at the same time in our ancestors' past… within a few thousand years.'

Samas didn't understand.

'Which means?' Jakan-tar asked.

'The same virus could not be naturally distributed across our worlds at that same time, so it's highly likely such a simultaneous manipulation to our genetic code was carried out by a sentient mind.'

Samas had lost his patience. 'That's great,' he said, 'I'm glad we're getting closer to finding out why we're here, but we must concentrate on our current situation.'

'These questions need to be answered,' Nine-five replied.

'We can't eat answers,' Samas replied and noticed the brothers chuckle.

Nine-five didn't respond and seemed focussed on the horizon. Samas saw lights flashing on his head and wished they still had Mihran's thought-cast system.

'My scouts are in constant communication,' Nine-five eventually said. 'They comb the immediate area around the dome, as they have done throughout the night, and are close to fully circumnavigating it. So far only one location has proven fruitful.'

'What have they found?' Peronicus-Rax asked.

'They have discovered a host of discarded transportation vessels.'

'And they'll be able to take us home?' Samas asked and felt all eyes turn to him.

He regretted the question instantly when Jakan-tar said, 'The time for returning home is long past, Samas.'

Samas was on the back foot but parried and hit back. 'It was always an option,' he said, 'and nothing can be ruled out in this world.' He desperately thought of a more useful question. 'So, these vessels – do they hold rations?'

John walked with Osayimwese and Crossley, following the leaders' path around the perimeter of the immense dome. As they walked, he could see more of the distant, solitary domes which lay in the opposite direction from the tower and cluster of domes.

Now, a new view had appeared: lines in the desert which were becoming rows of rectangular shapes.

'What are they?' Osayimwese asked.

'Well they aren't domes,' Crossley replied. 'Which makes a change.'

As they neared and the shapes became clearer, John recognised them.

'Aren't they the same as that spaceship we saw land last night?' John asked and pointed at the distant dome off to their right.

He squinted and could see that the cap on top of the dome was empty now.

'Yeah, they look about the same,' Crossley said.

'And they're lined up,' Osayimwese said, 'like a sleeping army.'

John thought back to the dead, mammoth-like creatures they had camped in when they'd met Peronicus-Rax. 'We can use them as shelter,' he said.

'If you can break into them,' Crossley said. 'If they travel in space, they've got to be airtight, so it'll be damn near impossible to break into them.'

'The Lutamek will find a way,' Osayimwese said.

'Maybe.'

'Do you think they'll get one to fly?' John asked.

'Who knows,' Crossley replied. 'Anything would be better than walking across that desert.'

They remained silent as the army veered away from the dome, down a long descent to the regimented spaceships. John guessed his mates were thinking the same as him: what was the point in all of this if they couldn't get home? If they had nobody to fight, what purpose did they have other than survival?

As they neared, John thought the long, rectangular, grey shapes looked like battleships out of water. Except these blocks didn't taper towards the bottom and were covered with scores of dark squares – portholes or doors perhaps.

'They're hundreds of paces long!' Osayimwese said.

'Pretty huge,' John agreed.

'Gather round!' Lavalle shouted as they joined the rest of the army where a rude camp had been constructed near the first line of spacecraft. 'All equipment here, please.' He gestured for the carts to be parked next to one of the craft – which loomed over them at least thirty feet high.

Samas addressed the group. 'Have a drink and take a rest, we'll be here overnight, so make yourselves comfortable.'

'We are studying the starships – please do not touch them,' Nine-five said.

'And be prepared for guard duty,' Jakan-tar added.

'Over to you,' Samas said to Lavalle then shouted, 'John, Crossley – with me.'

Crossley gave John a quizzical look but they both dumped their bags and marched over.

'What is it?' John asked.

'Seeing as how inquisitive you two were when we found that castle, we found something I thought you might want to see,' Samas said and gave a smile.

John smiled back, feeling warmth for their captain. If only some of his officers had been more like him, he thought as they wound their way around the rows of identical-looking vessels. Even though each craft had been parked twenty paces apart, it felt to John like he was back in the trenches. He stared at them in awe.

'This had better be good,' Crossley whispered and started his echo-location coughing.

'The Lutamek have been busy and found something important,' Samas said as they walked.

Around the next corner, John saw Ten-ten with an orange-shouldered Lutamek he didn't recognise.

'Right then,' Samas said.

'Are you ready to enter?' Ten-ten asked and gestured at what looked like a door set in the grey wall.

'What, we're going *in* there?' John asked.

'Yes,' Samas replied to John and Ten-ten, and Crossley gave John another look.

The orange-shouldered Lutamek touched a panel to the left of the huge doors. John saw a wave of blue energy dance between the robot's huge finger and the black square, which flashed with red and green lights in response. With a low clunk and a long hiss, the door of the huge spacecraft opened.

'Confirmation,' the orange robot spoke with a creaking voice, 'this craft was assigned to sector 684, section 832, quadrant beta.'

'What does that mean?' John asked, ignoring Crossley's coughing.

'It means,' Samas said, 'that this is the ship which brought us from Earth.'

Chapter 3

The smell hit John as soon as he stepped into the gloom: a mix of tarnished metal and excrement that reminded him of the cramped belowdecks on the ship his battalion had crossed the English Channel in. He squinted and tried to get his bearings.

'The Lutamek confirmed only one ship was used for each species,' Crossley said as he led John by torchlight down a long tunnel lined with walls of white ceramic. 'And Samas said it was every soldier's right to visit our own pod.'

'I'm not sure I want to,' John replied, running his fingertips along the smooth wall.

'Listen, we spent more time stuck in here than we did in our entire life on Earth, so it's an important place to visit.'

'I guess so,' John replied. 'Are you sure it's safe?'

'Yeah, they opened it up easy enough, and Ten-ten already sent a crawler drone in and didn't find any booby traps.' Crossley laughed. 'And who's gonna give up a chance like this? I mean, explore a *real* working spaceship? Ha!'

John looked back down the long corridor at the rectangle of light where they'd entered and felt a wave of claustrophobia wash over him. 'But why us?' he asked. 'We're expendable, are we?'

'Probably…' Crossley said slowly, distracted by something up ahead.

John craned his neck and made out dozens of curved lines reflecting the light from Crossley's torch, reminding John of the domes outside.

'These must be the pods Samas talked about,' Crossley said as John followed his torchlight around. 'This place is huge!'

The corridor funnelled out to the full width of an incredibly long room housing scores of egg-shaped metal pods lining the side walls. Each pod was as high as John's chest and had to be seven foot deep, capped with a glass shell.

'I can't see the other end of the room,' John said, wishing he had his own torch.

'So this is the stasis hall,' Crossley said. 'That's what Ten-ten called it.'

John remembered the term but he'd focussed on what Ten-ten had called 'live technology' within the ship, and he now had visions of being pulled back into his pod by tentacle arms. He shivered at the thought and walked to the nearest pod.

'So we spent thousands of years asleep in one of these?' John said, not understanding how such a thing was possible.

Crossley shone his torch into the pod, lighting up a host of pipes and wires splayed out across what looked like a soft, red bed. 'I always imagined us frozen in a block of ice… hard to think we were laying here for millennia.'

John felt a cold chill creep up his back, like when he'd been strapped to Panzicosta's torture table. 'Why can't I remember this place?' he asked.

'I'm guessing we were knocked out by the flash and put straight in here,' Crossley replied.

John stared at the bed inside the pod and thought about the people and events he'd missed at home since being taken. While he'd been asleep in one of these pods, his war had carried on like a merciless death machine, and his parents would have received a letter from the army, saying he was missing and presumed dead. How long would they have waited before telling Joe? Did they wait until after the war? Did they have a funeral? Was his name engraved under Rosie's on her headstone? Did Joe put flowers on the grave every year just like he did at the Cenotaph?

John sighed. The world had moved on while he had been stuck in this machine. While it floated above Earth, Joe and Crossley's war had raged across the globe, followed by Li's war, Delta-Six's war and countless others... Lost in his thoughts, John gazed at the panels and buttons. His hand reached out...

'Don't!' Crossley shouted. 'Samas said we can't touch anything, remember?'

'Yeah, sorry,' John said, pointing at the glass panel below the button. 'But look at this.'

Crossley aimed his torch and they crouched to get a better look.

'Mihran ibn al-Hassan.' John read the name shining through the glass plate in yellow font.

'This was Mihran's pod,' Crossley said and stood up. 'They're named! Come on, let's find ours.'

'I'll take this side,' John said and squinted to read the first name: Sir William Lavalle.

'Euryleia's over here and some I've never heard of,' Crossley shouted over.

John shook his head as he read a new one. 'Never heard of him,' he said and carried on along the long line, noticing other details on the panels which lit up the front face of each pod.

'There's no pattern here,' Crossley said. 'I mean, they're not in chronological order or sorted by continent; it doesn't make sense.'

'They've all got name panels though,' John said. 'Do you think it left Earth when they filled all the pods up?'

'Maybe,' Crossley replied and shone his torch into the darkness. 'I guess we'll find out when we get to the end.'

John checked the next pod, which had belonged to Althorn, and heard a distant knocking sound and froze. 'What's that?' He crouched and aimed his gun-arm at the narrow corridor they'd come down. 'Is someone stuck in here?'

'I can see a silhouette,' Crossley said and moved forward, his gun gripped under his torch.

John could see a shape moving up from the corridor. 'Who's there?' he called out.

The torch beam lit up Samas and John relaxed.

'It's just me,' Samas said. 'The Lutamek are restoring power, so I thought I'd join you. What have you found?'

'We've just got the pods the crawler drone found.' Crossley shone his light on the pods nearest to Samas. 'And they've got nameplates.'

'We're just working our way down the rows,' John said as a low humming noise ran up the ship.

'Cover your eyes,' Samas said.

John slapped his good hand over his eyes as a brilliant white light exploded around them. Tentatively, John peeled his fingers back and let his eyes adjust.

'Well, it's less intimidating with the lights on,' Crossley said and stood, hands on hips, surveying the long room, which ended closer than John had supposed.

'Right, well, we'll need an inventory,' Samas said and handed Crossley what looked to John like a sheet of metal. 'Just hold it in front of each nameplate and it will send the names to the Lutamek.'

'Okay,' Crossley said with a wry smile and a shake of his

head. 'I'm still getting used to their technology, so God knows what it's like for you.'

John could tell Samas wanted to keep a brave face, but he glanced at John's gun-arm and his shoulders dropped.

'It's a lot to take in, if I'm honest, but we adapt, don't we?' Samas said and looked around. 'Seeing as I'm here, why don't we find our own pods and then I'll leave you to it?'

'Okay.'

John turned back to the line of pods. There were at least another eighty to check, so he carried on reading the names. He recognised most as he sidestepped along the line, remembering those they had lost in battle, like Tode and Sakarbaal, as well as those who were alive and well, waiting outside the ship. He was getting into the rhythm of it, listening to the echoing steps of his robot foot and Crossley's and Samas' footsteps, when he saw two words which sent his heart racing.

John Greene.

He'd known his pod would be here, but seeing it made his head rush. He felt his cheeks warm as he said, 'I've found mine.'

John peered inside the pod as Crossley and Samas joined him. He'd half expected to see something different in his – maybe something that would trigger a memory – but it contained the same red bed and wires as the other pods.

Crossley put his hand on John's shoulder. 'Strange feeling, hey?'

'Yeah,' John replied, 'like seeing your own gravestone.'

'Who were you next to?' Samas asked and checked the neighbouring pods. 'Isao and… oh.'

John rushed to Samas and read the panel: Samas Labashi. 'It looks like we were neighbours,' John said and recognised the look of shock and acceptance he had felt on Samas' face.

'Yes,' Samas replied softly and moved to check his other neighbour.

'Okay, I've got to find mine now!' Crossley said with a tinge of annoyance and rushed off to check the remaining pods.

John walked over to help, casting a glance over his shoulder to remember where his pod was.

'Wait!' Samas shouted and John froze.

Samas was pointing to a new pod, which looked the same as the others, except that the name panel was green instead of yellow.

He was wide-eyed as he whispered, 'Someone is still in this pod!'

Delta-Six scanned the long, grey spacecraft before him, dozens of circles and squares of varying colours flashing before his eyes as his systems analysed markings and materials. The Lutamek upgrades were kicking in, boosting his systems to scan in more detail and at twice the speed of their previous capacity. The only price he'd had to pay was giving them his remaining mini-sat and sharing any new information he gleaned.

He paced around a corner of the spaceship but didn't expect to see much – these had been automated craft, so needed no driver or viewing plate, which would only have degraded the ship's structural integrity. More red squares flashed before him, in a symmetrical pattern this time.

'Ten-ten,' he radioed across the frequency the Lutamek had selected, 'looks like the engines were more powerful than we expected.'

'Which means our calculated maximum acceleration and deceleration rates can be increased,' Ten-ten replied.

'So the journey time may have been shorter,' Delta-Six said. 'But still many years.'

A pause, then Ten-ten said, 'We've received more data from the astrophysical analysis.'

A white diamond shape appeared on the left of Delta-Six's view field and he registered it with a glance, allowing the data to upload. He sat down to concentrate on the three-dimensional map of the stars which appeared before him. He recognised star patterns as seen from their current location and focussed in on the highlighted stars. Pulsars and neutron stars. Numbers beside each point of light suggested their current age in relation to their known age as predicted from Earth, the Sorean world or Lutamek space. The projected ages were similar, which gave them a clear date, but it didn't seem possible.

'Are you *sure* these figures are correct?' Delta-Six asked Ten-ten.

'Affirmative. All data points have been rechecked multiple times.'

Delta-Six held back his initial response and flicked the star model away. 'Then we need to get everyone together.'

Euryleia stretched her arms – all four of them – and changed her position as she sat and watched the rest of the army set up camp in preparation for another night outside the dome. They still had half a day left but, being one of the first to arrive, she'd picked a prime spot next to the wall of a spacecraft and had finished building her shelter with Lavalle before the last carts of supplies had rolled in.

Now, she took in the comings and goings of the humans, the cat-like Sorean and the huge, robotic Lutamek, who she hadn't forgiven for blasting off her hand, even if it had activated her ability to regrow damaged limbs. Euryleia closed her eyes as images of another deadlier explosion came back to her. The blinding light and lasting imprint of flying silhouettes remained strong in her mind from when Ethan had self-destructed, taking the Brakari soldiers surrounding them, along with her original arms. She sighed and pushed the painful memory away. The arms had grown back quickly enough, just double this time.

She spotted Lavalle joining Nine-five, Jakan-tar and the two giant creatures Althorn had befriended. Her relationship with Lavalle had picked up from where they had left it after their quarrel, and Euryleia hadn't mentioned Lavalle's 'Black Sword' alter ego since. Although she hadn't forgiven him, she accepted him for what he had been and could tell he'd been humbled. In the end, as she knew from the moment they'd first met, they'd been well suited in the final battle against the Brakari.

The group of leaders were still talking with Lavalle, and she didn't want to wait to hear the information at second hand, so she joined them.

'Ultimately, it doesn't affect our current situation,' Lavalle was saying as Euryleia approached the small gathering next to a makeshift table covered in paper. 'We need provisions before we starve.'

'No, we must find the Ascent that this one spoke of,' the cavalry captain, Gal-qadan, replied in his harsh tones, with a nod toward Peronicus-Rax.

Euryleia looked at the one-eyed giant who stood a few paces back from the group. She felt unnerved by him but wasn't sure if it was due to his silence or the weapons strung about his body like jewellery.

'Our priority now,' the Lutamek leader, Nine-five, spoke softly, 'is to gain as much information as possible, whether it's from the spacecraft, or the dome. Then we can fully assess our situation.'

Euryleia looked back at the immense grey–green shape of the dome looming over them. How could they get information from that?

'In the meantime, we starve!' Lavalle thumped the table with his fist. 'We need water *and* food.'

Seeing Lavalle lose his temper made Euryleia cringe – she had to help him. She stepped forward.

'We're not going back into the dome,' she said. 'Whether it's for information or for provisions – we can't go back now.'

Eyes fell on her and, for a second, she felt the heat of their gaze. She returned each stare as she waited for a response.

'This discussion–' Gal-qadan started but was cut off by Lavalle.

'Should be open, with everyone,' he said, staring at the Mongol. 'No one is planning on going back into the dome.' Lavalle looked at her. 'But there is another way to get the information we need.'

Samas peered through the glass shell at the dark shape of the human inside. Wires and tubes were leading out of the body at a variety of angles, and lights blinked on a panel to one side.

'Is that a mask?' John asked when he joined him.

'Yes,' Samas replied, 'but it doesn't seem as advanced as Li's helmet.'

The visor was black, like the rest of the soldier's suit, which showed no sign of electrical activity like Delta-Six or Li's suits, but Samas knew he was hardly an expert on future technology.

'Who is it?' Crossley asked, bounding over. He crouched by the green nameplate and read it out loud. 'Steve Smith? But...' He peered into the pod and coughed a couple of times.

'What are you looking for?' John asked.

'A shield,' Crossley whispered back.

Samas held his tongue. This wasn't the kind of soldier you would expect to be armed with a shield.

Crossley stopped and peered up. 'Or was it Rogers?' He

shook his head and looked at Samas. 'So what do we do to wake him up?'

'I'll find out,' Samas said and tapped the plug in his ear, resulting in a crackling sound, as the Lutamek had explained. He just had to say the name of who he wanted to speak to and he would be in direct communication. 'Ten-ten,' he said.

'Yes, Samas.' The deep voice of the science officer sounded like it was speaking inside his head. If it hadn't been for Mihran's thought-cast system the device would have confused Samas but, if anything, this method was slower than Mihran's. Samas looked to John and Crossley to see if they could hear it too, but they didn't react.

'We have a live human in the ship. Please advise how to resuscitate them.'

'The systems showed no life signs,' Ten-ten replied and almost sounded confused. 'Our diagnostics suggest the pods are deactivated when the ship docks at the dome cap, but I cannot access the feed externally. There must be a manual override.' The Lutamek paused for a second, during which Samas guessed Ten-ten was accessing vast amounts of data from its huge brain. 'Information from the crawler drone's scans suggests the manual controls are below the identity plate.'

Samas ran his fingers across the smooth white surface of the pod where it tapered to merge with the floor. 'Nothing here.'

'Apply pressure a hand's width directly below the identity plate,' Ten-ten said.

Samas pushed, using his natural hand, felt the surface indent and, with a quiet pop, a fist-sized door opened to reveal a panel of lights and buttons.

'Got it,' Samas said and heard Crossley and John sigh.

'The deactivation process should be simple,' Ten-ten replied.

Easy for you to say, Samas thought as Crossley sidled up beside him.

'There're no markings,' Crossley said, peering in, 'but if I was a betting man, I'd say this,' he pointed to a silver handle set in a black rectangle, 'controls the temperature, and these buttons must be the release mechanisms.'

'Yes,' Samas said and nodded, knowing it was time to relinquish control. 'Please start the revival process,' he said, trying to maintain his authority. .

'I'd better see if there are any more,' John said and walked off down the aisle with his gun-arm tapping against the pods.

The communicator in Samas' ear beeped and Ten-ten said, 'We are reconvening for briefing. Nine-five requests you join us.'

'I'll be there soon, don't start without me,' Samas replied, wondering what new news they had now. What could be more important than finding new soldiers? 'The army are having another debrief but I need you two here,' he told Crossley and John.

'Right, don't worry about us,' Crossley replied. 'I'll have Steve unfrozen in double time!'

Euryleia gazed at the galactic map in awe, but tried to hide her amazement. The group's leaders stood beside one of the spacecraft while a Lutamek projected the map. Euryleia didn't understand everything but knew she was a part of this. She had been *chosen* to be part of what was happening here and it was huge!

Jakan-tar stepped forward and raised a paw to quieten the murmuring crowd. 'We have decisions to make, none of which we will make lightly... and some new information which may help you decide when it comes to a vote.'

Nine-five gestured at the spinning cloud of stars. 'We have

left our home worlds behind, so any new information may seem irrelevant, but we share it all the same.'

Euryleia shifted her weight from foot to foot and crossed one pair of arms.

'These spacecraft,' Nine-five said and pointed at the metal hulk behind the leaders, 'were designed for interstellar journeys. But even at the speeds they're capable of, they should not have reached here in the time we now know them to have taken. Still, our calculations of the current year are certain, so it is undeniable that they did.'

'What does that mean?' Osayimwese called out.

'It means our journey here was quicker than the laws of physics allow,' Delta-Six replied.

'And?' Osayimwese asked.

'And our current date is earlier than we thought possible,' Samas said.

'Pah!' A Chinese soldier shouted and flicked his hand. 'What has passed has passed.'

'But if we want to move on, we must know what we are letting go of,' Jakan-tar replied. 'Over here is the ship which brought the Sorean,' the cat-like warrior pointed to a ship, partially hidden by the crowd. 'Over there is the Brakari ship and here,' Jakan-tar nodded at a ship whose entrance was visibly open, 'is the humans' vessel.'

Euryleia saw movement in the doorway.

'There are spacecraft like this beside every visible dome,' Nine-five said.

Delta-Six said, 'Although we don't know how we cheated the speed of light – some kind of warping of space itself maybe by way of the anomalies Ten-ten mentioned, we don't know – we have enough information from our star-aging analysis to show we are approximately in the Earth year AD 3000.'

Mumbles ran around the group but for many, like Euryleia,

the number didn't mean anything. Being frozen for 1,000 or 2,000 years made no difference.

'That's four acre, nine-ways,' Jakan-tar explained to the Sorean contingent.

'As we said before,' Nine-five said, 'this date makes little difference to our current situation, which we need to focus on now. Starting with resources.'

Lavalle stepped forward and Euryleia raised her chin and gave him a smile when their eyes met.

'Our supplies are low but we have been fortunate.' Lavalle looked at the spacecraft with the open doorway. 'Ten-ten has discovered the location of nutrition and water stores within each ship.' He raised a container holding a light-brown liquid, which he swilled around. 'I am told this contains all the goodness we need to survive.' He took a sip and Euryleia noticed how his jaw clenched. 'Not the best taste, but—'

'It will give us everything we need,' Delta-Six cut in. 'Vitamins, minerals, proteins and so on.'

Jakan-tar said, 'A similar liquid has been found in our ship, and the Lutamek will extract what they need when they find their vessel.'

'And the same will happen for Peronicus-Rax and Das and Pod,' Lavalle said, 'once their ships have been located.'

'But we must leave now!' Gal-qadan shouted from the back of the crowd, seated on his tocka and surrounded by his horsemen.

'Please listen.' Nine-five stepped forward. 'We need time to locate the vessels and extract what we need, during which time we propose a mission to the dome cap.'

'As I said before,' Euryleia insisted, 'many of us refuse to go back into the dome.'

A bang from the direction of the open spaceship made half of the crowd turn, but Euryleia was focussed on Nine-five.

'We propose a small party will ascend the dome from the outside,' the Lutamek leader said.

'How?' Euryleia asked, feeling her anger rise.

They should not be jeopardising their freedom, she thought, as an orange Lutamek strolled into view and deposited one of the large metal eggs the Lutamek had carried out of the dome.

'This is–' Nine-five started but was cut off by a disturbance at the humans' spaceship.

A figure clad in black and wearing a dark helmet was stumbling away from the doorway, followed by Crossley and John Greene.

'Steve, come back!' Crossley was shouting. 'We'll explain everything.'

'Steve Smith!' John cried out. 'Please stop!'

But the new soldier was clearly panicked and ran towards the gathering without looking up.

'It's the soldier they found in stasis,' Samas said and stepped forward to greet the newcomer with his palms held out. 'Please, take your time and stay calm.'

The new soldier paused for a second, looked Samas up and down and scanned the crowd around Euryleia, tilting its head when it saw a Sorean. Its gaze moved up to the nearest Lutamek and it stepped back, turning to see Crossley and John closing in from behind.

'Please,' Samas said, 'we can explain everything…'

It was too much. The soldier let out a cry, muffled by its helmet, and sprinted away between the spacecraft, out of sight.

Samas turned to the crowd. 'We have other news – as you can tell.' He raised an eyebrow. 'A human soldier was found in stasis on our starship and,' he gestured at Crossley and John, who now stood beside him, 'thanks to these two, has been successfully restored back to life.'

'If you can call that successful,' Euryleia heard Crossley say.

John looked anxious, she noticed, as he was almost hopping from foot to foot.

'So, to add to what Nine-five said, we also need time to search every ship for survivors.'

The crowd were mumbling around Euryleia again until Delta-Six shushed them.

'This is in our vital interest,' Samas continued. 'We may find new allies and, maybe... new weapons. Who knows what new tests we will face out in the desert?'

'I agree,' Nine-five said. 'We *must* be prepared.'

John tapped Samas on the shoulder and, by the look on his face, whispered something important.

'What is it, Samas?' Euryleia asked.

Samas guided John forward and said, 'I'll let John tell you.'

'It's... well,' John stuttered, still not keen on speaking in public, Euryleia thought. 'While we were in the ship I checked the other pods and,' he looked around from person to person, avoiding eye contact, 'there are more frozen soldiers.'

Chapter 4

Gal-qadan was bored and had been since the end of the battle inside the dome. He was fed up with listening to the meetings, like the one going on now, annoyed with following orders and tired of milling around these old metal ships. The tocka seemed jaded too. They wanted to run free as much as he did, he could sense it. There was so much out there to explore and yet the leaders kept the army close to the dome like children clinging to their mother's skirt.

He looked at the leaders – he was one of them yet he had no real power. He had the tocka and those men loyal to him, but he no longer had the powerful weapon, having handed it over to Peronicus-Rax. He felt further away from taking control of the army than ever. And what an army! The Sorean he could take or leave, but some of the humans, like Mata, were worth a hundred horsemen in battle, and the Lutamek were worth a thousand each. Since leaving the dome, Gal-qadan had daydreamed of riding into battle alongside those metal behemoths and commanding where to strike with their devastating force.

The discussions had gone on long enough, Gal-qadan thought. He stroked his metal-strong skin. Strange how it felt normal yet it could repel blades and arrows. He cast a glance down at the foot soldiers around him and spotted Isao. The samurai had once held his fascination as the Lutamek did now, but Isao was no longer a ghostly power. In fact, he seemed no different to any other swordsman: fast and technically efficient but with no signs of any useful mutation. Plus, Isao avoided Gal-qadan and sent furtive glances his way, suggesting he knew more than he should, which put him high on Gal-qadan's watch list.

Nine-five and Delta-Six were still talking to the group about new missions and hadn't listened to Gal-qadan's suggestions. Their resources were limited, and the way Peronicus-Rax kept looking at the distant domes made Gal-qadan sure there was far more out there than just armies of freakish soldiers. Peronicus-Rax had openly talked about the Ascent when they had first left the dome, so why did the leaders ignore their existence? The leaders were warming to the idea of sending out a scouting party, but they needed a push.

A couple of soldiers were talking to Samas about frozen warriors held inside the metal ships, including the masked soldier who had run out in front of them. He had the right idea, Gal-qadan thought. Get away from all this nonsense and strike your own path.

Gal-qadan sighed and wished he still had Tode to talk to. Although it had been frustrating having to express himself with words, at least Tode had understood the ways of their people and hadn't infuriated him with questions or suggestions. But no, Tode was dead, along with a quarter of Gal-qadan's original army, those who had been with him when he resurrected the tocka. He stroked his tocka's neck and remembered seeing Kastor's broken body on the battlefield, still wishing he had been able to deal the fatal blow.

Movement in his peripheral vision made Gal-qadan turn

to see Peronicus-Rax prowling behind the crowd. Gal-qadan eyed the plethora of weapons swaying from the array of belts and straps which criss-crossed the huge alien's body. Among the silver blades and coal-black guns swung the lightning machine Gal-qadan had handed over, hoping his good behaviour would lead to more trade in the future, so he couldn't shake off the feeling he was still owed something.

Tapping his tocka with his heels, Gal-qadan silently left the back of the crowd to follow Peronicus-Rax through the maze of metal hulks to the far edge where the tall soldier stood, aiming a metal box at the nearest dome.

Gal-qadan gave him a minute before asking, 'Contacting your allies?'

Peronicus-Rax didn't flinch, which suggested to Gal-qadan he'd already sensed his presence.

'Allies, no,' Peronicus-Rax replied, 'but maybe if we choose.'

'The Ascent?' Gal-qadan asked, shrugging off the itch of irritability he always felt during his conversations with the big alien.

Peronicus-Rax lowered the box and stared at Gal-qadan with his one, unblinking eye, then at their surroundings. 'I met them on my first journey.'

'Are they why you returned to the dome?'

Peronicus-Rax looked away. 'In a sense, yes. But now I search to complete my task.'

'I see,' Gal-qadan replied, sucking air through his teeth.

Peronicus-Rax would be dangerous if pushed too far, Gal-qadan thought. Even with metal skin as protection.

'I will join you, if you wish to travel,' Gal-qadan said, knowing he had to get to the Ascent before the rest of the human army if he was to gain any position of power.

Peronicus-Rax nodded and walked back the way they had come. As he rode beside him, Gal-qadan knew Peronicus-Rax was his way into the Ascent; then he could claim the alliance army as his own and offer them in return for co-leadership. Finally he would have his rightful authority.

They returned to the meeting at the perfect time, it appeared.

'...with limited rations,' Delta-Six was saying, 'to scout into the desert and rendezvous with the main army at a chosen point.'

'My men will do it,' Gal-qadan said. 'The tocka will give us speed.'

'And I will join them,' Peronicus-Rax added. 'My knowledge of the terrain will be required.'

'Any other volunteers?' Nine-five said.

'How can we turn down another adventure?' Das said, volunteering himself and his brother.

Several Sorean hands were raised along with a small group of human hands.

'I will select the best riders,' Peronicus-Rax said, 'and reserve tockas to carry provisions.'

'Maybe a cart would be better,' Gal-qadan said, focussing on one of the Lutamek carts.

In the back, under brown sacks, the telltale glint of metal caught his eye, and he recalled seeing the cargo in its glory when they had left the dome. If Gal-qadan was to get the power he demanded, he would need Lutamek technology in his arsenal.

'It's not like they're going anywhere,' Crossley said with a smirk as they stood, waiting for the conference to finish.

'You didn't open their panels, did you?' Samas asked.

'No,' John replied, feeling guilty after what had happened

with Steve Smith, 'they're still in their pods. I saw the green light, so I knew someone was inside.'

'Crossley is correct,' the metallic tones of Nine-five made John turn, 'there is no harm in leaving them in stasis while we discuss our options.'

'How come nobody got into these ships before?' Crossley asked.

John felt his stomach tighten as the whole crowd turned to them.

'They have,' Ten-ten said. 'Numerous incursions have been made but the spacecraft's self-defence mechanisms have proved sufficient.'

'Until now, right?' Crossley said.

'Yes. We have disabled their defence systems.'

'So why don't we just fire them up and fly out of here?' Crossley asked.

'Lack of fuel to breach the planet's gravitational pull, and we have detected signs of an authority-based access grid defending all airspace,' Ten-ten replied.

'Right,' Crossley replied, giving his head a scratch.

'How long will it take to check every ship?' Samas asked.

'Two days,' Nine-five replied and John heard groans from the army. 'Which gives Gal-qadan's scouting party time to explore and gives us another opportunity.'

John felt the mood lighten but couldn't shake the feeling the army would be weaker divided. They needed to be strong if they were going to find who had brought them here.

'I require volunteers for the data-retrieval mission,' Delta-Six said as he stepped forward, joined by a short blue Lutamek who placed one of the hip-high metal eggs on the dusty ground.

'What kinda mission?' Crossley asked with arms folded.

'You were in the spacecraft when we discussed it before,' Delta-Six replied and looked up at the immense dome behind them. 'We intend to travel to the dome cap to gain more information.'

John followed his gaze up. Even from half a mile away, the flat building which capped the dome was out of sight.

'Well that's okay for you,' Crossley said, 'because you've got a jet pack – what about the rest of us?'

Delta-Six gestured at the Lutamek beside him who was pressing buttons on the egg, which lit up, reminding John of the Lutamek box he'd saved from Abzicrutia.

'This is where our newest member of the army comes in,' Delta-Six said.

Crossley was coughing, scanning the Lutamek, as an arm-sized section of the egg popped out and those nearest took a step back. John stared intently, trying to make sense of what was happening as another section opened up, still connected to the egg, and another. The short blue Lutamek stepped back and left the egg to its own devices. Through the gap revealed by each moving piece, John could see more flashing lights and a dense muddle of metal inside the egg.

'This is the first of our new generation,' Nine-five said, 'and the first to be born on this planet.'

'Born?' Samas said and, like many of the soldiers around John, human and Sorean, watched the moving contraption with fear and confusion as two new slabs of metal pushed out of the egg's base, raising it up on two short legs.

'But how's such a thing possible?' Olan, the Viking, asked.

'This is how we reproduce,' Nine-five replied. 'In accordance with Lutamek reproduction protocols, DNA was selected from four individuals and tailored to fit its first mission's needs,' Nine-five said.

John was wide-eyed, as the number of protrusions coming from the egg multiplied.

'Components have been donated by every Lutamek and new metals added.'

The changes were speeding up now as sections of metal twisted and folded to create appendages, and new areas of the smooth, curved egg popped out to reveal even more shapes of silver metal.

'In our naming tradition, given the date and location, I hereby name our newest soldier One-eight-seven.'

The top of the egg twisted and enlarged to reveal two eyes and, as sections raised out of its metal shell, to form a perfect, if small, Lutamek head. John instantly thought of Joe and felt his eyes water. The head swivelled and One-eight-seven's eyes fixed on John's, sending a shiver through him.

This was new life, he thought, built and born.

'As you will see,' Delta-Six said, 'One-eight-seven has a few inbuilt tricks, which will help us on our journey.'

One-eight-seven was still expanding, and John saw a matt-black box protrude from its back.

'So who will join us?' Delta-Six asked and scanned the soldiers around John. 'A chance to see what's really going on inside the dome.'

Althorn stepped forward. 'I'm always ready for a new adventure.'

'No.' Samas held up his hand. 'We need you for scouting duties.'

'We need four,' Delta-Six replied.

'One must be Sorean,' Jakan-tar said and faced the section of Sorean warriors.

Eight Sorean soldiers, adorned with different weapons and physical adaptations, stepped forward and John watched Jakan-tar, whose muzzle wrinkled while studying each soldier.

'Tar-sone,' Jakan-tar snapped, 'you are still under observation, as are you, Bray-tae.'

Two of the larger Sorean bowed their heads and stepped back into the throng of the army.

'You five know your skills are required here,' Jakan-tar waved a clawed paw to dismiss the line, leaving the smallest Sorean. 'Rar-kin, are you sure this is what you want to do?'

'Yes.'

The voice was deeper than John had anticipated for such a tiny warrior.

'Ain't his head too big for his body?' Crossley whispered and John shrugged.

'Very well,' Jakan-tar said and turned to Delta-Six, 'Rar-kin has excellent memory and mathematical skills and will be of great use on your information-retrieval mission.'

'Glad to have you on-board,' Delta-Six replied, then asked, 'how about human volunteers?'

Osayimwese was the first to step forward. 'I would like to see the dome from above,' he said, 'and discover why we are here.'

'Great,' Delta-Six replied.

John wanted to know more too: why they were here and why they were evolving strange powers. But he couldn't think of anything he could add to the mission.

Crossley nudged him. 'Hey, why don't we volunteer? It'd beat hanging round here.'

'But what about the new soldiers?' John asked. 'Someone has to rejuvenate them.'

'After the last one, I'm not sure it should be us!' Crossley said, eyebrows raised.

John felt a hand on his shoulder and turned to see Samas.

'Let the Lutamek take care of the frozen soldiers,' he said, and pushed John forward with Crossley. 'How about these two volunteers?' Samas said as he walked them forward to Delta-Six.

Delta-Six looked them up and down, and John felt his gaze

pause on his arm. 'Yes, good choice. Crossley's engineering skills may be of use,' he said and turned to Nine-five. 'We're ready when One-eight-seven is.'

'One-eight-seven is ready now,' Nine-five replied.

John studied the Lutamek. Although not as big as any of its parents, One-eight-seven had grown considerably and looked strong, with two large arms, thick legs and a set of odd protrusions from its lower back. The black box John had noticed earlier was now high up on its shoulders behind what John still considered a cute robotic head.

'I can make my own way to the cap,' Delta-Six said and his propulsion system unfolded from his back. 'But you four,' he looked at Osayimwese, Rar-kin, Crossley and John, 'will travel with One-eight-seven.'

John heard a click, followed by a hissing sound as the black box on One-eight-seven started to expand. The sides folded out to produce more sides, and expanded again to create an ever more-sided shape which increased in size to loom over One-eight-seven's head.

Crossley coughed and said, 'Oh, I see. Very neat.'

The whole army were watching in silence, like waiting for a magician's next trick.

'Expansion 50 per cent complete.' One-eight-seven spoke for the first time, its voice a tinnier replication of Nine-five's robotic tones.

As the black box expanded more, John noticed One-eight-seven getting taller, then realised its feet were slowly lifting off the ground.

'I'm not sure about this,' he whispered to no one.

John jumped as three hooked appendages fired out of One-eight-seven's sides, anchoring it to the ground even as it rose into the air.

'Seventy per cent complete.'

John cast a glimpse over his shoulder at the immense dome and shivered at the thought of what he had volunteered for.

'What is that thing?' Osayimwese asked Crossley.

'My guess is at least 50 per cent helium,' Crossley replied.

John saw a look of confusion on Osayimwese's face and nudged Crossley.

'Oh,' the American said, 'it's a balloon – we're going to fly up to the top of the dome.'

Isao Yakamori watched the discussions from the back of the crowd, near Gal-qadan and his tocka, which fascinated him more than the talking did. Isao had ridden horses from a young age, learning to ride his grandfather's mares before graduating to the stallions. He had been so close to two horses – Lightning and Nightshade – that he had thought of them as friends, even allies on the battlefield. Nightshade had died in battle after Isao was dismounted by a fellow samurai, but his replacement, Lightning, had been more than adequate, seeing him through the scores of battles that followed.

Isao tensed, realising he would never know what had happened to Lightning after the flash that had taken Isao away.

He stroked the nose of one of the nearest, unmanned tocka and felt himself relax. The tocka's dark top lip vibrated, giving Isao a glimpse of the carnivorous teeth which lay beneath, but they didn't faze him. He, after all, carried a sheathed sword of equal power.

Isao kept one eye on Gal-qadan, who mostly stared at the foot soldiers nearest the tocka but occasionally fixed his glare on Isao. From the shadow world, Isao had seen Gal-qadan kill two of his own men, so didn't trust him, yet he knew he had to fight under the Mongol's command if he were to ride a tocka. He pictured Gal-qadan's wide smile when he had despatched the soldier at the cliff base, using his blood to rejuvenate the tocka. Although he'd seen it through the mists of the shadow world, the look was unmistakeable – Gal-qadan enjoyed murdering. Isao had known men like that and knew their thirst for murder was unquenchable. They *always* wanted to kill.

A cold rush ran over Isao's shoulders at the thought of the shadow world he'd been trapped in inside the dome. It had slowly washed away after every battle, giving him and his fellow samurai, Hori and Masaharu, the impression they could return to the real world if they fought well. So they had fought hard. When the main battle had arrived, they'd roamed wide, killing Brakari at will, but their prowess had been diluted across such a large area. They'd fared better during the battle outside the ruined fortress, where the Brakari and their allies had been packed into close quarters and Isao's sword sang true.

But their victory had been poisoned: as the fight turned in their favour, they'd remained in their physical form and become vulnerable. Hori had been killed by a freakish Brakari with poisonous spike-claws, and Masaharu had succumbed to the gas the enemy had pumped out as the battle drew to a close.

Isao cricked his neck and scanned the survivors who surrounded him now. They had endured many changes – John Greene with his gun-arm and Olan with his chest shield – but the Lutamek had given them explanations why those changes had taken place. Nobody could tell Isao what had happened to him, or if it would ever happen again even though, since walking through the silver gates, Isao had remained in his physical form.

Isao felt his pulse racing and turned back to the tocka. His heart steadied when he stroked it. He needed answers but he also needed to remain calm. A memory pain struck his stomach and his hand moved to his belly where the ritual dagger had sliced into his abdomen when he, Hori and Masaharu had committed seppuku. Strange how there had been no scar. Why had he been healed and allowed to continue this life? Would he eventually be pulled back into the shadow world?

Raised voices at the front of the crowd drew his attention again as the new metal man unfolded like a reverse origami to reveal new levels of beauty with each turn and twist: silver arms, sculpted ribs and a large, ink-black balloon shape, which lifted up the young Lutamek. Isao watched Crossley, as he pointed and chatted to Osayimwese and John, and followed the American's finger to the top of the imposing dome. Maybe they would answer his questions, he thought.

Isao looked to Gal-qadan and said, 'I will ride with you. Keep this tocka for me.'

The Mongol's face remained stony but he gave a sharp nod and Isao patted the tocka's muzzle before heading off through the crowd, weaving through to Crossley and John.

'Excuse me,' he said, tapping Crossley on the shoulder.

'Hey, we've already got enough volunteers,' Crossley said and gestured at the new robot. 'That thing can only take a handful of soldiers, okay?'

Isao gave the robot a glance and nodded. 'Yes, I see. I have questions… for your mission.'

Delta-Six had overheard and walked over.

'I wish to know how I was taken from this world,' Isao said.

'Well, we all want to know that,' Crossley said but Delta-Six held up a hand to silence him.

'No,' Isao continued, 'in the dome, I and my fellow samurai were taken into a shadow world and came back to this,' he swept an arm out, 'normal world after each battle. I need to know how.'

'So you can use it again?' John asked.

'It would be useful in a combat situation,' Delta-Six said.

'No,' Isao replied. 'I need to know to make sure I never go back again.'

Althorn looked out over the desert and distant domes. He'd sped away from the meeting and now sat by one of the outermost ships, where he slowly chewed on a chunk of dried meat he'd hidden in a weapons container. Samas had forbidden him from joining the dome-cap exploration party, and he needed energy if he was to be scouting this vast landscape. It was immense, and studying it had proven useless so far. Still, best to be prepared, he thought, and took in what he could with his one eye.

Raised voices from a few ships back caught Althorn's ear. He didn't turn, but listened. More voices joined in, arguing, followed by the deep tones of a Lutamek robot. Althorn sighed and stood up, feeling obliged to help out.

Saving his energy and remaining visible, Althorn strolled around the starships until he found a group of six or seven red-coated soldiers confronted by a Lutamek, who towered over them.

'You are forbidden to use any until an agreement has been made,' the Lutamek stated.

'I don't care about these agreements,' one soldier said and pointed to a cart laden with metal contraptions and boxes. 'We need fuel and we'll take what we can find.'

Althorn recalled these warriors were from John's clan, although he hadn't joined them, and the boxes were full of what Crossley had called gadgets and gizmos.

'Carter's right,' another soldier said, his thick coat slung over one shoulder. 'This is free for anyone. Nobody's property, just like what we found inside the dome.'

'Apart from the robot bits,' Carter replied.

'Of course,' the soldier replied and held a finger to his lips.

'All resources are to be rationed,' the Lutamek said.

'Look, I don't care for your authority here, right?' The new soldier said.

'You tell him, Elliott!' Another shouted.

'We can access the fuel and we'll take what we need,' he continued. 'Report it if you want but it's for the use of the whole army, right?'

The Lutamek stood still for a few silent seconds, then turned and strode off back to the main camp. The redcoats laughed and returned to the side of the starship, where a tiny, metallic dome had been placed on the side of a cylindrical tank.

'Fire her up, Wallis!' Elliott shouted and a separate box burst to life, coughing and spluttering grey smoke.

Althorn walked over, intrigued.

'Oi, you're not goin' to tell us what to do neither!' Carter yelled at Althorn.

'No, no,' Althorn held his hands up. 'I'm just interested. What are you doing?'

'Draining the fuel,' Carter replied. 'Ain't no wood here, see? Or diesel, so we can't get our machines running.'

'Defensive mechanata,' said another soldier, wearing circular shields over his eyes. 'Mostly steam-driven but some are operated with counterweight mechanisms... we work with what we have.' He said with a shrug.

'Ramsholt here's full of ideas and we don't use none of that electronic gubbins!' Elliott said. 'Don't trust it!'

'I know the feeling,' Althorn replied.

'We've improved our weapons,' the goggled soldier, Ramsholt, said, gesturing at a cache of wooden-handled rifles covered in an array of various metal projections. 'And I've made plans for a mobile defensive fortification – just need the materials.'

'Good,' Althorn said with a nod. 'Well done.'

It was too much for Althorn to understand – different types of metals and chemicals working together to make objects move. It was like magic. He didn't know if it was the words or the smoke but his head was hurting.

'Good luck with the fuel,' he said and walked away.

Maybe going scouting was a good idea after all?

John's shoulders felt heavy as he watched the samurai walk away. Now he had more questions to answer. They hadn't promised much but he'd seen a glimmer of hope in Isao's eyes, which was something he desperately needed. Maybe the Lutamek were right and every question they answered – every detail they clarified – took them one step closer to finding out who had brought them here.

He felt his gun-arm click and tried to relax.

'Come on,' Crossley said, gesturing at the starship. 'Samas says the Lutamek are going to resurrect the frozen soldiers – we've got a few minutes before lift-off.'

'How are they doing it?' John asked and stepped in with Crossley.

'They've accessed a connection from outside,' Crossley gave his fake laugh, 'not like that'll change things, right? The new guys'll just run off like Steve as soon as they see us lot. Hey, I would've done!'

John nodded and remembered the forest they had been deposited in and how he'd thought it was a strange dream at first. If he had found himself in that white spaceship he would have wanted to get out sharpish.

'Maybe we should try to find someone they would recognise next time?' John said, but they were already at the entrance to the ship and Crossley was inside.

'Come on!'

John ran his good hand along the smooth white walls again as they walked up the corridor to the main pod chamber and saw Lavalle at the end of the long room with Euryleia, intently watching the furthest green-lit pod: one of the last frozen humans.

Lavalle turned, nodded and said, 'Samas thought it best they were greeted by a couple,' he glanced at Euryleia. 'Less threatening.'

'Yeah, sure, a pretty face,' Crossley said. 'You might want to hide a pair of arms though, hey?'

Euryleia glanced at the American, then at her four hands. 'Maybe,' she replied, seeming proud of her adaptation rather than ashamed, and pulled her shawl forward. 'The Lutamek have started the rejuvenation process,' she said, 'slower this time, to allow them to get used to their surroundings before we open the pod.'

'Keep them trapped, you mean?' Crossley said. 'Yeah, that'll work.'

'You should wait over there.' Lavalle pointed. 'Just make sure they don't get past us.'

'It didn't work too well last time,' Crossley said.

'I wasn't going to stop Steve Smith with that weapon!' John said, remembering how the first thing Smith had done was to pull a mean-looking gun from a shelf inside the pod and aim it at his face.

Crossley nodded at John's gun-arm. 'It's not like you're not armed yourself.'

'Yeah,' John replied as he spun a couple of spiral shapes inside his gun-arm, allowing them to dissipate back into heat. 'But that doesn't mean I'll be able to stop the next one.'

'Who's this one anyway?' Crossley asked and leaned over to check the nameplate.

'Yarcha Chakava,' Lavalle said.

'Sounds Asian to me,' Crossley said.

John remembered seeing her serene face and strolled back over for another look at her long eyelashes and soft lips. 'She's a warrior?' he whispered.

'Come on,' Lavalle said, 'back in position in case she runs.'

'Yeah, sorry,' John said and blushed when he caught Euryleia glaring at him. Yarcha wasn't the first female soldier in the army, but she was always going to be an attraction.

'So where's she from?' Crossley asked John when he returned.

'India, I'm guessing.'

'Pretty too, going by the colour of your cheeks.'

John sent Crossley a quick glance and tried not to look hurt.

'Don't worry,' Crossley patted him on the shoulder, 'I doubt she's my type.'

Lavalle held a finger to his ear then spoke. 'I understand.' He looked to Euryleia. 'She's waking.' Then to John and Crossley, 'Be prepared.'

John heard a high-pitched hissing sound, then the green light on Yarcha's nameplate faded out.

'Here comes sleeping beauty!' Crossley whispered.

John watched Lavalle and Euryleia's faces as the glass lid of the pod unclipped and slowly drew open. The pair smiled and John imagined Yarcha's eyes opening. Were they dark brown like Rosie's? Or light brown like the desert sands? The thought of Rosie made John feel ashamed.

A voice like a screeching cat erupted from the pod. 'What is going on here?' The voice filled the long chamber.

John took a step back and watched Lavalle do the same. Euryleia remained poised as ever and moved forward to blow the spores of the translation mushroom into Yarcha's face.

'Where am I and what is that damned powder? Don't you know who I am?' the screeching continued.

'Greetings,' Lavalle said and bowed. 'Welcome to...'

'How dare you address me, you albino giant.' Yarcha cut Lavalle off and sat up, giving John a view of her long, dark hair. 'You!' She pointed at Euryleia. 'What's the meaning of this powder?'

'It gives you understanding of our languages,' Euryleia replied.

John saw her shoulders relax.

'You are from foreign lands,' Yarcha said, her voice calmer now as she held Euryleia's gaze. 'This room? Am I prisoner?'

'No,' Euryleia replied. 'We are all foreigners here.'

'In some way we may all be captives,' Lavalle added. 'But you are welcome among us.'

John could see Yarcha's breathing slowing as she calmed. Then, as she scanned the room, her eyes met his. He held them and breathed deeply. Then her gaze flicked to Crossley and back to Euryleia.

'Are there many of us here?' Yarcha asked.

'Several hundred,' Euryleia replied, 'and some soldiers not from our world.'

John wondered if Euryleia had pushed it too far, but Yarcha seemed to take the news in her stride.

'Gods?' she asked.

'Some might say,' Lavalle replied, 'but soldiers none the less.'

Crossley leaned in to whisper to John, 'I don't think this one's gonna be a runner.'

'No,' John replied, waiting for Yarcha to look his way again.

He heard a noise behind him, from the entrance, but didn't react.

'Well, I'd like to meet them,' Yarcha said and pushed herself up out of the pod then leaned back in to pull out what looked like a whip hanging down to her feet. 'My Urumi,' she said to Euryleia, who nodded.

John turned to see Osayimwese. 'It's good to see new recruits.' His deep voice made Yarcha turn and stare at him for longer than John liked. 'But it's time for us to start our mission.'

'Right,' John said and felt his stomach tense.

'One-eight-seven is ready and Delta-Six is getting impatient, so…'

'Okay, let's get the show on the road!' Crossley said and was off back down the white corridor.

John gave Yarcha a glance then jogged down the corridor and back into the sunlight, where One-eight-seven's black balloon floated impatiently, pulling at its anchors. John eyed up the four upside-down t-shaped sticks hanging from the Lutamek's balloon.

'Are they…?' he asked.

Crossley nodded and strapped a satchel of provisions across his back, then swung his legs over one of the swing-like seats. 'Come on!' he shouted, 'this is gonna be one helluva ride!'

John rubbed his fingers on his remaining palm, feeling the dampness, while his gun-arm clicked and he wondered how on Earth he was going to hold on.

While the young Lutamek established its balloon, Gal-qadan had watched Delta-Six run around the camp in a fuss, acquiring provisions for his mission. It gave Gal-qadan the perfect opportunity to acquire what he needed before he and the cavalry set off on their scouting mission.

'I'm seeking soldiers with riding experience.' Gal-qadan spoke loud and clear and purposefully ignored the Sorean who looked his way. The last thing he wanted was more of the mangy creatures with their bizarre fighting style and weak shield technology. He needed people he could trust, like Tode, if he were still alive, and Peronicus-Rax and the two brothers, Das and Pod, who had returned to their foot-high size to share a tocka. 'We have provisions and greater opportunity of finding more,' Gal-qadan continued his pitch as several soldiers stepped forward. 'And who knows what treasures we may find out there.'

He stared out between starships to the sliver of the desert which lay beyond.

'You,' Gal-qadan shouted to a turbaned, Afghan horseman, 'fix two tocka to that cart and lead them.'

The Afghan nodded and set to work.

'You,' Gal-qadan shouted at Isao, 'fill the cart with water barrels and dried meats.'

'And the new food?' Isao asked, pointing at the white cuboid containers the Lutamek had filled with a gooey liquid found in the tubes of the starship.

'Yes,' Gal-qadan barked.

He wouldn't eat it, but if the Lutamek said it was nutritional his men could have it.

Gal-qadan watched his men work or ride their new tocka, depending on his orders. Yes, he thought, this was a good unit. Strong men with strong horses. After checking that Delta-Six was keeping the Lutamek busy, Gal-qadan rode to the cart and lifted the sacking covering the Lutamek technology.

'Ah…' he gasped as the shiny metal beneath was revealed.

He let the sacking drop and casually rode away, holding his face rigid as he fought the surge of elation that ran through his body. He was about to steal a prize greater than he had ever imagined – one that would ensure his army were truly formidable.

'Riders!' he shouted. 'Move out.'

'See you at the rendezvous point!' Samas shouted, but Gal-qadan already had his back to him.

He kept his tocka at the rear, behind the heavily laden cart, and kept his eyes forward. They wound their way through the starships, to where Gal-qadan saw the distant silhouette of Peronicus-Rax, already crossing the immense desert.

Gal-qadan felt the feeling of boredom disappear with the warm wind, which smelled of freedom. He could feel his tocka relax too. So many possibilities now! He found the communication device Nine-five had given him in his pocket and gave it a nudge with his elbow. It would fall out soon enough, he thought.

No one would have a hold over him.

Chapter 5

John had never been scared of heights. In fact, he and Rosie had climbed up inside the Monument on one of their first dates because he'd loved the view so much. Funny, he'd thought, how a tower built to memorialise a tragedy hundreds of years previously was now a tourist attraction.

'Are you sure it's safe though, John?' Rosie had said, gripping his hand as they climbed the spiral stone staircase.

'Safe as houses,' John had said and gave her hand a squeeze. 'You'll love it, I promise.'

When they stepped out, both had held their breath, taking in the view and enjoying the cool breeze. Tower Bridge and St Paul's were dominant, but John's eye soon picked out other landmarks he knew from his rounds on his delivery cart.

'Gives you an idea how much was burned down,' he said. 'During the Great Fire, of course.'

'But it made room for so much more, didn't it?' Rosie replied and was soon picking out church spires and factory stacks John hadn't noticed before.

'We should do it again one day,' Rosie had said when they left, 'when we have children. To show them their city.'

John smiled now just like he had done back then. He

watched the horizons of this new world expand around him as One-eight-seven carried him and the team up beside the curved side of the dome.

Would he change anything if he could go back? The doctors had said Rosie would have died even if she'd made it to hospital and his world wouldn't have felt complete without Joe in it, who'd made the loss of Rosie bearable. But what about the war? If he'd known what would happen – being brought to this strange land – would he still have gone? Or would he have stayed at home, vilified as a coward, but able to bring up his son?

'Hey, look at that!' Crossley shouted from the trapeze to John's side.

John followed Crossley's finger to the needle-like tower they'd seen before. 'Wow!'

'Looks bigger from up here,' Crossley said.

John turned to Osayimwese and Rar-kin behind them, who were also taking in the view, dangling underneath the balloon on their tiny trapezes. Delta-Six was long gone and One-eight-seven had yet to communicate with them, so it felt like it was just the four of them.

'It looks like the tower's central to all the domes,' Crossley said, 'like a control tower… I mean, I haven't seen any other towers, have you?'

'No,' John replied, 'just more domes.'

'I think the domes are closer together around the tower as well,' Crossley said.

John squinted, remembering how the numerous towers of London had looked squashed together from the Monument, when he knew some were miles apart.

'No, it's just a trick of the eye,' John said. 'They're probably spread out equally.'

'I don't know,' Crossley said and turned back to the dome for more coughing.

Peering down, the neat rows of starships seemed tiny next to the immense dome, and John could no longer see the gang of tocka crossing the vast desert. They were drifting over the dome itself, whose clean, almost-iridescent green clashed with the dull, sandy brown of the land outside.

'Well, the shell's damn thick, I'll tell you that!' Crossley said after another coughing burst.

John peered up and around the balloon to see a dark line running around the dome.

'We must be nearly there!' he shouted and pointed.

'No, it's just the bottom of the dome cap,' Crossley replied. 'A little further yet.'

'Oh,' John said and turned to Osayimwese, who was talking to Rar-kin.

The wind sweeping off the dome was making it hard for them to hear one another.

'And once they've scouted that dome,' Osayimwese was pointing at various domes, explaining the planned route for Gal-qadan's cavalry, 'they'll meet us at that dome.'

'Yes,' Rar-kin replied in its gruff voice, 'an equilateral triangle... they will travel twice the distance on the tocka.'

Osayimwese smiled and nodded. 'Yes,' he replied, 'but we'll have to walk the whole way.'

John tried to gauge how far they'd have to walk. Without any obvious features, the desert looked no bigger than the plain of battles they had crossed before they fought the Brakari, but if the distant domes were the same size as theirs, it was at least three domes' wide, which would mean weeks of walking.

'The tocka travel ten times faster than us,' Osayimwese said.

'Eight and a half times faster,' Rar-kin said and tilted its head.

'What are you? Some kind of mathematician?' Crossley asked.

Rar-kin's muzzle wrinkled in response before replying. 'The Lutamek tell me various visualisation lobes in my brain have been enhanced.'

'So you're good at geometry?' Crossley said with a laugh. 'And I thought my skills were useless.'

'What happened?' Osayimwese asked, ignoring Crossley. 'Were you hit? Was it something you ate?'

'I do not know,' Rar-kin replied and looked up at the dome cap. 'But I hope to find out.'

'Worry about our mission first,' Crossley said.

'It's important,' Osayimwese said. 'I want to know more about these powers.'

'Why?' John asked, sensing Osayimwese was holding back. 'So we can reverse them?' he asked, hoping he might be able to heal his gun-arm.

'No, I…' Osayimwese looked away.

'It's because you don't have one, isn't it?' Crossley asked.

Osayimwese nodded.

'These changes aren't always good,' John said and nodded at his arm.

Osayimwese looked at John then away again. 'Those who died didn't have new powers – Kastor, Tode. They died.'

'Yeah, but so did Mihran,' Crossley said.

'Many of our lost warriors were enhanced,' Rar-kin added.

'And Sakarbaal died,' John said, remembering when the crazy Carthaginian had been the first human he had met in this strange world. 'Li as well.'

'Yes, maybe.' Osayimwese still looked glum. 'But I would be grateful for anything to aid me in our next battle.'

'From what I heard, you didn't need anything extra,' Crossley said and gave Osayimwese a smile.

'Look,' Rar-kin said and pointed with its furred hand. 'The curve of the dome suggests we will be reaching the cap soon.'

John sensed One-eight-seven slowing down.

'I just hope Delta-Six made it past any gun emplacements,' Crossley said. 'This thing's gonna be protected, you know that, right?'

John looked from Crossley to the dome. What if Delta-Six had been shot down or if One-eight-seven strayed into enemy fire and they fell onto the shell of the dome and slid all the way down? He gripped the metal pole tight and kept his eyes fixed ahead. A flash of light and a dull thud made him turn.

'Some kind of explosion,' Crossley said, 'but it wasn't near the cap... more like in the sky.'

'Was it Delta-Six?' Osayimwese asked.

'Hell knows,' Crossley replied. 'But something's happening up there.'

John craned his neck to look around One-eight-seven but the black balloon was in the way. His gun-arm clicked and the knuckles on his good hand were turning white as he gripped tighter.

'Shit!' John yelled as a whooshing sound made him jump and swing out his gun-arm in defence.

'Hold tight!' Delta-Six shouted.

'Don't bloody jump up on us like that,' John shouted back.

'There's no time,' Delta-Six replied, his dark eyes showing he was in a fighting mood.

'What was that explosion?' Osayimwese asked.

'Nothing to do with me,' Delta-Six replied. 'A new ship's coming in. The explosion was high in the atmosphere.' He looked away for a second and John saw his eyes flicker as though he were reading a book. 'Looks like a starship – unidentified – tried to follow the first but was destroyed.'

'What?' Crossley almost screamed. 'There are other spaceships up there?'

'It doesn't affect our mission – I'll send Ten-ten the video recording, then we must maintain radio silence. You understand, One-eight-seven?' he asked, looking up to a face John couldn't see.

A series of bleeps responded.

Delta-Six floated beside them. 'We're in luck. It looks like a ship docked on the dome last night, so we'll get to see everything in action. I'll cut a hole for us to climb in and One-eight-seven will attach to the outside, okay?'

'Sounds good,' John said with a nod and turned to see the others agreeing.

Like him, he guessed they just wanted to get their feet back on something solid.

Delta-Six nodded and gracefully flew out of view.

'Let's hope he doesn't get shot or we're screwed,' Crossley said loud enough for John to hear.

As One-eight-seven drifted closer to the metal of the dome cap, John could see how it matched the images the Lutamek had taken from information in the sample ships: the dome cap was a torus-shaped building of five levels, sitting on the flat top of the dome, supported by numerous huge, red, granite pillars: the red cliffs John and the army had seen when they had sailed their rafts through the waterways of the dead centre of the dome. The hole in the centre of the doughnut shape gave the dome cap access to the inside of the dome.

'Here we go,' Osayimwese shouted as they drifted over a sloping wall.

'Nearly there…' Crossley said in between coughs.

John braced himself for impact as One-eight-seven connected to the metal wall of the cap, then saw that Delta-Six was directly below them, standing inside the dome cap itself, under a perfect circular hole cut in the curved metal.

'Just drop down!' he whispered and beckoned.

John let Crossley go first, then swung his legs off his trapeze and dropped, landing with a metallic thump on the pleasingly solid floor.

John took a sip of water from Crossley's canteen and studied the inner wall of the dome-cap structure. Delta-Six had covered the hole with what he called a chamelo-cloth, leaving One-eight-seven outside, and John couldn't see the join.

'It's lighter in here than I thought it would be,' Crossley said.

'Just like inside the starships,' Osayimwese said, stroking the white, ceramic-like walls which curved up to a flat ceiling.

John stared down the curved corridor which led in either direction away from them and, he assumed, circled the entire cap. White from ceiling to floor, the inner walls were punctuated with rectangular panels which flashed with coloured lights.

'The air quality's the same as outside,' Delta-Six said.

'What? You didn't check that first?' Crossley asked.

'There's nothing to suggest organic life inhabits the dome caps,' Delta-Six replied. 'But why would the designers go to the effort of creating a vacuum if they didn't need one?'

'So how come we have all these species from across the galaxy breathing the same air?' Crossley asked, arms folded.

Delta-Six squinted at the American, then said, 'My guess is, this planet was adapted to house oxygen-breathers and other habitats were created to host other air-breathers... look, we don't have time for this.'

'Right,' Crossley replied, 'I thought we were here to answer questions, so...'

Delta-Six ignored him and gestured for them to huddle closer. 'We have four hours before the docked starship leaves, and we need any information we can find, okay?'

John nodded.

'We're in the top level, so I suggest we make a complete circuit then descend to the next level where we can split up. John and Osayimwese – you collect data. Anything this place holds about our different species: home-planet coordinates; biology; names; anything. Save it on your storage units.'

John fumbled his satchel open and pulled out a metal strip, feeling its cool, smooth surface through his fingertips.

'Good,' Delta-Six continued. 'Crossley and Rar-kin, I need you to observe the new species coming in on the ship. Find a good place to observe what happens to them.'

Crossley nodded and Rar-kin's eyes widened.

'In the meantime,' Delta-Six said, 'I'll infiltrate their systems, searching for future plans.' He gave a nod. 'Right, follow me.'

Delta-Six strode off down to the right and the others followed. John strapped his gun-arm tight and stepped as lightly as he could, worried the sound of his Lutamek leg would betray their position. Not that there appeared to be any signs of life here, he thought.

The corridor was a perfect circle, so the angle didn't change, giving them a clear, but unchanging view for a few hundred feet ahead of them.

Crossley coughed and said, 'The floors are way thinner than the walls and are pulsing with electrical activity, like energy waves or information flows.'

'Is there a way down?' Osayimwese asked.

'There's a service hatch here,' Delta-Six replied and leaned into a rectangular hole to scan. 'There's activity below,' he said. 'I'll go first and signal when it's safe.'

John looked around nervously and asked, 'So what's this floor for then?'

'Storage?' Crossley guessed. 'Extra capacity?'

'But for what?' John whispered.

Osayimwese tapped Crossley on the shoulder and motioned for him to be quiet, then pointed to his ear. John leaned forward to listen down the hatch, but all he could hear was blood pumping in his ears. What if Delta-Six had been captured and whoever guarded this place was already surrounding them? A flash of light caught his eye. He looked down the dark hatch and caught a double flash again.

'That's the signal. We're good to go,' John whispered and slid down.

On the next level, Delta-Six was waiting with a finger on his lips. He pointed down the corridor, which looked identical to the one they'd just left. Shadows danced on the curved wall, suggesting movement beyond. When the whole team arrived, Delta-Six guided them to another hatch, gesturing for them to repeat the process.

'Right,' Delta-Six whispered once they'd regrouped on the next level down. 'We're on the middle level away from the activity and,' he pointed behind them and John turned slowly, 'this is where we'll retrieve our information.'

John's mouth dropped and his eyes widened as he took in a fantastical view: the whole inner wall of this level was transparent, peering out over the hole inside the doughnut-shaped structure. Looking up, John could see the belly of the starship docked on top of the cap – its dark-grey surface was identical to that of the ships they'd found, though half hidden by a swarm of moving tubes and robotic arms which extended from the inner cap walls. Looking down into the swirling mist, John saw clear patches revealing glimpses of the red crag rock and blue waters.

'Wow.' Crossley was the first to speak, leaning on the long silver desk which ran along the inner wall, beneath the window.

'I suggest we work here,' Delta-Six said. 'Collect data from these banks,' he tapped the metal desk, 'and watch the new species on the visual links.' He pointed at a glass pane set in the desk. 'Meanwhile, I'm going to observe the activity above.'

Crossley and Rar-kin were already pressing buttons, but John felt lost. He turned to Osayimwese, who looked equally confused, then at the panels of coloured buttons and shiny screens. John didn't have the faintest idea where to start.

Delta-Six breathed a sigh of relief as he climbed out of the hatch and back onto the fourth level. It was good to be on his own again. He'd spent his military career working in teams and had trusted every member completely, but that was because they had literally been bred together – to complement each other. The group of soldiers on this mission made Delta-Six feel like a babysitter and he was growing frustrated with having to explain everything to them.

He took a second to calm down. He had distracting questions rushing around his mind, like how they had travelled to this world so fast. The spatial anomalies Ten-ten had mentioned intrigued him, but he didn't have time to investigate now, so he concentrated on the readings coming in from his sensors. Signs and lights blinked in his view but, since his suit had melded with his body, his direct connections with its various motion, wave and radiation detectors enabled him to sense the world around him in a new way.

Using the map the Lutamek had given him, Delta-Six created a visual representation of the torus-shaped level he stood in and laid it over his visual view. He fed in the information from his sensors to create a three-dimensional moving picture of his surroundings and up to fifty metres around each corner. Concentrating on the movement he'd sensed earlier, he could now make out fifteen humanoid shapes around the curve to his left. Silent and fast, they were shorter than Delta-Six and moving around one another like choreographed dancers. He analysed their behaviour, discerning five distinct groups moving between the control panels on the inner wall of the cap.

Delta-Six crept around the corner to allow his sensors to pick up more detail. The only sound he heard was the squeaking of the creatures' rubber feet as they stomped from station to station, so he flicked through frequencies until he found a series of high-speed, short-burst emissions, based on a quinary system. His processors correlated it with the language used on the obelisks inside the dome and soon had the code reconfigured. He overlaid the speech as streams of text next to each individual as they communicated.

'Synchronisation complete,' one shape told another.

'Start local environment synchronisation,' it replied.

A third shape moved over and reported its completed work to what Delta-Six saw as the team leader – each group's leader gathered information and gave out new tasks.

'Synchronisation complete,' an individual from a different team reported back.

Delta-Six made a note to call these robotic creatures *Synchronisers*.

Keeping out of view, Delta-Six prised open a white panel on the inner wall, giving him access to the circuits and information relays within. A patch on his wrist glowed orange as it made a connection, and new information flooded into Delta-Six's view: he looked up to see the docked ship; then below, to an empty corridor, which suggested the dome's sensors hadn't picked the team up.

Delta-Six focussed on a huge doorway which had opened beneath the docked starship. Shapes of various sizes were being lowered down from the aft section, each one pulsing erratically as metal arms and scoops prodded and manoeuvred them into the empty top level where they'd entered the cap. Were these the new soldiers? Delta-Six thought. Is that why the top floor is empty? He focussed on the starship and, using the dome-cap sensors, could see rows of stasis pods, just like in the humans' ship, but they were still occupied. So what was being brought out?

The process of emptying the ship was efficient and fast, reminding Delta-Six he needed to speed up if they were going to get out of the cap undetected. He tried to match the Synchronisers' activity with the emptying of the starship and sent a variety of auto-viruses into the cap's data stream to find information on what plans were in place for victorious armies who had left the dome.

With the connections made, Delta-Six retraced the team's original path up a floor, checking the chamelo-cloth on their entrance point was still in place, and scanned the new beings brought in from the ship. They were diverse in size and solidity, but the information was limited so, with a sigh, he set his suit to camouflage and crept around to get a direct visual check.

'What on Earth?' Delta-Six found himself whispering when he saw them, and backed away slowly.

John yawned as he swiped the thin metal sheet across the glass screen. The top right corner of the sheet glowed orange, showing it had absorbed the information, then he pressed the button to change the screen. The first twenty had been interesting – those with pictures – but these were full of alien writing that made no sense, even though he could read it. In fact, he wasn't totally sure if these pages were different to the last screen, but he wasn't going to tell Osayimwese that.

'Three more rows,' Osayimwese said and sounded as bored as John felt.

'And then what?' John asked.

Osayimwese shrugged. 'We find another panel or we see what Crossley and Rar-kin have found?'

'Are the other panels different?' John asked. 'If each one's like a book it'll take us forever to get the information out.'

'We don't have forever,' Osayimwese replied.

'I know,' John said and looked up at the array of huge metal arms which was systematically removing more panels from the belly of the starship. 'Okay, let's find Crossley.'

With only one way to walk around the circular building, it didn't take long for them to find Crossley and Rar-kin, who had a visitor.

'How did you get back?' John asked.

'There are hatches everywhere,' Delta-Six replied. 'I'm not sure what data you've got, but this is what we're really after.' He nodded at the screen in front of Crossley. 'It's a mirror system, monitoring the new soldiers as they're brought out of stasis.'

'What have you found?' Osayimwese asked.

Delta-Six pressed a few buttons and changed the images on the screen before he replied. 'You remember that shark in the dome?'

'Who could forget it?' Crossley said.

'Well it looks like the ship brought us here with extra cargo.' He pointed up through the window. 'The level we arrived on is currently full of the most dangerous creatures from this species' home planet.'

John frowned. 'But how did they keep a shark up there without any water?'

'And the giant eagle,' Osayimwese added.

Rar-kin cleared its throat and said, 'I believe they were adapted to this new environment.'

'That's some adaptation!' Crossley said. 'How on Earth did they make a fish breath air?'

'It appears the systems activate genes within each creature's DNA,' Delta-Six replied.

'So they can fly through the air?' Osayimwese asked.

Delta-Six shrugged. 'Something must have pushed them beyond their natural abilities.'

'Is that what happened to us?' John asked. 'Did they change us when we were brought out of the ship?'

Crossley shook his head. 'Doesn't make sense. I mean, I didn't get my abilities until days later.'

'Mine took five and a half days to establish,' Rar-kin added.

Osayimwese said nothing and stared out of the window.

'My theory,' Delta-Six said as he tapped more buttons, 'is the time we spent in stasis had a degree of influence on how we adapted. One of the transmissions from the Synchronisers mentioned telomeres – they're part of our DNA molecules.'

'Synchronisers?' Crossley asked.

'The creatures running the dome cap,' Delta-Six snapped, clearly feeling rushed. 'They were measuring telomere latency, so let's search for any information on that,' Delta-Six said.

'What a minute,' John said, and rested his gun-arm on the panel, 'if the top floor is full of dangerous creatures, how are we going to get back to One-eight-seven and back down to the ground?'

'That's what I need to fix,' Delta-Six said, and looked to Rar-kin. 'I need your help.'

Rar-kin's eyes dilated and it moved its head in a triangular motion.

'We need to fix the hole from the outside and bring One-eight-seven down a level.'

'Those Synchronisers must know we're here,' Crossley said. 'They're way more advanced than us.'

Delta-Six shook his head. 'The security systems aren't set up like that. All I've seen are external weapons pointing upwards and the odd pulse weapon pointing down into the dome... probably the one that shot me down.'

'To stop anyone flying up to the cap?' Osayimwese said.

'Most likely,' Delta-Six replied.

'But they hadn't banked on anyone climbing up from the outside?' John said, remembering an aerial attack he'd seen in the trenches, trails of dots dropping from a biplane. The machine guns had been fixed on the enemy trench, so they'd been defenceless.

'It seems that way,' Delta-Six replied. 'So once we've patched up the hole, there'll be no sign we were here.'

'Look at this!' Osayimwese called out.

He was at a new set of panels covered with screens.

John leaned in for a closer look, resting his gun-arm on the metal panel, and jumped back in pain.

'Shit!' he shouted and grabbed his arm with his good hand.

'Quiet!' Delta-Six hissed and peered around the corner.

'I just got bloody shocked!' John growled through clenched teeth.

The pain hadn't been as bad as when Delta-Six's automatic defence systems had shocked him, but his gun-arm tingled with pins and needles. He spun a bullet in the chamber to make sure it was still working, then let the energy spin away.

'You okay?' Crossley asked.

'Yeah,' John replied.

'You got the panel working,' Osayimwese said, turning dials beneath a screen which now flickered with images.

'It's showing inside the dome,' Rar-kin said.

Delta-Six moved forward to take a look. 'There must be cameras inside the dome... and they're preparing the land for the new species. They're called the Tathon according to the records.' He pressed more buttons and the whole array of screens flashed into life. 'This is great – we need anything you see on how the new species are brought in.' Delta-Six looked to Rar-kin. 'Let's go. We'll be back within the hour.'

'Right then,' John said as he, Crossley and Osayimwese sidestepped from screen to screen, zooming in and around to get the best views of what was going on.

'I'll take this one.' Osayimwese's screen showed the lines of glass pods inside the docked starship.

'Mine shows where they'll deposit the soldiers,' Crossley said, pointing at his screen. 'So far they've built a hill, covered it in some kind of algae that's spreading like wildfire.'

'And there's the obelisk,' Osayimwese said, peering over at a black obelisk identical to the one John had seen on their hill, only instead of humans it addressed the Tathon.

John searched for a suitable screen and found an image of a symmetrical shape which looked familiar to him.

'Be careful with your arm,' Crossley called over. 'No more shocks.'

'Yeah, okay,' John said and pulled his webbing straps to tighten his numb arm against his chest.

He swiped his metal strip over a red light and played with the dials, zooming in. The shape was ovoid, with a small blue circle in the centre with a thick red line on its right edge. The blue lines thinned then radiated out to create dozens of islands.

To the left of the central circle, John saw a swathe of brown marked with hundreds of tiny white dots.

'It's a map!' John said.

'What?' Crossley was soon by his side, followed by Osayimwese.

'A map of the dome,' John said. 'These islands are where we started out. Over here's the lake we sailed on the rafts, through the red cliffs here.'

'And that's the plain of battles?' Osayimwese asked and pointed at the area of brown.

'I think so,' John replied, 'but I can't work out what these white dots are.'

He twisted the dial to zoom in but the dots didn't come into focus.

'How about this one?' Osayimwese said and touched the screen with his forefinger.

A line of text flashed up straight away:

On this spot, the Nama-Gametiads and their allies were victorious over the Ilanos.

'They're battle obelisks!' John said.

'Jeez, it looks like we only passed through a quarter of them,' Crossley said.

'Can you see anyone down there?' Osayimwese asked.

Crossley laughed. 'Sure. Like it's a live map?' He took a step back. 'This is great, but we don't have time for heading down memory lane – let's get the info and scram before those Synchronisers work out we're here.'

Osayimwese shrugged and pointed at his screen. 'Look, they're waking up the new soldiers.'

John glanced over to see a white robotic arm pressing buttons on a pod and what looked like a needle pressing into something white and gelatinous that reminded him of tripe. What were these strange Tathon creatures?

Delta-Six lay the newly cut metal section of outer wall on the floor and double-checked his scans: no new movement or activity to suggest the breach had been registered.

'Right.' He turned to Rar-kin. 'I can fly us up to the next section so you can bring One-eight-seven back down while I fix the hole.'

'I understand,' the Sorean replied.

'Sorry, but I'll need to carry you,' Delta-Six said, and the small, furred creature thrust out its arms like a small child waiting for a hug. 'Thank you.' He picked the Sorean up, fired his propulsion system and glided out of the hole and up to where One-eight-seven swayed silently, attached to the cap wall.

'The curvature is low,' Rar-kin said as Delta-Six placed it on the trapeze.

'Pardon me?'

Rar-kin pointed to the horizon. 'The curvature is less than expected for a world this size.'

'I'll calculate it,' Delta-Six said and opened up an analytics window to scan the horizon, then apportioned 2 per cent of his processing systems to calculate the size of the planet. 'I'll get the results shortly,' he said and drifted up to One-eight-seven's head to ask it to move to the new hole.

A series of lights flickered and a click signalled the release as it drifted away from the cap.

All good so far, Delta-Six thought, and leaned in to focus on the chamelo-cloth stretched across the hole. There were no signs of damage but he couldn't risk leaving it here with the creatures roaming inside the top level.

Ten minutes later, and despite the attentions of a flock of inquisitive, hummingbird-like squid, Delta-Six had fixed the hole from the inside and gathered footage on the creatures and the processes they had undergone. He'd seen a series of robotic devices, controlled by the Synchronisers, injecting and spraying the creatures with a host of chemicals Delta-Six's systems hadn't recognised. He presumed the same processes were taking place on the soldiers inside the ship, so he navigated through the dome-cap systems until he found a list of active systems used by the group of Synchronisers.

That's interesting, he thought and focussed on a task labelled 'Acceleration'.

John concentrated on the screen and rubbed his forehead as the buttons he pressed refused to work in the same way they had done five minutes ago. He was desperate for answers but couldn't make sense of the diagrams and numbers.

'We haven't got long until the new soldiers are ready,' Osayimwese hissed.

'I know!' Crossley replied before John could. 'I'm still searching. Delta-Six said telomere latency, right?'

'Yeah,' John replied and Osayimwese nodded.

They'd found records for all species brought into the dome and needed to transfer any info about humans, Lutamek and Sorean onto the thin sliver of metal Ten-ten had given them. Just thinking about it gave John a headache; his reading had never been great, and after he had left school he hadn't had much need for it delivering veg or defending his trench.

'It would be quicker if Delta-Six was here,' Osayimwese said.

'Sure it would,' Crossley replied, 'but he's off on another of his missions, so...'

John looked around the curved room for any telltale shadows. Rar-kin was outside, tending One-eight-seven, so any shadow would belong to Delta-Six or one of the Synchronisers he'd mentioned.

John stared through the window above the computer screen at the docked ship. He was still amazed by the thought that he and his friends had gone through the same process as these squid-like creatures when woken from stasis.

'Ah, what's this?' Crossley said and John leaned over to see a list of names.

'Looks like us,' John said with a smile and tried to find his name.

'Just save it to that... piece of metal,' Osayimwese said.

'Already on it,' Crossley replied and swiped the grey sheet as Delta-Six had shown them. 'Just move that there and some more files here... Lutamek, Sorean and the new guys, the *Tathon*. Here's the Brakari,' he gave John a wink. 'Might as well have them too, eh?'

John looked away and wondered what ever happened to Millok, or General Panzicosta? He glanced at the screen with the map, but a sound made him turn.

'Do you hear that?' he whispered.

'Yes.' Osayimwese was already in a defensive position, holding his spear and eggshell dagger. 'Someone is running.'

'What do we do?' John asked. 'That's the way out.'

'I'm still saving the information,' Crossley said.

An elongated shadow appeared on the distant, curved wall as the rapid footsteps came nearer, followed by a distant shout.

'Retreat!'

'That's Delta-Six,' John said and looked at Crossley. 'Come on, something's up.'

'Alright, alright!' Crossley replied.

Delta-Six rushed into view and sped up to them. 'Come on, we're running out of time!'

'Is it the Synchronisers?' Osayimwese asked.

'No,' Delta-Six replied, 'the Tathon. I... there's been a malfunction and I need to communicate with Command.'

A flashing light on one of the screens caught John's eye and he saw an image of the new hilltop in the dome, now covered with the Tathon, huge, octopus-like creatures whose skin flashed with waves of colour. They were all shaking and writhing in a way that reminded John of Doctor Cynigar, the Brakari who had mutated himself.

'What happened?' Crossley asked.

Delta-Six looked away as he spoke. 'I attempted an interface with the sequencing technology to understand how the rejuvenation process may have stimulated our mutations, only,' he looked at each of the men, 'I inadvertently increased the parameters and now the Tathon are…'

'You boosted the power?' Crossley asked.

Delta-Six nodded. 'We have to get out of here before the Synchronisers work out what's happened.'

On the screen, John saw the results of the boost as the Tathon's tentacled, large-eyed bodies warped in size and shape, their mutated DNA struggling to assert itself.

'They're mutating right now,' John said.

'Shit!' Crossley stayed rooted to the spot and ran a hand through his hair. 'This is bad. I mean, we thought we had some tasty powers, but these guys…'

'I know,' Delta-Six stood impatiently, 'which is why we have to leave – we'll deal with the consequences after, okay?'

'Sure,' Crossley said and swiped his metal sheet over the screen to capture the recent footage.

'Let's get out of here,' John said, eyeing both ends of the corridor nervously, trying to keep up with Delta-Six, who jogged to his new hatch in the wall.

'Right,' Delta-Six said and peeled back his chamelo-cloth to reveal the distant desert vista and a waft of fresh air.

He stuffed the cloth in a pocket and stuck his head out, looking left and right, then up.

'Come on,' Osayimwese said, 'where are they?'

Delta-Six turned back and, for the first time John could remember, looked genuinely shocked. He took some effort to open his mouth and whisper, 'They've gone.'

Chapter 6

Samas toured the camp and found himself staring at the variety of shimmering trinkets the Sorean had pulled out of their starship. His understanding of this new technology was limited, and when Ten-ten had tried to explain their workings, Samas had to remind the Lutamek that he had been fighting against Alexander the Great's army just a few weeks ago as far as he was concerned. Thousands of years might have passed for others, but that was how it felt to him. Everything here was new – a culture shock, as Li had called it. Just like going into battle for the first time or your arm turning to stone, it took time for your mind to make sense of events and to accept what had changed.

Samas clenched his stone fist, feeling the strength it held, and remembered that, despite the advances in weapons and armour, tactics on the battlefield had changed little – as the battle against the Brakari had shown – and he had been chosen as leader of the human army because of his experience.

'Are these essential?' he asked Jakan-tar, who was overseeing the loading of carts the Lutamek had constructed from external parts of the starships.

'We have few rations,' the Sorean leader replied, 'so we'll need goods to trade.'

It sounded like an answer Mihran might have given, but without the accompanying sneer.

'Good,' Samas replied. 'The Lutamek say the light patterns on the tower suggest activity around its base.'

'Where else would they have gone?' Jakan-tar asked.

Samas looked around and nodded. Just like the obelisk on the first hill, the tower was a beacon for anyone leaving their dome. He looked up at the imposing shape of the dome and squinted at the dark-grey cap on its top. Maybe Delta-Six and the others would bring them the answers they needed?

'We've had no communication from them.'

Ten-ten's metallic voice made Samas turn.

'Delta-Six said they would maintain communication silence,' Samas replied. 'We should only hear from them when One-eight-seven is returning.'

'Our scans suggest the ship is nearing the completion phase,' Ten-ten said, 'which means they are running out of time.'

Samas wasn't sure how to read the Lutamek, with their lack of expressive face and tone, but he knew they were essentially animals inside their metal bodies, which would explain why Samas had the feeling Ten-ten was sad.

'I'm sorry to hear about your ship,' he said.

Samas had been taken to the broken ship with a burned, torn hole on one flank, like it had been peeled open. It had proven to be devoid of any Lutamek technology, let alone hibernating soldiers like they'd found in the other ships.

'We didn't expect looters.' Ten-ten turned to look through a gap between the nearest ships and across the desert to the cluster of domes.

Samas could never read the Lutamek but wondered if *they* had taken something from the ship they didn't want him to know about. After all, if it had been looters, why hadn't more ships been destroyed or ripped apart?

'Are your new recruits adapting well?' Ten-ten asked.

Samas laughed and remembered Steve Smith running off into the desert. 'After our first attempt we managed a little better, thanks,' Samas said and pictured Yarcha and the other new recruits. 'Four in total and I understand you have woken several other species?'

'Yes,' Ten-ten replied, 'the slow rejuvenation worked well. Also, we found sufficient rations for our journey, so we're on course to leave tomorrow at sunrise.'

'Yes,' Samas said and paused. Ten-ten seemed distracted by the dome. 'What is it?'

'We have received transmissions,' Ten-ten replied.

'The team made it out?'

'No, we have a message from One-eight-seven and Rar-kin. They are returning,' Ten-ten said, pointing high.

'What about the others?' Samas asked and cupped his eyes with his good hand. He could make out a black dot near the top of the dome, which glittered a tint of orange, suggesting the sun was going to set in a couple of hours.

'One-eight-seven is still young, so its language is developing,' Ten-ten said. 'The message was… ambiguous.'

'Ambiguous?' Samas turned to face the Lutamek. 'Are my men safe or are they dead.'

Ten-ten said nothing for a few seconds and Samas assumed it was communicating with One-eight-seven. 'No confirmation,' it eventually said.

Samas sighed and glanced at the dot again. 'We'll have to plan a rescue mission,' he said. 'Delta-Six can take care of himself but the others will need saving and I'm not prepared to leave until they are found – dead or alive.'

The army would be leaving in the morning and he wasn't

prepared to abandon any soldiers. For the army's sake as much as the individual's. Having Gal-qadan's men split off from the group had weakened them enough already and who knew what they would face when they travelled between the domes?

Ten-ten's head twitched but remained silent.

'In the meantime, I'll make sure we're prepared for tomorrow's departure.'

'Yes,' Ten-ten replied.

Samas strode off and pushed away any thoughts about what Mihran or Li would have done differently. He gave Euryleia a nod as he passed her and one of the new human soldiers, who sat, weapon in hand, as their new situation was explained in the simplest terms possible. Althorn was nervously pacing nearby, chewing on a piece of dried meat. He would be eager to get going across the plain, Samas thought. At the far end of the camp, Mata was using his branch-like arms to lift trunks of weapons and barrels of food onto the new carts, while Olan, Dakaniha and Bowman helped pack and organise the bizarre types of liquid nutrition the Lutamek were extracting from the starships.

'Nine-five!' Samas called out. 'Jakan-tar!'

The two leaders turned and walked towards Samas.

'Have you heard the news?'

'Yes,' they replied.

'But we must not delay our departure,' Nine-five said and Samas cast a glance back at Ten-ten, who looked away.

'Your troops are safe,' Samas said, 'so I need to retrieve mine.'

'It'll be dark soon,' Jakan-tar said.

'I'll rescue them in the dark if I have to–' Samas was cut off by a distant, hollow boom.

The group looked to where the grey starship had lifted off the dome cap and was now descending gracefully.

'So now they're stuck in the cap?' Samas asked.

He spotted the small silhouette of One-eight-seven, cruising down through the air. 'Let's get some answers,' Samas said and strode to where the young Lutamek was due to land.

Soldiers of all species joined Samas as One-eight-seven came closer, with the looming shape of the new starship close behind. It carried Rar-kin on one arm and floated down feet first, with the black helium balloon fixed to its shoulders like a parachute.

'They'll have to hurry or they'll be knocked out of the sky!' Althorn said and pulled his hood up.

As if in response, Samas saw the black balloon shrink and One-eight-seven zoomed towards them at a faster pace, allowing gravity to speed it up. A few soldiers stepped back, but Samas held his place at the front.

'Where are the others?' Samas shouted as One-eight-seven made a soft, gliding landing using jets from its feet.

Samas held a hand to his eyes and, by the time the dust had settled, One-eight-seven's balloon flapped around its shoulders like a black cape. It looked different to the other Lutamek: lithe and gangly like a teenager, Samas thought.

One-eight-seven lowered Rar-kin to the ground then spoke for the first time. 'We have returned with new information.'

'Information received,' Nine-five replied.

While Rar-kin bowed to Jakan-tar in the Sorean manner, the grey block of a spaceship manoeuvred in the sky behind them, turning as it descended to slip into an empty position just a few rows from their camp.

'We must check the new vessel,' One-eight-seven said and walked away.

'Wait!' Samas shouted and took a step forward. 'What happened to my men?'

'We must check the new vessel,' One-eight-seven repeated.

'Not now,' Samas said and looked to Nine-five and Ten-ten,

who were walking towards the new ship with the rest of the crowd.

Samas was about to raise his voice and demand an answer but stopped. Patience, he told himself. He walked with long strides, pushing to the front of the throng, and was one of the first to see One-eight-seven tapping on a panel near the rear door identical to the one they'd accessed on the humans' starship.

With a click and a hiss, the door slid away and shapes appeared from the gloom. Samas squinted as four distinct individuals stumbled out.

'Now that was a helluva trip!' Crossley said, slapping John Greene on the shoulder.

Osayimwese was behind them, followed by Delta-Six, who carried a handful of metal slips. He walked straight to Samas and handed them over with a stony look on his face.

'Mission accomplished.'

Gal-qadan and his cavalry were on a water break when the starship detached from the dome cap and floated to the ground. From here the dome was still monstrously big and far larger than the domes they were heading towards.

'I hope their camp wasn't in its parking spot,' Das, the brown, scaly alien said, sitting on the side of one of the carts.

'I'm sure Mata can deal with it,' Pod replied with a laugh.

Gal-qadan grimaced and looked away. Other than these two, the soldiers under his command rarely spoke, which suited him well. Most of those who had ridden with him in the dome had remained loyal apart from Dakaniha, who had chosen to stay with the foot soldiers. In addition, he had several Sorean, who had proven their prowess during the Brakari battle, and Isao, the Eastern swordsman who had flitted in and out of existence like a ghost. But Isao remained an enigma, as did

Peronicus-Rax. Although there was mutual respect between Gal-qadan and the tall, one-eyed alien after their deal over the weapon in the dome, Gal-qadan knew Peronicus-Rax had his own agenda, so he watched him carefully. He was starting to doubt his stories about 'the Ascent' were real after all.

Gal-qadan looked back at the cart, eyeing its contents. He would wait before checking on his newest recruits and hoped he remembered the sequence of buttons he had seen Ten-ten press on One-eight-seven to activate it. A surge of energy rushed through him at the thought of having those two metal warriors under his command, and he took a sip of water to cool his throat and survey the land ahead. There was a dark patch on the horizon. So far, they had followed Peronicus-Rax's directions, which led towards that patch rather than any particular dome. Gal-qadan had asked why but had simply been told, 'It is the way.'

'You say we should reach the next marker by sundown?' Gal-qadan asked.

'Yes,' Peronicus-Rax replied.

'And Das and Pod, you haven't been this way before?'

'No,' they replied in unison, without offering any further information.

Gal-qadan felt the urge to draw his bow and shoot the two scaly rodents off the side of the cart, but he knew their giant alter egos could appear in an instant and flatten him.

'So be it,' he said and watched Peronicus-Rax return his water to the half-cart which had allowed him to scoot along at a pace not much slower than the tocka.

As he checked his cache of weapons, Peronicus-Rax cast a glance at the nearest soldiers, as he had done a hundred times before. Watching. He was always watching, Gal-qadan thought.

Then it struck him.

Gal-qadan had finally worked out what annoyed him about Peronicus-Rax. He was too involved in the group, asking about every soldier before their journey and suggesting other members who could join – even that newcomer, Smith. Riding ability was never mentioned, just prowess and weaponry. It felt to Gal-qadan that the tall alien was collecting his soldiers like he collected the weapons that swung on his belts. Remembering how Peronicus-Rax had used the weapons as bargaining chips with the gang of thugs at the silver gates, Gal-qadan felt the cold realisation that he was being used.

John drank from the metal tube Althorn handed him and winced at the bitter taste. He gulped down what he could stomach, forcing the liquid down his throat without it touching his tongue.

'It's better than dying from starvation,' Althorn said as John gave a fake smile.

'I know, but I'd rather have a roast chicken any day,' John said and Althorn's stomach seemed to growl in response.

'Best not to think about it,' Althorn replied and returned the half-empty canister to Lavalle, who was still in charge of supplies.

'We'll have to ration these when we start the journey,' Lavalle said to Samas, who was inspecting the array of containers on the cart.

'Yes, but we still need empty containers for water and salt,' Samas replied. 'This may keep us alive but I need to make sure we have the strength to fight.'

Lavalle nodded back and John walked to where Crossley was regaling a group of soldiers, human and Sorean, with their dome-cap adventures.

'So I said to Delta-Six, why doesn't he carry us down one by one? But he looked like he was just going to make a jump for it, then the Synchronisers started–'

'The who?' Dakaniha asked.

'The Synchronisers,' Crossley said, 'the creatures who bring the ships in and govern the dome… anyways, they were done with their work so had started cleaning up the corridors and that's when John said, why don't we get in the starship?'

Crossley looked over to John, who felt fifty pairs of eyes turn to him. His cheeks flushed. 'Well, it made sense. It was empty and we knew it would land near the camp.'

A solid hand patted John on the shoulder and he turned to see Lavalle. 'That was quick thinking, John, well done.'

John looked to the ground. 'It was nothing, just made sense, that's all.'

'So we climbed back up,' Crossley continued.

'And the whole cap was empty,' Osayimwese added.

'We walked straight into the spaceship like we were catching a bus,' Crossley said. 'We sat on the floor and that thing zipped us down here quicker than a flash.' Crossley pointed at the new starship, surrounded by Lutamek, checking various panels and info-ports.

John turned to see Rar-kin walking with Nine-five and Jakan-tar.

'Rar-kin!' Crossley called out. 'Are you gonna tell us what happened up there? Why'd you leave us in the lurch, hey?'

The Sorean didn't show any emotion. It looked to its leader, Jakan-tar, who turned and said, 'A new mission became apparent.'

'What new mission?' John asked calmly before Crossley shouted.

'Rar-kin,' Nine-five said, 'would you like to explain?'

Rar-kin stepped forward and looked from soldier to soldier

as it talked through what it had seen. 'When we ascended the dome I noticed anomalies in the curvature of the horizon.'

Crossley raised a finger and opened his mouth but Nine-five lifted its hand to silence him.

'I explained to Delta-Six, who set his processors to calculate the angle and estimate the size of the planet, but I already had a theory – I just needed to go higher to see for myself.'

'So you took One-eight-seven and flew up?' Crossley asked.

'Yes and One-eight-seven's readings have confirmed my theory.'

'Which is?' John asked, feeling his pulse speed up.

'We are not on a planet.'

John frowned and looked around at the equally confused faces. 'Then what are we on?' John asked.

'It appears we're on an immense disc,' Rar-kin replied.

'Which are clearly not found naturally in our galaxy,' Nine-five added.

John imagined a huge coin with scores of domes on the surface, but the image didn't stick.

'So you're saying this whole place was *built* by someone?' Crossley asked. 'So how did they create the atmosphere? And gravity? You can't just *build* gravity, you know?'

'We are well aware of that,' Nine-five replied. 'We have sensed a constraining barrier – possibly to restrict spacecraft entering the atmosphere – but we don't have all the answers yet. However, we do have some information from the data you brought back from the dome cap.'

'Do you know who brought us here?' John asked.

'No,' Nine-five replied, 'but we have a greater understanding of how our biological components developed new abilities.' The great Lutamek held a hand up. 'Before you ask, no, these changes will continue to work outside the dome and are irreversible.'

The next morning, as the great army walked into the expanse between the domes, John couldn't shake off that night's dreams. The temperature had dropped again, but they had been sheltered amongst the starships and Ten-ten had set up a low-level dust dome to keep some heat in. Those dreams though... John had been back in the trenches with the rats, the dirty water and the stench of death. Only in this dream, John had his gun-arm, and the soldiers in his trench were a variety of bizarre creatures of every size and colour, animals and robots everywhere. Great shadows loomed over him and, when he finally saw the enemy trench, it was manned by hundreds of the same large, dark-blue creature: General Panzicosta.

John's gun-arm clicked as he walked with the army and spun shapes in the chamber. The more intricate shapes felt easier to mould now and the muzzle had more manipulative ability. He let the energy fizzle out and took in the mass of human, Sorean and Lutamek soldiers trooping across the red powdery soil with him. Althorn had taken the left flank and Delta-Six was scouting on the right, while several Sorean raced ahead on tocka with Lavalle and Euryleia, behind a vanguard of the fastest Lutamek.

John felt safe.

In the distance, past the carts and swarms of Sorean, John recognised Ten-ten's shape and made a beeline towards the Lutamek science officer.

'Ten-ten?' John called out as he neared.

'John Greene,' the metal behemoth replied.

'I... erm, I'd like to find out more about my gun-arm.' John shot a glance up at Ten-ten, then looked nervously away.

'I can scan it for you.'

'Yes, that would be good, thanks.' John hesitated then said, 'Can you scan it when I fire it?'

'To ascertain the composition of your bullets?' Ten-ten asked. 'Yes. Let's get ahead of the army.'

'Alright then,' said John. He tightened his gun-arm to his chest and started jogging away.

'Allow me.'

'Woah!' John shouted as Ten-ten lifted him by the straps and rushed him forward. He let out a yell of excitement like when he'd ridden the tocka; in fact, it was just like riding an invisible horse!

When they were out of range and his feet were back on the ground, John spun a few bullets for Ten-ten.

'Initiating scanning,' Ten-ten said and a blue light flickered across what remained left of John's Lewis light machine gun.

'Right, here's a couple of stubby bullets,' John said as he fired. 'Followed by some gnarled smashers… and a few long-range snipers.'

A series of dust explosions a distance away in the dirt signalled the endpoint of each shot, proving his gun was still working.

Ten-ten's light cut out and it stomped over to the impact points.

'Well?' John asked, jogging over.

'Your gun-arm is still changing,' Ten-ten replied. 'Partly due to the loss of material and partly due to a recent acceleration event.'

John frowned and stared back at the army and dome. 'Oh! I took a shock when I was in the dome cap, would that be it?'

'Yes, any excess energy could stimulate the process.' Ten-ten held out its left palm over the ground and John saw several thorn-thin slivers rise up. 'The structural change has been minuscule, but material has been lost with each shot.'

Ten-ten twisted its hand around for John to see six shards of white: two short, two ridged and two long and slender.

'These are your bullets,' Ten-ten said.

'But what are they?' John asked.

'Fairly crude but densely constructed shards of calcium-encrusted steel.'

'Calcium?'

'From the remnants of your arm bone,' Ten-ten replied. 'And the steel has been taken from the body of the gun.'

John swallowed, then asked, 'So if I keep firing these bullets, what'll happen to my arm?'

'Eventually the material will be used up.' Ten-ten started walking again, keeping ahead of the army. 'But the firing mechanisms will cease to work effectively before all the material is totally depleted.'

'Right,' John said, jogging to keep up with Ten-ten.

His eyes drifted to the horizon as he tried to understand. Should he stop using the gun to save his arm? Could the Lutamek fix it? What would it become when it stopped working – a metal stump?

'New information is coming from the scouts,' Ten-ten said. 'I must talk to the leaders.'

'Okay,' John replied, 'thanks for your help.'

John strapped up his gun-arm again and focussed on the domes ahead as he resumed his stride, his feet crunching the sand with alternate sounds of metal and hard leather.

As John walked, his feelings rose to the surface. He felt anxious. Worried. There was a lot to think about, to be concerned about, yet there was nothing he could do. The changes to his arm, walking into unknown territory… he needed to focus. At the core of his emotions lay his determined need to find out why he'd been taken from little Joe, leaving him fatherless – an orphan – facing the world alone for his entire life. John's gun-arm clicked again, and he pictured the bone being chipped away inside, so stopped, breathed in and let out a deep sigh.

The scale of everything here was totally overwhelming. The domes, the spaceships, this world... how could he, John Greene from the Royal Fusiliers, find who was responsible for all of this? Back home, he wasn't even allowed into an officers' mess without written authorisation, let alone to address a brigadier or general. If he wanted to know what was going on here, he needed to talk to the highest command, and how was he going to do that in a world he could barely comprehend?

'Hey, John!'

John turned to see Crossley walking over with Olan, the Viking.

'You been taking potshots?'

'Oh, I was just getting Ten-ten to take a look at my gun,' John replied.

'Surely Crossley could do that for you?' Olan said.

'Well, I haven't tried my sonar on anything living yet,' Crossley said as they strolled on together.

'You never tried my chest plate,' Olan said. 'Do you think you could find out what it's made of?'

'No way,' Crossley said. 'I've heard about what that thing can do – you could see the Draytor for Chrissake, that's how you killed it – what if some weird crap bounced back and messed my head up? No thank you!'

'Alright,' Olan replied. 'I'll ask Ten-ten to test it, but what about John?'

'Don't worry,' John said, 'Ten-ten said my arm's still changing and what I thought were air bullets were actually tiny shards of bone and metal fused together.'

Crossley's eyebrows raised. 'So if you keep firing...'

'Yep,' John replied and held his gun-arm out, 'there'll be nothing left. Have a look.'

'Okay.' Crossley coughed at John's outstretched arm, then tried a few gurgling sounds John hadn't heard before. 'Well, it's hard to tell, but I can just about make out where the bone ends and the metal begins... a bit blurred, but let me have a look tomorrow and see if it's changed.'

'Thanks, Doctor,' John said with a smile.

'Maybe you should get another weapon?' Olan said. 'There are plenty in the carts.'

'We'll see,' John replied, not sure he could carry another weapon.

'I don't know why we don't hitch a ride with them walking trains?' Crossley said, pointing at the nearest Lutamek. 'Seriously? We'd get there in half the time and save our energy.'

John shook his head. 'You're forgetting what happened to them in the dome.'

'What the Brakari did to them?' Olan asked.

'They controlled them and turned them into beasts of burden,' John replied, remembering the sparking body of Two-eight-four, the Lutamek Millok had used to transport them from Abzicrutia. 'They were in pain the whole time,' he said. 'It was torture.'

'Yeah, well, we wouldn't do it like that, would we?' Crossley replied. 'We could build open-sided carts and... maybe not. Anyhow, I heard some interesting stuff earlier.'

'Go on,' Olan said.

John watched Crossley's animated face as they walked on.

'So I overheard Lavalle before he scouted ahead – apparently the cart Gal-qadan took had a couple of Lutamek eggs in it.'

'No!' John said. 'He stole them?'

'Probably,' Crossley said. 'But that's not the point. The Lutamek knew all about it.'

'What?'

'They know he's taken them and they're in constant communication with them.'

'How does that work?' Olan asked. 'They haven't hatched yet.'

'One-eight-seven wasn't much of a talker even after it *had* hatched,' John said. 'Can they be trusted?'

'Sure they can – they're Lutamek,' Crossley said. 'Anyway, from what I heard, the young robots can communicate before they hatch out and are covered in eyes and all sorts, just like their... parents.'

John nodded, amazed once again by the machinery and gizmos of other species. During his war, John had been shocked by the ferocity of industrialised slaughter – gas shells, cannon barrages, fixed machine guns and dogfights in the skies – but now he only had to feel how his Lutamek left leg fitted into his knee to see how technology benefitted him. The white ceramic walls in the dome cap and in the starships, the Synchronisers and the vast machine at work across the galaxy to bring this array of alien soldiers here were all a different matter.

John sighed and pictured the screen in the dome cap where he had zoomed into views within the dome. 'I wonder what happened to everyone left in the dome,' he said, thinking about Panzicosta as much as Millok and her children.

'Well, if Delta-Six's panic about the Tathon was anything to go by,' Crossley replied, 'anyone left in there is about to get a shock – there're some souped-up beasts ready to kick some ass.'

Olan laughed and said, 'I think I've had enough of fighting dangerous creatures.'

'Who knows what lies ahead,' John said, staring out at the

domes in the distance, which didn't seem to be any bigger despite the distance they had already covered.

He felt Olan's stare and the Viking asked, 'What was it like up there? In the dome cap? Delta-Six said it was like inside the starships, but what was it *really* like?'

'To be honest,' John said, 'I didn't understand much of it – the machines, the Synchronisers and what they're doing.'

'We were just there to get the information,' Crossley said, 'and get out.'

'Why?' John asked and saw Olan frown.

'I… I had ideas of what could be up there,' he replied. 'This place fits with the stories of my gods.'

'Odin and Valhalla?' Crossley asked.

John knew little about Norse gods, so said nothing.

Olan replied. 'This could be Valhalla.' He stretched his arm out to gesture at the domes beyond. 'The domes could be the 540 doors where the warriors enter and the plains could be the great hall where we battle…'

'But weren't the warriors reborn every morning?' Crossley asked.

'Maybe Loki is at work here too,' Olan said with a shrug and looked at the cat-like Sorean and the huge robots which walked with them. 'And this chest plate?' He tapped the golden metal with his thick forefinger. 'Something the dwarves would have cast.'

Crossley patted him on the shoulder. 'Well, you keep thinking like that, big man,' he said with a smile. 'Because it sure makes more sense than anything I've seen so far.'

John wondered if Olan's ideas made any more sense than the explanations the Lutamek had given them. Surely there was a single mind somewhere responsible for all of this. A one-eyed god or some advanced alien, did it matter?

'What's going on over there?' John said, nodding to where

three of the Lutamek on the periphery had stopped in their tracks.

'Who knows?' Crossley said and they ground to a halt.

John, happy to give his good foot a rest, rubbed his calf as the fighters on the edge of the army drew in, closing around the bulk of soldiers.

'Hey, what's going on?' Crossley shouted.

'Hold position!' Samas shouted.

John saw One-eight-seven rise up from the rearguard, its black balloon inflating.

'They're spooked by something,' Crossley said as he unclipped his weapon.

Olan had his axe in hand and was scanning the nearest region of desert, so John unstrapped his gun-arm and span a few long-range bullets.

'Fall back!' Samas shouted. 'Defensive positions!'

John jogged back, eager to be safe in the throng of warriors. Hundreds of soldiers were gravitating closer together, drawing weapons, and the redcoats were busy pulling objects out of their boxes.

'What's happening?' Crossley shouted at Samas as they met.

Clumps of warriors grouped up and shields were raised, a mass of guns and bizarre weapons pointing out of every gap.

'We've got reports of an attack,' Samas replied.

'From the scouts?' Crossley asked.

'No,' Samas replied. 'From the young Lutamek. Gal-qadan's men are being attacked.'

Chapter 7

Isao woke with a start. He'd been dreaming of the shadow world, the grey-cloud existence where people, trees and other physical objects stood as swirling, seaweed versions of their true selves. From what Gal-qadan had told him, Isao had been invisible when he and his companions had slipped away. Delta-Six had called it 'phasing out', but Isao still needed more details. What had really happened to him when he switched worlds, and why?

He sat up, reached for his sword and scanned the group sleeping around him. The morning light gave them a red glow as the sun crept over the distant domes. Tocka lay motionless in a circle around their leader, while the humans and Sorean lay scattered like fallen dolls.

'We should get moving soon.'

The deep tones of Peronicus-Rax made Isao turn. He had taken the silhouette for a cart but now could make out the large alien perched on his two-wheeled contraption.

'Yes,' Isao replied and searched for Gal-qadan, who was still asleep.

Isao still didn't trust the Mongol and had kept him in view, waiting for him to make another wrong move. Anything that betrayed his true emotions.

'Do you think the Ascent are really out there?' Isao asked, recalling the conversations he'd heard between Peronicus-Rax and Das and Pod.

'I know they are,' came the terse reply.

What was Peronicus-Rax holding back? He reminded Isao of a hermit monk he'd heard of who allowed disciples to ask him one question each but answered every question with a dog bark. Still, year after year, the young disciples asked their question in the vain hope they would be the one to receive true wisdom from the master.

'And they will help us?' Isao asked.

'They had better help us,' Gal-qadan spoke and pushed himself up to a seated position, 'or they will find themselves with a new enemy.'

The last thing the army needed was another enemy, Isao thought. They barely had enough provisions in this barren land and a battle could be disastrous. From what he'd overheard, the Ascent were a group of advanced soldiers with weapons and technology far more dangerous than anything they had witnessed in the dome.

'They may have what we seek,' Peronicus-Rax replied.

'So where do we find them?' Smith asked.

Isao turned to the soldier, weighing up his physical prowess, having never seen him fight in battle. His tight-fitting suit was similar to Li's, or maybe it was the reflective mask face that reminded him of the Chinese soldier, and his weapon was more advanced than most, suggesting he was from an age after Isao's time. As for fighting style, Isao would have to wait to see him in action.

Peronicus-Rax pushed his cart away, ready to set the path the cavalry would follow. 'We don't find them,' he said. 'They will find us.'

Gal-qadan's face turned sour. 'Everyone eat and pack to move out,' he growled.

Hours later, when the sun was at its zenith, the true scale of the dark patch of ground they had been heading towards became apparent.

'It looks like a tar pit.' Smith said.

'Something similar,' Peronicus-Rax replied.

Isao felt his tocka twitch as the sweet scent of the black lake wafted to them on a light wind.

'We must travel around–' Gal-qadan was cut off by a shrieking sound and the entire group of tocka collapsed to their knees.

Isao rolled off, eyes tight and hands over his ears. A pain pulsed deep inside his head, lasting long dreadful seconds until subsiding with a wash of cool relief through his head. He released his hands, opened his eyes and stared around in wonder and awe.

He was back in the shadow world.

Isao stood and stared at the silhouettes of his allies: humans, Sorean and tocka rolling on the floor in agony. Here, outside the dome, shapes appeared solid and kept some of their true colour. There was more too: in the chest of every soldier Isao saw the pulsing blood-red gemstone of a heart. And when he turned to the tar pit, he saw a shoal of shining hearts emerging and surrounding them.

Staring at the faint-blue sky, Gal-qadan felt glad it was no longer the colour of jade, as it had been inside the dome. He lay panting with his head resting on the belly of a dead tocka.

Strange how these banal thoughts came to him when he

was drained of energy, he thought. Was it because, at times like these, the repetitive sounds stopped filling his head? Was this how his soldiers always felt and why they talked such nonsense?

He could fight no more.

The creatures from the black-tar lake had been seen off and taken their dead with them – that gave him strength – but what had the victory cost his army? He turned his head to one side, then to the other, assessing the damage: the tocka were seeing to their injured, as were the few Sorean in the group. Going by the number of humans stumbling around, they had fared better than Gal-qadan had feared. They were still weak though.

He sat up and pushed his hair out of his face. He'd been saved by his impenetrable skin, but the army's saviour and strength had definitely not been human.

'Captain?'

The voice made Gal-qadan turn. It was the new recruit, Smith, who had fought well from what he could remember.

'Yes,' Gal-qadan replied as he stood.

'The dead are accounted for and Peronicus-Rax is tending to the injured.' Smith's voice was muffled due to the mirrored mask, which clearly didn't work the same way as Li's had done.

Gal-qadan's anger rose at the mention of Peronicus-Rax and he felt the urge to smash the mask, to crack the warped image it projected back of him and the dead lying around him.

'We have enough horses,' Smith continued, 'but the carts need to be fixed.'

'Tocka,' Gal-qadan said and looked away.

'Pardon, Captain?'

'The horses, they are called tocka.' Gal-qadan had despised the name as much as the man who had given it to them, but, although he hated to admit it, Kastor had been a strong warrior in the end. 'I raised them from the dead.'

'Right,' Smith replied.

Gal-qadan winced at the faceless soldier's reply and he felt his energy returning. It was time to build on his army's victory and reassert his authority.

'Where are Das and Pod?'

'The two small creatures?'

'Yes.' Gal-qadan recalled how neither of the brothers had returned to their full size during the fight, but had scurried under the carts for cover.

'No sign of them.'

'I need someone to fix the carts,' Gal-qadan said and walked away.

Strolling through his scattered army, Gal-qadan ran the battle through his mind. The disabling sound had died away when the dark humanoids rose from the lake – no, not *from* the lake, they *were* the lake. Each creature had fired a different weapon: blasts of sunlight, waves of pressure or pulses of fire. They were as diverse as the human-and-Sorean army had been against the Brakari.

Taken by surprise, Gal-qadan's army had split and fired back with whatever they could. Streams of energy had bounced off his skin as Gal-qadan rolled straight for his bow and arrow, cursing the loss of his lightning weapon, hanging limp on the belt of Peronicus-Rax now, who'd hidden behind a protective yellow bubble. What the army could have done with them!

After slashing one black creature in half, Gal-qadan had been fighting to catch his breath when an array of multicoloured lasers lit the sky and the two Lutamek eggs leaped into action, unravelling and twisting like metal snakes. Their attack had been too much for the enemy army, which had slipped back into liquid form and drained away, into the ground. Now, despite their victory, Gal-qadan knew he could not rest.

'Peronicus-Rax!' Gal-qadan bellowed as he neared the one-eyed alien.

'Gal-qadan,' Peronicus-Rax replied, remaining focussed on an injured Sorean, who lay prostrate on the ground as he sprayed its injuries with an orange mist.

'You have collected an impressive range of weapons,' Gal-qadan kept his voice sharp and clear, 'yet refuse to use them on the battlefield. Tell me why.'

Peronicus-Rax finished spraying, leaving a waxy residue on the Sorean's burned skin, and turned to face him. 'My weapons have many uses.' The tall warrior stood, looming several feet higher than Gal-qadan. 'And I choose when to use them.'

'But as part of my army, I expect you and every soldier to defend and attack AS ONE!' Gal-qadan felt the eyes of his soldiers on him and knew he had to win this argument if he was to remain the sole authority here.

'Well,' Peronicus-Rax lumbered over to his two-wheeled contraption and tucked his medical kit away, casually turning the security shield off and then back on as he did so, 'that's a matter of perspective.'

Gal-qadan kept his face rigid, knowing the weapons in that cart would double his army's firepower... but that was before the Lutamek eggs had realised their potential. He glanced over his shoulder at them. Maybe Peronicus-Rax wasn't as important as he had first thought?

'From my perspective,' Gal-qadan kept his voice low and clear, 'you are part of *my* army.'

'And I have served it.' Peronicus-Rax gestured at the Sorean, who was sitting up now.

'But rather than attacking the enemy, you only defended yourself,' Gal-qadan replied. 'Men were injured by enemy soldiers you could have destroyed with a single shot!'

The large eye of the alien turned on Gal-qadan and grew

dark. 'We all have our own reasons for being here, human. We may be stronger together but I won't be told how to fight.'

Gal-qadan felt his cheeks warm and the pounding in his head returned. He took a long draft of air through his nose and focussed on Peronicus-Rax's eye, wondering how he could save face in front of his men.

'No, I shan't tell you how to fight,' Gal-qadan replied. 'But I *expect* you to fight alongside your allies as we fight beside you.' Gal-qadan looked around for Das and Pod. 'That goes for you two as well,' he bellowed, knowing he would lose this argument with Peronicus-Rax. 'Hiding is not an option during battle.'

'We were guarding the supplies,' one of the creatures said.

'I don't have time for excuses,' Gal-qadan replied and turned back to Peronicus-Rax. 'And what of your intelligence? Were these your Ascent?'

'No,' Peronicus-Rax replied quickly. 'These are not the Ascent I am searching for.'

Gal-qadan tilted his head. The tall alien had just betrayed his true motive. It made sense now: the questions about each soldier's fighting ability; the collection of weapons; and why he was watching the battles in the dome... Peronicus-Rax was *delivering* Gal-qadan's army to the Ascent.

Gal-qadan fought to control the hundreds of new questions rushing around his mind. He slowed his breathing and focussed. Was this why Peronicus-Rax had returned to the dome? To bring back the most deadly soldiers he could find? Gal-qadan's chest swelled at the thought he had been chosen above others, but his anger remained – he would *not* allow his army to be hired out without being part of the discussion and, at the very least, being paid. He sighed. He couldn't afford to reveal he knew the truth... he had to maintain order and be prepared for what was to come.

'Then we will search for your Ascent,' Gal-qadan said. 'We share the same goal.' He looked at the tocka, some of whom were standing again and looked strong enough to carry on. 'Heal the injured,' he ordered those who could hear him, 'fix the carts and we'll resume our journey.'

Gal-qadan headed straight for the ration boxes near a broken cart, which Smith and another soldier were fixing. A strange feeling tickled the back of his neck and he turned sharply, but nobody was there.

Isao had watched the conversation between Peronicus-Rax and Gal-qadan in a state of mild amusement. Here he was in the shadow world, yet he felt comfortable. There was no tidal pull, as there had been in the dome, and only the slightest smoky distortion interrupted his view of the real world.

And he could see people's hearts.

There was more he could see, if he concentrated, but the most obvious feature of the soldiers around Isao was their beating hearts: the Sorean's large, multi-chambered heart; the humans' fist-sized organ; and Peronicus-Rax's three large pumps, which squeezed his thick bloods around his large frame. He'd seen the odd, triangular hearts of the enemy as well.

Isao had been unable to fight during the battle and had found it bizarre to have his fortune reversed. In the dome he'd fought in clarity, yet here he'd been stuck in the shadow world during the battle. No, he wasn't stuck now; he had *chosen* to stay in the shadow world. Isao simply concentrated on which world he preferred and he could slip into either.

Isao felt like a boy with a new toy. He toured the army, walking around the broken carts and fallen tocka, invisible to them all. He stopped to marvel at the intricacies of the horse-like creatures' inner workings of glowing organs and glittering vessels. He walked over to Steve Smith and waved his hand in his face but got no response. He pressed his hand on the man's shoulder and felt some pressure, but nothing like the real thing. Could he travel through matter? he wondered as he walked to where the group of Sorean were burying their comrade. The inert body lay in the scraping they had made in the desert floor and Isao saw nothing within.

An idea came to Isao and he jogged over to visit the two Lutamek eggs which had flowered into such violent war machines during the battle. Warily, Isao stepped close and peered deep inside their mechanical bodies. He wasn't disappointed. The colours were different to those of the other soldiers and the Lutamek's metal pump of a heart was clear to see, as were the biological components which were scattered throughout the metal and ceramic body parts: thick nerves twitching in tubes; fibres pulsing in boxes; and odd-shaped organs vibrating in time with a variety of twisting mechanisms. One of the shapes, which reminded Isao of Ten-ten's face, turned in Isao's direction and he felt an odd tingling sensation spread over him as orange lights appeared, floating between them.

As the lights grew into shapes – two twirls, a cross and a star – Isao wondered: was the juvenile Lutamek trying to communicate? The shapes twisted and moved as Isao stared at them. He found he could rotate them if he concentrated, and they changed colour when they crossed each other. Isao presumed it was a type of puzzle, but the lights faded before he could answer it.

Maybe another time? he thought and left the Lutamek alone.

Lost in his thoughts as he walked away from the group, Isao nearly walked into Peronicus-Rax, crouched behind his small cart with a box of lights which he pointed towards the nearest dome. Isao tiptoed around the huge warrior to get a better view. If the Lutamek had sensed him, maybe the technology Peronicus-Rax held could do the same?

A screen on the box of lights showed moving lights and, as Peronicus-Rax moved it from left to right, a grey image on the screen changed too. It was a map of the land ahead, Isao realised, which meant the groups of dots had to be soldiers. Were they the Ascent?

With a grunt, Peronicus-Rax swung the device towards the cluster of domes that surrounded the needle-like tower. On the edge of the screen nearest the tower, the collection of dots merged into one writhing mass.

If Peronicus-Rax had the ability to see an enemy coming, Isao thought, why hadn't he told Gal-qadan about the attack?

Gal-qadan resisted pressing any of the buttons which covered the intricate metal shells of the sleeping baby Lutamek. He reached out and saw a metallic graze on his wrist.

'You and I are more similar than you would imagine,' he said, looking around to make sure nobody was in earshot. 'A strong shell protecting a terrible fury deep inside.' He dropped his head. 'I admire that,' he whispered, and turned as he sensed heavy footsteps coming his way.

'We should change direction,' Peronicus-Rax spoke in his deep tone, 'and make our way straight for the rendezvous.' He pointed towards the tower.

Gal-qadan studied the tall alien for a few seconds before replying. 'Why now?' he asked.

'Our numbers are too low,' Peronicus-Rax replied, 'and the danger too high.'

Gal-qadan sniffed. With the Lutamek on his side they were a match for any army crossing their path, but Peronicus-Rax still wanted to lead them into his trap, which suggested the Ascent were even more powerful. There was little Gal-qadan could do. When the time came, they would fight, and his skin would save him. Maybe it was time to let go of this army and think about the next one? From within the Ascent, he would have a better chance of gaining power.

'So be it,' Gal-qadan replied. 'We switch routes.' He pointed at the distant tower and raised his voice so everyone could hear. 'We cut straight to our final destination.'

Gal-qadan threw his bags in the cart next to the Lutamek eggs, hefted himself over and made himself comfortable on a sack of spare gear. Not the same as being on a tocka, he thought, wondering how the herd would readjust themselves now they had lost their leader.

'Move out!' he shouted.

The cart wheels creaked and the tocka's hooves padded the ground, creating a hypnotic rhythm. Gal-qadan surveyed his army and spotted Isao riding in the distance. He tried to recall what the samurai had done during the skirmish, but a flash of movement caught his attention.

'Das and Pod,' he called out, 'ride with me.' He patted the cart. 'Tell me what you know about our metal friends here.'

The two pangolin-like creatures scurried over, leaped aboard the cart without a word and made themselves comfortable on a sack opposite Gal-qadan.

'What is it you wish to know?' Das asked with a twist of his head.

Gal-qadan leaned forward and said, 'What I wish to know is how to communicate with them.'

Pod shook his head. 'They hear all and see all,' he said. 'The trick is getting them to talk to you.'

'Obviously,' Gal-qadan snapped back. 'But why are these two not talking like the rest of the Lutamek?'

'They're children,' Das replied and gave the nearest egg a glance. 'Before they can talk they need to understand the world around them.'

'Lutamek develop fast but they still take time,' Pod added.

Gal-qadan sat back with an audible *humph* and cast a glance out at the horizon beyond. Time was one thing he didn't have.

Isao felt Gal-qadan's glare on him but kept riding. Their leader sat in his cart, like an emperor on his throne, chatting with those strange animals he had avoided since seeing them swell into giants during the battle against the Brakari.

Isao was paranoid that someone had seen him slip back into the real world, but he concentrated on the path ahead and the huge, needle-like tower which glistened in the distance, squinting for anything like the countless signs of life he'd seen on Peronicus-Rax's machine. Who knew what lay ahead? Were those dots on the screen allies or enemy troops?

Isao felt a twinge of shame, knowing he would be safe if they were attacked again, while his comrades would have to fight. He clenched his fist to control his anxiety and felt his eyes blur. Flashes of red lit up on the nearest soldiers: a Sorean riding a tocka and a Roman soldier beyond. He recognised the colour and shape instantly. He was still in the real world, but had seen the hearts of his allies as though he were in the shadow world. He tried it again, forcing his eyes to lose focus. But it didn't work.

Where did the energy come from? Isao thought. In the dome he had been pulled by a tide, yet outside it there was no pull… although there was a *weight*. It was strong, like gravity, yet rather than pulling him down and slowing his movements, it gave him strength. Thinking about it like that, Isao could feel it once more: a power beneath his feet. He tried drawing on it… and the vision returned. Red hearts and organs glowed and pulsed a variety of colours. Isao was still in the real world, but his eyes were in the shadow world. What if it affected him permanently? He scanned the horizon – and saw a low pink glow straight ahead of them.

Isao snapped his vision back to normal and steered his tocka towards Gal-qadan's cart.

'Captain,' he said, 'I see soldiers ahead.'

'Where?' Gal-qadan growled and sat up straight. 'I see nothing.' He took a moment to watch the army marching around them. 'And the tocka show no sign.'

Das and Pod were at the cart edge, staring as well. 'Nothing out there,' one said.

'Peronicus-Rax,' Gal-qadan called out. 'Any sign of movement ahead?'

Isao looked back and saw the isolated figure of Peronicus-Rax standing motionless some distance back. 'He's stopped,' Isao said and pointed.

'Peronicus-Rax!' Gal-qadan yelled.

'What shall we do?' Isao asked, feeling ready to slip into the safety of the shadow world.

Gal-qadan looked at Das and Pod, who were stuffing their possessions into a sack. 'What are you doing?' he asked.

'This is the place,' Pod said.

'What place?' Gal-qadan spat.

'Where we meet our followers,' Pod replied.

'Followers?' Gal-qadan's voice was growing louder.

Das and Pod laughed and shared a look, enraging Gal-qadan further. He drew his sword and slashed at the creatures, who dodged and jumped over his angry blade.

Isao slowed his tocka and let the cart continue ahead. He could see more pink shapes and they were spreading out around them. Their army was outnumbered five to one.

He heard Pod reply to Gal-qadan, 'Our followers are the Firstborn.'

'Firstborn? What are you talking about?' Gal-qadan yelled back.

'They have come to collect your army,' said Das, as both brothers leaped off the cart.

Gal-qadan dropped his sword, snatched up his bow and started firing arrows at them as they ran away, weaving away through the forest of tocka legs. Isao pulled his tocka away, unsure of what to do.

'I thought Peronicus-Rax was selling us out!' Gal-qadan yelled with rage, 'not you little bastards!'

Isao turned a full circle and let his eyes slip into the shadow world. The pink shapes were advancing on the stationary army, who had no orders now Gal-qadan was chasing the brothers, and a dust trail led to the ever-decreasing shape of Peronicus-Rax, who had fled the way they'd travelled.

This is not a time to fight, Isao thought. He jumped off his tocka, gave it a consoling pat and slipped into the shadow world before the pink shapes closed in.

Chapter 8

Delta-Six hovered at 300 feet with his suit set to camouflage, watching distant energy flashes in the direction of Gal-qadan's cavalry. Calibration had proved a problem since they'd left the dome, but his systems seemed to work better at altitude, giving him a clear view of the tocka on their knees and a dark army surrounding the cluster of human and Sorean soldiers.

Then an odd sensation washed over Delta-Six.

There was no beep or signal; he simply felt a vacuum open up, and instantly raised his alert level until he found the source... his communication line with the Lutamek had dropped out. Spinning on a slow rotation, he raised a sensor map over his vision to plot the location of every Lutamek on the landscape below. The nearest scouts had stopped moving.

'We have reports of martial activity,' one of the Lutamek's metallic voices spoke in Delta-Six's ear, a second after he felt the connection reattach.

'I see it,' Delta-Six responded. 'Suggest we hold position.'

'Affirmative.'

A green light flashed, pulling Delta-Six's attention to where Lavalle, Euryleia and the Sorean rode their scouting tocka at the head of the main army. His systems suggested something was happening, but he couldn't see what.

'The army are assuming defensive positions,' Ten-ten said. 'All scouts to return to formation.'

The Lutamek were able to communicate through a range of methods, so the communication channel was purely for the humans' benefit. So, why had the Lutamek cut off communications? Had it been a defensive move to isolate their systems, or an attempt to communicate with someone else?

Delta-Six scanned the desert and was descending slowly, ready to defend his comrades, when an orange blip flashed in his view.

Movement.

He pushed energy to his visual processors, and more orange dots appeared. Surely the Lutamek could sense them too? He extrapolated his scan and view until he saw hundreds of clusters of dots moving at speed towards the army. Why weren't the Lutamek doing anything? The Lutamek nearest the attackers remained motionless while those on either flank were retreating and appeared to be outflanking the rest of the army. In less than a minute they would have the entire group surrounded.

'Samas,' Delta-Six contacted his direct leader. 'Samas, do you copy?'

Silence.

The bulk of the army were moving on, seemingly oblivious to the oncoming threat.

Delta-Six triggered a set of chemicals into his bloodstream, forcing him to focus. It took a second to calm his heart, but then he could think straight, and immediately it was clear: he had been cut off, but why?

'Lavalle, do you read me?'

Silence.

'Rar-kin, can you read me?'

A new Lutamek voice blared in Delta-Six's ear, 'Delta-Six. Return to the army. Defensive formation.'

Delta-Six studied the incoming orange dots, then correlated them against the signals he'd picked up from where Galqadan's men were being attacked. They were substantially different – enough to suggest they were separate armies.

'Copy that,' he replied to the Lutamek. 'Returning for defensive formation.'

Delta-Six had to act normally. If the Lutamek suspected he had spotted their change in tactics, they would neutralise him straight away, so he muted the comms link from his end and fired off a ghost probe to mimic his signature and descend as ordered. He triple-locked his camouflage, reduced all outgoing emissions to zero, including his breath, which was captured by a face mask, and drifted up and away from the main army. If his calculations were correct, he would have to climb several miles up to avoid the Lutamek sensors, to where the strange force field scrambled their sensors. Maybe he could sit out whatever was about to happen?

Maybe he would survive.

A surge of guilt ran through Delta-Six, similar to when his mini-sat had sent back images of the army's battle against the Brakari inside the dome. He should help his allies now, but a quick scan showed they were moving into groups to defend themselves. Maybe they would be okay? He gave himself a new shot of battle-ready drugs and kept climbing.

As he ascended, his mind calmed. He was a mote of energy almost in space, indistinguishable from the other debris the Lutamek had sensed near the disc's protective net.

He stared into the dark sky above and, after some time, when he started to feel safe, his mind returned to the one question which had been bothering him for days now.

What would he choose as a real name?

John kept the long-range bullets spinning in his gun-arm's chamber and remembered what Ten-ten had said about using up the metal and bone every time he fired. His arm felt different since the shock in the dome cap, more flexible somehow, but he didn't know if that was a real change or in his mind.

'Get behind that cart!' Crossley shouted, and John followed.

Samas was directing the army to group up behind whatever shelter they could find. Carts were tipped over and Sorean shields were being projected over each Sorean contingent, like huge half-bubbles. Olan was behind a nearby cart and Mata and Yarcha were approaching.

'Look at that!' Olan shouted and pointed at the small red army of British soldiers who were throwing boxes onto the ground. 'More of Ramsholt's inventions!'

'What on Earth?' John said as each box erupted into life as it hit the floor, forming solid-looking sets of metal-sheet walls which automatically locked together with a clicking and ratcheting sound John could hear from thirty metres away. In less than a minute, they had built a crescent-shaped defensive shield which curved overhead to protect the riflemen within, who poked their guns through tiny holes.

John was as gobsmacked at seeing the redcoats' contraptions as he had been with any Lutamek or Sorean technology.

'They've been busy!' Crossley said. 'They swear it's just metal and levers, but I really need to find out how they build that stuff.'

'Shall we join them?' John asked, eyeing up the broken cart they had as protection.

'Guess it would get a bit cramped in there,' Crossley replied.

'This will be fine,' Olan said and patted the cart.

'Plus we've got Mata, right?' Crossley grinned as Mata and Yarcha joined them. He moved in to pat the Maori on the shoulder but pulled his hand away when Mata squinted at him.

'My strength is returning,' Mata said with a glimpse at the sun. 'But the Lutamek will defend us, I'm sure.'

'If you trust them,' Yarcha replied, stony-faced.

'I guess this feels like one long nightmare, right?' Crossley said. 'I mean, you only just woke up–'

'Nightmare or not, I'm always ready,' Yarcha snapped back.

John saw she had one hand on the hilt of her bizarre-looking sword.

'But not ready to trust everyone yet?' Olan said. 'Wise decision.'

'Trust is to be earned,' Yarcha replied.

John scanned the horizon beyond the Lutamek sentinels, who all remained motionless. New silhouettes were appearing.

'The enemy are coming–' he started, but an explosion made him turn to where a tiny, bright dot burned brighter than the sun for a second before fading to nothing.

John followed a vapour trail down to one of the Lutamek.

'Well that sorted that out,' Crossley quipped. 'They won't be sending more missiles, that's for sure.'

John frowned. He hadn't seen a trail coming from the oncoming enemy. A new, cracking sound made him turn as a criss-cross mesh of blue light flickered into life high above their heads.

'And now the shield,' Crossley beamed. 'Whoever thinks they can take on the Lutamek better think again!'

'Are you sure this will defend us?' Yarcha asked.

Mata remained silent but stretched his neck and spread his fingers wide, each one sprouting a green tendril.

'What do you see, Olan?' John asked.

'Nothing strange,' the Viking replied. 'The shield is like the one Li created when we fought the Brakari.'

John looked over to where Samas crouched behind a cart with Rar-kin, Osayimwese and a host of other soldiers. By his hand gestures, Samas was clearly frustrated. He was pointing out to the left flank, so John looked over. He could see movement: a ring of tocka, circling the same spot.

'What are they doing?' John asked and pointed.

'I guess they don't want to be sitting ducks,' Crossley replied.

'They need to move under the shield,' Olan said.

'If these were the guys who attacked Gal-qadan, they'd have to have moved pretty damn fast to be here already,' Crossley said.

'What if it isn't them?' Olan asked.

'Another army?' Crossley said. 'I guess all these domes must have been full of armies at some time.'

John watched Lavalle and Euryleia's group of tocka. They were splitting into two groups – one was heading back under the shield but the second was heading towards the enemy. A flash of light was followed, a second later, by a deep cracking sound which ripped through the air.

'What the hell?' Crossley shouted and ducked. 'Did you see that?'

'The battle's started!' Yarcha said.

John could tell by her face she hadn't seen such an explosion before, and he wondered what her wars had been like.

'No!' Crossley yelled, looking from flank to flank and back to where One-eight-seven hovered behind them. 'That was a bloody Lutamek missile.'

More cracking explosions ripped through the air and John peeked over the cart to see a line of white flashes popping in the direction he had seen the tocka heading.

'That's not the only thing,' Mata said. 'Look!' He pointed up.

John stared up at the blue sky shield.

'It's getting lower.'

Delta-Six scanned the air around him as he ascended and moved away from the events taking place around the human–Sorean army. He hadn't detected any Lutamek sensors or missiles since they had destroyed his ghost probe. The Lutamek would have analysed the explosion spectrally and, thanks to his preparations, the dense organic material inside the ghost probe should have given a convincing recreation of a human getting blown up. Still, the speed at which they had despatched him told Delta-Six everything he needed to know.

Trust no one.

An alarm flashed on Delta-Six's view and he looked up. The stars were clearer here, in the deep blue of close-space, as were the satellites and what his sensors told him were orbiting spacecraft – hundreds of them. But that wasn't what his systems had drawn his attention to. It was the force field keeping the atmosphere in and those spaceships out, giving clearance only to sample craft to land on their assigned dome.

Delta-Six slowed his ascent, hovering ten metres beneath the field, and looked down. From this height, the entire disc was visible. The edges were clear and the domes were more concentrated towards the centre, but with an empty ring around the central tower. Even at this altitude, Delta-Six didn't feel safe above the Lutamek, so he drifted towards the centre of the immense disc.

He started to map his visual info against the data files the Lutamek had given him and stopped. Anything originating from the Lutamek had to be treated with suspicion. False information, virus loads, trigger mechanisms – it all had to be quarantined. He set off a deep-dive analysis probe, looking for anomalies or trends among the numerous files on gravitational readings, star maps and the files he had stored.

Looking back down, Delta-Six could see a light-blue mesh covering where he'd last seen the army. The Lutamek had been joined by the new aggressors – the orange dots – who were slowly moving in, like fishermen drawing in their trawl net. Movement and explosions suggested some soldiers were attempting to escape.

Delta-Six scanned the new enemy army, careful not to give away his position. Scores of the fighting species didn't register on his databanks but each unit's leader did.

'No?' Delta-Six zoomed in to double-check his readings.

Visuals confirmed it and his spectral and radiation analysis backed it up.

The new enemy were being led by Lutamek soldiers.

'We can't run for it, John!' Crossley shouted. 'We're not fast enough.'

'I know,' John shouted back, feeling panic take a hold of his body. The muscles in his legs felt jittery, his gun-arm clicked and his metal foot tapped against the cart. He needed to do something – to run or... 'We have to fight!'

He looked to Mata, who was watching the blue net with his intense glare as it closed in on them.

'We won't have time to fight,' Crossley replied.

'Here they come,' Olan said.

John made out a silhouette walking up to one of the Lutamek guards and his eyes picked up more detail of the large-shaped creature.

'Isn't that another Lutamek?' Crossley said. 'That's why they're not firing. Jeez!'

'What can we do?' Yarcha asked. 'These metal men are too strong to fight.'

'Not for some,' Mata said and walked off, his arms already rippling with vines and spiked tendrils.

'No, Mata, don't...' John called out but it was too late.

A blue bubble, similar to the one the Lutamek had used on Li, wrapped around the green Maori, pulling his steel-strong vines and barbed thorns in until he became a solid mass of wriggling tendrils. The perimeter of Lutamek guards turned to face the army now, with their weapons activated.

'What can we do?' John asked. 'Are they going to kill us?'

'Where did the new ones come from?' Olan asked.

'It has to be their ship,' Crossley said.

'What?' John gave the American a quick look.

'What if the Lutamek ship wasn't broken into by looters?' Crossley asked. 'But some of the Lutamek broke out!'

'And they've been out here all the time the Lutamek were in the dome?' John said. 'What if someone's got control of them again?'

'Not like the Brakari did,' Olan said and shook his head. 'I would be able to see it.'

'What d'you see there then?' Crossley asked and nodded at the British redcoats.

John saw a patch of rough earth where the metal fortress had been and a cloud of dust.

'Some kind of land ship,' Olan said as the dust cleared to reveal a moving vehicle.

Smoke was billowing out of scores of funnels poking out from what, to John, looked like a squat train.

'How on Earth did they build that?' John said.

'No idea,' Crossley said with a bemused smile. 'That guy's a genius. Look, it's changing again!'

The Lutamek had noticed too, sending snaking missiles its way.

John squinted, catching glimpses of whirring shovels and a sharp point protruding from the front. Then, with a deep, metallic clang, the missiles hit home, exploding in a wild eruption of dust and smoke. John turned and covered his head, wary of shrapnel, and felt a wave of tiredness wash over him. When he looked back and the dust had settled, the desert floor was bare.

'You bastards!' Crossley said, turning away. 'They killed them all!'

'We have to fight,' Olan said, leaning on the cart.

John spun a thick bullet in his gun-arm's chamber, hoping it would penetrate Lutamek armour, and looked up at the blue net, following its arch to the floor, where it fizzed and sparked as it touched the ground, creating a fixed half-bubble over the entire army.

'We can't get out now,' Crossley said, biting his fingernails.

'Do not be afraid,' a metallic voice boomed inside the shrinking dome. 'You will not be harmed.'

'That's rich after you just blew up those Limeys,' Crossley muttered and crouched to pull a grenade from his thigh pocket.

John looked at him through heavy eyelids but couldn't raise the strength to stop him.

With all his effort, Crossley turned and threw the grenade at the advancing blue mesh, where it exploded and froze in mid-air like a mini-star surrounded by white spears of light.

'Dammit,' Crossley groaned and slumped to the floor.

In the distance, John could see soldiers falling down as the blue net swept over them. Tocka were collapsing and groups of Sorean looked like they were already sleeping. Crackles and muted thuds signalled some fighting back, but it was all too little, too late.

'We welcome you all.' The voice seemed to echo as John's vision blurred.

The light from the blue mesh dazzled John, so he closed his eyes and knelt down to rest. His head was heavy and he soon felt the dusty earth against his cheek as he listened to the robotic voice.

'You are now the guests of the Ascent.'

Chapter 9

Praahs cantered through the Tathon army encampment, sending up clouds of dust as her clawed feet bit into the dry ground. 'Kno-lib, one of the three Tathon leaders, had summoned her, which was a good sign: she was needed. But, as benevolent as they were with their enhancements and endowments, they didn't appreciate being kept waiting.

For a moment, Praahs thought back to the lake: to her natural environment, where she'd mastered her own destiny. She tried to imagine herself deep in the dark water once more, her seven sets of light receptors and her rudimentary motion-sensitive eye, all on the top of her head, feeding her information. Her past was as murky as the waters had been though, no different to that of the other large beasts which had inhabited the lake, all forced to adapt to a new world and given little choice but to kill to survive.

Praahs imagined she could still taste the blood of the last set of animals she had fed on, and a pang of hunger tensed her stomach. It had been days since her last feed. In the lake, no sign of food for this long and the predators would turn on each other. She didn't miss those days.

Praahs could see the three huge shapes of the Tathon leaders, the nearest being 'Xit, who rarely conversed with non-Tathon, then the other two generals, 'Kno-lib and 'Brin, who discussed tactics openly, knowing none of their minions would disagree. She lowered her elongated, armoured skull submissively and slowed to a trot, then stopped with all but her foremost set of eyes open.

'Praahs,' the familiar, deep voice of her leader spoke directly to her through the ossicle bones of her sonar gills, the vibrations echoing in a tight air chamber at the rear of her brain, 'we have a mission for you.'

'I am ready, as ever,' Praahs spoke out loud.

'We have learned more of the mechanisms at work in this land and will soon vote on a new course of action,' 'Kno-lib said.

Praahs kept her head low in respect. Having been so easily subdued by them in her first encounter, she had never considered attacking even the smallest of the Tathon: the gelatinous soldiers who made up the majority of their army, and whose stories told of their accelerated development.

'We no longer desire to travel to the silver gates,' 'Kno-lib's voice echoed in her head, 'but believe there are resources worthy of acquisition in the land ahead.'

Praahs felt her wet teeth tingle in anticipation.

'You have command of the Cirratus.'

One of Praahs' eyes turned to the swathe of smaller, hard-shelled Tathon, who had proven almost indestructible when attacked by those who had naively opposed the Tathon expansion.

This marauding army of tentacled soldiers had only been unleashed for a matter of days when they'd captured her and, in the few days since she'd been assimilated into their ranks, hundreds more soldiers of various species had also been brought into their ranks.

'We need your speed and skill, Praahs,' the voice continued, 'to bring us new recruits. Return within four cycles, with the region's weapons and any soldiers of use.'

'Yes, 'Kno-lib,' Praahs replied. 'We shall pick the bone clean.'

As she ran across the plains, the wind rushed over Praahs' long body like the waters of her youth. Only the bitter tang of air in her gills reminded her this wasn't her natural environment, and that gave her strength – it showed how far she had come! She was flanked by a platoon of formidable, rock-hard, squid-like warriors who fought at her command as they scoured the land for a set of survivors the Tathon scouts had seen near a rocky outcrop. These warriors needed to be brought into the fold, or killed.

Despite all of the changes wrought on her by the generous Tathon, the thrill of the chase had never left her. If anything, it had been enhanced now she had masters to impress as well as a stomach to fill. Praahs hungered for their praise as much as she yearned to feed and sink her teeth into the warm, wet flesh of prey.

On the day they captured her, Praahs hadn't fed for weeks. Vibrations travelled to her deep, underwater cave and, slowly, she had drifted into open water, tensed her long abdomen to balance her swim bladders and unfurled her antennae-like sonar gills from behind her jawbone. She'd been as close to defenceless as she dared be, so she'd had to be quick as she absorbed the pulses of sound, processing the waves and clicks into pictures of movement in and around the lake and, more importantly, up the red cliffs to the hollow construction which sat high above her world. Deep vibrations told her a vessel had just left the building, which meant a new set of creatures had been brought in. New, softer vibrations had suggested the other deep dwellers were also ascending from their energy-saving stupors in their hidden caves. In a few days there would be a migration to where the water entered the lake, and she hadn't wanted to attract any attention from larger hunters.

In the end, Praahs had been late to the feeding party, as her urge to stay alive had clashed with her desire to feed on fresh flesh. These new soldiers had been quicker than any which came before them, she thought, as a new waft of blood-heavy water swept across the hairy sensors at the end of her long snout, each gill-full of water tainted with death.

Praahs had navigated upstream towards the kill zone, hoping the other predators had full bellies and were in no mood to fight. Better to have scraps than to be someone else's meal.

She'd ascended towards the green light, opening new pairs of eyes, and set her six fighting appendages flush against her side, keeping her muscular body streamlined as it wove through the water, following the trail of blood up a path to one of the inlets which fed into the lake. She'd *needed* to feed. She swam fast, concentrating on her surroundings as the channel funnelled into a thin red canyon. Praahs whipped her tail harder and kept low. New scents ran across her: fresh water and fresh blood. Then the canyon opened and she dived into the deep water beyond.

Praahs had known there were other small lakes like this, beyond the channels, but had never ventured into them. She could feel the shape of an island some distance away. She felt the movements of hundreds of creatures in the water just off the island's coast and opened her mouth to let the strains of blood rush over her tongue, which detected a bitter tang she hadn't tasted before. The other flavours were recognisable from those dark days when the predators of the lake had turned on one another, which suggested it was happening again.

Or had they been killed by the new creatures?

An ancient emotion, far stronger than hunger, took control of her and old instincts kicked in. Food could wait. She had to survive. Praahs turned around and headed back to safety.

But something had changed.

Praahs couldn't see or taste it but the entrance to the canyon was different to when she had exited it. She slowed and drifted. A shadow moved and, as quick as her reflexes allowed, Praahs shot off in the opposite direction, zigzagging away. The light sensors on her tail-tip registered shadows and shapes, so Praahs swam for her life. Now she knew what her prey felt like, she thought, as she used every ounce of energy to dart back around and make a last effort to speed down the canyon.

But she didn't make it.

She felt nothing, but her speed slowed and her muscles tightened. She readied herself, storing up what energy she had left, but, as a shape loomed from the darkness, Praahs was drawn to it through no effort of her own. She fought hard, but her body was numb. None of her weapons were any use.

Then a dazzling, multicoloured eye appeared from the gloom, bisected by a line of midnight black, and Praahs knew she wouldn't escape.

Praahs shook off the cold sensation her memories had given her and focussed on the land ahead.

Her array of sensors, now adapted to catching airborne scents rather than aquatic ones, had picked up a group of soldiers over the next ridge. Scores of them. Several species. All armed.

Without slowing, Praahs told her Cirratus officers to split into three groups. She would have fun with this kill, she thought. The tiny Tathon needed to feed as much as she did after travelling so far. Out of respect for any enemy soldiers that managed to survive the onslaught, she decided she would let five individuals live to join the ranks of the Tathon army. They would have earned the honour.

Praahs monitored the range of clicks and whistles coming from her horde of Cirratus fighters as they excitedly chatted amongst themselves, sharing tales of glorious battle. None overexaggerated and all gleefully embellished their war stories with graphic descriptions of how their enemies had been disembowelled or beheaded. It had been a quick victory with no losses and the enemy had died quickly. Plenty to be proud of, but after hearing the fifth mention of the taste of one of the species' innards, Praahs stopped listening. She was full to bursting having gorged herself on the warriors.

She allowed the Cirratus the pleasure of released chatter and social behaviour only after victory. The rest of the time, they were stoical and obedient. Maybe this was their natural way? she wondered. Before the Tathon leaders mutated and hyper-evolved their clan. Did they remember life before they'd had adaptations thrust upon them, as she did, or did their memories only go back as far as the tortuous pain of the forced changes?

After being captured by the Tathon, Praahs had regained consciousness in the oxygen-poor waters of the shallows, where her lake lapped against marshland. She'd never ventured this far from deep water and despised the taste of the almost-dry land which the creatures crossing the lake were always desperate to get to. The stench of mud and dead plants filled her gills and the edges of her scales itched as the thick water washed over her, coating her skin and sensors with a dirty film.

Praahs remembered trying to summon energy to her aching muscles and managing to cough out her gills and pull her dorsal fins out of the poisonous air. With a flick of her tail, she'd jolted off the mud and glided into deeper water where she could feel her way around, using the bell-bones in her snout to get her bearings. She was in a channel parallel to the coast, she'd found, blocked in by a solid bank of mud. She'd panicked. The water was barely three times as deep as her body's thickness and the pool was only wide enough for her to turn around.

A shape arrived in the water beside her. Instinctively, she attacked, firing barbed scales from her flank and a bolt of blue stun-energy from her mouth, but the shape was impervious to the attack and Praahs' energy was drained in an instant. She couldn't move. Scores of tubes had wrapped around her, holding her tight, and she'd felt the odd sensation of something reaching under her scales and into her flesh. For an instant she felt pity for those she had killed, powerless and overwhelmed by a larger beast. This was what they would have felt, along with searing pain when her formidable teeth had torn them limb from limb.

Warm flushes had run through Praahs and her internal organs had twitched in response. Her sonar had given off bizarre readings and her eyes had been almost useless as dark shapes moved around her, in and out of the water... tentacles and clouds. Then the eye again. A thousand colours. Staring. Hours of torture until Praahs felt the tug of the tubes and the sting of the air as she was raised out of the water.

Praahs had struggled and screamed for help, but it had been useless. Her body felt weak here in the unsupporting gas. Was this what death felt like? Her gills had clamped tight inside her to give her an extra minute of life in the poisonous air as she stared at her captor, fixing the image of her killer in her mind: an immense, octopus-like cephalopod, twice her size, which held her in two of its numerous tentacles, while the other sinuous limbs dexterously manipulated jars of liquids and powders.

The Tathon's skin was constantly changing with writhing colours, like its eyes, which focussed on her as it produced a long tube and poured a thick liquid over her head. Burning oil enveloped every crease of her face and head, running down her long neck and body. It scorched as it ran, finding every nook and breathing hole as the wave of pure pain shocked her body. Seconds felt like minutes, until a cooling sensation ran down her, from nose to tail. She was exhausted and fell limp when the concoction and burns had finally completed their tour of her entire body. Her gills flopped out, free from her control, and started to swell in the oxygen-rich air. Nitrogen tingled every square centimetre and her vision blurred. She waited for the sharp knives of death or the crush of jaws to kill her, but neither came.

With a body-shaking crash, the creature let go, discarding her on the moist mudflats, where she shivered and twitched. Waves of electricity flickered across her body and limbs as she counted down her last seconds, feeling the air slowly poison her. She stuck a forelimb into the mud to pull her body back to the lake, but the creature was there, blocking her path. It raised a tentacle, which splayed out to reveal a fan of thousands of tiny white lines, and aimed it at her.

'Struggle less. Let the changes occur,' a voice spoke inside her head.

'Changes?' She thought back but received no reply.

A calming sensation washed through her mind and body. Was this the ecstasy before death? Images flashed in her tired mind: her first kill; the sensation of being chased and escaping; her love. How could she forget her love? The hunts they had enjoyed together and their offspring, the joy of leaving them behind to fend for themselves, never knowing what would happen to them.

Praahs had rolled over and opened her eyes, ready for death.

Strange, she'd thought, she had been out of water for far longer than she thought possible. Her gills had withdrawn to their internal cavities and no longer ached with pain. With great effort, she'd rolled onto her belly, pushed herself up and looked at the creature, who studied her with equal measure.

'You are welcome,' the Tathon voice had said in her head.

Praahs looked now at the four captives as they bobbed and shook, tied to the backs of the broadest Cirratus. She'd said the same words to them when she had let them live at the end of the battle. There would have been five, but one had an energy-freezing mutation which allowed it to break out of its bonds, so Praahs had let the Cirratus kill it. The look of terror in their eyes was similar to what Praahs had felt when she'd been captured. Wait until you ascend, she thought. Then you will know true fear. And when the pain subsides and your strength returns threefold, you will know the meaning of power and of redemption. Praahs felt that power in her legs as they ran, and the energy deep within her chest, and knew she had been saved.

After a post-battle rest, Praahs and her unit of Cirratus crossed the parched prairie, returning to the Tathon army with their spoils of weapons and soldiers, who were ready to be enhanced. Praahs' unit wasn't the only team scouring the land for new recruits and materials. The army was growing by the hour, consuming all resources in their path as it marched on like a relentless machine, absorbing every living thing as a soldier or as food.

In the days since Praahs had left the water – her moment of rebirth – she'd learned a great deal about the Tathon, who had raised her up and who now marched forth to master this land and its peoples. They were generous with their knowledge and skills, enhancing new recruits with powers just as they had done with her. Weedy bipeds and hunched white beings now walked tall and broad amongst the ranks.

The more she learned about the Tathon, the less she feared them. Praahs had spent hours watching the huge, bulbous bodies of the three leaders, shining and reflecting the evening fires as they talked for any open mind to hear. The echo in their voices was due to their symbiotic nature – half-cephalopod, half-fungi – but both had evolved in water. Maybe that was why Praahs felt drawn to them? That and their triumph against the odds. Despite being waterborne, they had adapted to thrive in another beast's environment.

Praahs had also learned a lot about herself. Whoever had snatched her from her home ocean all those years ago had selected her to be a hazard for their chosen soldiers to face. She was nothing more than a danger to scare and test the land-crawlers who fell into her sea. But she could be so much more! She was far more dangerous than the puny warriors who fought here. The Tathon had showed her that. Praahs would take every opportunity to grow, adapt and learn. She would show everyone she was more than just a wild, dangerous creature.

Now, they crossed the mighty battle plain. Praahs had been surprised to find so much land here – and she'd never realised how many had made it across the sea successfully. One of her Cirratus scouts sent her a message, and she slowed her troops, so she could take in her surroundings. They were just a few hours from returning to the Tathon fold and it was tempting to ignore her scout, but her instincts told her not to ignore any opportunity. The tiny Tathon had sensed a presence near the debris of a recent battle, in the shadows of a stone-tower forest, which she was told was a ruined fortress.

'Corral the prisoners,' she ordered her unit, who tightened

their formation around the myriad warriors they had harvested from this dead land.

Praahs unfurled her sonar gills and opened all enhanced light sensors. She sensed movement deep in the shadows of the stone pillars. With a nimble bounce she leaped and twisted through the air, clearing a wide trench from a previous battle. Rotting biped bodies and empty blue shells tried to distract her, but her senses remained fixed on her quarry as she closed in. More information came to her: the creature was bulkier than her, as broad as 'Kno-lib, but not as long as she was. Probably less well armed too. The sonar reply told her it was covered in an external carapace, tinted dark blue. Looking at the shells around her she could see it was a survivor of the battle.

Praahs paused, surprised by the shape's change of direction and pace. It had left the shadows and was coming *towards* her. She pulled in her gills and unhitched the new claws which had proven so useful on this dry land.

The creature advanced and charged, leaping from the shadows.

Praahs raised her front limbs and prepared to defend herself, but the creature landed way short, scattering broken stones under its claws. She weighed the newcomer up: her predator mind searching for weak spots where she could tear the dark shell off and feed on its innards. But she also felt an affinity with this large, solitary soldier. Another loner lost in this world. They could fight, she thought, and test her new adaptations, but could she risk injury?

She remained silent and motionless, unsure of which course to take and, in the end, her opponent decided for her.

'If my shell had regrown to its full thickness I would have killed you and sucked your guts through your eye sockets,' the blue creature snarled, then crouched in submission and lowered its head.

141

Chapter 10

'It's a long, long way to Tipperary,' Joe's sweet voice sang.

John pictured his son on the side of the old horse cart, swinging his legs as he sang.

'Goodbye, Piccadi-lly! Fare-well, Leicester Square!'

John wanted to join in – he wanted to rush over and give Joe a big hug and tell the boy everything was going to be alright – but his feet were stuck and a mist was rolling in.

Joe's voice faded. 'But my heart's right there...'

John's temples pounded. He slowly became aware of his surroundings. He didn't have the energy to prise his eyes open yet, but he could tell it was dark and recognised the damp smell of mould. He'd been awake here before, but it was like the memories were on the end of wires dipped in water and he needed energy to raise each one up.

His cheek pressed against the rough bed he had slept on and drool had dried in the corner of his mouth. As had happened so many times in this bizarre world, people from John's home flashed through his weary mind: Joe; Rosie; his parents; his grandfather. With a deep intake of breath, John wiped his mouth and raised his head, followed by the rest of his aching body. He shuffled to lean against a cold, damp wall and slowly prised open his eyelids.

Light dripped from a grey rectangle high on John's left, coating the small room in a muddy brown. His mind raced back to Panzicosta's torture cell and a rush of adrenaline shot through his veins, popping his eyes completely open, hunting for signs of danger… weapons, torture implements, aliens. But there was nothing else here apart from the large sack in the opposite corner.

The shape shuffled and spoke. 'It's no better than the last time you woke up,' the voice croaked.

A hundred thoughts and swear words ran through John's mind, but his lips remained sealed.

'There's water in the trough,' the voice said.

John searched the empty corners of the dim room until he saw a clay bowl of water. He squinted and shunted his body across the wooden pallet, leaning down to dip his fingers. Coolness tingled his fingertips as he brought them to his dry lips. It was far from sweet, but his body needed more, so he dipped and scooped until he felt his head clearing.

John coughed, then asked, 'How long have I been here?'

'That's what you asked last time,' the voice replied with a throaty hack that John took for a laugh. 'Two days… but it took longer to get you here.'

Images of tall circles on sticks, bent silhouettes in red fields, grasping hands and staring eyes came to John, but he couldn't hold onto each memory and they slipped back into the dark water of the past.

John asked, 'What about everyone else?'

'I have no idea.' The shadow in the corner clicked as it moved its long arms or legs. 'There are many possibilities: working on the farms or in the mines. If they're lucky they'll join a scouting party, but if they fight back, they'll be thrown into the arena. Or worse... they'll be eaten.'

'Eaten?' John almost screeched and felt his stomach tense.

'There are many mouths to feed and not much to go around.'

John squinted, trying to make sense of the shape that was speaking to him. The voice clicked and trembled, so was clearly alien, but his brain's translation gave him no idea of whether it was female or male, large or small; he just had a sense in the shadows of long limbs and a small head.

'You may have noticed it's a desert out there,' the voice continued and John pictured the red fields again.

He tried to remember what had happened after the Lutamek's blue mesh had descended on them. He remembered a line of carts pulled by tocka – who wore hoods – and the domes... bigger domes. He remembered the tower too, like a giant needle pointing at the sky. But nothing else.

'Those bastards betrayed us,' he whispered.

The creature shifted its weight, rustling the dark sheet, which slipped over its body. 'I could count the number of soldiers here who haven't been betrayed on one hand,' it said, as an elongated, three-fingered hand slipped out to grip the pallet. 'Everyone is out for themselves. Even you if you are honest, human.'

'How do you know I'm human?' John asked, feeling a surge of panic rush through him.

'They told me when they dropped you in,' it replied.

'So why am I here?' John asked, looking up at the grey window.

'Same reason as me.'

'Which is?'

'They have a plan for us. The Ascent don't want us dead yet, or we'd be fighting in the arena or on someone's plate... so there must be some adaptation or mutation they think could help them with their quest.'

'Their quest?' John asked.

'You'll find out soon enough,' the voice replied as its body shifted again and the sheet revealed four long legs hanging over the pallet edge, glistening in the light like metal, or a Brakari shell.

'Who are you?' John asked, trying to hide any panic in his voice.

'Falen,' the voice replied. 'I am Drauw… a species you may not have seen before.'

John shook his head, not remembering the name from any obelisks in the dome. 'We met a few different species in the dome, but–'

'I meant before coming here,' Falen said. 'Despite being in the same region of the galaxy I doubt our species met.'

John laughed at the thought. 'We hadn't met any aliens at all before I came here!' He thought of Delta-Six and was pretty sure he'd never met other species before either.

Falen clicked and sighed. 'Well, we Drauw were a young species but traded with scores of other sentient species – mostly closer to the core thanks to a convenient SJ point.'

'I see,' John said, as ever not understanding everything. He wondered how different London would have been with aliens wandering around. How different life would have been with the new technologies he'd seen here, he thought, and pictured Rosie's dead body on the bloody sheets.

'And your name?' Falen asked.

'John,' he replied. 'John Greene.' He thought about offering a hand to shake but kept his good hand to himself.

'That's an interesting weapon you have there, John,' Falen said. 'Most weapons are confiscated.'

'Well, I can't go anywhere without it.' John lifted his gun–

arm up to show it in the dull light, noticing it had changed once more. He could still feel the chamber inside, but the barrel of the gun looked thicker, and if he squinted he was sure he could see three lines running towards the tip.

'They confiscated mine,' Falen replied and held a burned stump for John to see.

He gagged. 'Looks nasty,' he said, unable to tear his eyes away from the dark grey arm, which looked half-Lutamek, half-Brakari.

'I think they have a thing against female soldiers,' Falen said.

'Really?' John said. 'I haven't seen many female fighters around.'

'Some species more than others,' Falen replied. 'But the Ascent are governed by males, so…'

John wanted to know more about the Ascent, about what they had in store for him and how he could find the rest of his army, but his head felt weary. He stared at his pallet and an odd thought came to him.

'You said it's a desert out there,' he said.

'Yes.'

'No plants to eat?'

'No.'

'So where did this wood come from?' he asked and tapped his pallet with the tip of his gun.

'That's not wood,' Falen replied.

John felt the rough texture again with his good hand.

'It's made of bones.'

When John woke again his bladder was ready to burst.

Ignoring the swaying floor and his pounding head, he stumbled to the nearest corner of the room, unbuttoned his flies and felt a sharp nudge on his shoulder that turned him against the other wall. Urine streamed until, with a sigh, he finished, struggled to button up one-handed and sat back on his pallet.

'Last time you pissed in the trough,' Falen's rough voice said.

Her bony claw of a hand had shoved him in the right direction.

'Thanks,' he whispered and leaned down to scoop some foul water for his mouth.

'The pills they gave you stopped the motions for a few days,' Falen said. 'Stops the hunger too.'

'Right,' John said, feeling less dizzy, so scooped up more water.

The light through the grey rectangle was growing stronger – either that or John's eyes were becoming accustomed to the dark – so he could see Falen's outline now: four long legs and two thicker arms shone a gunboat grey, while her torso and head looked like artillery shells. Falen lowered her bullet-shaped head away from the wall to where John could see her four black eyes, which focussed on him. He tried to make sense of the knobbly rings and circles which made up Falen's skin: swirls within swirls, never-ending swirls.

'Now we have seen each other,' Falen's voice rasped and John saw the drill-like teeth lining her mouth, 'I trust you. We should make plans.'

'What?' John moved back onto his pallet, ignoring the fact it was made from some huge soldiers' remains. 'Trust? You said everyone was only out for themselves.'

'True,' Falen replied. 'And I trust you would kill me if it meant saving your life. I also trust you would do anything to get out of here and to find your comrades, so I trust you want to listen to me when I tell you I know a way out of here?'

'You could be lying,' John said. 'Or a mole… a trap… someone trying to get me to talk.'

'Believe me, if the Ascent wanted information out of you, they would have had it by now.'

John looked at his arm and remembered how the Lutamek had collected information on every soldier: age; skills; mutations. 'They need my arm,' he said softly.

'Possibly,' Falen replied. 'But they need you with it or they would have ripped it off.'

John shivered and felt his metal leg wobble. That was Lutamek, he thought. Did they have any control over it? He felt the urge to pull it off his stump and smash it on the wall, but he needed it desperately. It felt like part of him now. Whole.

A sudden thought came to him and John shifted his position to look around from wall to wall.

'There's no door,' he said.

Falen gestured up, and John saw that the roof, some ten feet above him, was made from a thick material. Spots of light dotted it like lines of stars where strips had been roughly sewn together.

'We're in a pit,' Falen said. 'And the only way out is up.'

John felt his shoulders slump. His grandfather's voice came to him, as it did when he felt weak: *Get up boy! Grow some muscle, show some backbone and fight!* The harsh tones melted away and John pictured the old man's eyes. Desperate eyes, John knew that now. Eyes that had foreseen John's future on the battlefield. The old man had known war was coming and had forced him to toughen up. John wondered if his grandfather had lived long enough to be around while Joe was growing up, and if he'd been as harsh with him? Joe had gone to war too. Had being an orphan toughened *him* up? Given him a strong will and determination that could have saved his life in battle?

John would never know.

Rosie's voice came to him, no words, just her tone, her delight and wonder at seeing new things and her endless positivity. Nothing was all bad. Every cloud had a silver lining, she used to say.

What a great mother she would have made.

John sniffed and looked at Falen.

'Alright then,' he said, with thoughts of Millok, realising this was the second time he'd been captured and given himself into the hands of an alien. 'I'm ready to hear what you say, but first...' He paused, not knowing how to explain.

'Yes, human.'

'First, I want to know about the worlds out there.' He nodded up at the skin roof. 'Not the Ascent and whatever they've built here, but about the real worlds. The planets and people of our galaxy.'

Even in the gloom of the pit, John could sense the light failing. Falen had been talking for hours. While she talked, John had traced his fingers over the carvings in the mud wall of their prison and tried to make sense of them in the poor light. Were the prisoners who carved these long dead? As Falen described bizarre creatures and dangerous soldiers, John linked them to the swirls and patterns scored in the mud: parallel lines he thought were a warrior's name; triangular marks which must have been made by a type of claw; a set of three dots around a circle.

John let the conversation die down then asked, 'Do we get food?'

'In the morning,' Falen replied. 'It won't taste good, but it will keep you alive.'

'Right.'

'We should sleep now,' Falen said, and John realised her injury must have taken a toll of her.

John tried to make himself comfortable on the dry slab of

bone he had for a bed. When he closed his eyes he saw the swirls on Falen's face and could still hear her voice. Images of the galaxy came to him – the spinning fog of stars the Lutamek had shown them – and he tried to make sense of what Falen had explained.

The galaxy was full of what Falen had called *sentient* species. Aliens, thinking creatures, like humans, who had evolved over millions of years. Again and again, life had sprung up across the galaxy. John didn't understand when she talked of comet dust and basic proteins and, when he mentioned God, Falen had been quick with her response: religions were as varied as the peoples of the galaxy and caused many wars.

As she explained more, it was clear that humans were a tiny part of a range of societies of which Falen admitted she only knew a fraction. Compared with Earth, the Drauw's planetary system was closer to the galactic centre, where the stars were closer and civilisations lived in close proximity. Their territory encompassed a few star systems either side of an SJ point, which, from Falen's description, sounded like a kind of doorway in space that allowed them to travel further, quicker. The Drauw had become proficient traders with several surrounding empires, including the Scarpinelloss, who John remembered had defeated the Brakari in their first battle, alongside the Ladrof. The Drauw trading network had collapsed though, Falen had explained, when civil war erupted on her home planet. That was where she had been fighting when she was taken from battle, in a flash of light, just like everyone else on the disc.

'So you travelled in space?' John asked.

'I spent most of my adult life on my home planet,' Falen replied, 'but as a species, yes.'

'Then why didn't you find the ships?' John asked.

'Which ships?'

'The ones that brought us here,' John said, fighting his tiredness – he knew this was important. 'If you had ships in space, why didn't you find them?'

Falen was silent for a while before answering. 'I don't know.'

'From what the Lutamek said, we were taken from our home planets and brought here, but they must have been in orbit for thousands of years picking us off one by one.'

Falen sounded quieter than before. 'We failed to register them.'

She was clearly ashamed, so John had let it go, but he wondered if any other species had managed to detect a ship and follow it to the disc? He took in a deep breath as he felt sleep taking him.

John was building a picture of the new galactic world which included the other species Falen had met: Korax, Greems, Stur-Morches and Rassums. Each was completely different to the rest, as were the Lutamek and Sorean, he thought. Insectoids, androids and humanoids. All air-breathers, all had been taken from their home planet and, despite the thousands of years of development and space travel, nobody knew who had brought them here or why.

Thoughts blurred in John's head as he slipped away, but a new, stubborn thought remained.

The Scarpinelloss.

Falen had mentioned them, and the Lutamek had said the domes were placed across the disc according to where the species were located in the galaxy. He had little trust in the Lutamek after they'd turned on his allies, but the theory made sense. If that was true, Falen's home planet must have been near the Scarpinelloss, which meant she would have been in the same dome as them.

It didn't add up. Falen was hiding something.

A shaft of white light woke John and he had a bullet spinning in his gun-arm's chamber in a second, aimed at the roof.

'Relax.' Falen's voice sounded less muffled.

The skin roof of their pit had been peeled off, allowing sunlight to pour in.

In the brilliant light he could see Falen in all her alien glory: her face of a thousand tiny swirls and her six long grey limbs splayed out like she'd been dropped from a great height.

John looked up as a leather bucket descended on a frayed rope. Beyond were two, lumpy silhouettes. The bucket tipped its multicoloured contents onto the floor and was quickly hoisted back up. The cover was slapped back over, returning John and Falen to near darkness, and leaving John with the silhouettes imprinted on his eyes.

'Eat,' Falen said and flicked a pink spongy cube at him.

John picked it up and turned it over in his good hand. 'What is it?' he asked.

'Thoraxian pears. It's protein. Some minerals. You'll need it.'

'Why?' John asked. 'What do they plan to do with us?'

'What do you remember of this place?' she asked as she nibbled the edges of her cube with her needle-like teeth.

John smelled the cube and bit a corner off. Fishy, he thought, but not bad. He sat back to think as he chewed. 'I remember lots of domes,' he said, 'and red fields... then small buildings and the tower, that's it.' A memory of men dressed in white, playing cricket came back to John and, not for the first time, he wondered if this was another trick of the Frarex.

No, he thought, this was too real. Too dirty.

'The red fields are where the food comes from,' Falen said. 'Few plants are grown and, with such a need for protein, the Ascent devised a way to farm the larvae of a flying insect–'

'What?' John sat forward and stared at the food in his hand. 'Bugs?'

'They photosynthesise sunlight and eat the soil. They just need water which they collect in hydro traps.'

John remembered the huge rings in the desert, like immense bubble blowers. 'So the Ascent have a whole system working here? Do they have money?' he asked.

'In a way,' Falen replied. 'They have a trading system at least.'

'How long have they been here?'

'You said you didn't want to know about the Ascent,' Falen replied.

'I think I'll need to know,' John said with a glance at the roof before he cautiously nibbled the blended maggot cube.

'Firstly, the Ascent aren't one species.'

John stayed silent, filtering the Drauw's words more carefully now he knew she was hiding something.

'Nobody knows the first species to win freedom from their dome,' Falen's voice fell into the easy rhythm it had had the previous day, 'or how long ago. But all victors drift to the centre of the disc eventually, drawn by the tower.'

John pictured the needle-like shaft of diamond which pierced the sky above the cluster of domes: one of the first things he had seen when they had left their dome.

'With no way off the disc, the number of victors grew,' Falen continued, 'and with resources scarce, factions arose, controlling the sections of land surrounding the tower. One of these called themselves the Ascent.'

'Why?' John asked.

'They're named after the message—'

A rustle above made John look up as the roof skin was peeled back again. He raised his gun-arm to shade his eyes and squinted to make out shapes moving on the lip of the pit.

'Time to see if you can pick the lock,' a deep voice bellowed, followed by laughter.

A dark, square shape descended, heading straight for John, who shuffled into the corner as fast as he could.

'Bugger off!' he shouted.

'Come on,' the voice replied as the square transformed into a giant hand, moving in to grab John.

'You can't fight them, John,' Falen said.

John sneered and spun a snub-nosed bullet to blast the hand away, but he knew it would be another waste of his bone and metal.

'Go down fighting!' His grandfather's voice rang in his ears, and he fired the bullet, only to find it popped out impotently.

Something in his gun-arm felt different. He stared at the smoking muzzle as the giant hand gripped him around the chest and dragged him out of the pit. He looked down at Falen, who seemed tiny now.

'What was the message?' John shouted, 'the one they're named after?'

'If you're going to the lock,' Falen shouted back, 'you'll see it for yourself!'

Chapter 11

Samas punched the granite wall with his rock-fist and felt the satisfying crunch as the stone cracked and crumbled, falling to his feet. One more punch, he thought, and stretched the muscles in his shoulder. The clay covering Li had fused onto his broken arm might be harder than any natural substance, but the parts of Samas' body outside the rock – his biceps, shoulders and chest – were unenhanced and he could feel it.

'I'm done,' he whispered to Rar-kin, his Sorean partner, who shuffled in to clean up the debris.

Samas squinted to see in the poor light, then dropped to sit on a rock and dipped his crudely carved stone cup into an equally crude bucket which had collected water dripping off a long stalactite.

'Remember, that liquid is condensed sweat and breath from scores of different species,' Rar-kin said in an almost-happy voice as it swept the rock chippings away.

Samas wondered if punching Rar-kin into the rock would soften the repetitive blows but shook the irritating thought away. 'Do you have any better suggestions?' he asked. 'That mud they give us tastes of metal and faeces.'

'That's because it is mostly—'

'Yes,' Samas cut Rar-kin off, 'I get it.'

He let his head drop, closed his eyes and drew his breath deeply. He couldn't smell it now, but when they'd first descended into the mines, all he could smell was the rank odour of decay and death. According to older miners, the masters had only agreed to ventilate the shafts after three Greems had died in a cloud of their own waste, so it could have been worse.

'If we resume at a ten-degree angle,' Rar-kin spoke between pickaxe swings as it chipped away at the wall Samas had been demolishing, 'we will increase our efficiency.'

Samas felt sorry for the small, furred creature. Rar-kin was putting every ounce of energy into the project – mind and body – as though it were its own master plan, yet one smash from Samas' rock-fist was the equivalent to half an hour of the Sorean's pickaxe chippings. Samas sensed Rar-kin knew that too but carried on.

'Ten degrees then?' Samas replied, feigning interest.

The masters hadn't even told him what they were after. Metal ore for weapons? Digging for a water source? Or hidden treasure? Samas couldn't remember what the mine guards had told him; he'd been in shock at regaining consciousness after the Lutamek's blue net had descended. He'd been given a brief look at the makeshift city which leaned in the shadow of the immense tower, at the centre of this world, then they were led below ground, into the dark.

He sighed. Half his army were missing, every human miner had had their head shaved and the Lutamek were nowhere to be seen. They'd been sent straight into the dark pits, told to dig down, and after the first Sorean who asked why was beheaded, Samas had kept his questions to himself. Still, with Rar-kin's mathematical abilities and his enhanced fist, in the days they'd been here their zigzag shaft had delved deeper than any other pit.

'I'm going up for food,' Samas said and clambered up the ladder of finger- and toeholds he'd clawed into the shaft wall.

As he climbed, switching walls every ten steps as the pit zigged and zagged, Samas felt a tingle in the back of his neck: his pin. A little welcoming present from the Ascent – every miner had an explosive device inserted in each species' kill spot and the masters frequently blew an insubordinate miner's head off to keep the rest in check. Samas often daydreamed about what he would do to the guards if he got free, but deep down he knew they were obeying their orders and were as much prisoners as he was. He'd seen the gleam of metal on their necks too.

Samas took a second to catch his breath before climbing the last stretch to the main corridor, from where all shafts descended. As much as he hated the labour, the terror of imminent death and the lack of sleep, it was the look in his men's eyes which haunted him most.

He had let them down.

It had taken Samas days to come to terms with it, but at some level he'd known it all along: he shouldn't have been in charge. He was no Mihran. He lacked foresight. He'd been unable to protect his army and had led them straight into a trap which had cost many lives and put everyone's future at risk.

He let his face relax, trying to hide his anxiety, and climbed the last stretch to greet the host of alien miners who lay tired, broken and possibly dead along the weakly lit rock corridor. A dust-covered human nodded at Samas, and he nodded back while his mind raced to recognise the soldier. He'd lost so much weight. Egyptian. But his name? Samas walked on, grateful talking was prohibited. He strode to where a gang of miners of varying body types – insectoid, humanoid and android – scooped liquids from stone jars under the watchful eye of a tall Ladrof master who looked almost as weakened as the slaves he governed.

Samas paused as vibrations ran through his sandals, and he immediately thought of Crossley. From what he'd gleaned, the Lutamek must have studied every soldier from the moment they'd met and had given the Ascent information on each individual's capabilities so they could be assigned to the tasks most suited to them. Not only could Crossley 'see' through rock, but his legendary skills with explosives, as demonstrated in the battle with the Brakari, made him ideal for mining.

Samas joined the queue. Eyes watched him and he felt the glare of the Sorean as much as the humans. The eyes reminded him he had let them down. But there was something else there too, if he looked closely.

Hope.

Samas knew he was no general but he *was* a leader of men. His words before battle strengthened his men's arms and when it came to battle – in the wild moment of steel, tooth and claw – there was no one better than him at reading and reacting.

Then Samas saw her.

The shaved head, the sack clothing and skin covered in the toxic dust of the mine made her look like any other biped, but two hollow eyes fixed on Samas and he felt an energy run through him.

Yarcha.

The Lutamek had little information on her and she had no mutation from the dome, so they'd dumped her in the mine. Samas had barely talked to her, and knew little about her, but her eyes spoke to him. They didn't blame him, or ask anything of him. One emotion shone through.

Defiance.

In that moment, Samas knew his task. He would save what

was left of his army and, even if it meant dying, he would free them.

Delta-Six knew his diversion might not have fooled the Lutamek. If they were as clever as they seemed to be, they would pretend to accept his apparent death – blown up in the sky – and come back for him later but, if that was true, they were tracking him right now, he thought, and climbed a little closer to the energy shield which protected the entire disc, hoping it would distort any scanners.

He'd survived four hours since the fake assassination but knew he couldn't stay in close-space for much longer before his breathable oxygen or fuel cylinders ran out. He had two choices: confront the enemy or hide from them.

He felt a desire to rescue the rest of the humans – even the Sorean – from their incarceration. During his war, with his crew, they had fought and died for one another like brothers and never deserted each other. No one got left behind. Part of that instinct stayed with Delta-Six but he had to be realistic. He was outnumbered and outgunned. In order to survive he had to hide – travel to another dome or find shelter in the desert.

He focussed his enhanced optics on the high-speed convoy of prisoners being led by the Lutamek and their new allies: a host of alien soldiers Delta-Six hadn't seen before. From his vantage point, his guess was they were heading for the tower beyond the domes.

From this height, he could see a segmented city lying around the tower. Each wedge shape lay with the pointed end by the tower and its outskirts fanning out towards the desert and domes. His systems suggested the nearest wedge was the Ascent segment and that the city was fringed by farm complexes.

More questions came to Delta-Six about the nature of the domes, the tower and whoever had orchestrated this whole bizarre system, but he needed to survive. Maybe he could both hide *and* find the answers to his questions?

An orange light blinked to the right of his view.

Strange, he thought. Something was trying to communicate with him but it couldn't be his mini-sat. He fired his jets and set them on a series of random manoeuvres while he filtered and decoded the message. It was an audio file which had been damaged en route, possibly by the disc's shield.

'...an. If you can hear this, we can extrapolate your position and–'

Delta-Six deleted the file as soon as he heard 'position' and killed his jets, sending his body into freefall. He rotated until his head pointed at the ground and descended with speed, switched his systems to maximum alert with maximum energy sent to his data walls: physical defence awareness and sensors. It was too realistic to be real, so had to be a Lutamek trap!

His head, shoulders and chest warmed as he zipped into the disc's thicker atmosphere.

A thought came to him. It was too late now he had discarded the file, but he was unsure whether it had been translated from its original language or if it had originally been in English.

Samas woke as a brush of fur ran across his leg and his hand scratched the dust for his knife. He sat bolt upright. Dark shapes moved around him and it took a few seconds for his dehydrated brain to catch up. The light was poor, but he recognised the arched roof of the main chamber of the mine and his current situation came back to him like a wave of cold water.

Samas shivered and drew a sharp intake of breath.

The chamber was the only place the masters kept ventilated at night, so the miners were marched from their pits for their allotted sleeping time. Each exhausted species kept themselves to themselves, so the Sorean slept in a hairy pile, with the humans lined up nearby. New to the mines, both species had the least comfortable area, away from the heat source and closest to the open latrines.

Alien crap smelled worse than elephant dung, Samas thought, as a deep horn sounded at the other end of the chamber and the sleeping shadows around him twisted and groaned. If that was the first call, who had walked past and woken him?

'Morning, Captain.' Crossley spoke between yawns and stretches. 'Another day in paradise, hey?'

Samas found himself smiling and licked his dry lips. 'Something tells me we might be the lucky ones,' Samas replied, not sure if Crossley would take it as a joke or not.

As commander of the troops, Samas couldn't be seen to make light of their situation.

'Silence!' one of the masters bellowed as the others prowled through the chamber, kicking sleepers awake.

Crossley gave Samas a shrug.

The morning call was the only chance Samas had to check on his men – to see if they had lost anyone and, through whispers in the food queue, learn of any developments. So far there was little Samas could tell the troops, but now he was resolved to finding a way to escape he needed to build their morale. After one group hadn't returned from their shift, Samas had started the rumour they had found a passageway and managed to escape. The lie gave his men hope while he figured a real way out of the mines.

Morning breaths, squeaks and grunts echoed along the long hall of a cave, peppered with the hollow laughs of the guards.

Every soldier here belonged to a victorious species who had made it through their dome's silver gates, Samas thought. So who ruled the Ascent? He'd heard from other miners there were three main species. He didn't know which species had made it to the tower first, but over time the most ruthless species had risen to the top to protect their own – he was pretty sure he wouldn't see any of the leader species down here as a miner or a guard.

A shout from the distant entrance drew his attention and scores of heads turned in unison. Nobody was stupid enough to speak but something odd was going on. More shouting was followed by a crashing sound and a wail. Samas saw his men's clenched fists and the Sorean group beyond, who sat with wide eyes and tall ears. Their moans were clear when a guard hobbled around the corner, dragging the limp body of Jakan-tar, the Sorean leader.

Samas recognised the guard as one of the Bensha: broad-shouldered, ape-like creatures whose heads were covered in protective plates of brilliant white bone.

'What happened?' the Ladrof master, Pek, asked.

Although less fearsome in appearance, this particular Ladrof had a reputation for spitefulness and, physically, reminded Samas of a badly carved sculpture: angular shapes, not finished off properly. The Ladrof had great strength too, so were rarely tested, and their army had beaten the Brakari, Samas remembered.

'We caught it trying to escape,' the large Bensha said with what Samas assumed was a grimace. 'It managed to kill Fliit and Ren.'

Pek stared at the guard, then at the limp body of Jakan-tar. 'Really?'

The Bensha moved its head in a manner Samas guessed meant 'yes'.

'This cannot go unpunished,' Pek said and looked at the Sorean group. 'We can lose one miner but two guards?' Pek swayed from side to side.

Samas watched intently, pressing his rock-arm into the ground, ready to leap up and attack. Was this the moment? he wondered. Two guards already dead and it was probably dark outside.

'The commanders will need to know what happened,' Pek continued, 'so we punish now and get back to work.' He nodded at the Bensha. 'Kill it.'

Quicker than anyone could react, the large Bensha pressed the controller on his belt and, with a tiny flash of light and an audible crack, Jakan-tar's head dropped onto the floor, leaving a spout of blood in its place.

Samas knelt up, caught Crossley's eyes and felt the other human eyes staring at him: pleading with him to make a stand – to stop this madness. They were ready, Samas thought, they would fight. Maybe they should fight before they lost more men or got weaker?

'Silence!' Pek bellowed and tapped his belt, quietening the low hum of whispers. The stone-like Ladrof paused to think for a while, pacing a circle, before saying, 'One is not enough for two guards... we need two more,' and gestured at the gang of Sorean, who scrambled behind one another to the safety of the cave wall.

Both of Samas' fists were clenched. The other species in the cave remained silent in their respective groups and watched calmly as though they had seen it a hundred times before. Maybe they had? Samas thought. Which was why they knew not to fight back.

At a tap on his shin, Samas looked down to see that Crossley had smuggled a slip of explosive out of the mine. The American talked with his eyes and it was clear what he had planned. They hadn't been able to fight back when they were captured, so this was their first chance. Samas shook his head. As much as he wanted to fight – as much as he knew they could take these masters – this was not the time. The explosive pins were too deadly and he'd lose too many men.

Samas looked back at the Sorean, who had stopped struggling and, through some unheard call, started to form a ring, which had confused the Bensha, who had halted its approach. The Sorean were whispering and clicking claws with one another, which reminded Samas of a war song he had heard the men of a mountain tribe sing in the Persian army. The Sorean sped up but the sound was getting quieter until, with a solemn groan, the group sat down in unison, leaving two Sorean standing. Samas gasped as he realised what was happening.

With their eyes fully open and teeth bared, the two Sorean walked over and knelt before the stunned Bensha, who looked to Pek.

'Do it properly,' Pek snarled and walked away.

The Bensha drew his long, curved blade, took one step back and, with a flash, the two Sorean were despatched and two thuds echoed around the chamber. Another Bensha walked forward and carried the soldiers' bodies and heads to where the body of their leader, Jakan-tar, lay in full view of the miners.

Samas kept his eyes on the Sorean group, who had remained silent throughout. When he was sure he had enough eyes on him, Samas closed his eyes and lowered his head in respect for their loss. When he opened his eyes, what was left of the Sorean army were blinking in response.

Samas breathed in deeply. He felt the weight of their loss more than any other human in that cave.

He was responsible for both armies now.

Delta-Six finally had what he'd longed for – a given name.

In truth it wasn't a given name, it was a chosen name: a name he'd chosen for himself. But for the past few days, as he had toiled in the fields, eaten with the slave-farmers and slept in the pest-infested huts, he'd become known as Lucien Thomas. The field masters called him Lucien Thomas and, when they were out of earshot of the guards, the workers who shared this agricultural prison with him also called him Lucien Thomas.

Despite the hardship they endured here, Delta-Six smiled every time he heard his name, even if it was a simple 'Pass me the hoe, Lucien Thomas,' or 'Get out of my way, Lucien Thomas, you piece of Rassum turd.'

Despite this, Delta-Six didn't allow himself to relax. He was confident his true identity hadn't been discovered by the Ascent, but he was yet to set eyes on a single Lutamek.

After plummeting from near-space, Delta-Six had taken a haphazard route to the cultivated lands of the Ascent. Since then, combining information gleaned from the farmer's small talk with images he'd taken from near-space, he knew the other wedges of land radiating from the tower belonged to other factions who governed their segments of land like gangsters.

Using a combination of a chamelo-cloth and clothes he had found on bodies desiccating in the desert, Delta-Six had constructed a basic but effective disguise that gave him the look of Lucien Thomas: a broad, bald-headed humanoid warrior of no specific origin. After a day of reconnaissance, he had infiltrated a line of new captives and had fashioned a fake tag in the back of his neck. He knew he had been accepted as part of the group when guards beat him. It took a great deal of self-control not to fight back, but Delta-Six's defence systems protected him while tricking the attackers into feeling muscles being pounded and ribs cracking.

'Lucien Thomas,' a guard yelled, 'there's a blockage in the corner field's air pipe.'

Delta-Six tapped his head, dropped the metal tub of larval seeds he'd been sowing and limped across the dusty red field. His leg was fine, but the guards had given him a good going over the day before and his systems told him the bruising from a real beating would take days to heal.

Even with his disguise on, Delta-Six could sense his surroundings as he had done before – his visuals were enhanced when needed, and he could sense movement from any direction at all times. As he crossed the field of almost-ripe Thoraxian pears, which wriggled a few centimetres beneath the desert soil with their black breathing tails pointing skyward, a red light flashed in his field of view. He slowed his pace and zoomed in on the signal – a cloud of dust on the horizon: an Ascent scouting party. He zoomed in further and recognised the shapes: Lutamek. He groaned. The last thing he needed to see. But they were heading away – probably defending the edge of the Ascent's territory like good little robots – and had disappeared from view by the time Delta-Six made it to the far corner of the field.

This was the border between apparent civilisation and probable death in the desert. This place reminded him of the pictures of regenerating Europe he'd seen during training, where the poorly performing soldiers were retired. Images from his old dream came back to him – of the Elysium plains and his promised wife and kids – then the sharp reminder kicked in. It had all been a hoax.

He looked at the wriggling tails of the field. With this crop so close to fruition, the guards would act harshly if they lost a single pear, so he set to work, crouching to check the filtration unit, a small beige box covered in flashing lights. The filters were fine. He scanned the corrugated hose which ran from the box. It had to be just a pipe blockage. He grunted, detached the tube and tapped out a pile of desert soil. Strange, with the filters working fine, there was no way that soil could have infiltrated the air system. He fixed the tube back together and made sure the air was pumping again, like the water-irrigated fields of Earth.

He stood to stretch and raised his arm to show any guards watching that the problem was fixed. He didn't receive a response, but his systems picked up three guards' reactions and recorded their conversation, knowing he had been marked for a beating tonight. There was little he could do to prevent it, so Delta-Six gave himself a second to think. He had so much information now – from the dome cap, from the Lutamek, if that could be trusted – and from communications he had picked up from various scouting groups in the desert. Yet every answer led to more questions.

He pretended to urinate into the desert to buy a minute more thinking time and set a portion of his systems' capacity to building theories to answer his questions. He ran his toe through the pile of soil as he added another question: How did this disc have gravity?

He stopped. Something in the sandy soil had caught his eye. It looked like a corner of cloth. Carefully, he teased it out with his foot and flattened it out. Three shapes were printed on the cloth in red ink. Three shapes: human and Sorean handprints, beside the print of a tocka's clawed hoof.

That answered Delta-Six's most anticipated question.

Someone else had survived the Lutamek attack.

Chapter 12

John had been awake the whole time, watching and waiting. Even though he had enough energy to escape, he knew it was pointless. He was on an open truck pulled by a small electric engine, similar to the ones that had transported men and ammunition to and from the front line in John's war, travelling through the centre of a huge town – there were no towers or great buildings like in London so he couldn't call it a city – which hummed with life and activity. The train of open metal trucks full of mining materials and half-dead captives meandered towards the looming presence of the huge tower.

John hardly noticed it though, now it was so close, his eyes on the metal shacks and stone buildings, which were far more advanced than the mud domes of Abzicrutia, and the inhabitants – this place was teeming with hundreds of alien soldiers of every species imaginable! John had thought the variety of warriors in the dome had been bizarre, but what he saw here was way beyond that: humanoids of every size brushed shoulders and knees with arthropods and insectoids, like the Brakari and Falen, who scuttled beside seemingly impossibly shaped multi-tentacled blobs, legless worms and bent-over trees. Mechanoid creatures flashed and beeped, some with their organic parts proudly on show behind glass covers, others pure metal as far as John could tell. Nothing flew – everything crawled, walked or ran – and it was hard for John to tell what was normal and who had been enhanced by the Synchronisers. At one point, the giant silhouette of a Lutamek stalked through a marketplace, and John felt his stomach drop. Knowing the level of their technology, John would have no chance of hiding from them.

It was while his train cut through the market that John had a glimpse of what made the town work. He'd seen the farms where, if he trusted what Falen had told him, newly captured soldiers were put to work or eaten, but what made this place run – other than fear – was trade. Small transactions involved payment with tiny canisters of water and food cubes, while the biggest payments were made with weapons. John smiled when he worked it out – it was so obvious. Other than their life, what was the one thing every one of these thousands of soldiers had? Their weapon. Metal for making new weapons. Ammunition. Explosives.

This was a martial society in the truest sense.

John's gun-arm twitched, and he felt grateful they hadn't ripped it off, as they'd done with Falen's weapon. He tried spinning a bullet again but couldn't quite get it going. The ridges on the outside had deepened as well, which concerned him. Once again, John had no way to defend himself, and he had no idea what was happening to his body.

The train screeched to a halt, jolting him.

'End of the line!' shouted a large, gorilla-like soldier with a white bony head. It pulled a captured warrior out of the first truck and threw them to the ground, then pointed to a ramp of soil which descended into a dark tunnel. 'You're diggers,' Bonehead shouted. 'Grab a pick and get moving, or I'll take your head off!' It tapped its belt and then the back of its neck.

172

John watched the broken creatures crawl and squirm, carrying what they could, and saw the glint of metal on each of their necks. Funny how he didn't have one, he thought, and reached round with his good hand.

'Shit!' he gasped as he felt the cold disc of metal protruding from his neck.

His shoulders sagged.

'If this doesn't work,' a metallic voice made John turn to see a huge, solid block approaching him, 'you will end up in there, John Greene.'

'Ten-ten?' John asked and pushed back against the side of the truck.

'The arena,' said Ten-ten, pointing at a broad building on the other side of an open square. 'It's where they send the lucky ones to fight to the death.' The Lutamek stared at John's gun-arm. 'But maybe you have the key to getting us all out of here?'

Olan tested the weight of the axe in his right hand, swung it round to loosen up his shoulder, then repeated the process with his left hand. The axe was heavier than his original weapon, which the Ascent had taken from him, but it felt well-balanced. He swung and spun the axe, with his eyes fixed on the metal door three strides from his face. The anticipation coursing through his body felt similar to a boat raid, just when the ships glided up to a riverbank. But instead of standing perched on the ship's side, listening to his men vomiting and making their prayers to Odin and Thor, Olan was stuck in a metal box. All he heard was the pounding thump of blood through his ears and the bizarre yowls and screams of the alien crowd outside.

They were waiting for him. They wanted to see him fight. They were desperate to see him *die*.

Olan scratched a mark on his leather belt: seven times he had entered the arena since his capture. Any humans or Sorean who hadn't been carted off for other uses had been brought here and thrown into the arena to fight in a melee against whatever wild creatures the Ascent had managed to cluster together. The first had been a free-for-all designed to show off the new captives and root out any weaklings. Confused and leaderless, the allies had fought in clumps and without purpose. Many, including Olan, tried to use the skills they had evolved, but others were simply outgunned by the vicious other-worldly beasts.

Olan could still smell the giant, toothless worm which had consumed him whole. Swept into its stomach, Olan's chest plate had given him a clear vision of his surroundings and, holding his breath, he'd had enough strength to cut through the stomach lining and muscular wall. Bursting free with his skin tingling from the stomach acids, Olan had never felt more alive! After twenty more deaths though, every creature in the arena had been trapped by an unseen force and the bout signalled complete.

Since then, the survivors, including Olan, had endured day after day of deadly combat in the arena. All to raise the morale of the crowd of soldiers – the hundreds of warrior species, like the Lutamek, who had agreed to be part of the Ascent. They were the lucky ones, safe in their protected world. Or so Olan thought, until he fought against a species he recognised from the stands. Each individual's position here was precarious. That, he realised, was why passions ran so high in the stands. Tomorrow, any spectator could be beside Olan, spilling their blood on the dusty floor.

Olan sighed. Through the metal door, the crowd's bellowing peaked with a roar, which signalled another fight ending, giving him less than a minute. He tapped his golden chest plate – despite their efforts and technology they hadn't managed to get it off him – and pushed his helmet down tight.

This was it. He cleared his mind, touched the hammer around his neck and breathed in deeply. The metal door slid back with a swish and Olan stepped out, eyes wide open, ready to face whatever or whoever the Ascent had prepared for him. Yesterday he'd killed a bone-headed Bensha, a long, lizard-like creature with acid spit and three stout creatures he had thought of as trolls.

He strode forward purposefully, ready for action, but what he saw this time made him pause.

The scarred floor of the arena held no aliens or trained robots. The other doors were open and there, equally confused, stood four humans.

John remained still while a graceful, long-limbed soldier solemnly removed his shackles. He tried to remember the soldier's species – Ilanos maybe? Or maybe this soldier was from a different dome? When it turned its head, John saw the coin-sized silver disc on its neck and sighed.

Was anyone free in this city?

'This way,' Ten-ten ordered and John hesitated before jumping out of the carriage.

The last time they'd spoken, Ten-ten had explained how John's gun-arm would eventually run out of ammunition – the bones of his arm and the metal of his gun – and stop working. Then Ten-ten, and the rest of his clan, had sold them out to the Ascent.

A roar from the crowd in the distant arena made John jump and he looked straight at Ten-ten, who didn't seem to register it.

'Follow me,' it said and strode away.

John tried to calm his breathing and found his good hand caressing the tin soldier hanging around his neck. Ahead, the ground rose up to the base of the glass tower. He was finally here – in the centre of the disc where the tower seemed to grow out of the very bedrock itself, shooting into the sky like some enormous glass tree. John squinted to see inside the tower, but the dark glass only reflected the buildings and desert around it. John had heard Crossley talk of the tall glass buildings of New York – the skyscrapers – and imagined this was similar, although he struggled to picture a city full of them.

'Security is tight here,' Ten-ten said and pointed to a metal wall which ran in a ring around the rock platform, leaving an empty circle half a mile wide. 'Access is only granted with full cooperation of every faction,' Ten-ten continued. 'So our time is limited.'

That would be why nobody stood at the tower base, John thought. He could see the metal fence which ran around the tower had sections leading away into the desert, dividing each faction's territory. John remembered what Falen had said about the various groups and wished he'd asked more. Would he be safe if he escaped into their territory?

'So it's a no-man's-land then?' John asked.

'A peace has been issued here,' Ten-ten's deep tones sounded solemn, 'although the Platae ignore it.' He pointed to a dark area on the left-hand side of the tower base.

The stain shimmered like dark water. John remembered the kite-like shapes in the salt moat around the ruined castle and the drawings of the battle, but couldn't make sense of the smudge on the tower.

He looked up at Ten-ten and said, 'They're the ones who defeated you.'

'Yes.'

As they walked nearer to the dome, John started to see definition in the dark shape. It was the entire surviving mass of Platae – foot-long flatworms – spitting their young at the glass wall of the tower, just as they had done to the castle and to the Lutamek. Back in the dome, these polyps had secreted acid and broken through stone and metal with ease, but here they were thwarted by a more advanced technology.

'What's that?' John asked as a silver line vibrated down the side of the tower, cleaning the stain away.

'A defence mechanism,' Ten-ten replied. 'Our studies show the surface remains untarnished, yet the Platae continue to reproduce and attack.'

'Won't they run out of soldiers?' John asked, picturing the line after line of soldiers running through mud, being cut down by waves of machine-gun fire.

'In twenty-six cycles they will have depleted their resources.'

'Cycles?'

'Each time an adult dies it produces a kernel, which needs nutrition and water to germinate a new body. It's essentially the same adult with the same knowledge but, with their resources reduced, they can only repeat the process a number of times.'

John nodded. A new group of aliens caught his attention. Eight broad, white-skulled, ape-like creatures carried two throne bearers on which two creatures relaxed: one a mass of fur and limbs; the other a long creature which reminded John of the stick insects he used to collect as a boy.

'This is the one?' the giant stick insect clicked.

Once again, John felt grateful for the mushroom he'd eaten when he first arrived here and pictured Crossley's smiling face. John straightened his back and concentrated. These had to be the Ascent leaders. Whatever he did here could have consequences for everyone in his captured army.

'Affirmative,' Ten-ten replied.

'You are sure it can open the lock?' the hairy beast asked.

'Modification is required,' Ten-ten replied and turned to John. 'Show me your gun-arm.'

John held his gun-arm back. He tried to spin a stub-nosed bullet but the heat wouldn't build.

'There is no point in resisting,' Ten-ten said.

'You can easily be manipulated,' the insect clacked, sounding impatient.

John breathed heavily. He was clearly trapped but felt he had to do something to escape – wasn't that his duty?

'Do it,' the furred alien ordered.

John's gun-arm swung round and up to Ten-ten as though it had been pulled by a rope.

'No!' John shouted, but it was futile.

A metal tube popped out of Ten-ten's forearm and three drops of oil fell onto the gun-arm barrel. It warmed immediately and, held tight by the Lutamek's immobilising field, John couldn't shake it off. A tickling itch, like a thousand tiny spider's feet, ran down and inside the gun-arm.

Finally, the holding field dropped, allowing John to scratch the muzzle.

'What's happening?' he asked, staring at his arm in horror.

'The next stage,' Ten-ten replied coldly.

John yelped as what felt like a hundred tiny bites ran through the inside of his gun-arm. The internal mechanisms were changing. Where fingers and tendons had been merged with firing mechanisms and bullet chambers, these were swiftly reforming and moulding into something new.

'What next stage?' John asked when the pain subsided to a dull ache.

'Everything changes,' Ten-ten replied.

'No, it doesn't,' John argued back but knew the comment was ridiculous given his circumstances. 'It shouldn't do anyway. A gun should just be a bloody gun.'

'We were set on a path,' the furred Ascent leader said.

John looked to the immense glass tower.

'And we have our destination.'

'We are just tools in the grand scheme,' the huge stick insect clacked.

'And our bodies respond to external stimuli,' Ten-ten said. 'On arrival, we were each endowed with the genetic plasticity to take us on a new course. Yours is nearly complete, John.'

'What?' John replied.

Images came to him: the electric blast from Delta-Six; the Synchronisers preparing the new species; the shock from the display board; the Tathon writhing as their bodies fought their changes.

'Why can't it just stay like this?' John asked and felt a looseness in his arm.

He stared at it as, almost imperceptibly, the stunted machine gun started to change: ridges grew deeper and the barrel shrank, the metal flowing up his arm.

'Mutations have many advantages,' Ten-ten said.

'Or disadvantages,' the insect clicked.

'And although no mind is at work here,' Ten-ten continued, 'the potential can be seen in every change and, if required, ushered to a chosen destination.'

'You did this?' John raised his voice. 'When you scanned my arm before you betrayed us, you… you screwed my arm up?'

'No,' Ten-ten replied. 'Our brothers in the Ascent gave us requirements and your adaptation was the closest match, so you were preserved while I prepared–'

'Enough!' The insect screamed. 'The doors are opening and our agreement won't hold long. Get him to the lock.'

'Agreed,' Ten-ten replied and gestured for John to follow him through the door in the metal fence.

John paused, caught between watching his hand in horror

and the desire to know what was in the tower. Ten-ten's force field gently nudged him along and he found himself following the giant robot. He tried to spin a new bullet but the chamber was in pieces now – one segment was on what felt like his palm and others were inside his fingers.

Fingers?

John turned his wrist to see four darkening lines running up the broadened muzzle like cracks. He tensed what felt like a thumb and the section split away.

'You should find the new changes useful,' Ten-ten said as they walked through the gates, guarded by two more broad, white-headed gorillas. 'Now we require silence,' Ten-ten said and gestured at the crowds of bizarre-looking alien soldiers congregated around numerous other gates in the metal fence.

Their bizarre body types reminded him how the other domes had been filled with martial species from more distant regions of their shared galaxy. Floating blobs, metallic cuboids and large-eyed, fish-like creatures were all focussed on him and Ten-ten as they climbed the incline to the tower. John cast a look back and could see a crowd was forming inside the city as well.

All eyes were on him.

John's cheeks reddened and he stared at his gun-arm again. It had stopped itching and looked more like a hand now. He stretched what felt like tendons and four fingers snapped free, just as his thumb had. It was like having his old hand back, he thought, and gave the shadow of a smile. It felt like a hand but was so much larger. It felt stronger too. And the mechanisms of the Lewis machine gun were still imbedded somewhere in his wrist and forearm.

How on Earth did they expect him to open a lock with something that looked like a human version of a Lutamek hand?

The ground levelled off and John saw their reflection, his tiny body next to Ten-ten's hulk.

'The lock,' Ten-ten said and pointed at a silver ring set into the glass of the tower wall, a few feet off the ground.

Ten-ten gestured for John to carry on alone.

John gave his surroundings one last look then shuffled towards the tower, cradling his metal arm.

How many people had made it this far? he wondered. Was he the first human? What would happen if he couldn't open this 'lock'? A cold shiver ran through him and he scanned the floor but couldn't see any body parts or piles of dust.

As he came within two strides of the dark glass, it cleared and John could see inside the tower with absolute clarity.

'Shit,' John said.

Inside was another obelisk.

Olan took a step back. His opponents had paused as well. He hadn't expected this. Usually he would have some half-crazed animal rushing at him or a wily alien soldier with a head full of battle rage. The first could be tired out given time, while the other was too full of resentment to fight naturally and would eventually make a mistake Olan could seize upon. But this time he knew each of the four men, standing sixty paces from each other. He had fought alongside them and he knew their strengths and weaknesses, just as they knew his. Bowman, Osayimwese, Steve Smith and a Chinese warrior, Rae. Like him, none of them had their original weapons, but that didn't make them any less dangerous.

Olan searched for guards in the crowd, wondering what they would do to get them fighting. He'd seen pacifists killed before and the crowd wouldn't stand for a battle without death. The oval-shaped arena dipped at one end so the full majesty of the glass tower could be seen by everyone and, for a second, it caught his eye.

A swishing sound made Olan duck to one side as an arrow buried itself in the red soil behind him. His ear burned where it had clipped him. Bowman had already singled Olan out as his most dangerous opponent. Good thinking, Olan thought, as he weighed up the men. Bowman had great eyesight, but his 'thinking' arrows had been confiscated, while the Chinese soldier, if Olan remembered rightly, was endowed with the ability to heat his body to great temperatures, so was no threat from a distance. Smith, on the other hand, was armed with a lightning spear Olan had seen used by a tall, metal-clad soldier some days back. No problem with that, because Olan could see the energy pulses rising and falling before each strike, but what tricks did Smith hold within his visor? It had to be fixed to his head or the guard would have ripped it off.

Another arrow flashed past as Olan ran at Smith, to the pleasure of the crowd, the volume of which rose a notch. He stepped around the huge lumps of metal strewn across the arena floor, hoping some might deflect the arrows. The Chinese warrior had been waiting for someone to make a move and now closed in on Smith, presumably hoping Olan would distract him.

'Choose your own battle,' Olan hissed, too far away to be heard.

Steve Smith was already lowering his spear at Olan, who remained focussed on the energy patterns in the shaft. His chest plate was at work again, he thought, as a surge of blue rushed up to the spearhead. Olan dived to his right and rolled away, leaving the blast's crater behind him. With a curse, he was back on his feet, ignoring the taunts and laughs from the alien crowd. The rise in volume accelerated his heart rate and gave power to his muscles. He used it, just as he had in previous battles, and rushed at Smith, but the Chinese warrior was nearer, warming up like he had a cauldron in his chest. Olan was tempted to strike him down first, but a set of new arrows came thudding down between them.

'Bowman!' Olan bellowed. 'Fight like a real man, or don't fight at all!'

The crowd loved that and Bowman responded with a low, fast arrow which glanced off Olan's chest plate with a solid clunk, just missing his cheek. Olan knew he had to keep this entertaining or the evil bastards in charge of the arena would send in new creatures. Smith was busy keeping the Chinese warrior at bay with energy bolts, so Olan turned to Bowman and ran at him.

From this distance it was hard to concentrate on a small figure when there were hundreds of shouting, sparking and yelling aliens in the stands behind, but Olan tried, dodging when Bowman's bow was loaded and running straight when his arm bent for a new arrow. In the time it took to cover half the distance, Bowman had released three arrows, one of which clipped Olan's forearm, which dripped warm blood down his wrist.

Olan knew this was wrong, but he closed in just as he had done in foreign lands. Don't think of the man you're killing, he told himself, just think about the consequences. It was instinctive – he *had* to stay alive. As he closed in, Olan felt a lull in energy. Bowman had noticed it too and paused shooting. No time to be weak, Olan thought and raised his axe, ready to leap and swing at the English longbowman. But Bowman wasn't looking at him any more. Neither were the crowd, whose roars had shrunk to a wave of low murmurs.

Olan cast a quick look over his shoulder and saw Smith and the Chinese soldier staring into the distance as well. He skidded to a halt, checked Bowman's bow was empty, then followed the gaze to the tower. Tiny silhouettes could be seen at the tower base. A metallic crash made him turn as the arena entrance doors smashed open and the guards came rushing out for a better look. The crowd were leaving in their droves.

'What's going on?' Olan shouted to Bowman.

'Not sure,' Bowman replied and climbed one of the metal hulks. 'But you see those people?'

He pointed and Olan squinted to make out a huge shape walking next to a tiny humanoid.

'Lutamek?'

'Yeah,' Bowman said, 'and that little one is John.'

Olan gripped his axe tighter. It was the first time he'd seen or heard about anyone else from their army, other than those who had died in the arena.

'What shall we do?' he asked, with a glance at the guards, who had left the doors unattended as they tried to get a better view.

Bowman shrugged. 'Could be a good time to make a move?'

Olan nodded at the nearest exit and they walked over as naturally as possible. So far so good, Olan thought, as the guards stared at the tower base. Olan sidestepped the decaying bodies from previous fights and slipped into the darkness of the exit. If they could get through one more set of doors they could mingle with the crowd and disappear.

'Stop!' A white-skulled Bensha guard stepped out of the gloom, blocking their path with its long sword. 'Nice try,' it growled, 'but that's far enough.' It tapped the back of its neck. 'I'd hate to lose tomorrow's entertainment so cheaply.'

Olan held his axe tight as the two of them stared each other down for long, silent seconds until finally, knowing he couldn't win this one, he let the axe drop. Their captors always had the advantage over them, but Olan felt he and his comrades had gained something extra today. They knew the rest of the army were alive, which gave him hope there would be a way out of this hellhole.

John rubbed his forehead with his good hand and reread the message carved into the stone of the immense obelisk inside the glass tower. It was written in the same script as the obelisks inside the dome and, like those messages, remained equally cryptic:

Enter to complete your path of ascendancy.

Seven words? John thought. All the battles and the deaths were all for these seven words? And this was why this group of kidnappers and pirates called themselves 'the Ascent'?

John scanned the glass wall of the tower for other locks or entrances – anything that would give him a clue about what to do. But there was nothing. Just one metal circle in the side of the tower. He was beginning to feel the frustration the Ascent leaders had shown and he wondered how long they had been here, stuck outside the tower, knowing they were one final step away from completing the puzzle.

A creaking noise behind him made John turn to see Ten-ten, who gestured at the lock again.

'Right,' John said and stepped forward, lifting what had become of his gun-arm.

His metal fist looked about the same size as the dark hole at the centre of the metal ring. Nothing around it showed signs of a door or hatch; it was just a depression in the glass ringed with metal. John held his breath and slowly pushed his hand into the hole, feeling a tingle of excitement run through him.

Was this it? If this worked, he would become a hero. Thousands of soldiers from countless worlds would know his name… his shoulders sagged at the thought, remembering how his mates had treated him after the night of the crater, setting him apart and always expecting more heroic exploits from him.

No, John thought, this was way bigger than just him. If he opened the lock all these species would be led to the next level, and humans would be known across the galaxy for the part they had played.

John felt a click and bent down to peer into the dark tube, where his little finger had magnetically linked to a small tab at the back of the lock. There were four others and when John's digits connected his fingertips warmed. Here we go, he thought, and pushed his hand forward.

Nothing.

He twisted his wrist to the right, hoping the lock would turn with him, but it didn't budge. The same happened when he twisted to the left.

John felt his cheeks flush. All eyes were on him and here he was with his hand stuck in the wall. He pushed again, and twisted. He was starting to feel desperate. Why had the Lutamek chosen him? Surely their metal arms could be changed to fit the lock? Was it because his arm was a gun too? John started the process of spinning a bullet. The parts which used to make up the chamber were separate now, but he could still feel them. He let energy build and, although he couldn't visualise it like before, he could see a light glowing inside the lock.

'Something's happening,' he said to Ten-ten, who didn't reply.

John wasn't sure if it was the heat, but he was sure he felt a new itching sensation now. It tickled, like when Ten-ten had put those drops of oil on the muzzle.

'Oh no,' John whispered and peered into the lock tube, where a grey oil ran along his fingers and over the tabs in the lock.

John pulled his arm, but it was still magnetised. Something felt wrong, so he let the energy dissipate and pulled harder. It was stuck. Panic was setting in and he felt his heart racing. He put his metal foot on the tower wall and pulled on his arm as hard as he could.

'What have you done?' John shouted at Ten-ten, who took a step forward.

'It won't work like this if—'

A flash of light and a wave of winter cold rushed through John. He felt himself flying through the air. Then all was dark.

When he came to his senses, John saw shapes moving around him and heard the insect leader of the Ascent barking orders.

'Too much time has been wasted,' it clacked.

'It was our strongest response yet,' Ten-ten replied.

'Enough,' the Rassum leader barked. 'Throw him in the mines.'

Chapter 13

Isao leaned against a rock to catch his breath. Just as he had done countless times before, he waited to make sure the coast was clear before slipping into what had become his home these past few days.

The cave was an air pocket hidden under the rock, large enough for him to crouch in and lie down. He'd only found it after a close encounter with a scouting party who'd been scouring the land for survivors from Gal-qadan's army. He had dived into the sand at the rock's base, only to find his head pop through into the hollow.

Isao knew he could slip into the shadow world if he was seriously threatened but, if the armies saw him, they would hunt him down for knowledge of his true abilities. Slipping his eyes into the shadow world was useful enough, he found, and had given him enough advance warning when an enemy approached, their hearts glowing like red coals.

Since finding shelter, Isao's main focus had been finding food. No animals lived in the desert outside the domes, and the only plants able to scratch a living out here must have arrived as broken stems or seeds stuck to some victorious soldier's boot or claw. From his tiny sanctum, Isao was able to search the land for discarded food and tools, and to keep an eye on his comrades, now imprisoned by this faction of desert dwellers who called themselves 'the Firstborn'. From what Isao had seen, the Firstborn lived in a string of forts which led from the open desert to the huge tower.

Isao ducked, pushed through the sand which blocked his cave's entrance and kicked a pile back in place once he was inside. It was dark, but he could see clearly when he let his eyes slip away. Here were the meagre rations and weapons he had scavenged from what was left of his army's supplies after the Firstborn had ransacked them. Anything of use and small enough to secrete away – clothing and blades, storage tins and bottles – had been stashed here.

Isao unscrewed the lid of a metal canister, carefully poured in a vial of water, reclosed it and tapped the last drip into his mouth. He unwrapped a piece of cloth and picked out a leather-like strip of tocka flesh, which he wiped the inside of the vial with, searching for any hidden moisture, before chewing. This was what he had been reduced to: sipping water squeezed from roots and chewing on dead allies.

Now, as he prepared for another excursion, Isao let his thoughts wander as he would whilst meditating. Nothing was new, so his thoughts took him back to when Das and Pod had given them to the Firstborn. This feeling of betrayal was new to Isao. He had seen former allies change sides during many of his long wars, but that was in reaction to the political dynamics of their Daimyos. What had taken place with the Firstborn was a cold-blooded trap. For their own gain, Das and Pod – and maybe Peronicus-Rax – had led them into slavery.

When Gal-qadan's soldiers and tocka had been chained and marched to the nearest fort, Isao had trailed them from the shadow world and watched as Das and Pod were welcomed like heroes. Victors, returning with the spoils of war. The pair had told tales of their prowess and the hard-fought battles won, how they had bravely entered a new dome, located the strongest army and made sure they won their battle. Throughout it all, Gal-qadan had squirmed, unable to break from his chains. Isao had been close to attacking when they had slit the throat of the first tocka, but managed to hold back, knowing he was more useful if he was free.

As the days passed, Isao had learned about the Firstborn's territory. They governed a wedge of desert radiating out from the central tower and guarded both borders with passion. What lay close to the tower, Isao didn't know, but here, in the desert, their string of black metal forts were complete with moisture absorbers to water the soldiers.

No food production though.

Isao sighed. His rations were meagre and wouldn't last long. Soon it would be time to leave this refuge behind. There was little he could do for his comrades on his own. He needed help.

As he curled up to sleep, one last vision came to Isao: Peronicus-Rax. The tall soldier was an enigma to Isao, like a piece of a puzzle that never seemed to fit. He had been aloof during their journey and had returned but sat apart from Das and Pod after the army's capture. Since then, Isao had seen him talking with members of the Firstborn, and on one occasion he'd given them one of his many weapons.

What deal has he struck? Isao wondered as he drifted off to sleep.

Althorn sped away from the metal behemoth, wondering why one Lutamek was out on its own so far out in the desert. He had to slow down or he would run out of energy, but avoiding capture took precedence after what had happened back in the dome with Belsang and the Brakari. He paused to catch his breath, took a sip from his canteen and adjusted the headband which covered his missing eye. His depth of field was still poor, but he was amazed at how his balance and senses had adjusted.

He took a second to scan the horizon. There was nothing in sight here in the featureless landscape, but that didn't mean he wasn't being watched, so he ran off again before anything spotted him. He painted a wide arc around where he had spotted the Lutamek and found no sign of other scouts. His curiosity was too strong – he had to find out why it was here. Was it a deserter? Had it been cast out? If it was, Althorn was torn between drawing it towards Euryleia and Lavalle's bandit group and destroying the metal beast for being a traitor.

When Althorn found the Lutamek again, his anger rose. He remembered the slaughter these robot giants had carried out. He remembered the line of carts carrying their new slaves. He remembered his lost friends. But there was no way he could take it out by himself.

This one did move awkwardly though. Was it damaged?

Althorn closed in, trying to keep his movements snappy so he didn't register on the robot's sensors, a method he'd tested with Ten-ten during their time camped by the starships. As long as Althorn had the energy, he could remain invisible.

Closer up, Althorn could see this Lutamek was larger than any he'd seen before and moved with less grace; it jolted and clunked along like it was about to fall apart. Then there was the sound. The clicking and crunch of metal was clear to Althorn from a hundred paces away, and he heard new sounds the nearer he got: whooshing and ticking, along with what sounded like voices.

Althorn rushed past and caught a muffled voice say, 'More oil on the caspet!'

'Ease up the falloo-finator,' said another when Althorn sped past again.

It was hard to tell, given the language fungi which translated all communication in Althorn's brain, but he was sure they were human voices. He took another run past and tapped a grey leg with the hilt of his knife, then sped off and watched from a distance.

The Lutamek stopped and a hatch opened in its back, followed by a pair of human eyes. The hatch slammed shut again, followed by a call of 'Forward!'

Althorn laughed for the first time in what felt like months. How had they managed this? He ran to stand in the path of the mechanical giant.

'Stop right there!' Althorn shouted and stood, arms folded.

A stifled voice called out, 'Slow to halt!', which was followed by a tiny bell ringing.

A puff of steam belched from an unseen pipe in the robot's back and a dozen portholes opened up across its body, revealing a number of gun muzzles.

'Name?' A distorted voice called out.

'Althorn. And you?'

'I am Troy,' replied the voice.

'Troy?' Althorn asked. 'There's no need for weapons – I'm a friend. Do you recognise me?'

Silence.

'I'm Althorn. We met when you were siphoning fuel from the ships,' he said, remembering the red-coated soldiers. 'I'm with a band of survivors from our army. You can join us if you wish.'

The Lutamek wobbled on its feet and buzzed as its crew shuffled within, discussing and chatting.

'No, Carter,' one voice raised a level above the rest said, 'Elliott's right…'

Althorn pressed on. 'You are the soldiers in red coats, am I correct?'

'We fight for our majesty's empire!' came the response.

Althorn remembered something Crossley and John had said about these soldiers belonging to an empire, but he couldn't recall the details. The group had kept themselves aloof, insulated from the events which surrounded them, Althorn thought, so did they really know what was going on here?

'Our mission is to remain alive and fight when needed,' the voice shouted.

'But we're stronger together,' Althorn replied. 'Surely you can see that?'

Silence.

'How did you escape?' Althorn asked.

All he knew of these soldiers was the bewildering gears and gizmos they were always playing with.

'Guile and deception,' the voice replied.

Althorn raised an eyebrow. Maybe one of them had an adaptation he was unaware of?

'Like this metal man… this Lutamek you're travelling in?' he asked.

'Yes, no real bits of course – they can track them – but it's our way of blending in.'

'And seeing off would-be attackers,' said another voice.

Althorn shook his head and decided it wasn't a good idea to disagree with them. 'Where are you headed?' he asked.

'We need supplies. Move aside now, our quarrel is not with you.'

Althorn sighed and shook his head.

'There's nothing out there,' he said, casting his arm out to the empty desert, 'apart from domes.'

A bell rang out, followed by the cranking of gears. The forest of gun barrels slipped back through its holes, and the hollow Lutamek resumed its bizarre, clunking walk.

Althorn stood to one side as it strode past him.

'Good luck,' he heard a voice call out from within.

'Signal if you need us!' Althorn shouted back, though he had no idea how they would ever find each other in this vast wilderness.

Althorn's shoulders slumped. It was time to return to base and explain what he had found. Lavalle would berate him for not convincing the redcoats to join their cause, but the group had more important goals. There were more important missions taking place after all.

Euryleia held herself as close as she could to the cliff face, gripping tight with every finger and toe. She kept her breathing steady, with her head close to one of her right hands, as she stared out at the shapes moving across the desert.

Scouts.

Their presence had slowed her party down, so their timings would have to shift, but that was why she always added in a little leeway. The scouts were unexpected, which meant the Ascent had either changed their scouting routine, or something big had drawn their attention. As far as she or Lavalle knew, their team of tocka-mounted resistance remained undiscovered and free to roam the desolate spaces where territories blended into the desert.

Or maybe they had simply been left to die? Euryleia thought, knowing that was what her subconscious had been trying to tell her for days. No. Leaving this group of warriors to roam freely was a big mistake, she thought, as the tiny silhouettes of the scouts merged with their dust trail.

Her eyes drifted and focussed on the back of her hand, sending an odd sensation through her. She twitched a tendon to remind herself this was her hand. It *was* her. It looked just like the hand she had lost when Ethan had blown himself up, but so did her other right hand. Her forearms, elbows... identical to before, just as it was with her left arms. Her real arms were lost in the explosion and these were just... tools. They felt the same, but she didn't have the same affection for them. Euryleia smiled at the idea of explaining her thoughts to Lavalle.

The dust cloud was far away now, so Euryleia turned her head slowly to scan the horizon.

'Nobody in sight,' she whispered and leaned back to see the rocky cliff face come alive with camouflaged soldiers, scaling back down.

'Cheng.' She called her second in command.

A solemn man, with greying temples, Cheng was leader of the party of ancient Chinese warriors in the dome and they obeyed no one else.

He nodded.

'We must speed up to avoid capture.' Euryleia thought fast as she spoke. 'We'll split into two parties to deliver the messages.'

Cheng nodded again, then spat a series of lightning-fast orders to his crew, who split evenly and without sound.

Euryleia took the left posse and handed Cheng the cloth.

'Back here before sunset, or return to base,' she said and the groups set off.

They jogged with soft feet in an ever-changing formation, hoping to avoid disturbing the telltale dust or attracting the distant eyes of scouts or guards. Their clothing had been dyed to match their surroundings, but one of the group, Guang, had an ability which had come in useful many times. He could manipulate light to shield his compatriots, just as he had done during the battles in the dome, which was why Euryleia hadn't seen the Chinese contingent fighting. In fact, if Cheng's men hadn't been between Euryleia's group of tocka and the

Lutamek, when they had turned on the army, they would have been captured.

'Guang, create a haze,' Cheng ordered.

Euryleia felt what she could only describe as a *softness* rise up from the ground itself and set a shimmer in the air around her. She had seen the practice at work from a distance and those shielded had simply vanished from view.

A few minutes later, Euryleia gave Cheng a nod as they ran and the group split in two. Their destination was nearer, she thought, so they could do without Guang's protection.

A grey line wavered on the horizon ahead: their target. Euryleia raised a fist and her group lined up behind her.

'Nearest guards?' she asked.

'One on the far right,' Sancha, a Chachapoyas warrior with the ability to focus on distant objects, replied. 'The half-blind one with a keen sense of smell.'

Euryleia relaxed a little. They had bypassed this guard before. The barbarians who ruled this land believed in demoralising and splitting up captured armies, and several humans had been discovered in the isolated farms which lay on the edge of their inhabited regions. Lavalle had said what Euryleia had been thinking: to destroy an army you divide and conquer. So, if they were going to fight back, they had to reunite.

They were getting close now and, without Guang's protection, Euryleia was concerned they would be seen. 'Any movement?' she asked.

'No,' Sancha replied.

Euryleia held her lower right hand out and flattened her palm. They would crawl from here.

The sun was low in the sky when the group made it to the edge of the plantation, where rows of stubby red bulges tipped with black spikes made patterns in the desert sand. They had been here before, and although Euryleia was keen not to duplicate their methods, she knew their contact would be active here tomorrow, during the harvest.

Leaving her group behind, Euryleia crawled forward, imagining she looked like a giant ant on her six appendages. The guard had made his pass minutes before, so Euryleia headed for the nearest row of almost-ripe crops. She dragged her body between two rows, dug a hole beneath what looked like a swollen beetroot and pushed the cloth inside. She covered her marks and scuttled backwards, erasing her tracks as she crawled.

The most dangerous part was over, she thought, but no time for complacency. Steadily, keeping her eyes on the field, Euryleia reversed into the open ground. The message Cheng was delivering was different to hers, but just as important. As she crawled back to her team, ready to make it back into the open desert, she pictured the words and made a quick prayer that their contact would get the message and know what to do. Two simple words which made it sound easy but, if anyone could do it, she had faith this man could.

Free Mata.

Isao kept himself in the shadow world but let his hands appear in the real world as he filled his canteen with water from a filter trap. The Firstborn army who ran this segment of land were frugal, he thought. No city to administer, control and feed – just a series of forts manned by loyal warriors, supplied by raided food and these water filters.

Since leaving his hollow, Isao had tracked a scouting group to a hidden food store, marked with an infrared circle, which he could easily spot with his shadow eyes.

Keeping a safe distance back, Isao listened to the myriad species talk while they rested.

'But I'd be safe in the city,' a reptilian soldier said after openly suggesting she could defect.

'You can't just walk over the line and become Ascent,' a tall creature covered in horned armour said, 'they would interrogate you – torture you, to make sure you weren't a spy.'

'Controlling the land means almost as much as the tower,' a third, small, squat creature added.

'I could give them information,' the reptilian said.

'And they could sell you back as a traitor – it's not worth it,' the armoured soldier replied.

After a pause, the squat scout said, 'I've heard there'll be another swap soon.'

The others looked at him.

'Some of the scrawny runners Das and Pod captured – the Ascent want them and we can get our troops back. Easy trade.'

'They should get rid of that thing as well while we have the chance,' the armoured one said. 'It stinks and uses up food.'

'They're holding out for a better price,' said another.

'Well, let's get rid of it now,' the tall one said. 'Keep the runners. Use them as scouts. I'm fed up with this constant travelling here and…'

Isao turned and let the words fade in the wind. He'd heard enough and knew he had to travel to the fort on the border with the Ascent land. It overlooked the lush fields the Firstborn soldiers longed to plunder and only the constant presence of Ascent guards prevented them taking the fresh food for themselves.

It took Isao a day to reach his destination.

Despite the hostility between these two groups, Isao could tell by the well-trodden sand between the fort and the Ascent guard post that this was a trading station. Isao waited, remaining in the shadow world. Then, with the sun at its zenith, the fort door creaked open and a posse of Firstborn soldiers strolled across to the border, placed a long-barrelled gun in a box and returned with a set of boxes full of fresh food: red bulges; green leaves; and yellow stalks. This was why they captured new armies. They needed weapons to pay for food.

Isao was tempted to sneak into the fort as he crept behind the soldiers, and would have snuck in through the gate if his instinct to survive hadn't cut in. He had to avoid capture. He circled the fort, listening to cries of torture and whimpers of hunger from within the ramshackle building, the rusted walls and open roof of which gave little protection to those inside. From the red hearts he could see, scores of prisoners were held in fetid pits in the ground. Then he glimpsed a pair of eyes on a wall and froze. Who knew what abilities some of these species had? He couldn't risk being sensed by any of them, so crept away to a rock, behind which he crouched and waited some more.

Noise rose from the fort by the evening, and Isao was rewarded with new activity. He remained in the shadow world, watching the glowing red hearts in the inky silhouettes. More soldiers left the fort: two rows flanking new creatures, dragging crates and boxes, followed by a trail of chained prisoners. They must have emptied the fort, Isao thought, as the line of dishevelled beings was ushered and beaten along the path to the Ascent border.

On the other side, on Ascent land, stood a welcoming committee of four individuals of such varied nature it made Isao smile. He crept forward for a closer look: one was a human-sized mass of fur; another stood bulky and broad with a white skull beside what looked to Isao like a many-legged bamboo puppet; and there was the huge, unmistakeable shape of a Lutamek soldier.

'We give thanks for your offerings,' said the foremost Firstborn guard.

'And we appreciate your timely payments,' replied the hairy beast.

'We have much to trade,' the Firstborn guard said. 'Do you have our kin?'

'Yes,' the insect puppet clicked.

A screening device Isao had been unaware of, even from within the shadow world, dropped to reveal a gang of more than twenty aliens behind the Lutamek, some of which matched the styles and features of the Firstborn guards he had seen.

'We are told these humans are valuable,' the Firstborn guard struck the nearest human, who didn't respond but took a step forward, allowing Isao to see his face.

Isao gasped: it was Gal-qadan!

'These are not your most valuable assets,' the Lutamek boomed.

'No,' the Firstborn guard replied. 'We expect all of our comrades in return for these humans and your kin.'

Two boxes were toppled over and two spheres rolled out: the Lutamek eggs Gal-qadan had stolen. Isao couldn't see the Mongol's face clearly enough, but he could imagine how he looked. Not only had he been betrayed and his army captured, but his prize assets were being bargained away before his eyes.

'This is a fair trade,' the insect clacked and gestured for the swap to take place.

'Yet there is more,' the Lutamek said and pointed at the final box.

'Ah, yes,' the Firstborn guard rubbed its claws against its hips, 'for this we expect a greater trade... a cycle's worth of fresh food would suffice.'

'No,' the furred beast growled and turned, showing Isao some of its muscular strength.

'The price is too high,' the insect clicked.

The Firstborn guard waited a few silent seconds, then said, 'You have already scanned the contents and know its value.'

The comment was addressed to the Lutamek, who took a step forward. 'Yes.'

Isao felt his heart speed up. Why was the Lutamek acting strangely? Normally they were quick-witted and one step ahead, but this one had been caught out. What was in the box? With his shadow-world eyes, Isao could see a silhouette inside with a green diamond shape for a heart.

'And its worth?' the Firstborn guard asked.

'It is a good trade,' the Lutamek said. 'We will cover the costs,' it said, before walking away from them, in the direction of Isao.

'What is it?' one of the Ascent asked.

'A Velluta,' the Firstborn guard said. 'I doubt you've seen one before.'

'Out trade is complete!' the Lutamek shouted, and raised a hand to start the swap, but carried on walking towards Isao. 'No more questions.'

Isao watched the humans walk into Ascent territory and the Firstborn soldiers pass back into their realm. He moved to one side to peer around the Lutamek but it changed direction with him. Isao paused and looked up at the metal giant. He spotted a grey sphere between its eyes and found it familiar.

'But I still have questions,' the Lutamek said, apparently to no one.

An orange beam flashed from the Lutamek and Isao dropped out of the shadow world. He tried to run but his legs felt heavy, like stone.

'For you, human,' the Lutamek said, reaching down to grab Isao, 'I have many questions.'

Chapter 14

John rubbed his eyes with the rough fingers of his good hand as his vision adjusted to the dim light. He was in an enormous underground cave rich with body-odour stench, where dishevelled aliens stumbled in lines under the gaze of huge, white-headed guards.

'Get up!' a voice cracked.

John saw a new species looming over him. Spiky, but not as bulky as the other guards, this one held a weapon in his hand, aimed at John's head.

'Alright!' John said and raised his hands.

The tall, stone-like alien seemed to glow, as John saw its eyes fix on his mechanical hand. Was this one of the Ladrof which had defeated the Brakari?

'Has it been checked?' the Ladrof shouted over its shoulder.

'The Lutamek said it's fine,' a voice shouted from around the corner.

The Ladrof stared John in the eyes. 'Failed the test, did we?'

'I…' John looked from the guard to his metal hand and back again. 'It wasn't the right fit.'

The Ladrof holstered its weapon and mumbled, 'This is your new home. You need to know the rules. You dig, sleep, eat and shit. Anything else and,' he tapped its neck, 'you die. Got it?'

John nodded and opened his mouth to ask what they were digging for.

The Ladrof tapped him on the forehead with a rectangular finger. 'No questions – just walk,' it pointed to one of the scores of dark passages which led from the main chamber, 'and dig.'

John set off, with his head low, and felt the air thicken as he walked into the descending, narrow cave. Lights glowed from scoops in the wall every twenty strides, and passing places had been carved every fifty. John received a nudge in the shoulder to walk past any branching caves, reminding him the Ladrof was behind him. How could anyone find their way around these warrens?

'Don't even think about running off and hiding down here,' the Ladrof said, as if reading John's thoughts. 'We tour the tunnels every night and set off the primers.' It tapped the pin in the back of John's neck. 'So if you're not where you're supposed to be, you end up dead.'

'Right,' John said, feeling what little energy he still had drain away.

'Keep moving!'

John sped up and turned the next corner to where a small cave opened up, its floor littered with holes two strides' wide, each with a strange symbol carved next to the opening. Between the rows of holes at the far end of the cave, a white-skulled guard patrolled the narrow walkway. A green light shone on each symbol as the Ladrof scanned for John's assigned workplace until…

The light on the floor flashed red.

'In here,' the Ladrof ordered, then spoke to its comrade. 'A new one for you. I've heard Bensha have taken a liking to human flesh.'

The guard responded with a deep laugh, and John felt the white-headed guard's eyes on him as he sat down and dangled his feet in the hole.

'He's another one of the Lutamek's chosen ones,' the Ladrof said. 'Another failure.'

John looked into the hole to see a short drop down to some rudimentary steps and a dim light.

'I don't tolerate trouble here, failure,' the Bensha growled. 'Just keep digging and you'll stay alive… unless I get hungry, of course.'

The Bensha let out another laugh as John dropped into the hole and scrambled down the steps, out of view, where he waited and listened.

'Get digging!' the Bensha roared and stomped off.

It was too cramped to stand, so John shuffled along, crouched, around three corners, spiralling down the narrow path, and stopped as a shape appeared.

'I thought I heard someone coming,' a voice said.

John recognised the voice but squinted at the face a few feet away. It was gaunt and marked, but the eyes hadn't changed.

'Yarcha?'

'Yes,' she replied and ran a hand over her dusty, shaved head. 'You were one of the men who woke me?'

'John,' he replied, feeling relief at finding a friendly face here. 'Are there more here?'

'Silence!' a voice boomed from above.

'We must whisper,' Yarcha said, in a voice John hardly registered, and beckoned him down the remainder of the passage to a small chamber with a hole at its centre. 'We have to carry up debris every hour or they think we have stopped,' she said, nodding at the piles of rocks lining the walls.

'What are we digging for?' John mouthed.

Yarcha ignored the question and tapped three times on the edge of the hole.

John leaned over, peering into the darkness, and, after some scratching sounds, a pair of eyes glinted back and grew in size. He pulled back as a species of alien he'd never seen before, like some oversized beetle, crawled out of the hole on six legs. Its antennae twitched as if sniffing John and its eyes flicked from Yarcha to John and back again.

'Yam-mit,' Yarcha said, 'this is John. He's human like me.' She looked at John. 'And this is Yam-mit, a Korax.'

'Hi,' John said with a timid nod, his heart racing as he stared at the Korax with a mix of intrigue and fear, being in close proximity to another bizarre-looking alien.

Yam-mit gave a wave with two hands and grunted a vowel. It pointed at the rocks and scampered back into the hole.

'We're a team now,' Yarcha said with a nod, 'so we'd better shift some rock.'

John nodded back and set to work, trying to make sense of what he'd seen. In the poor light his eyes could be playing tricks on him, but he was sure he'd seen a symbol he recognised on the chest of the Korax. It was identical to the one he'd seen carved into the wall in the prison he had shared with Falen: a disc circled by three dots.

Although Praahs enjoyed her elevated position in the Tathon army, she longed for the freedom of the chase. She longed to fight once more. She had enjoyed her time capturing scores of rogue soldiers from the far reaches of the plains, and had felt bored stuck with the main Tathon army. Until now. A troop of blue arthropods had been terrorising the Tathon army and, according to her Brakari captive, Panzicosta, they were led by a rebel Brakari. The shelled fighters tore into their rear ranks, then their right flank – attacking with no apparent plan – and had set numerous traps in their path. None had been captured and only one killed, which had earned them huge respect in the eyes of the Tathon leaders.

A tingle ran through her long body when 'Kno-lib ordered Praahs and her platoon of small, hard-shelled Cirratus to track the guerrilla force and, if they couldn't be captured, destroy them.

'And Panzicosta?' she asked the Tathon leader.

'He has potential and will be developed,' 'Kno-lib replied with its echoing voice. 'We will camp at a new location–'

A map flashed in Praahs' mind, sent from 'Kno-lib. She recognised it but wasn't sure why a curved boundary ran along one side.

'–and will start our next project, which must remain uninterrupted.'

'Yes,' Praahs replied, remaining prostrate before the large gelatinous creature, whose adaptations and abilities exceeded anything Praahs had thought possible.

'You did well bringing us soldiers – especially those lingering near the silver gates – but ridding us of this blue nuisance will be more beneficial to our cause,' 'Kno-lib said and raised the tip of one of his enormous tentacles.

'Yes,' Praahs replied and took the cue to crawl away.

Her Cirratus were waiting for her, resting in a symmetrical pyramid shape which, she had been told, provided rest time for over half the troops whilst maintaining maximum defensive capabilities. The Tathon doctors had given Praahs a new organ – she visualised it as a slip of red liver lying beneath her digestive tract – which she used to communicate directly with her group of efficient warriors.

She had often wondered how she would defeat a Cirratus in

battle. No teeth could penetrate the shell and they could hold their breath for hours. A gaseous poison followed by crushing was the best method, she had concluded, and had had four individuals' sensory arrays enhanced accordingly.

'Move out,' she whispered through her abdomen, and the pyramid pile collapsed with a tinkle of shells. 'Open-jaw array,' she ordered and they followed, spread out into a wide U-shaped formation. 'Now we hunt.'

As they left their army behind, Praahs saw the vast array of mobile vats of the liquids on one flank and winced. They had been put to use on so many new soldiers to enhance their abilities and create new physical attributes, but Praahs could only remember the pain. She had been told of the codes within each soldier and how the Tathon masters scoured every new species' code for fresh snippets of information, which they used to enhance themselves and their army, but her understanding was limited.

Between the vats, Praahs caught a glimpse of Panzicosta's blue shell covered in fungus vines, holding him in place as the doctors prepared their machines.

She bowed her head and saw an eye blink in return.

John hadn't felt this tired for days. His body ached, his head was a blur, his eyes itched and his lungs rasped with dust.

'It'll be our turn for a break soon,' Yarcha whispered when John returned from carrying another load of rocks up the twisting shaft.

The air had been cleaner at the tunnel's opening into the cave, where John had watched the other holes, hoping for a glimpse of the other miners – maybe a human or Sorean from his army – but long shadows had reminded him of the prowling guards and he'd soon clambered back down.

John nodded at the dig hole and asked, 'How long until Yam-mit returns?'

Yarcha shrugged and stared at John, making him turn away. Her presence had made it easier to bear the conditions these past few hours, but she hadn't answered his questions – too worried about the guards overhearing, he guessed. She shrugged whenever he asked what they were digging for, how long they'd been here and where Yam-mit had come from, so he soon gave up.

Only when Yam-mit climbed out of his hole, pushing a hoard of rocks ahead of him like some kind of tunnel spider, did they finally speak. Yarcha held a finger to her lips and nodded at the Korax, who rubbed two antennae together to form a blue bubble that expanded to encompass the three of them.

'Now we can talk freely, John,' Yarcha's normal voice sounded incredibly loud.

A hint of a smile curved her lips and John found it hard to tear his eyes away from her.

'I,' he forced himself to turn to Yam-mit, 'I'm glad to meet you. I'm John, John Greene – a human.'

'Yes,' the Korax's voice was lower than John imagined it would be for a Sorean-sized insectoid. 'I have heard about your battles,' he glanced at Yarcha, 'and heard that your species were unfortunate… a bad choice of ally. Betrayal is not warrior-like.'

John sighed. 'Everyone changes,' he said, remembering his conversation with Ten-ten.

'Some more than others,' Yarcha said, and nodded at John's metal hand.

'The Lutamek used some liquid to… transform it,' John said. 'It could still be changing for all I know.'

'But it was not enough for the lock?' Yam-mit asked.

209

John shook his head. 'The lock nearly blew my arm off,' he said with an embarrassed laugh. He tapped his metal leg and said, 'It's not the only thing the Lutamek helped me with.'

Yam-mit stared at the patch of material where John's cauterised leg met the Lutamek tech. 'I see,' he said, apparently in deep thought.

'Did they take you to the lock?' John asked.

'No,' Yam-mit replied. 'But many in here have been taken.'

The Korax's antennae wafted softly and John wondered if he was listening out for the guards.

'Are there more of us in here?' John asked, looking at Yarcha.

Yarcha nodded. 'You'll see tonight when we return to the main hall… humans, Sorean… many other species from other domes.'

'Anyone the Ascent has no other use for,' Yam-mit said.

'And this,' John pointed to the symbol on Yam-mit's chest, 'what does this circle and three dots mean?'

'It's the sign of our system,' Yam-mit replied. 'Three species, three planets, one star… in my time we never physically met or even saw images of one another, but we knew their names and formed an alliance… we vowed to work together to defend our system.'

'Who?' John asked.

'We, the Korax, lived on the innermost habitable planet, the Drauw lived on–'

'The Drauw?' John asked. 'But…'

'You know of this species?' Yam-mit asked as his antennae started swishing. He held a claw to his mouth, mimicking Yarcha's earlier gesture, and the blue bubble shrank and disappeared.

John clenched his fists and listened to the echoing steps above.

'Keep digging!' came the call from above.

Yam-mit disappeared back down his hole and Yarcha stacked up the new rocks, leaving John wondering why Falen, the Drauw, had mentioned nothing of her home system or the Korax. She'd talked at length about trade and her species, yet never mentioned other species in her system.

John picked up rocks and thought back to the prison. Falen could have carved the sign in the mud wall, but what if someone else had done it? A Korax maybe, but what if it was a soldier from the third species?

Samas punched the wall again, feeling it shatter in response. Shards of stone scattered on the floor and he pulled out loose rock with his good hand. One last assault, he thought, then they could rest... before starting it all again tomorrow.

This truly was a living hell.

He couldn't let the situation weigh him down – there were too many people relying on him. He had to keep up the morale of his troops, which included the Sorean contingent after Jakan-tar's execution, and there were other wheels in motion which he had to help keep moving.

He *had* to stay positive.

The Ascent leaders assumed they had demoralised the miners by splitting up species, enforcing their silence and keeping them weak with poor food, but Samas knew otherwise. There were many unseen skills at work in the mines, building, exploring and communicating. The humans and Sorean hadn't joined a slave army; they had become a new link in a vast network of what was, literally, an underground resistance movement.

Samas loaded the last pile of rocks onto the basket and hefted it up for Rar-kin to take.

'Any progress?' he whispered.

'Three weak spots complete and marked,' Rar-kin replied with a faraway look in its eyes. 'The map is nearly complete.' It tapped its head with a clawed finger and blinked.

Rar-kin had been mentally communicating with three other individuals scattered across the mine network and the energy drain was evident. They had sent him mine-layout information which he pieced together to form a map, which would be a vital part of Samas and the other leaders' plans. Samas had left the Sorean to its own mathematical devices for too long, he realised. Each soldier had to use their strengths if they were to escape from the mines, but it was no good if they left brain-dead. There was more fighting ahead of them, Samas was sure.

'You can start the digging tomorrow,' Samas said.

'But…'

'You need to keep your physical strength up,' Samas replied.

'Yes, but the rocks are heavier the deeper we dig,' the Sorean complained.

The original miners had been exploring ways to escape for months, but rumours of other factions' tunnels coming into Ascent territory had given Samas the idea. Crossley had been set to work and, sure enough, had detected a faint echo of a chamber towards the border with the neighbouring group, the Firstborn. They had been directing mine shafts towards the area ever since.

Through various communication methods, the leaders of each species had discussed the plan under the noses of the guards. Many leaders didn't want their soldiers to leap from one prison into another, especially those who had experienced the ruthlessness of the Firstborn, but in the end the majority agreed to give Samas' plan a chance. Regiments were created and knowledge shared. It was a risky plan, but Samas had his troops placed in the most dangerous positions, so any mistakes and the humans and Sorean would pay the highest price.

There was just one thing stopping their plan – the neck pins.

Samas knew the guards wore pins too and was sure if he could get one of the controllers he could kill them off one by one. But one thought nagged at Samas – what if the guards didn't have to die? Maybe he could get the guards on their side? They wore pins because they were captives too. Maybe a little soft and compliant given their guard status, but wouldn't they join an uprising if they could? The army would be stronger with them.

'You are tired too?' Rar-kin asked.

Samas stared at the Sorean for a second before registering its question. He could hear the guards calling above, rousing the miners from their shafts.

'Nothing some sleep won't fix,' Samas replied and forced a smile. 'Come on, one last load and the day will be over.'

Rar-kin climbed the zigzag shaft ahead of Samas and said, 'Yes, another day closer to the end.'

Samas wasn't sure whether Rar-kin was talking about their escape or their death.

They were soon up in the fresher air of their shaft's mini-chamber, where the guards lined up other miners ready for the walk back to the main cave.

Samas made a quick headcount, checking his own soldiers as well as those of the other leaders so he could report back. This chamber was just one of the scores of caves currently in use, and they lost men every day to accidents or the whim of the guards. Even though they outnumbered the guards ten to one, if they were going to mount an escape they needed to know their exact numbers.

Crossley was in one of the other groups and winked at Samas when their eyes met. The lines of tired miners funnelled through the narrow, rock-walled corridors, giving them the chance to whisper if they lined up in the right order.

Samas let a tall, shiny-skinned humanoid go first so that
he would be near Crossley. The guards didn't allow the same
species next to one another, so he kept Rar-kin in front of him.

'What news?' Crossley whispered as they filed through the
corridor.

'All three points are ready,' Samas replied, checking the
guards weren't close behind.

'You?' Samas asked.

'The deepest one yet,' Crossley said, referring to his mine
shaft, 'and it's getting dark… heavy. I can't see further down.'

'And the rocks?'

'More granulated the further down. Contain patches of
something… dense,' Crossley replied.

That fitted with what Rar-kin had said about the rocks being
heavier, Samas thought, but still didn't explain what the Ascent
leaders were looking for. Every rock they excavated was sent
out, labelled by depth and position, and, according to new
recruits who had seen the plant outside the mine entrance,
analysed by Lutamek soldiers.

'Later,' Samas whispered.

The end of the tunnel was soon in sight, and raised voices
suggested the guards had pulled someone out of line for a
misdemeanour. The line slowed and soldiers grumbled as they
backed up into one another.

'Keep moving!' A guard shouted and the line sped up again,
as it led into the main chamber.

They passed the argument, where a bone-headed Bensha
guard held a small miner against the wall by the neck. Samas
couldn't see the creature but recognised Yarcha, who knelt
beside the guard, and what looked like a six-legged Korax
lying half dead on its back.

'I don't care for your reason – silence must be obeyed,'

the guard said and knocked Yarcha to the ground while the throttled creature gargled nonsense.

Samas felt obliged to help Yarcha.

'Guard,' Samas said, stepping out of the line but keeping a safe distance back, 'may I help?'

The Bensha looked Samas up and down, then barked, 'Another noisy human? How many do I have to kill before you understand your position here?'

Samas lowered his head. 'I mean no disrespect,' he said calmly, 'only to help. The more miners we keep healthy, the sooner we achieve our goal.'

Samas had to play on their shared hatred of the mines.

'It's his first day,' Yarcha said.

'Be quiet!' the Bensha growled, keeping an eye on the line of miners passing, and another on the guards who were scattered along the cave. 'Is it true?' he asked.

Samas looked up as it pulled the limp body from the shadow and presented it to him. It was John Greene!

'Yes,' Samas replied, staring at John with a mixture of joy and concern. 'He's one of my men… how did he get here?'

'It doesn't matter,' the Bensha said, distracted by a disturbance down the cave. He dropped John on the ground and said, 'If he speaks tomorrow, I kill him.' He patted the controls hanging from his belt and stomped off.

Samas ran over and cradled John's head.

'John?' he whispered.

Yarcha turned the Korax over, who jolted a couple of times before rising.

'Are you injured?' Samas asked.

John shook his head and rubbed his throat.

'Let's get him back,' Samas said.

'And I must return my soldiers,' the Korax said, apparently

healthy again. 'We have much to discuss.' It scuttled off to join a cluster of Korax.

Samas put John's arm over his shoulder and Yarcha helped to carry him into the main cave, to the strip of floor the humans occupied in the evenings.

'Keep back,' Samas whispered at the soldiers crowding in as he gave John a drink. 'Give him air.'

'John!' Crossley was first by his side. 'How the hell did you get here?'

'Quiet,' Samas hushed.

Crossley's voice had some effect on John, who blinked and came round. He squinted, smiled and coughed.

'Don't speak,' Samas said, eyeing the red marks at John's throat.

'What's happened to his arm?' Crossley said. 'I mean the gun was useful and all, but–' he twisted his head as he stared at John's metal arm.

Samas looked too. He'd always felt an affinity with John, seeing as their enhancements were similar, but had thought the changes were the endpoint, yet John's gun-arm had completely transformed into what looked like a small, metal Lutamek hand.

'It's changed again?' Samas asked.

'Well I like it,' Crossley said, 'very handy.'

John coughed in response, or was it a laugh? This was good, Samas thought. Good for morale. Another soldier in the group, adding to their numbers, and it meant there could be more out there. Soldiers who had escaped.

'You've arrived at the right time,' Samas said, patting the young Englishman on the shoulder. 'Rest now and get your energy back up.'

Samas looked up to meet the eyes of Crossley, Yarcha and

the other human soldiers watching and whispered, 'Tomorrow we escape!'

Praahs had considered not returning to the army, but knew her own Cirratus would be sent after her if she did that. She would make a good go of it – return to the lake if she had to – but that was weakness talking. As much as her survival instincts told her to hide and wait, she would have to face 'Xit, 'Brin or 'Kno-lib eventually and explain how the enemy had got away.

They had been fast. They had been clever. They had known Praahs and her army were coming.

Five Cirratus dead and two injured. Praahs thought about what she would tell the leaders. Images of the Brakari rebel leader ran through Praahs' mind: the speed and agility; the flashes of lightning; the piercing calls coordinating the army, who cracked the shells of the Cirratus with vicious smashes of their hammer claws.

Praahs and her unit ambled back to the rendezvous point at the pace of the weakest, allowing them to maintain their defensive formation at all times. They had been harried from the rear twice but repelled the enemy and expected no more attacks now they were close to the full army. The map flashed in Praahs' mind as they climbed a long rise in the featureless landscape. Beyond, the clouds were thick, but Praahs was sure they would see the Tathon army from the summit. In her mind, she imagined the circle-shaped conclaves of soldiers resting or sleeping off the effects of their rapid enhancements. Red Comglo worms, white loping Frarex and humanoid bipeds mixed by ability rather than species.

'If I come within ten strides of a human,' Praahs remembered Panzicosta saying, 'I won't be responsible for my actions.'

Praahs wondered what it felt like to have an enemy like that.

That level of pure hatred. The power from that emotion would feel amazing, she thought, its strength intoxicating.

The cap of the shallow hill curled to reveal the land beyond. The furthest stretch of desert was coated in a thick, wavering mist, but the nearer land was clear and dotted with the circular formations Praahs had expected. The sight of the huge structure in the centre of the army was not anticipated though and caused her to stop.

'Leader?' a Cirratus asked, sending a vibration through Praahs' abdomen.

'What is that?' she asked.

'A shell,' the nearest Cirratus replied.

The Cirratus had been in direct contact with the Tathon leaders all along, Praahs realised. She felt dread constrict her muscles – the leaders already knew she had failed. Her muscles relaxed – they knew but hadn't punished her. Not for the first time, the power the Tathon had over her, and the feeling of always being an outsider, irked her.

'A shell for what?' she asked, staring at the large, clear structure which curved up from the ground.

'Defence,' came the obvious answer. 'And a place to strike from within.'

The shell was an immense, curved shield constructed of a clear glass which rose to over ten times Praahs' height, resting on an array of wheels. Behind it, at its centre, stood an enormous ramming device: a huge slab of metal hanging from six hefty arms. The sharpened end of the ram protruded through a hole in the shield's centre.

'And what is that for?' Praahs asked, staring into the mist for answers.

'The leaders have found a weak point,' the Cirratus replied.

Praahs had no idea what it was talking about until a map flashed in her head showing their current position. It zoomed out, allowing the curve of mist to expand. Praahs recognised landmarks as it zoomed out further – the fort where she had found Panzicosta, the battle plain and her lake, surrounded by red cliffs, which proved to be at the centre of a perfect circle. The whole land was hemmed in by the circle. A border. A net.

They had been trapped the entire time!

'Kno–lib's voice filled her head. 'And now we will break free.'

Chapter 15

Dakaniha stood to stretch his back. He and the rest of his farming crew had been plucking crops for half a day now and deserved a rest. Looking across the field, he could see they had a handful of rows left, so he knew the guards would work them until they were finished.

The sound of an electric whip charging up drifted across the silent field and Dakaniha got back to work, pulling the large red tubers from the sandy ground. Each one needed leaves stripping into the sack on his back, before the swollen root itself was placed in the box he dragged along the row.

Surely there was a better way to do this? Dakaniha thought. What with all the technology the Lutamek and countless other species within the Ascent had at their disposal.

Today will pass, he told himself, and carried on plucking and stripping.

He was close to the edge of the field, on the outskirts of the farm, facing the open desert. He pulled his headband down to dangle around his neck and opened his second pair of eyes. He tried not to do it often in front of the guards because, although his adaptation was nothing special, they punished anyone using their new skills.

Dakaniha slowly plucked leaves as he scanned the horizon, his new eyes searching for life signs, when he noticed patchy nuances of colour in the soil by his feet. Nothing lived underground here, so any soil disturbance had to have been made by the farmers. He checked the nearest workers weren't close enough to notice. Dakaniha looked down and scraped the sandy soil with his foot but couldn't see anything. He picked the nearest tuber and stripped it, while still digging in the soil with his toe. He could tell by the colour something was hidden – there! A corner of fabric poked out. Bending down for the next tuber, Dakaniha pulled the piece of cloth free and folded it into a handful of leaves.

Dakaniha breathed in deeply and felt his heart pick up speed. He bent down again and opened the material to see two clear words: Free Mata. He pictured the large Maori warrior who, rumour had it, was held on the other side of the farm. He'd seen guards carted off to the city bearing slash marks identical to those he'd seen on Brakari shells during the battle in the dome. When the number of injured guards slowed and eventually stopped, he had assumed Mata was dead.

Dakaniha stuffed the cloth into a pocket and continued to pluck and strip. His mind was racing. Someone from their army had survived! They were not abandoned, as he had feared. Not only that but they were mounting some kind of resistance. But did they have a way to counter the neck pins? He pulled his headband up, tight around his head, then picked up his box and returned to the pile of crates for a rest.

That evening, with another field harvested and the farmers finally allowed to rest, Dakaniha sat leaning on the brittle wall of his crew's mud hut, sipping from his metal canteen. He was safe here with his back to the wall, staring up at the kaleidoscope of alien stars. His birth eyes were amazed by the clarity of the bizarre constellations and patches of colour, but his new eyes peeled back layers and created a whole new picture for him. Up there, as close as the moon back home, he saw scores of objects. Metal, if the colour match with the Lutamek was to be accepted. They each took strange orbits while others remained still and could have been mistaken for distant stars with his normal eyes.

Talking was prohibited, yet the darkness allowed some clumps of soldiers to form and spread news or barter with their meagre rations. Sounds were magnified in the desert night. He could hear the distant laughs of the guards, the solemn whispers and moans of his fellow captives, and he could see all around him, which was why he didn't jump when the silhouette appeared.

'You have something of mine,' the shadow said with a distorted voice.

Dakaniha focussed and unfocussed his eyes, reading various wavelengths in the low light, until, with a flicker, he recognised the true shape and relaxed. Here was one of the most proficient warriors Dakaniha had ever seen in battle. Forget Gal-qadan, he thought, this man was one to learn from.

'Free Mata,' Dakaniha said, still looking at the stars.

'When?' the shape asked.

Dakaniha scanned the wide fields of the farm, noting every guard's position, and turned to face his ally. 'With you by my side, Delta-Six, the best time is right now.'

Euryleia waited in the dark, listening to the chorus of soft breathing that surrounded her, human and tocka.

'What if he doesn't know where Mata is being held?' Lavalle whispered, close to Euryleia's ear.

'He'll know,' she replied.

They were ready to attack, to start the uprising. There was no going back. No food or water.

Sancha had watched Dakaniha find the message and one of Cheng's scouts was adamant he'd made contact with Delta-Six. Once freed, Mata could occupy the farm's guards on his own, and Euryleia was confident the farmers would join their guerrilla group. It was what came next that worried her.

A shuffling sound behind signalled the return of Cheng, who had been with the bulk of their troops beyond the nearest rocky outcrop.

'My last scout has returned,' he addressed Lavalle.

Normally, that would have irked Euryleia but she had grown used to it.

'The tocka station has been located,' he continued, 'in the strip between the farm and city.'

'Then we can pick them up on the way,' Lavalle said.

They hadn't confirmed their exact course of action after winning the farms, but Lavalle clearly had his mind set on pushing on to attack the city and free more slaves.

'What is their state?' Euryleia asked.

'Many tocka are dead and the survivors are weak.'

'They will need food before we fight,' she replied.

'Which they will have in surplus when we attack!' Lavalle said with a smile, reminding Euryleia that, despite their domestic nature, the tocka were carnivorous beasts.

She patted her tocka and asked, 'Any sign of Althorn?'

Lavalle breathed in before answering, 'No. As ever, he's scouting ahead.'

He was clearly still perturbed by Althorn's interaction with the British soldiers who had stalked away from the city in their steam-driven Lutamek. They needed every soldier, he reminded her on an almost-hourly basis.

'Good,' she replied, not wanting to bring up the event. 'We should move closer to see what has been happening–'

She was stopped by Lavalle's hand on her arm.

'Look,' he said with a nod at the far edge of the farm.

She squinted at the distant light, which radiated a steady glow, followed by the echo of small-scale explosions.

'It has to be Delta-Six,' Euryleia said with a smile.

'He'll draw every guard to him if he's doing that!' Cheng said and Lavalle nodded.

'Then we must act now,' Euryleia replied. 'Mount up!'

She looked at Lavalle, who seemed transfixed by the lights.

'Even after all of this,' he murmured, 'such a vision I never thought I'd see.'

Euryleia turned and, in the distance, saw the white, glowing shape of a man ascending into the sky. With his arms outstretched and legs straight, his body formed a cross.

Althorn ran for his life. His legs burned and his stomach tore at itself, but Althorn was running on pure adrenaline. More pain would come later, but now he just had to stay alive.

He hadn't meant to travel this far into Firstborn territory, where their defences grew denser as their territory tapered into the thin end of their wedge of land by the tower. The closer he got, the narrower his options for escape. He'd been spotted and managed to avoid the first watchtower, but they were all on the alert now, so he pushed on towards the tower at breakneck speed.

His surroundings blurred as he rushed past, right up to the building he'd heard about. He slowed down to make two circuits, making sure it was empty, and then he was inside. From the outside, it looked like a rough, metal-walled shack identical to the hundreds that made up the Ascent city, only this shack stood completely on its own in the shadow of the tower. Inside, dusty steps lined with relics and rudely carved statues descended. Althorn followed them down into a cool cave that dog-legged right to where a rope hung across at waist height, designed to keep visitors – or pilgrims, Althorn imagined – from touching the main shrine. A large scoop in the rock wall was lit by a handful of orange lights, glowing like tiny setting suns around the main sculpture of two figures, hand in hand. Althorn stared at them and at the offerings of weapons and ammunition which lay about the statue's feet. A sign above them read:

Revere the Firstborn.

These two? Althorn shook his head.

A scuffling sound at the cave entrance startled him and he ducked under the rope and slipped into the shadows behind the shrine. Out of the light, Althorn controlled his breathing as he listened to the footsteps, the murmured prayers and the clatter of metal. More offerings.

By the time the pilgrims had scuttled back up the steps, Althorn's eyes had adjusted to the dark enough for him to see a low passage in the shadows which bent around the shrine, deeper underground. He crawled through, hoping to find a water source or discarded rations, but was greeted with another set of roughly hewn stone steps. A light further down gave shape to Althorn's surroundings as he descended deeper, the path twisting down to yet more steps – less rough, with straight edges and a solid feel – then finally levelling off and leading him through a series of rooms to a sight that took him completely by surprise.

'So that's who you really are,' he said and stroked the shiny metal.

Delta-Six felt nausea rise in his stomach and signalled his system to inject a 5mg medistrone burst into his bloodstream. He glanced at Dakaniha, who had all four eyes wide open and was almost panting as his pulse rate rose rapidly.

'Relax,' Delta-Six whispered. 'We will fix this.'

Dakaniha didn't turn, but nodded.

They were hidden behind a pile of crates full of the slender, protein-rich stems the Ascent farmers grew on the far side of the farm, where the soil was stonier. The smell reminded Delta-Six of the porridge they used to serve as breakfast in the Himalayan training camp, and he thought of his old unit. No time for nostalgia, he told himself, the smell would conceal their odour from alien senses, he hoped. The guards here were no different to those across the farm, but who knew what adaptations these individuals had gained since arriving here?

Dakaniha signalled and Delta-Six watched one of the three guards stroll away, only to be replaced by a fresh guard – this one a stocky, four-legged beast. A Graifar according to the dome's databanks, which he had been slowly digesting through his time in isolation on the farm. He'd taken his time, knowing the real reason the Lutamek had sent One-eight-seven to the dome cap with him was to limit any data he found on them. They had been clever, sending well-camouflaged mining worms into his systems to remove the knowledge, but Delta-Six's systems had retained shadow data.

'We must attack,' Dakaniha mouthed.

He was right, but Delta-Six wasn't ready yet, so held up a hand. He looked at Mata's prostrate body again: a sprawling mess of vines and roots stretched out over a ten-metre-wide circle, trapped in a series of metal straps and vices. It could have been just a bizarre plant experiment, but the tortured face at one end and the rough shape of a humanoid body at the centre proved it was Mata. Bottles of liquids bubbled beneath roots, encouraging hundreds of yellow growths, while scores of flowers and an array of bizarre fruit hung from the myriad vines.

Mata was being harvested.

'Right,' Delta-Six whispered and projected his plan of action on the side of the nearest crate for Dakaniha to check.

The warrior's eyes widened.

'We must fight,' Delta-Six said, 'and this is where the rebellion starts.'

'But…' Dakaniha gestured at the metal disc at the back of his neck.

Delta-Six hadn't been captured so had no explosive device nestling under his brainstem. He had given the issue a great deal of thought and created an ingenious solution.

'All taken care of,' he whispered but could see anxiety written in the Aniyunwiya's expression.

This mission would be one of reassurance as much as revenge, Delta-Six thought. He gestured to some distant crates and said, 'I'll show you.'

Dakaniha hesitated but silently crept through the shadows to a safe distance.

Delta-Six pulled the cloak back over his head. With his disguise back in place, he set his new frequency-detection system to mirror all signals. With a grunt and a groan, he limped out of the shadows and into the sight of the sleepy guards.

'Halt!' a Bensha yelled, waking the other dozing guards.

Delta-Six maintained his forward shuffle, mumbling, 'so hungry… no food…'

'Halt now or we will expel you,' the guard said, as it walked around the sprawled, vegetative mess of Mata to intercept Delta-Six.

Delta-Six stumbled forward and fell to his knees near where one of Mata's vines had been coaxed into producing bulbous, apple-like fruit. 'Just one would keep me going!' he said and coughed.

Before he could reach the nearest fruit, the Bensha was on Delta-Six, kicking him in the gut, sending him into an empty crate.

'You are not allowed here, Lucien Thomas!' the Bensha yelled.

'Just zap him,' the Graifar said while the other guard – a tall biped with glowing blue eyes – stalked over to join the Bensha, its claws clasped around the pin-control device.

'No.' The Bensha held him back. 'I could use a little fun first.'

The Bensha picked Delta-Six out of the broken crate, showering the floor with splinters.

'What about its body?' Blue Eyes asked.

'Fertiliser,' the Graifar replied with a nonchalance suggesting he'd done it many times before.

Delta-Six let the Bensha throw him to the ground and take its aggression out on him. His systems compensated for each blow with a force-field push designed to mimic the body, so he remained uninjured.

'I just want food,' he murmured.

'We feed you enough, you filth,' the Graifar shouted, reclining and enjoying the fight.

'You should have been stronger,' Blue Eyes said. 'If you weren't caught you wouldn't be here.'

'Like you?' Delta-Six said, with his normal voice and pushed himself off the ground.

Blue Eyes fingered the silver disc on its chest and the Bensha stepped back.

'Who are you?' the Graifar demanded, springing up to join its comrades.

Right where I want you, Delta-Six thought as he stood to his full height and let his cloak slip to the ground. He felt an energy rise inside him – a power – and decided he would make a show of this. He pushed energy into his jet and lifted a few inches off the ground.

'I was never captured,' Delta-Six said, 'but I have been chosen.'

He spread his arms out and set his suit to emit a white glow as he ascended.

'Kill him,' the Graifar said and Blue Eyes clicked the button.

Delta-Six's suit mirrored the signal, deflecting it back, and created an energy shield for biological debris as Blue Eyes' pin exploded in his chest, covering his comrades with guts and brains.

'You shall die!' the Bensha yelled and leaped at Delta-Six with his long sword, while the Graifar simply turned and walked away on its four stout legs.

Delta-Six rose higher and sent a replicated version of the guard's signal to the Bensha, whose head disappeared in a mist of blood and pulverised bone, leaving his headless body staggering into a pile of crates.

The Graifar was twenty paces away with what looked like a pulse-rifle as it turned to Delta-Six, who sent the pin signal to take off its head.

Nothing happened.

'Like you, I was never captured.' The Graifar sounded louder now it held a weapon. 'I have never fought your species before... I hope to enjoy this battle.'

Delta-Six set his shield to maximum and fired three laser bursts at the horse-like warrior. It was more agile than he had expected and shimmied away, then returned fire, sending an array of orange globules at Delta-Six. He gave himself a shot of what his unit had called 'war-blood' – an enhancement drug which enabled them to make a series of lightning-quick decisions based on their system's analysis. A sudden burst from his jet sent him above the globules, which looped over the crates and into the desert, sending sprays of dust and fire into the air. Delta-Six fired back, catching the Graifar on a front foot, causing it to roll closer to Mata. He dodged another blast from the gun and replied with four laser shots at the ground, which all missed the Graifar, but hit metal boxes, sending showers of sparks across Mata's twitching body.

'More guards will arrive soon,' the Graifar said, as it changed the settings on its rifle.

'Good,' Delta-Six replied and slowly descended from his lofty position.

Predicting the Graifar's next move, Delta-Six weaponised his suit and sent an energy blast at the four-legged creature, sending it stumbling backwards. Movement behind it told Delta-Six all he needed to know. He fired another shot, sending the rifle spinning out of the Graifar's claws, then aimed more bursts at the ground, where jars of liquid toppled over, pouring their contents into the sand.

The Graifar picked up the Bensha's sword.

'Do you dare face me in mortal combat?' the Graifar growled, swinging the cumbersome weapon.

'No,' Delta-Six replied and turned in Dakaniha's direction. 'My comrade will deal with you.'

Dakaniha's silhouette split from the shadows and the Graifar faced him.

'Then I will kill you both,' the Graifar said and rushed forward, only to find his rear feet were fixed to the ground.

'Oh, no,' Delta-Six said and held up a hand to halt Dakaniha's attack, 'not that comrade.' He gestured at the sprawling mass of Mata's vegetative body, which he had freed from its prison. 'This one.'

The Graifar's face contorted into a picture of pure panic as Mata's tendrils wound up its back legs, thorns digging into its flesh. The Graifar slashed and sliced, but a bark hardened on the vines as they pulled it towards Mata, into a deadly embrace. Ten seconds later, the Graifar had been engulfed by a mass of roots and leaves.

Delta-Six saw Dakaniha wince as a series of deep cracks signalled the end of the Graifar.

Every tendril of Mata was free now and, somewhere inside the huge mass of writhing plant, Delta-Six knew Mata's eyes still existed. He hoped the Maori's mind was in one piece as well as he projected images onto him: crashing waves; snowy mountains; green hills; wide, grey, stony rivers. Images of Mata's homeland.

'You are free,' Delta-Six said.

Dakaniha stood beside Delta-Six, still shocked by the sight and said, 'Next time, I will join you.'

'And I will protect you,' Delta-Six replied. He pulled the sheet of fabric from a pocket and unfolded it for Dakaniha to see, then cast an ultraviolet light on it. 'I had another message.'

It was a hand-drawn map of the farm and surrounding area, covered in an array of white points of light, which sparkled like constellations.

'These are our comrades,' Delta-Six said, 'human, tocka and Sorean. These are who we will free next.'

Chapter 16

John woke up coughing and tasted gritty dust in his spit. He rubbed his dry eyes and took in the sleeping bodies around him. In the dim light he could make out a few faces he recognised: Samas; Crossley; Yarcha. Beyond them sat the vibrating ball of Sorean fur, as the cat-like creatures slept huddled together, and clusters of other alien huddles beyond them.

It felt like he'd been fully aware of his new surroundings all night: sleeping on the cave floor with the echoing sounds vibrating in his ear and the thick stench of hundreds of creatures desperate for fresh air wrapped around him. Exhaustion must have taken him in the end, drawing him into a deep, dreamless sleep. Just like sleeping in the trenches.

'Wake!' A distant shout echoed along the long cave and the wall lights flickered.

By the cave wall, Samas stirred and rubbed his beard. It had been barely noticeable in the dome, when they shared every day together, but now John noticed how many men had grown beards or moustaches. It aged them. Or maybe they looked older because every human soldier apart from John had

had their head shaved when they entered the mine. Or maybe it was the fear?

During John's war, even the youngest men had aged terribly in their first year. He'd tried to grow a moustache himself, like most of his mates, trying to look older, like the officers, but he'd failed miserably. He ran his palm over his chin, felt the thin stubble on his top lip and tried to remember the last time he'd seen his face.

Crossley sat up and stretched. He was clean-shaven, so clearly had a razor stashed away somewhere.

'Right,' Samas whispered after the guard had strolled past, 'same as any ordinary day.'

The miners around him nodded.

'Don't behave too well – act normal,' Samas ordered.

'Easy for you to say,' Crossley replied. 'We're the ones who cop it if it fails.'

'It won't fail,' Samas replied with a smile.

John sensed it was a forced smile, but it did the job for the soldiers, who slowly rose and filed to the cauldrons of watered-down porridge awaiting them for breakfast. A couple of fights broke out in the queue and again when the miners were ushered to their shafts, but, according to Crossley, it was normal stuff. No one was killed.

Once he was back in the enclosed, dusty chamber with Yarcha and Yam-mit, John waited, not sure what to do. He hadn't been given specific instructions, so he waited for the noises of fighting above, when he planned to climb back up and escape with the masses.

Yam-mit disappeared down his hole and Yarcha started shifting rocks, so John studied his metal hand in the dim light. He was sure he could see the grey liquid Ten-ten had dripped onto it, flowing between the gaps and joints. It was probably inside as well, although he couldn't feel it. If it was still a firing gun-arm he would be expected to fight, he thought, and felt reassured he wouldn't have to today.

Yam-mit's head reappeared at the top of the shaft and his antennae twisted a blue bubble of protection around them. 'Everything is in place,' he said. 'We must descend now.'

'What?' John asked, looking to Yarcha. 'We have to go down there?'

The hole was wide enough for a human to climb down, but he couldn't see any handles or steps.

'Our shaft is one of the three exits,' Yarcha said, raising her chin with pride. 'Our neighbours will break in here and follow us.'

'Right,' John replied with a wide-eyed nod.

Yam-mit stared at John for a second before saying, 'You must have faith in your allies.'

'Oh, I know, sorry!' John raised his hand. 'It's not that I don't trust you–'

'You have given me faith,' Yam-mit said, his antennae constantly weaving the bubble around them. 'I know my eternal allies – the species who share our solar system – are among us. I don't know what they look like but our bond is unbreakable. Knowing they are here gives me strength.' He paused and seemed to sniff the air. 'Your allies are here, John,' Yam-mit said.

The bubble shrank and disappeared, and the three remained silent, waiting.

The escape was suddenly feeling very real to John, who imagined scores of alien miners scrambling through into their tiny chamber and the crush of bodies as they tried to get into Yam-mit's hole. He felt a high-pitched sound at the back of his head and Yam-mit jumped into action, forming a bubble to seal up the entrance to the chamber, before dropping into his shaft. Above, the guard's echoing steps faded away.

Yarcha shuffled to the side wall, pulling John with her, and whispered, 'It's fine. Yam-mit has thought of everything.'

The floor of their square mini-chamber, some five paces wide, suddenly dropped away with a deep rumble and a cloud of dust.

'Let's go!' Yarcha shouted.

Where Yam-mit's hole had been, a stone staircase now descended into the gloom. Yarcha leaped over and stepped down, so John followed.

This was what Yam-mit had been constructing all this time? It was amazing. The steps curved and twisted, reminding John of the steps in an old castle or church he'd visited as a child, he couldn't remember which, but as his head dipped under what had been the floor he saw new holes in the walls and new faces from adjoining shafts.

'Keep going,' Yarcha said. 'Yam-mit should have the exit open by now.'

As if to confirm it, John felt a cool blast of air rush up from the depths and a dim light appeared below, giving shape to the last ten steps to the floor, where silhouettes were already rushing past.

Yam-mit was waiting at the bottom, next to an arched exit which led into another tunnel. 'Keep moving,' the insectoid said. 'Through this last passage.'

John slipped through behind a troop of Sorean and made sure Yarcha was behind him.

'I'm here,' she said.

Images of Rosie came back to John and, although Yarcha clearly didn't need looking after, he still felt the urge to hold her hand.

The tunnel was narrow and short, causing them to stoop but, with no side tunnels branching off, there was no chance of getting lost. Everyone was silently shuffling along until they reached an opening where John saw them lining up, reminding him of people waiting for an Underground train. The crowd heaved and shuffled, but remained silent. Too much was at stake here. John tiptoed to peer over the aliens' shoulders and around shells. He saw human heads here and there, then spotted Samas and Crossley standing by a closed stone arch. By his stance, John could tell Crossley was coughing, using his abilities to 'see' through the rock. The American gave a nod, and Samas plunged his rock-fist into the wall, which was only a couple of inches thick.

John held his breath as Samas peered through the hole. After a few long seconds, he turned back and nodded. This was it! Time to break through and escape.

Five humans stepped forward and, in unison, smashed a piece of rock from high up and passed it back to a Sorean, then smashed another piece and repeated the action until a wide hole was formed and a pile of rocks had been placed out of their way.

'To freedom!' Samas said softly, his whisper echoing as the group surged forward and through the new caves.

John linked arms with Yarcha, who responded by gripping him tightly as they stepped forward with the silent throng. John was watching his step and wondering who had built these new caves when the first sounds reached them: the horrific sounds of pins exploding and heads and bodies being torn apart.

'No!' John shouted and looked to Yarcha, who was equally shocked.

A cold wave rushed through John. This wasn't going to be the heroic escape they had dreamed of.

They were trapped.

'What's going on?' Yarcha asked as the crowd surged forward.

John shook his head as he searched for Crossley in the throng ahead. In the distance he saw grinning Bensha and stone-faced Ladrof corralling the first wave of escapees, and randomly exploding pins, killing the miners at will.

Panic ensued as the crowd turned on itself to get back into the mines they had been escaping from. John gripped Yarcha tight and pushed against the crowd to get away from the guards. In the confused melee of pressed bodies and fighting, they managed to slip free and hide in an alcove. The guards advanced, rounding up survivors and blowing the heads off anyone stupid enough to fight back.

Peeping from their hiding place, John saw one of the guards – a long-tailed Scarpinelloss – stalk out of the shadows, turning to corner a group of soldiers. It was hard to see in the dim light, but John was sure Samas, Rar-kin and Yam-mit were in the gang, backing up against a wall, standing defiantly.

'Kill them,' a hoarse order came from one of the head guards.

Lava flew from the blackened palms of the Scarpinelloss and, when the glare of light had cleared from John's eyes, the cave was smaller. A thicker rock wall stood where the soldiers had been encased with the odd hand or foot poking out into fresh air.

Yarcha pulled John away, into the shadows, stumbling back to the stairs and up to their chamber. Yells echoed around them. Cries of defiance, pain and death.

'No digging today, you bastards!' Pek, the Ladrof guard, shouted. 'We deserve some entertainment.'

'We've got to get back to the main chamber,' John whispered to Yarcha. 'Safety in numbers.'

Yarcha nodded and led John out of their mineshaft to where the mayhem of a free-for-all battle raged. John stared at a cluster of miners' bodies splayed around the guard they had beaten to death. It was like being back in the trenches or crossing no-man's-land, surrounded by death and with the constant threat of the Germans' machine-gun fire hanging over them.

Yarcha was quick and keen-eyed, leading them around the centres of violence, back to the main cave, where hundreds of miners lay bloodied and wheezing.

'John, you made it!' Crossley was sitting in a dark corner and jumped up to greet them. 'And Yarcha… did you see anyone else?'

John shook his head.

'It didn't work,' Crossley said, not looking at either of them. 'We'll never escape as long as we have these.' He slapped the back of his neck. 'Fuckin' Lutamek tech.'

'We have to find a way,' Yarcha said.

Crossley's stare was intense as he said, 'I only survived because Pek said they need me.'

Yarcha's head dropped and she muttered, 'I'm sorry.'

More survivors joined them and the dark minutes continued. Eventually, it was clear the Ascent had known about the escape plan all along and had let the ringleaders show their full strength before ruthlessly cutting them down. Now they knew every adaptation the miners had at their disposal and the most dangerous soldiers had been killed. They might have lost a few miners, but the guards had gained a listening post in the Firstborn's abandoned tunnels.

As he lay on the rock floor, taking it all in, John pictured the soldiers dying… the explosions… the stone encasing his friends.

'Who will lead us now?' he whispered.

'Hell if I know,' Crossley replied.

'Who's left to lead anyway?' Crossley grumbled. 'The whole thing's fucked up.'

They kept their voices low.

'There's no army left,' Crossley continued. 'What were we going to do anyway?'

John tried to think of an answer.

'I would rather die breaking free,' Yarcha said, 'than remain a slave.'

Crossley closed his eyes, apparently out of energy.

'We would have carried on fighting,' John eventually said.

'And they would have blown all our heads off,' Crossley replied. 'We're just lucky they need some of us to dig out their goddam rocks.'

John pictured Yam-mit's bubble ability and wondered if that could be used to defend against the pin technology, then remembered the Korax had been killed by the lava Scarpinelloss, in the wall. Did they still have hope? he thought, remembering Yam-mit's faith in his allies.

'They have pins too,' John said, gesturing at the guards.

'Yep,' Crossley said, sitting up. 'Which means they must work on a different frequency or–'

'Look,' Yarcha said and nodded at silhouettes stumbling into the chamber from the main entrance.

'We've already got new recruits,' Crossley said. 'So whatever we're digging for must be pretty high up on the Ascent's list of priorities.'

'Like the tower,' John said, flexing his robotic hand, which still tingled with the memory of the explosion.

'Nothing trumps that,' Crossley said. 'From what you told me, every faction's trying to get in there, but nobody's tunnelling in.'

John watched the newcomers as they entered the light of the long chamber. 'No humans or–' he stopped when one figure caught his eye.

It was tall, with long, thin arms and limped on four

grasshopper-like legs. Only when she came into the full light of a nearby lamp did John recognise her and feel his spirits lift.

Falen.

Olan faced the metal doors once more, touched the hammer hanging around his neck and cleared his thoughts. He'd already scratched a line into his belt and tried not to think about the previous nine fights. They were a series of blurs punctuated by vivid islands of pain and anger. He had killed for no purpose other than to survive and now, looking at the weapon he'd been given, he wondered if this would be his last battle. He still had his chest plate, he thought and gave it a reassuring tap as he would a nervous comrade.

'One more time then,' he said to himself as the roar of the crowd outside raised a notch and the door slid open.

Olan swung the lump of bludgeoning metal up onto his shoulder and strode into the light, sounds and smells of the arena. He squinted and moved with irregular steps to avoid the flame balls he'd been showered with at the beginning of the last bout. The fact they'd let his opponent out in advance had suggested the Ascent still wanted to punish him for his escape attempt.

Olan scoured the arena for information: metal fences had been constructed in a formation he hadn't seen before and the opposite doors remained closed. To his right he saw Osayimwese, with Steve Smith a little further round and Bowman beyond him. Their weapons were equally basic.

'Looks like we're being teamed up!' Smith shouted.

'Maybe,' Olan said with a shrug.

They never knew what lay ahead in each fight – part of the entertainment apparently – but this was new. No weapons on the floor.

Smith jogged over and, reflected in his mask, Olan saw his own face for the first time in days.

'Who d'ya think we're fighting?' Smith asked.

Olan shrugged as a low rumble from the other end of the arena signalled the opening of the doors. Out came two rows of humanoid silhouettes, arms raised to shield their eyes.

'Are they human?' Smith asked.

'Yes,' Olan said with a grimace. 'They want us to exterminate each other… to weaken us until there are none of us left.' He turned to the crowd. 'Have you no other use for us?' he bellowed.

Some of the crowd shouted back alternatives but Olan ignored their insults. He squinted at the new soldiers, looking for any he recognised – most were human, some were Sorean. There was no point in trying to team up with them. The guards wouldn't allow it, so they'd have to focus on the most dangerous first.

'Gal-qadan!' Olan said, spotting the Mongol horseman.

Bowman and Osayimwese joined them and started picking out other soldiers they recognised.

'They left our old camp before we did,' Bowman said. 'I thought they'd been destroyed before we were captured.'

'Where is Peronicus-Rax?' Osayimwese asked. 'And the two brothers… Pod and Das?'

'No idea,' Olan said, still focussed on the arena set-up.

Something about the layout irked him and he couldn't tell why.

'Good,' Bowman said. 'I'd rather take these guys on any day.'

'I vote we focus on the right wing first then–' Smith was cut off by a new rumbling sound.

A strip of land in the centre of the maze of palisades between the two sets of fighters shook and collapsed on one flank. A dark line five paces wide cracked open and the ground descended. Seconds later, in a cloud of white dust, a herd of wild-eyed tocka rushed up the ramp, out of the darkness and into the centre of the arena.

'What the hell?' Smith mumbled and stepped back.

'Are we supposed to fight them too?' Bowman asked.

Olan shrugged.

Who knew what the vindictive Ascent overlords expected of them? Olan had thought of them like his gods – wielding great power and choosing who should live or die – but now he knew they were just weak mortals. The Ascent were trapped here, like everyone else, and fought for what power was available. They'd become big fish in a little pond, nothing more.

'I think the only thing we're required to do,' Osayimwese said, 'is die.'

'Not today,' Bowman replied.

The tocka calmed their pace and circled the centre of the arena, crossing the dusty ground where the ramp had locked back to form a seamless floor.

'They're carrying something,' Osayimwese said.

'Weapons,' Bowman said and took a step forward, then looked at Olan like he was their leader. 'Come on! We have to get there first or we'll be totally outgunned!'

Olan took a moment to scan the crowd for any of the Ascent elite. No Stur-Morches or Rassums present as far as he could see. No Lutamek either, but they had rarely been seen these past few days.

'Let's get the weapons,' Olan said, 'but watch out for mines and other traps.'

No sooner had the small party advanced than a hole appeared in the arena floor.

'That was close!' Bowman said, sidestepping the dark pit that had nearly swallowed him.

'This is different to before,' Osayimwese said. 'Why don't they just let us fight?'

A distant crackle made Olan turn and raise his bare shield arm, but nothing appeared.

A new voice cracked into life, creaking like a falling tree. 'Now we witness a great moment from the human army's past,' the voice boomed across the arena through unseen speakers, and the crowd jeered. 'We witness the taming of the tocka.'

Olan winced. He had no idea how these horses had been tamed – he had only heard rumours spread by Crossley and the odd mention from Dakaniha that Kastor, the Spartan, had been the soldier to tame them, but he was dead, so what could they do?

As they neared, Olan caught the metallic glint of various weapons strapped to the backs of the tocka, whose eyes remained wide with panic. Wet marks on their back showed why. Olan recognised the barbed cuts of the whip weapon the Bensha guards liked to use. They'd literally been whipped up into a frenzy.

The crowd's roar picked up as Olan peered over the nearest palisade to watch a Sorean from Gal-qadan's side leap on the back of a tocka. Hanging on for dear life, rather than subduing the animal, the Sorean desperately fiddled with a buckle, trying to release the weapon.

'Another one's up!' Bowman shouted.

'We've got to get in there,' Smith said.

'Be my guest,' Olan replied.

The last thing he wanted to do was run into a wild pack of carnivorous horses and jump on a back! Olan hadn't been part of Gal-qadan's army but had spent time with the tocka and knew their normal behaviour, and something about them now reminded Olan of what he had seen when they'd saved the soldiers from the Frarex. Whether it was his chest plate working for him, he didn't know, but he recognised the distant look in the tocka's eyes.

'They can't see us,' he said, turning to the nearest soldiers, shouting to them. 'The tocka can't see us! They're under a Frarex spell.'

Nobody replied.

Olan didn't have time to explain and shook his head. 'We have to use everything we have to get the tocka to calm down and stop... every power available to us.'

Osayimwese looked away. Olan was well aware the Oyo warrior had no adaptation, as Li had called their powers, but what about the others? Bowman had his sight, but Steve Smith?

'Smith,' Olan called over, 'if you've had any changes since we found you in the ship, now's the time to tell us.'

The shiny screen of Smith's helmet gave Olan no idea of emotion – only a warped version of his own concerned face.

Smith shook his head and said, 'The Lutamek told me those changes only happened to those who travelled through the dome cap... something to do with the Synchronisers?'

'Right,' Olan replied and took a lungful of air. 'Then we'd better get on with it.'

Olan pictured the monstrous Brakari he had fought with his axe, the huge, dead puppets he had leaped off to cut the puppet strings from Belsang. This would be no worse, he told himself.

'With me!' he shouted, as he had done to his men on countless raids, and jogged to the last metal palisade next to the central oval where the tocka thundered by.

Gal-qadan's men were holed up on the other side, but Olan only had eyes for the tocka.

'They slow on the turn,' Olan said and ran out into the open.

The crowd cheered as he opened his arms and ran with the tocka, ready to jump and grab one around the neck. But these beasts were not docile pack animals and no sooner had

Olan made his intentions clear than two tocka separated from the wild herd and barged him to the ground, to the obvious pleasure of the crowd.

Olan rolled to a stop and scrambled back as two new shapes bore down on him. These tocka looked wild – their teeth bared and front hoof claws unsheathed. Olan raised the lump of metal to defend himself as they reared up, then heard a shout.

'No!'

And the tocka skidded to a halt.

The tocka remained precariously balanced above Olan and the crowd had gone silent. Had someone stopped time? he thought, watching as the tocka's eyes rolled up and closed. Their muscles relaxed and Olan rolled away before the pair collapsed on him.

The crowd burst back into life with a wild roar and Olan turned to Osayimwese, who leaned over with a hand on each tocka. As he pulled back, a crackle of blue energy rippled across his palms.

'How?' Olan asked and Osayimwese replied with a shake of the head.

'Can you do that on the others?' Bowman asked and Osayimwese shrugged.

Olan got to his feet as Smith and Bowman unstrapped the weapons from the sleeping tocka.

Osayimwese stood dumbstruck, staring at his hands.

'This looks good,' Bowman said, holding a black crossbow with a string of green light.

He pulled the string back, turned and fired towards Gal-qadan's soldiers.

Nothing happened.

Olan could see that some Sorean and Gal-qadan himself also had weapons and were struggling. Was there someone else they were supposed to fight? Olan wondered.

'What's that guard doing?' Osayimwese asked, coming out of his trance.

On the other side of the arena, at the midpoint, a guard had pulled a cloth of camouflage down to reveal an entrance Olan hadn't seen before. The Ascent had sent various enemies through every combination of gateways, so there was no way to predict who was coming out, yet this suggested something new.

'And now,' the voice on the speaker boomed back into life, 'we witness the humans' first contact with a new species.'

The crowd gave a half-hearted cheer as the tocka slowed their circle of panic and the two parties of soldiers scrambled to the nearest lines of metal fences, still fiddling with their weapons. The door opened and two large metal balls rolled out.

'Oh shit,' Smith said.

The crowd were silent for a long second, as though processing what they could see, then exploded into a wild frenzy of sound. The crowd fired their weapons, lasers tore colourful lines in the air, metallic gunfire erupted and the beating of shields echoed around the arena.

Olan felt the muscles in his back tighten.

'For their first training mission,' the voice boomed, 'these young Lutamek will take the place of their forefathers.'

The two Lutamek eggs unravelled like spooled snakes.

Olan looked to his comrades. 'We'd better get these weapons working right now!'

'We find ourselves in a new prison, John Greene,' Falen said.

'Yes,' John replied, sitting beside the tall, insectoid Drauw, the pair of them leaning against the cave wall. 'Only this time I get the feeling it'll be our last.'

'Maybe,' Falen replied. 'And maybe this whole world is a prison?'

John looked at her. The light was better here than in the pit, so he could take in the bizarre spiral markings which covered her head while they talked about the lock and how Ten-ten had adapted John's hand.

'We are both failures,' Falen said with a sigh. 'Rejected.'

There was so much John wanted to ask her – about her time in the dome, about this world and about life beyond – but he had something to tell her first.

'I met one of your allies,' he said and drew a disc and three dots in the sand of the cave floor. 'His name was Yam-mit. A Korax.'

John remained fixed on Falen but, as ever, couldn't read any emotions.

'Is the Korax here?' she asked, calmly.

'He was killed in the uprising,' John replied, picturing the rock wall Yam-mit had been entombed in alongside Rar-kin and Samas.

'That is a shame,' Falen said.

'Did you ever meet one?' John asked, feeling his spirits lift. 'Yam-mit said he came from an age when your species communicated but were unable to send images.'

'Yes, I come from a later time,' Falen replied, 'when our trading alliance had matured.'

John thought for a bit before asking, 'What about the third species? Who were they?'

'They–'

'Silence!' A Bensha guard shouted. 'Or we will reopen the games.' He growled and gave a gravelly chuckle.

John waited in silence, letting the guards wander away, before whispering to Falen again.

'If we don't escape soon we will die,' he whispered. 'But the pins,' he pointed to Crossley, who was curled up asleep, 'give the guards power over us.'

Falen's head cocked to one side, reminding John of a dog he used to see on his delivery rounds. She turned her dark head to John, scanning him from head to toe.

'This new leg of yours,' she said.

'Yeah,' John said, pulling his trouser down to cover the metal glint.

'Lutamek technology?'

'Yes, it talks to my nerves through my stump apparently,' John said and wiggled his foot.

'And the Lutamek oil is still present in your arm?' she asked.

'Yeah, I can see it in the joints,' John replied. 'Why?'

'Sometimes,' Falen replied, 'the greatest enemy is ourselves... and that might be the one lesson our Lutamek friends haven't learned yet.'

Chapter 17

Isao drank pink liquid from a metal tube and tried not to think what it was made from.

'It contains everything your body requires,' a Lutamek had said when it had handed it to him.

It tasted like meat and berries, Isao thought, trying to work out why he'd never seen that particular Lutamek before.

Isao sat cross-legged on the floor and studied his prison. From what he had been able to see when his group of captives had been transported in, he was in the centre of the Lutamek encampment, which sat inside the Ascent city. He was caged alongside four or five other unfortunate souls, in a building constructed from several starships, like the ones they had found outside their dome, and which was a hive of activity.

Some of the hibernation pods were still active by the look of it, but most had been ripped out and replaced with metal boxes of varying sizes covered with glowing panels and blinking lights. Lutamek and tall, thin, insectoid aliens Isao hadn't seen before rushed around, carrying rocks and vials of liquid.

'No, that depth has already been tested,' a Lutamek said to an insectoid. 'Label it and file it.'

What were they studying? Isao let his eyes slip into the

shadow world, hoping it wouldn't set off any alarms, and saw energy gleaming from the rocks. It was like nothing he had seen before: they sparkled with hypnotic waves, which ebbed and flowed erratically.

'Is that why they brought you here?' a whisper made Isao turn to his neighbour.

'What?' Isao replied, pulling his eyes out of the shadow world.

'Your ability?'

'How did you know?' Isao asked and shook his head.

Before setting his eyes back to normal Isao saw a green diamond in the alien's chest. The creature looked like any of the bizarre bipeds this world was littered with – two eyes in a round head and a thickset body dressed in lightweight body armour – only this one had an array of tiny antennae scattered across its otherwise bald scalp.

'You're the Velluta,' Isao said, remembering the box the Lutamek had taken from the Firstborn clan in exchange for food and weapons.

The Velluta cocked its head in what Isao assumed was an affirmative nod.

After being captured, Isao had stayed with the Velluta's box, while the metal Lutamek eggs and the majority of humans and Sorean had been diverted to a different destination. Gal-qadan had glared at Isao when they parted – his usual look – but Isao couldn't help feeling Gal-qadan was asking him to come back for him.

Peronicus-Rax had travelled with them too and left soon after arriving in the Ascent city, leaving Isao's mission in disarray.

'It's all about gravity,' the Velluta said and pointed at the hive of activity some twenty strides from their cells. 'Of course, they find new methods of nutrition here, through their experiments, but the Lutamek are only interested in this world's gravity.'

'Why?' Isao asked.

'Because it's the only thing they don't understand,' the Velluta replied, 'apart from me, perhaps, and it looks like I've caused a distraction,' it paused and seemed to sigh, 'which is why the Lutamek are congregating now… returning from their various missions. They all need to be here. Their religion dictates it.'

'Dictates what?' Isao asked, wondering how a group of robots could have a religion.

'They strive for perfection. We started adding components to our bodies when our planet grew inhospitable, but never thought it would get this far.'

'We?' Isao asked.

'I was on their ship,' the Velluta said. 'We share the same home world. We are the same species… but I don't consider myself one of them.'

Isao turned from the Velluta to the Lutamek and saw no obvious resemblance.

'How did you escape the ship?' he asked.

'A handful of Lutamek bypassed the extraction protocols when the hibernation system powered down and so avoided being taken into the dome. Then, once the ship landed on this world, they blasted their way out and we escaped. I managed to hide, convincing the ship I was dead, so the free Lutamek were unaware of my existence until the new Lutamek escaped the dome with your army and downloaded my information.'

'They said it had been destroyed from the outside,' Isao said.

'Of course! Your Lutamek were in contact with the escaped Lutamek from the second you won your freedom from the dome. The escapees had been busy… working their way into the Ascent hierarchy, gaining positions of power. I had managed to avoid them but...'

'So why am I here?' Isao asked, ignoring the Velluta's self-pity.

'The gravity and your ability are linked.'

'That doesn't make sense,' Isao replied, peering through a window, watching a large, dark quadruped pull a metal cart into the courtyard outside.

The Velluta shuffled away and said, 'I know, but that's what they told me to say.'

The cart was tipped into a metal-lined hole and what looked like body parts tumbled out.

'What did you say?' Isao looked at his drink and then at the Velluta. 'Who told you to say that?'

'He did.' The Velluta pointed to a dark shape in the courtyard.

Isao recognised this Lutamek: Ten-ten.

Millok did not take her decision lightly but the Scion, as she had come to call her brood of young Brakari, had been in the forefront of her mind when she had finally decided.

'We leave the Tathon to it,' she ordered. 'Maintain scout missions and double the guard.'

'Yes, Millok,' the officer replied and left without saluting.

When Millok had found them – the young Brakari army of Doctor Cynigar's experiments – they'd been fresh from the battle against the humans outside the ruined fort. She had explained their creation story and why they needed to fight against their own species to ensure their survival. Eager to follow their shell-mother, even though few of the sky-blue shells had hardened properly, they had fought valiantly. After the victory, Millok had taken the Scion off the battlefield and refused to leave the dome until she had found all of her offspring. In the days that followed, she'd developed an informal authority over her new army.

A new scout scuttled in.

'The contraption is primed and ready to fire.'

'I will see for myself,' Millok replied and signalled to her guards that she was leaving camp.

As she walked through her resting army, Millok looked at them through a mother's eyes. They were all so different, which was to be expected with such a variety of father lines, but they were *all* half her. She was mother to all because there had been no other female soldiers in the Brakari ranks. She felt proud. The pain had been worth it.

Many of her young couldn't communicate and some had trouble walking long distances, but they were all formidable fighters, thanks to Cynigar's tweaking, which had come in useful when facing the new enemy. The Tathon – these soft-bodied, bulbous octopeds – had appeared without warning, spreading across the vast landscape like a flood. Nothing stood in their path.

Not even General Panzicosta.

Millok climbed the incline with speed, up the well-worn path created by her scout's claws and walking legs. It wasn't good to stay in one location for too long – it would attract that freakish fish creature the Tathon had summoned from the lake and its legion of tiny, round-shelled warriors who had hounded her almost as well as she and the Scion had hounded the Tathon army.

Slowly, the view revealed itself to Millok. She crouched low and stretched her long-distance eyes on their stalks. The view had changed little: the huge contraption the Tathon had been building had shifted forward and was still moving forward… if her vision was correct. It was hard to tell at such a distance.

Now she was in charge of a team – and responsible for their very lives – Millok found she was always thinking. The feeling was similar to when she had looked after John, she thought, remembering the journey from Abzicrutia to the allied army, when she had had to think of every possible scenario ahead of them. She had succeeded, and they hadn't treated her well, but John had repaid her generosity. If he hadn't, she doubted she would still be here. Where the victors had gone, nobody knew. But now, having seen the Tathon's plans, Millok felt sure she could follow in their wake.

Let them do the hard work.

Millok scanned the almost-barren hillside for signs of movement. Just three of her personal guards as far as she could tell, which meant she could wait a little longer and watch.

On the valley floor, the huge contraption of metal and rock loomed tall; its strong, criss-crossed structure was starting to disappear behind the mist that fringed the landscape. Around its base, scores of creatures heaved and jostled, under the orders of the Tathon leaders, whose shapes could be seen some distance back, ringed by various levels of defence. A flash of lightning spat down from the heavens but dissipated on the enormous, clear shell, leaving the machine to roll on, into the thick fog. Then the contraption shuddered to a halt, followed by a deep thud a second later.

Shapes moved frenetically, and the huge machine started to twist and stretch, like a giant preparing to leap. In the centre, Millok could see an immense block of metal rising and pulling out of the mist. When it couldn't stretch any more, the mechanisms clunked to a halt and, following an unseen order, the nearest soldiers backed away as the contraption released its harnessed energy. With a flash of raw power and a crack that ran through the ground and made the clouds shake, the block swung and thrust into the mist, where it hit its intended target.

Immediately, the mechanisms jumped into life, pulling it back, setting it up for another hit.

For the first time in many weeks, Millok felt genuinely scared.

Isao hung upside down by his ankles, fixed to a wall by metal clasps.

'Now, I want you to try to slip into your "shadow world" again.' The deep tones of Ten-ten sounded detached and emotionless, but Isao had learned to follow the Lutamek's orders during the several hours they had been experimenting.

Isao wanted to know as much about his ability as Ten-ten did, although he wouldn't have chosen these methods. So he persevered and, although he answered Ten-ten's questions accurately, he didn't tell him everything.

So far, they had discovered several depths to the shadow world that Isao could access. Most, like when Ten-ten had been able to see Isao in the shadow world, were shallow and involved little effort to access. But others were deeper and, if Ten-ten was to be believed, out of his extrasensory sight's range.

'Of course, my sight doesn't use photons or radio waves,' Ten-ten said, 'but I have extrapolated a method using the readings from the mines, where mass and gravity are strongest.'

'And this is the *alternate matter* you mentioned?' Isao asked, using the Lutamek's terminology for what he called shadow matter, hoping to keep Ten-ten engaged so he could learn as much as possible.

'Affirmative,' Ten-ten replied. 'Which is why I have placed concentrated supplies of it around this building to inhibit any plans you have of escape.'

'Yes, I feel those,' Isao replied but held back the truth.

He'd long learned the secrets of how Ten-ten had hidden the soldiers on the border with the Firstborn and he'd drifted deep into the shadow world, where Isao felt the barriers with normal matter thinned to almost nothing. In that state, he was sure he could swim through any normal matter – go through living rock or the metal shackles if he needed to. The raw power he was harnessed to lifted Isao's spirits and he longed to test it out fully, but not yet. When it was time to escape he would glide through Ten-ten's gravity mass traps.

'And the cause?' Isao asked.

'I have gone through the recordings from the dome cap,' Ten-ten replied. 'It appears a safety system shifted the bodies of you and your companions into the new-matter range at the point of death, then shifted you back to regain physical form as we know it.'

'What went wrong?' Isao asked.

'The organic part of me suggests it was a system glitch, but my processors disagree,' Ten-ten said. 'A system this complex would have many fail-safe mechanisms. My theory is your DNA was still in a state of flux following the work of the Synchronisers, so it confused the system.'

'And only when it settled were we allowed physical form?' Isao asked.

The thought made him feel hollow. He, Masaharu and Hori had been convinced they were regaining their honour with each battle.

A light on Ten-ten's arm flashed and Isao rotated back to an upright position.

'Why did you do it?' Isao asked the question he'd held back. 'Why did you turn on your allies?'

It was the first time Isao had seen a Lutamek hesitate.

Ten-ten turned to face him. 'Despite what you think, Isao, the Lutamek are an honourable species. We have rules. Codes of conduct were created when we first took the path to automation. A belief burned in the very core of every one of us that we were an improvement and that we owed it to our ancestors, our kin, our comrades to constantly strive to be the best.'

'So you betrayed your allies for the sake of your kin?' Isao said. 'It's been done before.'

'We may have become more machine than animal, but we haven't lost the instinct to survive.'

'I see,' Isao said.

'Now I want to measure your sensitivity to the waves I have sensed in this alternate energy field,' Ten-ten changed the subject, 'before you become tired.'

'Yes,' Isao replied, knowing the Lutamek's apparent concern for his well-being was no more than anxiety for the validity of his experiments.

'The sensor array we constructed shows an alternate matter flow towards the tower, in the centre of this disc. The movement of currents distributes the gravitational force evenly across the disc and in one direction.'

Isao remembered the tidal pull he and his comrades had felt when they had first entered the shadow world. It was weaker here, but he didn't know if he should tell Ten-ten everything. Any clue to his real abilities would risk damaging his escape strategy.

'I have felt these waves,' Isao said.

'I need you to partially step out of this plane and inform me of each wave you see, while I take my readings.'

'Sure,' Isao replied. Confirming they were seeing the same thing shouldn't harm his plans, he thought, but one thing was on his mind. 'Just one question before we start.'

'Yes.'

'The Velluta… it said the Lutamek are convening for a purpose. Your religion dictates it?'

'Yes,' Ten-ten answered, focussed on a metal device with a black cone pointing to the ground.

'Will the Velluta become your leader?' Isao asked.

Ten-ten emitted a sound close to a Lutamek laugh, then said, 'No, we need to sever our links with our past.'

'What will you do?' Isao asked.

'The most obvious course of action – we will kill the Velluta.'

Panzicosta hadn't felt this invigorated since he'd expanded into his first adult shell. How many seasons ago had that been? So many battles won and lost since that day. So many memories, which felt clearer now, as though a window in his mind had been cleaned of decades of smudge and grime.

These Tathon truly were miracle workers. Panzicosta didn't have to look at his transformation to see that – the whole army the Tathon had formed was full of enhanced, confident soldiers from scores of warring species. The Tathon were far greater scientists than Doctor Cynigar, that malicious, shrivelled turd, not just in their abilities but in the way they boosted each individual according to their skills and powers, rather than just sticking on new abilities because their cause demanded it.

The Tathon were great leaders as well, far more intuitive than Belsang, yet more ruthless than Panzicosta could ever have imagined. They had swept up every single surviving soldier in this great, bizarre land and either transformed or killed them. Everyone had a purpose, either as a soldier or as food, and he was no different. Panzicosta had more power than ever before, yet he had dropped his title. General no more, but his potential was almost limitless.

He flexed his new shell, catching a shimmer of red reflecting in one of the protective bubble-glass domes the Deron insectoids had created for the Tathon. A hundred strides away, their immense contraption towered into the clouds, where lightning licked the shield. The hammer bit into the ground with its screw foundations and groaned and vibrated as it drew its power, then released its powerful thrust into the mist, shaking the entire world around them. This was the weapon of the gods that Panzicosta's Brakari ancestors used to pray to.

Panzicosta felt the urge to talk to his leaders – to learn more. He had served them well, but surely there was more he could do? Not only was he faster and leaner than before, but his mind was sharper too. He had fewer pincers but those he retained were more lethal than his previous ones. His red shell felt stronger and lighter.

The pain of change had been worth it.

Panzicosta moved towards the Tathon High Command and focussed on the three shapes of 'Xit, 'Brin and 'Kno-lib, whose large, globular masses stood tall over the nearest line of Tathon warriors. Panzicosta had learned that the Tathon, like their monstrous contraption, extended underground as well, with their mass of fungal hyphae, and he wondered what they could sense right now. As he drew closer, he caught a glimpse of Praahs' long body weaving through the Tathon commanders. For once she was free of her irritating mass of Cirratus, who seemed to shadow her every move.

Panzicosta diverted his walk accordingly.

'Praahs,' he called out as he neared, taking her attention from the huge battering ram overhead.

'Panzicosta,' she responded. 'Now is not the time for our duel.'

Panzicosta felt his scales rise, ready to snap down with annoyance, and took a moment to control his emotions.

'Indeed,' he replied, 'maybe another time.' His red scales relaxed and silently slipped back into place. 'I simply came to offer any advice on your pursuit of the rogue Brakari guerrilla force,' he said with clenched mouthparts as he thought of the turncoat, Millok.

'Your help is appreciated, but our venture has been postponed,' Praahs replied and turned to view Panzicosta with all her open eyes.

They may have been different species, but something drew Panzicosta to Praahs. He'd seen her in battle – a formidable sight – and respected her in a way he'd never felt for a comrade or enemy before. This wasn't lust. It was something else.

'Your improvements were successful?' Praahs asked as the giant ram flew above them, shaking the ground and vibrating the clouds.

'Yes,' he replied. 'I'm looking forward to the next battle.'

Panzicosta remembered seeing Praahs before his final procedure and the look she'd given him… that was it! She was a kindred spirit, an orphan who had endured the same humiliation he had.

'And the chemicals?' she asked, lowering her voice.

'Chemicals?' he replied and noticed one of her eyes had shifted in the direction of the Tathon leaders.

A soft haze wafted from a pair of antennae on the back of Praahs' neck and the sounds around Panzicosta became muffled.

'We can talk freely for a short time,' Praahs said. 'The Tathon give more than just new weapons and skills.'

Panzicosta remained silent.

'Do you think great warriors like us would be satisfied with a place in the ranks of an enemy army?' Praahs asked.

'No,' Panzicosta replied, 'but what they offer is–'

'What they offer,' Praahs cut in, 'is control. We have been conditioned into loving our captors.'

Panzicosta felt weak. His fighting eyes flicked open and he searched for imminent danger. Had he been fooled? Were these gifts just tricks to subdue him?

'Your defensive mechanisms still work,' Praahs said. 'Some instincts remain deep and must be trusted.'

'But we are safe here,' Panzicosta said but felt a conflict within.

The mist faded and Praahs said, 'We should talk of war now.'

Was Praahs right? Panzicosta thought. He looked at the Tathon army and the myriad species of soldier aliens and felt kinship with them. He looked to the three leaders and felt... love. He admired their successes and command, their decisions and their orders – Praahs was right! This was not his natural behaviour.

'What do we do?' he asked.

'We do what we do best – we fight,' Praahs replied.

The ram sprang into life again overhead and sent the world shaking about them. Only this time the clouds were pierced with a dark rain.

'Get under cover!' Praahs shouted and barged Panzicosta towards the centre of the protective dome.

Panzicosta's new eyes focussed as the rain hit the shield: huge shards of dagger-shaped glass shattered and splintered and bounced harmlessly to the ground.

'Some kind of shell?' Panzicosta asked.

'And soon we will be free of it,' Praahs replied.

'There is more,' Ten-ten said as Isao rested on a metal bench in the sunlight. 'The alternate matter is an energy source.'

Through trying to gain as much information about his

captured allies as possible, Isao had become Ten-ten's sounding board. Isao drank another tube of pink liquid, holding back his gagging reflex as he tried not to picture what it was made from.

'It powers the domes?' Isao asked.

'Quite possibly,' Ten-ten replied as he tinkered with more devices, 'but its unique properties have other uses, especially at these concentrations.'

Ten-ten had been open with his knowledge, just as the Lutamek had been when they had searched the starships parked outside the dome – how the disc had been built to orbit and harness the energy of the star – but very little had been given away about the fate of the rest of Isao's army.

'The starships which circle this world intrigue me – have you been able to contact them?' Ten-ten asked.

Isao put his empty container down and looked at the tall robot. 'No,' he said.

All the times he had entered the shadow world, Isao had never looked up. He'd been too concerned with the lights in each soldier's chest, or what they were doing. He'd looked down at the swirling mass, but he'd never taken the time to look at the stars.

'I could try,' Isao said.

'Yes,' Ten-ten replied.

Although he wasn't facing him, Isao knew the Lutamek was observing him as he let his eyes slip into the shadow world – or the alternate energy frequency – and stared at the midday sky. He took a sharp intake of breath and gripped the bench a little tighter.

'What is this?' he asked.

The star-scape he saw was more vivid than what he had seen during the clear nights: balls of sharp energy dotting the sky in an arc reminiscent of the night view, but interspersed with other lights of myriad colours, nearer and clearer than the stars.

'I predict you will see black holes as stars,' Ten-ten said, 'and other apparitions scattered throughout the galaxy.'

Isao nodded and remained silent, focussing on the coloured shapes. If he looked away, his peripheral vision could see full shapes – discs, tubes and boxes.

'And the nearest energy will be emitted by starships – either new sample ships waiting for their allotted dome, or – I predict – visitors from captured species' home worlds.'

'Really?' Isao said, transfixed by the orbits of the craft, which swarmed and dodged each other like fish in an ocean.

'I believe the mass of the alternate matter held within the disc is used to create artificial gravity for those on its surface and as a repellent force, keeping unwanted visitors at bay,' Ten-ten said. 'So if we are to gain freedom from this world, we must harness this source of alternate energy.'

Isao nodded and let his eyes return to normal and, as he did, noticed a strange ripple in the energy beneath them. Under normal circumstances he would have asked Ten-ten if he'd sensed it as well, but held off.

'Only once we understand it can we harness it,' Ten-ten continued. 'So knowledge is key.'

Isao was busy preparing. He set his eyes and the soles of his feet to the shadow world and felt another new wave pulse through his shoes. It was strange, but just what he needed to escape more quickly than the Lutamek could react.

'Good luck,' Isao said.

Ten-ten turned sharply and aimed his arm at him. 'Whatever you are planning, desist.'

Isao remained calm, seated on the bench, and said, 'Look down.'

Another wave, of what appeared to Isao as golden energy, washed beneath them, flowing towards the tower. Isao had timed the gaps between the waves, which were speeding up, so knew how long he had.

'Whoever is creating these has a greater knowledge than you,' Isao said and let his body drop, deep into the shadow world.

The explosions from Ten-ten's missiles and laser blasts could be felt in the shadow world but Isao rode them as he rode the incoming wave that pushed him through the shadow-energy barriers, into the reservoir of shadow energy beneath the crust of the disc and swept him away to the core, to directly beneath the tower.

Chapter 18

John had spent the entire day pushing carts of rocks up a long slope, along with the survivors of the failed mine escape. Crossley had been absent most of the day and John had tried to talk to Yarcha and share his water with her, but the guards were extra-vigilant now. They'd had their blood-fun and spoiled the miners' plans, but they were still prisoners of the Ascent, who wouldn't tolerate another rebellion.

He'd seen Falen limping heavily as she pushed her cart with her insect-like claws and the burned stump where her gun had been removed. John had tried to work out what she had meant by our worst enemies often being ourselves, but the lack of food and water had eventually got to him and the rest of the day had turned into a blur, with their shift ending in what John guessed was the evening.

'We're going deeper than before,' Crossley whispered to John as they queued for their bowl of soup. 'I had a quick look but can't see past a certain point.'

John gave him a look.

'Which means we've reached where the Lutamek need to be – not that we'll see any–'

'Stop!' A guard yelled and stomped over to the line. 'No

human or Sorean contact,' he bellowed and, with a swipe of the shaft of his spear, sent Crossley stumbling backwards into a group of Korax.

John kept his head down and, for once, Crossley didn't fight back or comment; he simply stepped back in line, keeping other species between him and John. When he received his unappetising soup, John meandered past the other groups of miners, spotting lone Sorean and humans. He felt a pang of guilt for the Sorean, who'd not only lost their leader but could no longer huddle in their furry pile at night. He saw Yarcha and gave her a nod, then Falen sitting in an indent in the wall and ambled over, happy to have someone to talk to.

'Crossley says we are getting close,' John whispered as he sat where Falen gestured.

'I doubt it will be soon enough,' Falen replied and lapped at her soup with a coiled tongue that reminded John of a butterfly he'd once seen feeding on the flowers of a French meadow.

'Why?' John asked.

'Change is in the air,' she replied. 'And if my plan works, the Ascent will soon have a new uprising to deal with.'

'But we've just failed,' John said and pictured Samas being turned to stone. 'We've been punished enough.'

Falen's head twisted back and forth before she said, 'The Ascent will pay.'

'I want to believe you, but–'

'They *have* to pay for their crimes. I was one of them once, as were these guards.' She looked at the nearest group, sitting on rocks, laughing.

'But it's too soon,' John protested.

'No,' Falen snapped, 'now is the ideal time.'

John thought about her phrase – our greatest enemy is ourselves.

'You want to turn the guards to our side?' he asked.

'No,' Falen replied. 'I mean to kill them, along with the Ascent leaders, but first I need something from you, John Greene.'

John swallowed the last of his soup and felt the urge to edge away.

'What do you want?'

'Give me your leg,' she demanded.

'What? No! I can't work without my bloody leg.'

'A drop of oil,' the Drauw continued, 'and your trust.'

John thought about it for a second then asked, 'How long?'

'Just this evening, while you rest.'

John felt exhausted, ready for sleep, and didn't have the energy to argue. Another sacrifice for the greater good? he wondered.

'And I'll get it back, fully working?'

'Yes, absolutely,' Falen replied.

John set his bowl down and looked around before unclipping the metal leg from his stump. The whole process felt bizarre because his leg really did feel part of him – as though his nerves ran all the way to the ends of his toes, as they did in his good leg. A cold tingle rippled over the end of his cauterised stump and he handed the surprisingly light leg to Falen.

'I will take care of it,' she said, and reached over to John's arm. 'Now…'

A long finger uncurled from beneath a claw and slipped in between the metal, darkening as it drew Ten-ten's liquid out of the arm's joints.

'Now you must rest,' she said.

John nodded and curled up in his usual sleeping position to let his exhausted body relax. Sleep took him swiftly but sometime later he felt a warm feeling at the back of his head, which mingled with dreams of hot baths and floating down giant rivers.

'What do you see?' Euryleia asked Sancha, the Chachapoyas cloud-warrior, who sat beside her on his tocka.

'No unusual activity,' the Peruvian replied. 'The guards are rotating as usual. No scouting parties and no Lutamek.'

'Good,' Euryleia said. 'No word of our incursion yet.'

Lavalle rode up beside her, with Cheng, their co-commander, and Euryleia smiled. Seeing Lavalle reminded her of the changes to her body. He'd acted differently since she had grown her new arms – which was understandable, and he would adjust given time – but Euryleia had other changes she needed to tell him about, changes which would affect both of them. Despite being able to heal, she was more concerned about getting injured in this battle than any before.

'Where on Earth is Althorn?' Lavalle hissed. 'He's been gone for days and we need him now!'

'My scouts will provide the information we need,' Cheng said. 'With or without Althorn, we can take this city.'

'I still think we should starve them out,' Lavalle said. 'We have control of their food source.'

Euryleia shook her head. 'Time is of the essence. We need to hit hard while the Lutamek are distracted.'

'For what gain? To save our comrades?' Lavalle asked. 'We can do more.'

'What need is there?' Sancha asked. 'We will never be stronger than them.'

'And we can't leave our allies prisoners!' Euryleia said, trying to control her anger.

This dithering was starting to work on her nerves. Since the Lutamek betrayal, the group had listened to Lavalle's experienced voice – taken their time to regroup, to assess their enemy and to plan the attack on the farms. It had worked, with few losses, but Euryleia knew they needed to use the element of surprise when attacking the city or the Ascent would be ready for them.

'Say we free our comrades and have a larger fighting army, what then?' Cheng asked.

'It wouldn't be enough to take command of the Ascent!' Lavalle said, shaking his head.

'But we could force a peace,' Euryleia said. 'An alliance which would suit us all... we could demand an end to the slavery and create new ways of food production.'

The silence from the three men spoke volumes: no one completely agreed with her, yet no one wanted to be the first to speak against her.

'You forget, we are stronger now,' Euryleia continued.

'With Mata?' Cheng asked and snorted. 'He was with us when the Lutamek turned on us and what use was he then?'

'Forget the Lutamek!' Euryleia replied, ignoring Cheng's derision. 'Your scouts said they have isolated themselves and won't fight.' She sighed. 'Besides, I was talking about our other new recruits.'

'The farmers will be little more than cannon fodder,' Lavalle said. 'Useful in a diversion maybe, but none show any mutations of worth.'

'I meant Delta-Six,' Euryleia said with a sly smile.

'Ah,' Lavalle said, 'the one they couldn't catch.'

'And that the Lutamek think they destroyed,' Euryleia added.

'That's what he tells you,' Cheng said.

Euryleia sighed and said, 'If his mission goes well, we could have the Ascent on their knees before the day is out.'

'Or we'll be captured along with the others!' Lavalle said.

'The truth is, we'll never know,' Sancha said.

Euryleia felt the weight of the argument moving her way. 'And there will never be a better time to strike,' she said.

Lavalle turned to the troops who waited behind them, resting in the ruins of the nearest farm huts. They were all hidden by the bent light shield Guang had created around them.

'Today it is then,' Cheng said, looking to Lavalle.

'We should wait for Althorn,' Lavalle said and turned to Euryleia.

She could see uncertainty in his gaze. He was a brave man who led from the front, she admired that, but he needed a reason to fight – or was there something else?

'Does it have to be a certain victory before you fight?' Euryleia asked, staring into his eyes.

'No, I...' Lavalle looked away.

'There is no shame in losing confidence,' Euryleia said, 'especially after the Lutamek's betrayal, but this must be done and it must be done now.'

'And there's no greater victory than winning against a greater foe,' Cheng added.

Lavalle nodded slowly. 'We will do what is right,' he said, 'no matter the cost. And I will pray to God that Delta-Six completes his mission before we attack.'

John woke to see Crossley sitting beside him with a thin metal tube in one hand and John's metal leg in another.

'Well, you've got to hand it to her,' the American said, his sentence peppered with the odd, tiny cough, 'this tech is pretty intricate... but she knew how to unlock it.'

John sat up.

'Falen?' he asked.

'A genius,' Crossley replied, then looked down the cave with a glare of fear. 'See you later,' he said, dropping the metal pieces and scrambling away.

Still half asleep, John strapped his leg back on as the guard Crossley had spotted walked by. The familiar cool sensation ran across John's stump as the cup of miraculous Lutamek black material touched his stump. He fixed the strap, flexed his toes and smiled – same as before, like having his old leg back.

Something did seem a bit off to John though and he couldn't put his finger on it. He looked at the tiny clumps of alien miners and lone Sorean and human soldiers lining the immense cavern. They were eating breakfast and preparing for another day's hard slog. Just like being back in the trenches after a rainstorm, John thought. Endless physical labour, slowly breaking your body, while the threat of imminent death or injury surrounded you like some poisonous gas.

Feeling a twinge of pain at the back of his head, John felt for the cold metal disc – but all he felt was the damp warmth of matted hair and a thick scab. The pin was gone!

He looked on the ground, where Crossley had been sitting, and fumbled the metal tube. It was half the length of John's little finger but tapered to a point, which felt sticky. The thickest end was finished with a coin shape he recognised instantly.

'Bloody hell,' John mouthed to himself and looked around for Falen.

How had she managed it? And where was she now?

Despite the rough night sleeping on the floor and the bone-weary feeling throughout his body, John felt a spark of energy run through him. He had been liberated. Without the pin, the guards had no power over him, other than their larger physical size and lethal weapons, of course.

'Get to work!' A guard shouted, followed by its colleagues throughout the cave.

The tired soldiers lifted their heads and forced their bodies to stand and move. John joined a line that reminded him of injured German captives he'd seen heading away from the trenches. The living dead, one of his mates had called them, but John had felt jealous. The conditions in a prisoner-of-war camp weren't much better than those in the trenches, but there was less chance of being blown up by a shell.

As the line meandered away from the fresh air of the distant cave entrance, John clenched his mechanical fist and felt strength. He flashed a look at his arm but was disappointed when he saw no physical differences. Still, his arm felt different. The inner workings – the chamber where he had formed bullets and the firing mechanisms – felt looser, as if a tube ran deep within his wrist, where he was sure he could manipulate shapes, if given the time to practise. The mechanisms felt stronger too, like they commanded a hotter source of energy now.

The line descended down the long ramp, past the piles of rocks from the day before. John peered over shoulders and through arms for a glimpse of another human or of Falen, but neither could be seen. He felt a scratch on his shoulder and brushed it away, but another identical scratch made him turn.

'Keep walking,' Falen's voice was quiet, 'and hold your hand back.'

John didn't question her and felt a coin pressed into his palm.

'Stick it where your pin was,' she said.

John could feel the weight of his pin in his pocket and shook his head. 'I'm not having that in me again.'

'It's a fake,' Falen said. 'Wear it or the guards will know we've broken the technology.'

John fiddled with the coin and took a peek. It looked like the thick end of the pin and one side felt tacky so, swiftly, he pushed the matted hair aside and stuck the coin on the wound.

The scab felt raw now and John realised the pin must have numbed pain when it was inserted.

'How many others have you fixed?' John whispered.

He didn't get a reply and, when he turned round, Falen was gone.

Delta-Six was taking every precaution possible. The Lutamek had almost killed him once and he didn't want to give them another chance. Plus he knew little about the other species within the Ascent. The farm guards and scouts he'd encountered were not their best warriors and, if their punishment regime was anything to go by, their top soldiers would be safe in the centre of the city.

Covered with his chamelo-cloth, and with 90 per cent of his energy set to defence and sensors, Delta-Six crept into the makeshift sprawl of the Ascent city. More like a slum, he thought, remembering the pictures he'd been shown during his training: the European asylum seekers huddled on the edge of their desolate continent, desperate to get to the oasis states of northern Africa and the Middle East. Here was no different. Soldiers, with their former lives behind them, forced to work and wait. For what, nobody really knew, but Delta-Six was sure the tower was the key to understanding this constructed world.

And that was where he was heading.

A group of gargling quadrupeds set his sensors off and information flashed in his vision: species unknown; danger level – low due to inebriation. At least someone was having a good time, he thought, and sidestepped into the shade of the nearest metal shack. After a quick scan of the sleeping occupants, Delta-Six pocketed a white object left on a table, then crept out again.

The sun was still low, which suggested the majority of the free workers would be rising now and would flow towards the main workplaces. From what Delta-Six had seen on his scouting missions, the Ascent might have built a society on fear and slavery, but the majority of the citizens were free as long as they worked in one of three installations: the hydration plant; the Lutamek research lab; or the entertainment arenas. In return, the free workers received credits for food, drugs or for visiting the same entertainment centres they worked in. The closest Earth culture he could find in his databanks was the ancient Roman civilisation. But every one of these citizens, Delta-Six forced himself to remember, was a warrior and had been victorious in their battles in their respective domes. He had to treat them all as dangerous.

Delta-Six crept further into the cluster of shacks and adjusted his clothing and shield settings to give him the shape and look of a Rhil, a species he'd seen in the farm, and which the guards had been wary of. Delta-Six hoped the species' reputation meant they were feared throughout the Ascent.

As the sun rose, more workers ambled out of their dwellings, soon outnumbering those heading back from their late-night entertainment. Delta-Six's stride mimicked the Rhil's powerful gait as he followed the stream of foot traffic past larger buildings – shops and food-distribution centres – towards the largest buildings near the tower, which overshadowed the whole city.

Everyone walked in silence, deep in their own thoughts, and Delta-Six was no different. His systems remained on high alert as he let his many unanswered questions circle his mind like vultures on the wing. He thought of the dome cap, pushing away feelings of guilt over his accident with the Tathon, and wondered why the Synchronisers had screens for accessing information if they communicated through data-waves? For that matter, why was the dome cap unguarded? Sometimes the most bizarre answer, Delta-Six thought, is the truth. Maybe whoever built this place – the discs and domes – was expecting visitors to the dome caps.

A series of towers up ahead marked a checkpoint in a fence, and Delta-Six pulled out the ID card he'd stolen from the sleeping workers' hut. There was no picture or species identifier but the colour coding suggested he would be limited to the next ring of the city and would have to find another way to get into the central area closest to the tower.

'Keep moving!' a guard in one of the towers shouted as the mass of soldiers funnelled through the gap, where other guards scanned the workers' cards with what looked like Lutamek technology.

Delta-Six held his breath as his card scanned. The machine bleeped and he carried on, maintaining his awkward and arrogant Rhil walk, and let his 360-degree sensors scan for any giveaway movements from the guards.

Nothing.

The crowd fanned out, so Delta-Six quickly chose a stream to follow. Anyone caught dithering or looking lost would stand out and attract the guards' attention.

In the distance he could see the Lutamek research centre, heavily populated with the turncoat robots. So many more than before, which suggested all their scouts had been recalled.

Fearing the sensitivity of their scanning systems, Delta-Six turned down his array. We'll get our vengeance, he thought and pictured the neck-pin mirrors he had created for the freed farmers. If they worked as planned, any guard triggering the device would receive a message directed at their own pin instead. That would give Lavalle and Euryleia's party a good chance of getting into the city and building an army of resistance.

Delta-Six concentrated on the alien soldiers around him. Very few were from his dome, but he recognised some from the farms, and soon realised why they were more excited than the other groups. They were headed for the arena, enjoying their free time. Poor mindless drones, Delta-Six thought. The fun would be short-lived and they'd soon be back working their shift. What sort of life was this?

'Payment here!' A set of guards stood by the entrance to the arena, which curved over their heads.

The card Delta-Six had pilfered was from the lowliest part of the city, so he doubted the owner had been flush with credit. He would just have to risk it, he thought, as he walked up to one of the white-skulled Bensha guards.

'Payment,' it barked and scanned Delta-Six's card, only taking his eyes off him at the last second. Something about his demeanour suggested this guard would invite a fight with a Rhil. 'Insufficient,' the guard growled and pulled a blade from an armoury hanging around his waist.

'That's Rassum shit,' Delta-Six replied, mimicking the gruff voice of the Rhil farmer.

It worked, catching the Bensha off guard long enough for Delta-Six to give the card a quick ultraviolet burst from his palm sensor. He raised it again and said, 'Try again.'

The Bensha's eyes were fixed on Delta-Six this time as he swiped his device over the card. A light flashed and the guard's face clenched.

'Proceed,' he said, turning the blade in his hand.

Delta-Six strode off, head held high, through the main gate and into the dank darkness of the building. He followed a set of ramshackle stairs to an opening where fresh air wafted over him. Long benches ran to his left and right, populated by scores of soldiers who were ready for the main event. All eyes were fixed on the oval arena, where a maze of palisades surrounded an open area in the centre.

'Here come the fighters!' a voice called out.

Delta-Six shuffled along to find a space on a bench and watched as doors opened in the arena walls, spilling out the gladiators… human and Sorean.

John spotted Crossley in the crowd and pushed through to talk to him.

'Have you seen Falen?' he asked, trying to get a glimpse of Crossley's neck pin.

'No, but I told you she's a genius, right?'

John realised it was the first time he'd seen Crossley smile in days.

'She fixed yours too?' John asked.

'Yep,' Crossley tapped an object in his chest pocket. 'It was my idea to stick the caps on everyone – I found a bar of metal and Falen did the rest. Did she tell you how she released the pins?'

'No.' John shrugged.

The crowd was slowly shifting forward and John kept his eyes peeled for guards.

'I'm still working it out, but I'm sure she used the neuro-connectors from your Luta-leg to talk to the pins, but I've got no idea how she switched them off.'

John thought back to the previous night with Falen and asked, 'The oil in my arm?'

'What oil?'

'The stuff Ten-ten poured inside to change it to this,' John said and held up his robotic hand.

There was an energy churning within, John could still feel it, but would it be able to fire like his old gun-arm had done?

'Falen took some,' he said.

Crossley nodded. 'Okay, must be some kinda pre-programmed manipulator,' he said, 'so she just told the oil what to do and it talked through the neuro-connectors. Neat.'

'But what now?' John asked. 'We can't risk another revolt.'

Crossley shook his head. 'Not until we're sure everyone's free,' he replied. 'And then we need to arm ourselves.'

'Kill one guard, take his controller and we can blow all their heads off,' John said, with a nod at the nearest guard.

'Sure,' Crossley replied.

John felt a vibration through his metal foot. It was subtle, so his organic foot barely registered it, but small puffs of dust fell from the cave roof. He gave Crossley a look.

'Probably just explosives,' the American said and looked cross. 'Although I told 'em not to do it too far down. I'd better check,' he whispered and sidestepped away and out of the cave.

Another vibration followed and this time other miners felt it. The crowd slowed and soldiers were pointing to cracks in the walls where small stones crumbled free.

'Keep moving!' a guard bellowed.

John had to get out. Crossley was long gone, so he turned around, searching for Falen and Yarcha or any face he recognised. Others were turning and walking back up the ramp to what felt like the safety of the main cavern. The guards looked confused too and were losing control.

'Stop!' one shouted. 'Stay exactly where you are!'

The miners listened and the whole group slowed to a standstill, waiting for the next rumble. John stared around and froze when he spotted the morose, one-eyed face of Peronicus-Rax. Had he been captured too? The last they'd heard, just before the Lutamek had betrayed them, Gal-qadan's mini-army had been attacked, so he thought he'd been killed.

John watched the large alien as he paced the top of the ramp, scanning the crowd of miners. When Peronicus-Rax saw a guard and talked in a friendly, but authoritative, manner, John knew he wasn't a prisoner. The guard pointed across the crowd and John stretched up to peer over the smallest species. He caught a glimpse of Yarcha's shaved head and... Falen. Two guards pushed through and grabbed Falen, pulling her uphill to Peronicus-Rax. Had they discovered her plan?

Peronicus-Rax pointed to a flat area in the next cave and started to remove his cache of weapons, piling them neatly by the wall.

John pushed through the migrating crowd to get a better view. Falen had been brought to the space and, to John's eyes, seemed bigger now. Swollen. New shell linings had thickened her arms and legs.

Peronicus-Rax threw a weapon on the ground before her and slowly, moving like a predator, she picked it up. Then they fought.

Chapter 19

Olan rolled to his right as an energy blast from the young Lutamek ripped into the spot he'd been standing on, spraying stones and red desert dust across the Viking's back.

'They're too powerful!' he shouted to Steve Smith, who was hiding behind a metal palisade.

'The weapons still don't work,' Smith replied, shaking his rifle with frustration.

Olan looked at the axe he'd picked up. Rusted and pitted, its single-headed blade had seen plenty of action, and had caused its own share of injuries no doubt.

'This doesn't need any power,' Olan said.

'Good luck,' Smith replied, 'if you can get close enough.'

Olan could tell he was smiling behind his mask and gave a little laugh, momentarily easing the tension. He took a deep breath and tried to block out the jeers and calls from the crowd. It was hard enough fighting against an unbeatable enemy without having a mass of alien soldiers baying for your bloody death. He rolled over to Smith and peeked through a gash in the metal; the two young Lutamek were sat back to back in the centre of the arena floor where the tocka had risen from the depths on their ramp. The tocka stood at the far end now, away from any flying debris, but Gal-qadan's army of humans and Sorean remained on the other side of the Lutamek, taking as much fire as Olan's side.

'I'll be in Valhalla before nightfall,' Olan whispered. Thoughts of his wife and children invaded his mind, his eyes welling up as he visualised their faces. A few seconds later, the rush of nostalgia passed though, and Olan blinked his tears away. As quickly as the emotion had come, it vanished.

What was happening?

Olan searched the crowd for anyone using their skills to influence the fight. He was sure his chest plate had just saved him from another attack. The guards were usually hot on that kind of thing – it affected the gambling conglomerates – so maybe it was a new power the Lutamek had created? Either way, it was affecting all the soldiers, who seemed ready to throw their lives away now.

Osayimwese rushed over, shouting, 'We must attack before they change the rules!'

Olan peeked through the fence as a metal bolt flashed off an unseen shield around the Lutamek. Shapes behind their shelters suggested Gal-qadan's group were moving in to attack the Lutamek, which was madness. Maybe the Ascent had released a fighting hormone? Olan had been in enough arena battles to know how the Ascent liked to do things – any sign of the crowd getting bored and they ramped up the stakes.

Bowman rushed over, carrying a bundle of grey and black weapons, and ducked as a red line of light ripped into his leather jerkin. He collapsed next to Olan with smoke coming from his lower back, though there was no smell of burned flesh.

'That was close!' he said and started rummaging through the weapons he'd collected.

'Anything working?' Osayimwese asked.

'Not that I can see,' Bowman replied. 'Of course there's

nothing here like Li's old rifle but I'm sure we can get something to fire.'

Lights were flashing around Smith's visor and he checked an energy-rifle. 'There's nothing wrong with the components, just the energy source.'

'So if we can get–' Another red flash burst in Olan's eyes and he stopped mid-sentence. He stared at Bowman, kneeling next to him, as two dark streams of black smoke poured from either temple. The archer's eyes rolled down at different speeds. Then he collapsed onto the sandy floor.

'This weapon's working!' Osayimwese shouted, oblivious to Bowman's death.

'They must've been waiting for one of us to die,' Smith said as he carefully closed the Englishman's eyelids.

'Bastards!' Olan growled, slipped the shaft of his half-axe through his belt straps and grabbed the nearest rifle. 'Now we can fight!'

'We'll make sure we're never forgotten!' Osayimwese said as he aimed his chunky grey rifle.

Olan felt his head rush with adrenaline as he pictured blasting the Lutamek apart. He took a deep breath. He had to stay calm and think straight. He searched the weapons and saw the tocka milling about at the far end of the arena floor, dodging the empty water canisters thrown at them from the crowd. One tocka stamped a clawed hoof and gave Olan an idea.

'There's only one way we can defeat them,' he said. 'And we need Gal-qadan's help.'

'But they're over there!' Smith shouted and ducked as a laser blast dented the metal wall inches from his head.

'Then we'll find a way to talk. Osayimwese?'

'Yes.'

'This new power of yours… can you summon the tocka?'

John pushed his way to the front of the crowd, watching in disbelief as Peronicus-Rax and Falen grappled and wrestled. Despite the size difference, the Drauw's strength was on a par with that of Peronicus-Rax's muscular frame. The crowd of miners and guards circled around them, reminding John of the scraps the boys used to have in the schoolyards.

'Why have they only got knives?' John asked Crossley.

The American shrugged and shook his head, then nodded at a guard. 'I think it's good timing though,' he said and slipped back into the crowd.

John's eyes were fixed on the fight and barely registered the response. Blue lines showed where Falen's shelled limbs had taken slashes from Peronicus-Rax's blade but the large warrior looked worse off, with pitch-black blood oozing from wounds on his bare arms. Both were tiring but had enough energy to taunt each other when they broke free.

'You should be ashamed,' Peronicus-Rax said, switching his knife from hand to hand, waiting to lunge in.

'For leaving the battle?' Falen replied.

'For the sins of your planet.'

Falen gave a caustic laugh and attacked with her bizarre dipping-and-rising style.

'My species is far older than I,' Falen said, 'and I do not carry their burden.'

'But you are the last,' Peronicus-Rax said, sidestepping with his bulky frame to find a better angle to attack.

'And you may be THE last,' Falen replied and ducked Peronicus-Rax's lunge, before leaping onto his back and slashing at his shoulder armour.

The crowd roared as Peronicus-Rax elbowed her off, along with his shoulder pad, which Falen now held as a shield. Free from the rule of the guards, the crowd were chattering and yelling.

Amongst the noise, John heard a guard say, 'They were both Ascent once.'

How could that be? John thought. Falen maybe, but how could Peronicus-Rax have been part of the Ascent if he'd been in the dome with him and the rest of the army?

John saw a group of Korax in the crowd on the other side of the fighting ring, talking inside a blue bubble similar to the one Yam-mit had used in their mine.

'After what your ancestors did–' Peronicus-Rax started but was cut off by another attack, which he defended, throwing Falen at the feet of the crowd.

'Is that why you sought us out in the dome?' Falen hissed back.

'STOP!' a voice yelled and all eyes turned to the group of squat, beetle-like Korax.

'What is it, Korax?' a guard yelled. 'You're spoiling our fun.'

'This fight must stop,' the Korax said and walked into the dusty fighting ring.

With a lower leg, it scratched out the sign John had seen in the prison: a circle with three dots.

'Three planets, one star,' the Korax said, looking at Falen and Peronicus-Rax, who stared back.

'In your time, maybe,' Peronicus-Rax said. 'But no more. The Drauw saw to that.'

All eyes were on Falen, who shuffled away and said, 'What my ancestors did was necessary for our continued expansion.'

'You wiped my species out,' Peronicus-Rax replied. 'I was there at our final battle, before I was brought here. I found everything I needed to know from my extraction vessel.'

'Was that why you returned to the dome?' Falen asked. 'After we met?'

'After seeing you here, in the Ascent, I had to be sure,' Peronicus-Rax replied, his eye turning dark. 'I needed to know you were the last Drauw in this world.'

John breathed in sharply. When the human army had met Peronicus-Rax, he hadn't been observing battles and saving weapons for posterity – he'd been searching for Drauw survivors from his battle, burying every soldier to make sure everyone was accounted for. He must have collected weapons along the way, knowing they were currency here in the Ascent city.

'Enough!' Falen said. 'One of us has to die.'

'But what of the union?' the Korax asked.

'It was a lie!' Falen shouted. 'You had nothing of worth, so we kept you inhibited on your shrivelled, volcanic planet while the Drauw developed and grew.'

The Korax were shaking, visibly upset as their spokesperson sidled back to the group and formed a new blue bubble.

'And after you kill me?' Falen said to Peronicus-Rax, stretching her long, armoured limbs.

'I will escape this world and return to your planet to kill every last Drauw,' Peronicus-Rax said in his deep, emotionless tones.

'So be it,' Falen replied and leaped at him and the knife fight resumed with greater intensity.

John felt useless. He didn't know what to think or who to support. Flashes of his old war came back to him; the futility of the fight and the loss of life weighed on him again. He was ready to walk away when he felt a tug on his shirt and turned to see Crossley smiling at him.

'I've done it,' the American said and gave a little laugh.

'Done what?' John asked.

'Just follow me to that big pile of weapons and you'll see,' he said with a wink.

Delta-Six watched the battle with interest, noting how the Lutamek eggs' fighting abilities had improved upon the Lutamek's standard tactics. Being so close to the metal behemoths made him wary, and he knew every minute here was a minute lost… but something stopped him from leaving.

Whether it was deep programming or something woven into his very bones, Delta-Six couldn't leave his comrades behind. He'd seen Bowman die and, if the fight continued the way the crowd wanted, all the humans and Sorean would bleed into the dusty soil of the arena floor before the hour was out.

He considered his options. Helping Olan and Gal-qadan's men would be too risky and he couldn't fire any weapons with so many alien soldiers around him. He looked to the exit, remembering the Lutamek station nearby, then turned to the looming tower – his goal. Maybe a distraction was what he needed? Something to keep the elite guards busy and to make sure the Lutamek stayed in one place while he completed his mission.

An orange light flashed at the edge of his vision. He triggered the warning: his air filters had detected low pheromone levels; not one it recognised but the parts per million were slowly rising. He pushed the alert away and concentrated on the battle. Osayimwese had crawled away, trying to attract the tocka, while Gal-qadan and his men had spread out on the other side of the Lutamek, taking potshots through gaps in the defensive fences.

'This won't last long,' a bulky humanoid a few seats ahead of Delta-Six said to a companion. 'We've paid good credits for deaths and what do we get?'

'One headshot,' a gangly grey mass of wires and hair replied.

'And a burning,' a scaly soldier covered in red spikes and belts stringed with weapons replied.

'The Sorean died slowly and loudly,' the first one said with a laugh.

'I've heard we've got new gladiators from the mines, so they'll finish these humans off soon.'

'Today, I was told,' the grey mess replied.

Delta-Six had heard similar chatter throughout the crowd and could see the guards grouping together at the arena gates. He watched Gal-qadan's group, who were fanning out, keeping low. Zooming in, he could see that each soldier carried a number of small grey objects. That's what they've been doing! he realised. But why were Olan's men wasting their time with the tocka? Maybe there was a way to help?

Delta-Six stood, drawing a few looks, and clambered to the top row of empty seats. From here he had a good view of the ramshackle city outside and the farms and desert beyond. Past them, the behemoth shapes of the domes dominated the landscape.

The orange light flashed again. The parts per million had doubled. But what was the chemical designed to do? He set a portion of his system's energy to analyse the chemical components while he searched for any signal from Lavalle and Euryleia.

Nothing.

Wait. Smoke was rising from a building close to where the small army were stationed. Delta-Six ran a spectro-analysis on the smoke and compared it to the predefined communication chart – an idea from Euryleia. The composition was high in phosphorus and heavy metals, which meant the attack was imminent. Delta-Six had to move fast to complete his mission! But first he could help events here a little. He carefully slipped the chamelo-cloth off his shoulder and launched two silent missiles into the sky, then walked back down towards the exit.

'A waste of credits,' he grumbled, using the Rhil voice, and slipped away.

Olan held his arm across his mouth as smoke poured from the tiny grenades Gal-qadan had lobbed at the Lutamek. A smokescreen wouldn't stop the Lutamek from seeing, Olan thought, so what were they up to? The crowd weren't sure either and had started howling even louder.

'Get close!' Olan shouted to the nearest soldiers. 'Power up your weapons!'

A series of explosions shook the ground and set Olan's ear ringing. He peeped through a gap and saw dark holes in the floor around the Lutamek.

'That was my idea!' Olan shouted, feeling the urge to run out and fight again. 'Aim for the ground around the Lutamek,' he shouted, controlling his instincts. 'Throw everything you have at it!'

He pushed the muzzle of the weapon Bowman had died with through a gap and fired energy pulses at the ground. Lutamek laser fire replied, melting the gun and rendering it useless.

'Fire at the ground!' Olan shouted, his voice sounding muffled by the whining noise filling his ears.

A second later, two enormous explosions tore into the arena floor and Olan felt the ground dip towards the Lutamek. Smith was looking at him, probably shouting, but he couldn't see his face, and Osayimwese was behind him, keeping the Lutamek busy with a mortar launcher.

'Keep firing!' Olan shouted, his throat hoarse now.

The sound of battle was coming back to Olan, along with Osayimwese's voice.

'It's going!'

Olan grabbed the nearest free weapon. The smoke was still thick but he knew where to shoot. The ground was moving, he was sure, so he kept firing until, with a deep groan and an earthquake, the section of ground the Lutamek were standing on finally gave way, crashing into the void below, taking the robots with it.

The crowd hushed as a cloud of dust and smoke rose from the giant hole.

'Where have they gone?' Steve Smith asked.

'Wherever the tocka came from,' Olan replied. 'They were on the ramp – a false floor.'

A lazy wind stirred the thinning smoke and Olan's bare arm touched his chest plate, feeling its warmth. He didn't remember being hit by a Lutamek shot, so why was it warm? The last time it had felt like that was just after the Draytor shape-shifter had blasted him with some godforsaken weapon.

The crowd were getting louder now, which meant Olan was getting his hearing back.

'Prepare to defend!' Olan shouted, feeling the urge to run out and leap into the hole.

Nothing came.

Olan felt his breathing speed up. What was going on? He touched his chest plate again. Warm still.

'We must finish them off!' Osayimwese shouted.

Humans and Sorean were appearing from Gal-qadan's side, weapons raised, sidling up to the huge hole in the arena floor. Their eyes were wide, almost manic.

'No!' Olan shouted. 'What are you doing?'

Movement caught his eye as Smith walked around the palisades, into the open. The crowd were cheering and jeering, and Olan could see the guards were busy keeping the peace where fights had broken out. Olan felt strange, then a wave of calm washed through his stomach and he felt focussed. The battle rage had gone and he could think clearly again. Smith was hopping from foot to foot, firing his rifle into the hole, and Osayimwese was beside him, also acting wild. Why was everyone getting so worked up?

A yellow blast of sunlight ripped out of the hole and Smith dropped to the floor.

'Get back!' Olan shouted, but knew it was too late.

A net of blue light flashed across the hole in the ground, trapping the young Lutamek in their new prison, and Olan rushed to Smith's body. The Lutamek shot had blasted him through the neck, severing his head instantly. Olan knelt and picked up the masked head, seeing his own reflection in the face mask. He wondered what Smith had looked like and felt the urge to pull the mask back.

'Did you know him well?' Gal-qadan's gruff voice asked.

Olan looked up to see that all the humans and Sorean were here now. He shook his head and said, 'No better than anyone else here.'

'The humans are victorious,' the voice crackled over the arena speakers. 'Reversing the fate of history.'

Olan placed Steve Smith's head on the ground beside his body.

'But we feel the bloodlust,' the voice continued. 'So, to honour our leaders, we open the doors to any warrior wishing to prove their prowess.'

'What?' Olan looked around for someone to speak to but the noise from the crowd was rising.

Wild screams mixed with manic howls as the bizarre menagerie of scores of alien soldier species – many hyper-evolved beyond natural limits – clambered over the barriers, onto the field of war. Many were fighting each other but some only had eyes for the humans.

The tocka had moved to the centre, huddled near the humans, who Olan thought still looked crazed.

'We must fight them all!' Osayimwese shouted and leaped forward.

'We must defend ourselves!' a Sorean replied, signalling for its kin to form what looked to Olan like a shield wall.

'You are acting hastily. What the hell is going on here?' Gal-qadan asked with his usual growl and scowl, looking to Olan. 'What are these mind tricks?'

'I'm not sure, but we can't trust our instincts,' Olan replied.

Gal-qadan stared at Olan. 'That's not possible.'

'We must think and act logically – or we won't make it out alive.'

Osayimwese pointed at the circle of alien warriors closing in around them. 'I don't think we're getting out of here alive, Olan. They want our blood!'

Olan eyed up the nearest enemy soldier and saw the guards had joined their ranks. He looked at his men and cursed their lack of decent mutations or abilities. Even the weapons they had were limited.

'We will do our best,' Olan replied and grasped the hammer amulet hanging around his neck.

Visions of his countless battles rushed past him, of warriors and victories past. Time and time again he'd stayed alive and fought again. He let out a wild laugh.

'After all,' he said, facing his men, 'what else can we do?'

John followed Crossley through the crowd of miners, checking each one for a neck or body pin as he passed. Many had their pins in place, and he checked that the false pinhead was still stuck on the back of his head.

Looking back, he caught glimpses of the fight between

Peronicus-Rax and Falen. The knives had been discarded and they were now using the mutations they'd evolved during their time in the dome: Falen's limbs were glowing red-hot and Peronicus-Rax emitted a white aura every time Falen attacked. They skirted around the back of the group and John caught a glimpse of Yarcha. He grabbed her arm, beckoning for her to follow.

'The guards!' she said with wild eyes, searching.

'It's okay,' John said and ushered her to follow Crossley.

'Have you had your pin removed?' Yarcha whispered back to John, who couldn't keep his eyes off the circular hole in the back of her shaved head.

'Yes,' he whispered, wondering if he should give her his sticky disc.

Crossley was chatting as he led them to a pile of weapons, '...and we can take them all.'

'Sorry, I didn't hear,' John replied.

'Forget the bloody fight, okay?' Crossley stared at him, then Yarcha. 'This is our chance to get out of here. We distribute the weapons while Peronicus-Rax and the guards are distracted, then we blast our way out of here, okay?'

'But... the pins,' John said, turning over the bulky brown pistol Crossley had handed him.

Crossley's eyebrows rose as he said, 'I've taken care of it.' He nodded at the fight. 'If Falen survives we can thank her, but we need to get these distributed now.'

John nodded and felt a tap on the shoulder. A Sorean looked up at him and gestured at the brown weapon, but John pocketed it and handed the Sorean a short, serrated sword. Another Sorean followed, who took a lethal-looking sword. Again and again, the diminutive furred warriors appeared to deplete Peronicus-Rax's stash.

Yarcha was helping to hand the guns and blades out but hadn't chosen a weapon for herself.

'What are you going to use?' John asked her.

'There's nothing like my Urumi here,' she said with a shrug and handed a rifle to a Sorean.

'But you must fight,' John said, feeling concerned, 'or at least have something to defend yourself with.'

'I…' Yarcha started and looked away. 'I've never fought in a battle before.'

'What?' John said a little too loudly. 'How's that even possible? You… who did you kill to get here?'

'I don't understand.'

'Everyone brought here has killed hundreds of warriors in battle,' John explained.

'My father was at war. He was a great general,' Yarcha had pride in her voice, 'and he sent many trophies back home as he expanded his kingdom: treasure; weapons; elephants; and captured soldiers.'

'And the soldiers taught you to fight?' Olan asked.

'Some,' she said with a tilt of her head, 'but mostly I defeated them in one-to-one combat.' Yarcha sighed, seemingly weighed down by her memories.

'That's incredible,' John replied, genuinely amazed. He'd killed his enemy from a distance, with his Lewis gun, and didn't have the stomach for any close, bloody fighting. 'You deserve to be here,' he said. 'What you've learned can easily be put to use in battle.'

Yarcha gave a solid nod and said, 'Their deaths taught me many things… how to defend, how to control one's anger and how to never underestimate even the smallest enemy. Especially the daughter of their enemy's king.'

'You're a princess?'

'Not out of choice,' Yarcha snapped, grabbing a long sword by the handle and testing its weight.

'Yes, but–'

'Okay, that's everything gone.' Crossley cut John off and checked his rifle. 'Let's watch the fight.'

'Right,' John replied, and he followed Yarcha back to the crowd.

John eyed up the nearest Bensha guard and kept his distance as he slipped into the crowd, but everyone was focussed on the fight. The first thing John noticed as his own gaze turned to the battle was one of Falen's arms on the ground. And she looked exhausted, while Peronicus-Rax looked as strong as ever.

'Finish her!' one of the guards yelled.

'And then back to work!' shouted another.

Peronicus-Rax wore a look of determination. John couldn't tell whether he was enjoying it or not but, from what he said earlier, this was vengeance for his entire species.

'Do you think it was chance we met on the battlefield?' Falen asked, clearly trying to enrage Peronicus-Rax and make him charge her.

'We had fourteen days,' Peronicus-Rax replied. 'And so did you. Our meeting was pure chance – unless you had already won a battle and waited for us?'

'Perhaps,' Falen replied.

John could see the Korax in their blue bubble, antennae wafting and flicking as they talked in private. One of the guards had spotted them and pushed through to the front.

'Cease!' he shouted and kicked the Korax apart, bursting the bubble. 'Get on with it,' he shouted at Peronicus-Rax.

Peronicus-Rax breathed in deeply and said, 'In my own time, unless you wish to be next?'

The guard instinctively raised his pin device but Peronicus-Rax shook his head.

'Unlike you, I was never a captive of your ridiculous army,' he said. 'I will deal with you after–'

Falen leaped in, slashing at his hand with a red-bladed arm, leaving a yellow glare in John's vision.

Peronicus-Rax responded by blasting Falen with energy, sending her skidding across the dusty ground towards the group of Korax. He took a look at his hand, where a finger hung limply on a thread of flesh, and bit it off – spitting it onto the floor.

'Korax,' Peronicus-Rax bellowed. 'This creature defied our pact and offended your world as much as my people.' He blasted Falen again and John could see the white energy pulse from the large warrior's belt. 'Your species was bound to your planet, held back by the Drauw. Generations were lost and the Korax weakened. What will you do?'

'They will do nothing,' Falen replied and leaped at Peronicus-Rax with a blinding flash of orange.

A blue light exploded and, when John could see again, Falen's long-shelled limbs, her body and bullet-shaped head, covered in spirals, lay scattered across the floor in a dozen inert pieces.

Peronicus-Rax nodded at the Korax, who nodded back, each of them extinguishing the blue spark on their antennae.

'And now,' Peronicus-Rax said, turning to the miners. 'Let the revolution begin.'

'What?' the guard next to the Korax said, still holding his pin trigger.

'I was talking to the resistance,' Peronicus-Rax said as he slowly knelt as if to pray.

A white glow shimmered around him as he said, 'Find your freedom.'

A second later, the cavern was filled with laser fire and explosions as every miner armed with Peronicus-Rax's pilfered weapons attacked the guards. John stumbled backwards. He saw a Bensha wrestling a Sorean to the ground, slicing into it with his jagged sword. Without thinking, John fired the pistol in his metal hand, hitting the Bensha in the shoulder, sending him rolling away. In a flash, the white-skulled soldier aimed his pin activator at John. He held his breath... but nothing happened.

'Not this time,' John said, breathed out and fired again, aiming between the Bensha's eyes.

Chapter 20

Althorn should have been better prepared after his experiences of being imprisoned by Belsang and the Brakari, yet here he was again, captured by the enemy. They'll be wondering where I am, he thought, as he bided his time, sitting on his tiny island of dirt at the centre of a pitch-black sea.

Unlike in the deserts of the dome, there was literally nothing to eat here, so Althorn had been reserving his energy, feeding off what little rations he'd manage to keep to himself as he tried to get back to Euryleia and Lavalle, with news of what he'd found hidden beneath the Firstborn temple. The trouble was, after the Lutamek withdrawal and the Ascent retracting their guard, the Firstborn scouts had spread further afield, and Althorn had fallen into their trap.

He'd sped past the dark figures and watched from what he assumed to be a safe distance, but their ability to drop into the ground and resurface metres away confused him. Their numbers grew and, no matter how fast he ran, Althorn was soon surrounded by them. Rather than waste energy, he slowed, ready to fight, but the shapes simply merged together and liquefied to form a moat around him.

That was the status quo. Althorn had no idea who they

waited for but he could see a shape in the distance. The tar creatures felt it too. The lake vibrated and a head popped up every now and then, two yellow discs focussing and slipping under again.

The shape was a Lutamek.

The last Lutamek Althorn had seen had turned out to be a shell of a robot stuffed full of steam-powered engines, counterweight gizmos and a group of sweaty British soldiers, but this one moved with the grace of a normal Lutamek and didn't appear to be producing smoke. Althorn sighed. His rations had gone, so whatever he needed to do had to be done now. He stood and stretched his legs.

Then two more shapes appeared. They were far smaller, but nearer than the Lutamek, running in between it and the lake. Althorn recognised them straight away – Das and Pod. They were in their armadillo body form, as when he'd first met them. Scampering at speed, they quickly reached the edge of the black pool.

'Ah, Althorn!' one of them, Das he guessed by the darker scales, said.

'You've come back to us,' said Pod.

'Yes,' Althorn replied. 'I have returned.'

Althorn wondered if the soldiers of the Firstborn knew the truth he'd discovered in the shrine near the tower and cast his one eye to the nearing Lutamek silhouette, then back to Das and Pod.

'Have you been busy?' Das asked.

Althorn shook his head. 'Not really. This desert offers little. I can see why you have grown bored over the years.'

Das twitched.

Pod narrowed his eyes and said, 'You were always so busy under your dome. Scouting here… spying there.'

'As were you,' Althorn replied, knowing he had to remain confident to get through this.

'Yes,' Das replied and motioned for the lake of tar to split and create a dry path for him. 'We couldn't save your eye but we guaranteed your victory.'

'So you could leave the dome safely and lead my army into slavery,' Althorn said.

Pod gestured and the path widened, allowing his brother to approach Althorn too. 'The whole army would have been more suitable, of course, but the Lutamek had certain demands and had become affiliated with the Ascent while we were in your dome.'

Pod's voice became more authoritarian… more leader-like as he spoke. So, he was finally seeing the brothers in their true form.

'And Peronicus-Rax had his own agenda, so we helped each other,' Das said.

The dry path opened all the way to Althorn's island, and the pointed heads of the tar soldiers rose in a ring around him. Eyes shining from the dark. Althorn noticed something new in the distance – a trail of smoke – and his confidence grew. All he had to do was bide his time.

'And you were here in the beginning?' Althorn asked.

Das and Pod both stopped walking.

'It is forbidden to enter the temple of the Firstborn,' Das said and the black heads around them slowly sunk down.

Pod looked to his brother and said, with slow intensity, 'This changes our plans.'

'You don't want your army to know the truth?' Althorn said, sweeping his arm around him. 'The truth about the Firstborn and–'

'Enough!' Das shouted.

'Army, be gone!' Pod yelled and the pitch-black lake of

warriors slipped into the ground, leaving the three of them in the open desert.

Das said, 'Your truths may cause offence.'

'You aren't even warriors, are you?' Althorn asked.

'Does that make a difference to you?' Pod said. 'When we kill you?'

The pair started to make jerking and twitching movements like just before they had grown during the battle with the Brakari. Could he outrun them? No, they would anticipate that, Althorn thought and glanced a few degrees off from where Das and Pod now advanced.

'Let's make this quick,' Das said, 'before our soldiers make it back to the nearest outpost and start spreading rumours.'

'They wouldn't dare,' Pod said as his legs ballooned, followed by his torso, arms and head.

Das followed suit and pulled a bottle of liquid from an unseen pocket. Althorn remembered the pills and liquids which had rejuvenated him in the battle and he sprinted off to one side, sure he had to stay clear of whatever they were about to use on him.

'Were you abandoned here?' Althorn asked.

Das leaped forward, covering the ground far quicker than Althorn had anticipated, and sprayed the liquid at him. Althorn dodged and sped away. Pod attacked next, pummelling his mighty fists into the empty ground each time Althorn zipped away.

'You will tire eventually,' Das shouted and attacked again.

'Maybe,' Althorn replied and leaped away once more. 'Tell me,' he said, 'why did you keep the shrine? In case they came back for you?'

The pair attacked in unison this time, dodging and weaving, giving Althorn little space to escape, yet he managed it. Just.

'Were you slaves or paid workers?' He teased them now,

buying every second he could. 'Labourers brought here to do the dirty work while the real masters kept their hands clean.'

'So what?' Pod replied and pulled a metal rod from his belt. 'We are the Firstborn – nothing can change that.'

'Your army follow you because you feed them lies... you concoct your own myths.'

Another attack.

Althorn felt his legs growing heavier with each sprint, but salvation was coming. He pulled out his own weapon – a small laser-pulse pistol Cheng had given him – and fired at the ground, creating clouds of dust, then ran again.

'You weren't the first victors to leave a dome at all!' he shouted. 'You were just builders–' Althorn was cut off and screamed as droplets of Das' poisonous liquid struck his arm, pricking his skin with fire.

'And you will tell nobody,' Pod said.

Althorn fired more shots, throwing up clouds of dust, and ran as a new shape joined the melee. As he sped away, Althorn heard an echoed voice.

'Forward shields to maximum, Carter! Elliott! Present arms and fire at will!'

Isao felt serenely calm, which was odd considering he was deep within the heart of a vortex of shadow matter which pooled and pulsed around him. To him it appeared golden, like he was floating in the sun itself, swimming in a swirling mass of vibrant energy.

This was the exact centre of the disc.

Every now and then, an eddy or surge in energy would pull at Isao, but he knew he was safe here. He felt the power and it fed him; it swelled and ebbed around him, reminding him of the tidal pull he and the other samurai had felt in the shadow world under the dome.

From what Ten-ten had said, the original material of his body, along with Hori and Masaharu's, had been switched with this strange shadow matter, to create a new version of him. The transition had been incomplete, hence the phasing in and out they had experienced in the dome, but he had been reborn and now was one with it.

Like a spider tending a web, Isao could feel movements from many leagues away across the disc, sensing its entire structure. He could feel the centre, the crust, the domes – even the pull of the star. He focussed his senses and felt a new starship locking onto the cap of a distant dome. Another dome's silver gates were opening, freeing the latest victors. He felt the Tathon; the shockwaves they'd created when they smashed through their dome wall still sent mirror ripples through the shadow matter. Isao sensed the Tathon probing this subterranean, golden lake with their stubborn hyphae – fungal spears which delved through the ground at speed, tapping and probing.

Isao looked up. He could still see and listen as he had done in the air of the soldiers' world. Above him, the tower reached up, sheltering the huge stone obelisk. From here, inside and under the tower, Isao could see the incessant attack of the Platae, who threw their acidic bodies at the tower wall, for no gain. Although deadly and tactically dangerous, they lacked the complex thought processes to see that their attempts were futile, or the ingenuity to try another tack.

Other factions of victorious armies were spread around the tower in their territories, each with boundaries like spokes on a wheel. Isao saw them all: the Firstborn's temple; the Ascent's complex of mineshafts; another group's boreholes. None of them had what it would take to free themselves from this disc.

Apart from the Tathon. Maybe *they* had the ability to break free of this egg?

Isao floated higher to where the golden sea thinned and mixed with the world of light and other matter. He was still wary of the Lutamek so kept an eye out for their telltale sensory waves as he spread his senses out across the shadow-matter reservoir, developing a mind map of every living creature floating above him. To him they looked like tiny fireflies, and slowly he learned to pick out different species. He identified a group of humans outside the Ascent city and another in the Ascent mines. The Sorean were visible, as were the Lutamek, who were grouped around their research centre. He found another pocket of humans and Sorean beside tocka, and two mechanical hearts that shone out to him. What were they doing here? He was drawn to them and sensed they weren't happy. They'd been woken and twisted, forced to do someone else's will.

Isao controlled the energy around him and floated closer to the two life forms. One was injured and the other had withdrawn back into its shell. He knew them. They knew him. Twisting the energy around him, Isao formed the four signs he'd been sent by the young Lutamek when they'd first met, and sent them up – two twirls, a cross and a star – overlaid to form a spiral shape like the image of their galaxy the Lutamek had shown them.

The shape dissolved and Isao felt a tube had linked up with them in the shapes' wake.

He asked, 'Can I help you?'

'Not safe,' the injured Lutamek replied. 'Enemies surrounding.'

'Do you need power?' Isao asked, staying in the safety of the ground.

The second young Lutamek flashed and replied, 'Human, leave us.'

A spark of energy leaped from the robot, shooting past Isao, grazing his shoulder. He reeled back and watched the wound heal itself with golden energy from the source. A memory flashed before him of the tiger he had killed with Hori and Masaharu, and shame washed over him. That creature had only been defending itself as these Lutamek were now.

'You have shadow weapons?' Isao asked and sunk a little lower, keeping his gaze on the Lutamek.

'Us only,' it replied.

'I am not your enemy,' Isao said. 'I can help you.'

'No more thinkings,' the injured Lutamek said.

Isao studied the injured robot more closely. He could see organic parts matched with metal and innate substances. Energy in the robot's circuits ran around its body like tiny rivers of power, combining with the organic conduits to create pathways of silicon, carbon and potassium. Two areas glowed red and Isao felt a warm pain emanating from both, so he focussed on them, allowing the light beneath him to rise and wash away the Lutamek's pain.

The red patches faded and the flow sped up.

'Words gone,' the injured Lutamek said. 'Orders removed. Protocol returns.'

Isao turned to the other Lutamek and performed the same motion, wiping the red smudges from its pathways, allowing the energy to flow freely until, slowly, the young Lutamek unravelled itself.

'Release. Protocols remain.' A rush of blue energy pulsed through its cortex. 'What we do now?'

'What any sentient creature does,' Isao replied. 'Survive.'

'And then?' the other asked.

Isao took a moment to think and let his inner emotions

settle. What was it he really wanted? What did anyone really want once they were safe and comfortable? Whatever answer he gave now could have long-lasting consequences with these two individuals.

'Explore,' he finally said. 'Learn, create and help those unable to help themselves.'

A noise made Isao look up and he focussed through the ground to where the other souls stood. Humans, tocka and Sorean. More were there now, surrounding them. Myriad species.

'Help those?' a Lutamek asked.

'Yes,' Isao replied. 'Let us help them.'

As he walked through the dark passages within the arena walls, Delta-Six changed from his Rhil disguise back to the basic costume he'd used on the farms. He was Lucien Thomas once more. There were no guards at the exits, and a wild roar from within the arena suggested events had taken a course of their own, so Delta-Six continued his walk with his head hung low.

The main lesson he'd learned during their time in the dome was that a battle would be far shorter if you removed the enemy's leaders. Delta-Six knew the Ascent's leaders were inside the final ring of the city, nearest the dome, so he headed for the nearest checkpoint. The second lesson he'd learned was never to trust the Lutamek. So, as he walked a curved path around the closed Lutamek research centre, Delta-Six dropped pebbles and watched the robots with care. Scores of transport starships lay beyond their research centre, clearly dragged here from the nearest domes, but he focussed on the robots, keeping his left-side shielding on maximum as he recorded the behemoth robots kneeling in concentric rings around a stone altar where a humanoid figure was tied to the stone.

There was nothing he could do to help. His mission was more important.

The pebbles contained tiny monitoring devices which would alert Delta-Six if the Lutamek left their compound. He'd given Euryleia a wrist-bound device that gave her the same information during their attack. Delta-Six looked back through the city towards the farms. No sign of any activity yet, so what were they doing?

The orange pheromone warning went off again: the pheromones were still being filtered by his system, but the parts per million had doubled again. A bleep in his ear signalled the completion of the pebble array, and he diverted his walk to the gate, analysing the three guards who chatted and argued with one another, gesturing at the arena.

'I say you stay here and let Hirat-que and I go battle,' a heavily furred biped shouted at a white-skulled Bensha.

'And I say if you demand anything again we'll have our own battle here,' it replied.

Delta-Six strolled forward, bent low and saw the flash of silver on each of their necks. He wondered how strong the hormones had been and if any guards had resorted to blowing each other's heads off.

'That's far enough!' the third guard shouted and blocked Delta-Six's path with its tall body. 'Name?'

'Lucien Thomas.'

'You don't have clearance for this gate, Lucien Thomas.'

Delta-Six offered the stolen ID card, hoping his manipulation hadn't triggered the security system.

The guard spat a globule of yellow gunk onto the ground and touched the card on his device.

'Ha!' he shouted and his comrades joined him. 'So they're letting stinking farmers in these days, are they?'

'Not a chance,' the Bensha said and unclipped his sword.

'I can pay,' Delta-Six said with a tired, rasping voice.

'The Ascent don't give credits to guards, so we can't be bought,' the Bensha growled. 'But there's nothing to stop us giving you a good kickin'!'

Delta-Six held his hand out again, this time with three silver coins on his palm.

'I offer you freedom,' he said.

The three crowded round.

'What is it?' the hairy one asked.

'It turns off your neck pin,' Delta-Six answered.

'Give it,' the Bensha said and grabbed a coin.

'It fits on the pin,' Delta-Six said, pointing to the back of his neck.

But rather than fit it to his own, the Bensha grabbed the tall guard and stuck the disc on his pin, then pushed him away and pulled out his device.

'Only one way to test it,' he said and pressed the button.

The tall guard gasped and Delta-Six held his breath… but nothing happened.

Delta-Six exhaled slowly.

'Looks like we're free,' the hairy one said as he and the Bensha took their coins. 'What are your plans, Lucien Thomas?'

'To see the tower,' Delta-Six replied. 'Before I die.'

The tall guard stared at him for a long second then said, 'Should we? I don't believe him.'

'And I don't care – we're free!'

'But the leaders…'

'Screw 'em. Let's go and fight!' the Bensha shouted and ran off to the arena, taking the other two with him.

Delta-Six shook his head and strode through the empty gate, into the inner ring of the Ascent city. Here, a host of well-constructed metal buildings sprawled out in even blocks, all overseen by the immense, glistening tower. He'd never been this close so, when he'd walked past the first row of buildings, he set his analysis systems to work on the stone within and its true purpose.

It was stunning.

'YOU!'

A voice made him turn.

'Lucien Thomas,' Delta-Six replied to a species he hadn't seen before.

It reminded him of a stick insect he'd seen during his humidity training in the tropics. Non-poisonous and inedible, yet it had held his fascination during his camouflage test.

'You are not a chosen species and you have no chaperone,' it stated.

'I have come to see the tower before I die,' Delta-Six replied.

The tall, long-limbed creature clacked and glowed an orange colour. Delta-Six's systems detected a surge of energy and reported huge spikes in life-threatening readings: heat; radioactivity; q-pulse; photons; infrared. Delta-Six held his arm to shield himself as a blast hit him, burning and saturating his systems. The blast continued to rage, switching currents and phases as Delta-Six's shields depleted fast. His thoughts were slowing too, so he initiated his fight hormones and hardened the outer shell of his suit.

'You are not what you seem,' the Ascent soldier said after letting the beam fade out.

Delta-Six cast aside what was left of his chamelo-cloth and stood tall as the creature advanced on its stick-thin legs.

Delta-Six sent stored energy to his weapons. His mind was quick, shutting down a cyber-attack and studying his enemy for weaknesses: joints; eyes; feeding parts. Either this alien was endowed with an array of adaptations, or it had help. A flash of movement picked up on his sensors suggested the latter, so Delta-Six waited for one more step then fell into a series of rolling shots at the tall soldier, who deflected each shot. Delta-Six signalled his system to attack at will and re-routed power to his propulsion system. If it got any worse, he could always fly straight up to escape.

Missiles blasted out of shoulder pads and lasers tore from his wrists as Delta-Six made evasive movements: rolling; dashing; sidestepping. Warning lights flashed around his vision as the other soldiers revealed themselves. He made another feint, and fired a looping shot, mimicking Bowman's arrows. Another roll and his enemy exploded, scattering its limbs and tubular head across the ground.

Delta-Six powered his jets and lifted off the ground as the new soldiers opened fire and more warriors streamed from the buildings. That was close, he thought, and felt a tug on his left leg. Something had him in an energy hold – a yellow line twisted round his ankle, pulling him back down.

'No!' he shouted, firing off his last missiles and shooting pulse blasts at the soldiers below.

Delta-Six fought on as his energy depleted and he descended into the growing mass of enemy soldiers. His warning lights blinked out and he tried to force the white energy through his system again, but there wasn't enough power. The jet on his back coughed a few times and stopped as a laser pulse ripped into his leg, freeing him from the yellow-energy hold, but sending him spiralling out of control.

With his remaining power, Delta-Six directed his flight towards the tower. More shots tore into his body, past his non-existent shielding and straight into his torso as he tumbled over the final set of metal fencing and towards the base of the tower. He tried to redirect his jets to slow his descent but, with a bone-breaking crash, he hit the ground in the ring of no-man's-land, where no faction could tread without joint permission.

Pain screamed through his body and his breathing was laboured as he lay on his back. But his view was clear, straight up the side of the crystal tower. No warning lights or messages. He didn't need them.

This was it.

He would die now.

Distant sounds pulled at his attention but Delta-Six was transfixed by his view. The shining tower loomed into the sky above like an immense rocket. Or a road. It led his eyes up and away.

Now, he felt the deepest, most protected program in his system set to work. Delta-Six's view merged with a view of a verdant landscape, which eventually took over his sight. Children were playing in the warm sun with a retro-dog and dark trees swayed in a breeze. For the first time in as long as he could remember, Delta-Six felt completely relaxed.

'Lucien Thomas.' A soft voice spoke his name and he turned to see the woman he'd known all his life.

His dream wife.

'Welcome home,' she said with a smile that made his heart skip its final beat.

Gal-qadan charged at the nearest group of soldiers with a laser rifle in one hand and a long, saw-edged blade in the other. He was in his element: his blood was hot; his skin was as tough as metal and his enemy had given up their weapons when they had entered the arena. All they had were their biological adaptations.

314

Some of the enemy diverted to attack a group of Sorean, leaving Gal-qadan with five warriors to face. He shot his rifle from the hip, taking one out and blasting the leg off another, then cast the rifle to the ground and leaped in with his sword held high. One swipe sliced through the shoulder of the first alien, whose claws impotently scraped Gal-qadan's chest. The second soldier was smaller and pummelled low into Gal-qadan as the third blasted them both with a bolt of heat from its chest.

Gal-qadan picked himself off the ground, casting aside his smouldering top. He felt good: his metal skin was free now, glistening like sword steel in the frost.

'You'll have to try harder than that,' Gal-qadan snapped as he retrieved his sword from the charred remnants of the smaller soldier.

'Everything has its melting point,' the bulky, dark-horned creature replied and released another blast of furnace-hot heat.

Gal-qadan rolled, but hadn't been quick enough to protect his head. Kneeling, he dusted his now bald head off with a handful of dry earth and was rolling away again when another soldier attacked, slicing with the sword, cutting into the aggressor's rear legs.

'I will show you the power of the sun,' the Firestarter said and blasted the soldier Gal-qadan had just cut down. Its screams mingled with the battle cries and explosions from the battle as it fried.

'And I will show you how day becomes night,' Gal-qadan said, turning to his opponent.

He dropped his sword and ran straight at him, throwing himself at the next blast of energy bursting from the alien's chest. Gal-qadan was covered in flame as he dived through the energy blast, straight at the alien, and crashed into him, sending him sprawling. His grabbed the warrior's scaled neck with both hands and squeezed. Still the energy poured over

Gal-qadan, pummelling his chest, sending his clothing up in brilliant flames.

'Time for night-time,' Gal-qadan shouted as the alien's neck grew smaller in his tight hands until, with a snap, he broke the creature's neck and let its body fall.

The flames stopped.

Naked, and feeling more alive than ever, Gal-qadan stood with one foot on his latest victim, searching the field for the next enemy fighters.

'Do not underestimate us!' he shouted.

The nearest soldiers avoided Gal-qadan, giving him time to survey the battle. He caught a glimpse of Olan and Osayimwese on the other side of the gaping hole in the ground where they had trapped the Lutamek. He grimaced as he saw the men mount the tocka.

'They belong to me,' he whispered and searched the ground for unused weapons.

But a new sight stopped him in his tracks.

Three glowing orbs were rising from the hole in the ground. Some soldiers stopped to gape in amazement, but most fought on. Gal-qadan felt an axe crash and splinter across his shoulders but he ignored the weak attacker – he only had eyes for the balls of light. Two were orange and slowly faded to reveal the Lutamek eggs he had long coveted, while the third remained white and formed a humanoid shape. When they reached two men's height above the ground, tiny blue bolts of energy shot out of the two Lutamek, striking soldiers with pinpoint accuracy.

Aliens of all sizes fell at Gal-qadan's feet as he watched on with no fear. When the shots finished, the only warriors standing were the humans, Sorean and tocka. Everyone else was dead.

The Lutamek eggs drifted down to a bare patch of earth and

unravelled to form their biped shapes, followed by the glowing human, who Gal-qadan finally recognised as Isao, the samurai.

The survivors gravitated towards them, weakened but victorious.

'Next time, do that earlier,' Gal-qadan said.

Olan laughed and looked him up and down. 'Long ago, I knew a man who liked to fight naked. Not for me though.'

Gal-qadan looked down at his body but felt no shame.

'Maybe take some garments from the dead?' Osayimwese said.

Gal-qadan wrapped a strip of cloth around his waist, grabbed a spear and rifle from a cluster of dead soldiers and said, 'I have what I need.'

'In that case,' Isao said, 'we should leave this place.'

'And?' Olan asked.

Gal-qadan pointed his spear in the direction of the tower. 'And we keep fighting.'

Althorn sat on the shoulder of the huge metal machine, Troy, as it had been named by its occupants. As it strolled across the desert at what, to Althorn, felt like an incredibly slow speed, he marvelled at how it had managed to take Das and Pod by surprise. His guess was they had assumed it was a standard Ascent robot they could control with the mechanical device Althorn had found discarded on the ground after the fight. But rather than being filled with corruptible wires and processors, Troy was full of human soldiers from various centuries of the British Empire, singing victorious songs about saving their queen or king.

Althorn had tried to fight the huge beasts alongside Troy, but his weapons were ineffective and their poisonous liquids too threatening. The false Lutamek fired scores of assorted missiles, but Das and Pod were more nimble and split to attack from both sides. Then, just as he feared Das and Pod would crush the soldiers inside their metal prison, the brothers stopped their attack and looked into the distance, sniffing the air.

'Resist it, brother!' Das had said.

'It's strong,' Pod replied. 'We must fight!'

'No,' Das said, 'we must return.'

And they ran off, leaving Althorn and a battered Troy wondering what was going on.

Hearing a knock, Althorn raised a flap of metal casing beside him and a hand holding a small metal canister of steaming liquid appeared.

'Cup of tea, Althorn?' a voice followed. 'Not the best, but it's the last of Elliott's supply and we could use one after that fight.'

Rude to decline the offer, Althorn thought.

'Thanks, Carter,' Althorn replied, taking the beverage.

'No milk of course. Sorry about that,' the soldier said and popped his head out to chat.

Althorn sniffed the aromatic drink and wondered why anyone would want to mix milk with herbal infusions. He took a sip and nodded. Not too disagreeable.

'Mmm,' Althorn said to Carter with a nod.

'You get used to it, I guess,' Carter replied. 'Of course nothing tastes like it did in India.'

Althorn nodded again, trying to remember what he could of his Earth's future. He'd managed to glean some information from John and Li, Crossley even, but not enough to understand everything Carter talked about.

'Do we know why they left?' Althorn asked and peered into the darkness within Troy.

He could see movement: shadows; silhouettes; a pair of eyes. Was that Elliott?

'Jenkins – the rear gunner – says a few of his dials perked up, but he's not sure what they're for.'

'Is it Lutamek technology?' Althorn felt his body flush with heat. 'They can track it!'

'No, no,' a voice piped from within. 'It *was* an air-quality monitor but something changed when we reversed the polarity.'

'Could be sensing anything!' Carter said.

Althorn looked him in the eyes. He was so young. How did he end up here? With his fresh face and eager eyes, he reminded Althorn of John. Eyes that had seen war were never young though, Althorn remembered.

One of the tall exhausts sticking out of Troy's back belched a puff of black smoke and a voice cried, 'Open lower vents!'

'We need to get back to the Ascent city,' Althorn said, pointing to the tower, which dwarfed the smudge of building beneath. 'We need your help, to break everyone free.'

'Well, we'd like to but–'

A shudder ran through Troy, making Althorn hold tight. He drained his tea and handed the canister to Carter as a deep voice within Troy shouted, 'Enemy approaching!' and the huge machine turned.

'Gotta go!' Carter said and slammed the flap down behind him.

Althorn had a good view up on the giant's shoulders but he couldn't see anything as the gears and cogs spun beneath him. Troy slowed and shifted as counterweights moved and sprang into action. The way Troy worked confused Althorn more than the way the Lutamek worked.

Then a dark patch on the horizon caught his attention. It was hard to gauge the distance with just his good eye, but Althorn had the impression of a swarm of creatures heading their way fast.

'ETA thirty seconds,' Elliott called out.

'Defensive manoeuvres!' another voice yelled and Althorn wondered if he'd been forgotten about.

Troy shifted to face the grey mass and a host of weapons appeared out of portholes.

As the newcomers neared, Althorn started to make out individuals – they were fast and big. Taller than a human but longer – six legs maybe? Like long beetles. He squinted and recognised a familiar shade of blue. His empty eye socket ached and he moved to climb down the back of Troy.

'You're safer here, Althorn!' Carter shouted.

Althorn gripped tight, peering over Troy as a host of Brakari headed straight for them. He drew his blade, ready for a fight, when a flash of light on the side of a grey lead soldier made him pause.

'Millok?' Althorn whispered.

John had trusted her, but nobody had seen her since the battle in the dome.

'Halt!' a voice from Troy bellowed and Millok and her horde of light-blue Brakari slowed, raising a haze of desert dust.

'We are allies,' Millok said, holding up her front legs.

Tiny clouds of moisture puffed out of holes across her body and those of her army as the exertion of their journey caught up with them.

'Are you Lutamek?' she asked.

'We are human,' Althorn replied and stood on Troy's shoulder. 'What news?'

'My Scion and I,' Millok explained, 'have escaped what many could not.'

'Speak plainly!' Elliott shouted from inside Troy.

Millok's head dropped as she spoke. 'The Tathon... the enemy of all armies. They are coming!'

Chapter 21

John stared through the cavern exit and shielded his eyes.

'Are you seeing what I'm seeing?' he asked Yarcha and Crossley, who stood either side of him.

'I can see an elephant,' Yarcha said. 'And the sun is in eclipse.'

'There's a scarecrow on a cross,' Crossley added. 'And a pond.'

'If you turn your head,' John said, tilting his and squinting, 'it looks like a giant face.'

A tall soldier pushed past them, spoiling the moment. 'You've been underground too long,' it growled.

John rubbed his eyes and looked again at the bizarre alien world of the Ascent city. Yarcha's elephant was a heap of fighting soldiers, Crossley's scarecrow was a body strung up outside the Lutamek research lab, which stood in front of a host of starships identical to those outside their dome, and the pond turned out to be a moving tar pit filled with bobbing soldiers.

'We're under attack,' Peronicus-Rax said and pulled a bulky energy-rifle off his back.

'From who?' John asked but Peronicus-Rax was off, running towards the nearest burning building.

'Hey, Peronicus-Rax,' Crossley called out, 'you got any more weapons stashed away?'

He was ignored too.

'Seriously,' Crossley said to John, 'I'd have gone for that one if it was on his pile of weapons.'

A steady flow of surviving miners was joining them. Most were armed, some were injured. John saw a group of Korax, and pictured what had happened to Falen. He stared back into the dark of the mine and remembered the others they had lost: Yam-mit, Samas, Jakan-tar and Rar-kin.

Explosions made him turn back to the burning city, where fighting seemed to be erupting from every corner.

'Look!' Yarcha said, pointing to two bulky shapes jumping on the roof of a small building. 'Weren't they with our army?'

'Das and Pod.' John said. 'What are they doing here?'

'Were they captured as well?' Yarcha asked.

'I doubt it,' Crossley replied with a sneer. 'Plus they're fighting with some guys I don't recognise.'

'Falen told me about the factions here,' John said, 'different armies holding ground around the tower. So they could be one of them.'

'If we join them to fight the Ascent, we'll jump from the frying pan into the fire. No, thank you,' Crossley replied.

'So what do we do?' Tar-sone, the Sorean, asked.

'Well, I'm not gonna defend these Ascent bastards after they put me in that place,' Crossley said. 'But if I'm fighting, I wanna know who I'm fighting for.'

The group huddled in the mouth of the mine entrance, armed, blinking and leaderless.

'If Mihran was here we could communicate with the rest of our army,' John said and looked at Crossley. 'You never know, some might still be alive.'

Crossley shrugged.

'But we must fight!' one of the humanoid miners said with a long intake of breath. 'I feel my strength returning.'

'Yes,' said another. 'Time to show our prowess… prove our worth.'

John could feel his spirits lift too. He had felt weak in the mine, drained. But now something rejuvenated him and pumped him up. He breathed in the fresh air and scanned the cityscape for signs of anyone he recognised, friend or foe. He pulled the brown gun from his belt and gripped it with his metal hand. They felt good together, like they linked. He felt a charge of energy rush down his wrist and through his palm and the gun glowed.

'We have to fight,' John said with a nod.

'Well, if I'm gonna fight, I'm on his side,' Crossley said and pointed to the far side of the city, where a new set of soldiers had burst through. Some were on tocka – John caught a glimpse of Lavalle's jet-black armour amongst the riders – but others were on foot. Or, in Mata's case, on root.

'What is that?' a Korax asked.

'He was one of us,' Crossley said as the gnarled and spiked, leafless tree crashed through a single-storey building, sending out lightning-fast vines to grab the Ascent soldiers running away.

John remembered the wolves Mata had ripped apart back in the pine forest of their dome as he repeated the skill with even greater strength and speed.

The tocka who escorted Mata were wheeling in a wide arc to avoid the Firstborn fighters.

'Look,' Tar-sone said. 'They're coming our way.'

The tocka looked magnificent, John thought, and he longed to be riding again and back in battle.

Dakaniha felt alive! The wind rushed over him as he and the rest of the attacking guerrilla army sped on their tocka across the ground between the Ascent farms and city. With his four eyes open, he felt the full force of their attack with him in the centre, behind Lavalle on point. Euryleia was beside him, with two bows already primed. Cheng and his men of China took the left flank, while Sancha and a host of freed farmers rode on the right. Beyond them, the bizarre form of a rejuvenated Mata strode and glided on his roots.

To give them a chance against their larger-numbered enemy, Guang, on Cheng's side, formed a field of bent light around them, hiding their approach. With his new temple eyes, Dakaniha squinted to see the process in action, white lines bending and converging as light waves were streamed around them. If he could sense it maybe someone else could? He worried, but it was too late – they were already attacking.

The plan was simple. They would take over the main centres of power – the water supply and the entrance to the tower – while Delta-Six handled the leaders. Anyone in their way would die. Euryleia had asked everyone to be mindful of the slaves with pins in their necks and handed out the deflectors Delta-Six had designed for the farmers.

'They will join our fight,' she'd said.

'But we won't be able to see their pins,' Cheng had replied.

'They'll be the ones not fighting,' Lavalle said with a hard glare. 'So if they fight, kill them.'

The herd of tocka ran a curve around a cluster of huts and aimed for the first gateway. It was manned by two guards, who were transfixed by something inside the city walls. Dakaniha sniffed the air deeply and felt invincible. Nobody could stop them, he was certain. He lifted his pulse-crossbow, squeezed his knees tight around his tocka's muscular back and fired.

Others followed suit, and the guards were blown to pieces, along with a stretch of the metal wall.

Mata was way ahead, ripping a string of metal fence panels out, creating a gap for tocka to stream through. The second wave of soldiers – the farmer slaves who travelled on foot – would be here soon, ready to support them if they ran into any serious resistance.

'This way!' Lavalle bellowed, guiding Dakaniha and the others towards a bulky building riddled with white pipes.

If they could control the water, they could control the Ascent. The problem was the Ascent knew their weaknesses and had placed a small platoon of soldiers to defend the water plant. The second Dakaniha rode into open ground, they opened fire. As tocka fell around him, sending their riders flying into the dirt, he fired back. Smoke billowed, and the group split as the tocka wheeled around to avoid the attack.

Only Mata didn't alter course.

The huge, tree-like soldier, whose face and tattoos could still be seen through his protective bark and spines, leaped at the enemy with vines. He pulled two soldiers away as the others turned their fire on him, giving Dakaniha time to turn and rush back in.

'From the left!' Euryleia shouted as the tocka cantered in the shelter of a low building.

She turned and led them in, firing her explosive arrows.

Mata had the enemy guard busy, but new Ascent fighters were joining them. One had no weapon and Dakaniha felt the tocka jolt when it saw the long-tailed, black-handed Scarpinelloss. It raised its hands and shot flaming lava from its palms, striking Mata's roots and lower trunk, fixing him to the ground in solid rock.

Dakaniha patted his tocka and whispered, 'So this is the soldier that entombed your army?'

He got no response – he didn't expect one – but the other tocka were grouping now, looking for their leader, and slowing their attack. Dakaniha knew they had to push on or risk defeat.

'Concentrate on the lava thrower!' he shouted at the nearest riders and fired his own weapons at the Scarpinelloss until it stopped attacking Mata and turned their way.

Plumes of molten lava sprayed from the beast, creating great arches of fire, which solidified into rock as they hit the ground. Some tocka were caught, trapping them or setting them on fire, while their riders rolled away, dead or injured, and, while Dakaniha's group panicked, the other Ascent soldiers took potshots with their laser rifles. They needed organising. Dakaniha couldn't see Lavalle or Euryleia, so shouted and corralled the group together, out of range of the lava flows and laser fire.

'We must take out the lava soldier,' he said to the other riders when they were clear, 'and free Mata. We need a two-pronged attack,' Dakaniha explained and continued his plan with one eye on the enemy.

The tree-like Maori was still fixed to the ground – his roots encased in rock – but had sent long vines into the water-reclamation plant to plunder the rare resource, which gushed out of broken pipes now. At his base, Ascent soldiers kept out of range of his spikes and lower vines but fired at his trunk, burning holes in his body.

Dakaniha's crew took off as one, with the tocka deftly dodging the dead and the piles of hot rock. Dakaniha stared at the rock with his new eyes and noticed a strange colouration that matched the ground beneath the volcanic soldier.

'Get him in the air!' Dakaniha shouted as sped in. 'He's drawing rock through his feet!'

As they came into laser range, the group split in two, the

riders rolling and dropping to form an infantry unit, shielded by a deflection bubble created by one of the freed farmers, while the tocka circled away in a feint movement which would lead them around a set of huts and behind the Ascent fighters. Dakaniha's plan would only work if they could absorb the fire for long enough.

They struggled forward, until the protective bubble burst under pressure and the soldiers ran for cover behind the blobs of still-warm rock. The Scarpinelloss moved to a new spot of ground, nearer to Mata, who had withdrawn his vines. Dakaniha fired his crossbow, drawing the ire of the Scarpinelloss, and molten rock soon splashed around him, burning his skin with orange globules as he rolled behind a large block of rock.

He brushed off the spots of liquid fire before they burned through his flesh, then waited as the battle rose in volume – more explosions and screams – then silence. The sudden change shook his nerves and Dakaniha slowly peered around the rock.

When he finally did, he smiled and exhaled.

Millok slid to a halt and waited for the humans to catch up in their lumbering hollow robot. She blasted acidic gas out of her spiracles and sucked in fresh air, cursing Doctor Cynigar for giving her speed and fighting adaptations but nothing to improve her sensory or scouting abilities. Still, her Scion showed a variety of useful skills suitable for reconnaissance and the long-range journeys that had been forced on them by the Brakari doctor while they were still in the egg. Despite the taint, she was proud of them, her own personal army. Her brood.

'Another hour and they'll need a rest!' Althorn shouted from atop Troy.

'We don't have time to rest,' Millok replied. 'Has nothing I said sunk in yet?'

Althorn didn't reply and, after a quick scan to make sure her troops were in position, Millok ordered them to fan out ahead of their advance, while she slowed to keep pace with Troy.

'I think you're underestimating the threat of the Tathon,' she said, for the benefit of the soldiers inside Troy, as well as Althorn. 'They took over the entire dome, and everyone in it, within days.'

'But not you and your army,' Althorn replied.

'No,' Millok replied, unsure how she could explain how close they'd been to capture and what she'd seen the Tathon do to their captives. 'They have General Panzicosta,' she said, 'among others… Maybe some humans too, I'm not sure.'

'And they develop them, you said?' Althorn asked. 'They force mutation?'

'And bend them to their will,' Millok said, looking ahead, where a change in ground colour and a scattering of huts signalled the beginning of the Ascent's farms.

'But they're just a bunch of losers,' a voice came from within Troy.

'Yeah, everyone left in the dome is a loser!' another voice said, followed by laughter. 'We can take 'em.'

'Silence, Carter!' A voice boomed.

Millok would have ignored them but their situation was too dire.

'The Tathon are incredibly intelligent – more so than any species I've met yet, maybe even of the level of whoever brought us here. They have such abilities… have you not felt the change?' she asked.

'What change?' Althorn asked.

328

'The rise in confidence,' Millok replied, trying to describe what she'd felt and seen in her Scion. 'An eagerness to fight.'

Althorn grimaced and shook his head. 'Maybe, maybe not. We're in a land of soldiers – everyone wants to fight.'

'But this is different!' Millok was losing patience. 'I've seen it before. It's overwhelming. The Tathon release a set of pheromones on the wind, set to infiltrate their enemy before they arrive. It emboldens them – makes them stand up for themselves and their beliefs.'

'Which leads to them fighting each other before the Tathon get there?' Althorn asked.

'Sometimes, but the hormones also coerce them into making reckless decisions… even in well-defended fortifications it leads to them coming out to attack. Then the Tathon capture, kill and mutate.'

'And you think the Ascent won't be able stop them?' Althorn asked.

'I'm not sure any army can stop them–' Millok replied but was cut off by her scouts, clicking in the pared-down, subsonic Brakari language they had developed while tracking and avoiding the Tathon.

The news wasn't good.

'I know little of your Ascent,' she eventually said to Althorn, 'and would say numbers are no factor in a war against the Tathon. Maybe some warriors have adaptations that could help resist their march but, from what I've heard, it's too late. Your rebels are already attacking the Ascent, along with neighbouring factions.'

She could see lines of smoke ascending from the grey smudge at the base of the tower, where tiny flashes of light spoke of hidden skirmishes.

'Then what choice do we have?' Althorn asked.

'We fight!' came a shout from Troy.

'And if we fight,' Millok said, 'we must fight to the death, or risk being in the Tathon's army forever.'

Praahs was running so fast through the thin air, across the bare landscape between domes, that she felt like she was swimming again. The hardened soles of her feet were almost numb to the surface she pounded along, and her aerodynamic form barely felt the air rushing over her. Huge domes swept past and the great glass tower loomed larger and larger.

She was well aware of the biological tricks and psychological games the Tathon were playing with her, but her mental conditioning and altered physical body gave her no choice but to go along with their plans. For now. She would fight to the death for them but, as soon as she had the chance, she would break these biological bonds and escape.

From what she had heard about the size of the army she and her Cirratus warriors were about to face, she would have plenty of opportunity to escape, with the right help.

Panzicosta was by her side, her second in command. Despite her authority, Praahs knew the Brakari had important qualities she could use. He was more ruthless than her, would take control of the entire Tathon army if given the chance, but Praahs needed that razor-sharp, selfish instinct if they were going to survive both the battle and the Tathon.

Praahs watched Panzicosta and could tell by the way he rested pairs of legs that he would need to take a break before they attacked. She wondered what he was thinking and whether he had created a plan for how they would break away from the Tathon army.

Small huts appeared ahead as predicted.

'Slow and rest!' Praahs shouted and her platoon of tiny Tathon responded.

Panzicosta followed suit too, blasting moist air out of holes in his shell.

Praahs looked back to where the bulk of the Tathon army advanced. They would be here shortly, but they expected serious damage before they arrived. Whatever Panzicosta had in mind would have to be put into action soon.

Praahs let her second in command rest before asking, 'Any new ideas?' She kept her questions open to avoid the Cirratus guessing their plans.

'Some,' Panzicosta replied, his voice low. 'The fog of war leads to many accidents, but I expect this battle will proceed swiftly.'

'Yes,' Praahs said, noting a tang of despondency in his tone. 'Sometimes events occur after the battle as well.'

'Which we must be mindful of,' Panzicosta replied, with one set of eyes turning to the Cirratus. 'Plus, after victory, who is to say what each soldier's true value will be?'

Praahs wanted to ask more but held back. For now, the mission was more important. She had been given specific instructions to attack the Ascent first and neutralise the most dangerous soldiers for genetic renewal, before moving around the tower, attacking each faction in turn.

She released her gills to cleanse her blood and wash away the acids from her muscles, and tasted the chemicals in the air. She felt strong. Invincible. They *would* be victorious. She gave her army another minute before reeling her gills in and setting her protective bones over her most vulnerable organs. She knew the rush of hormones giving her a buzz was orchestrated by the Tathon leaders, designed to subdue her fears. She knew her problems wouldn't go away. But the rise in energy and confidence felt so good. Addictive. Her worries could wait.

'Shields up,' she ordered, feeling ready for the fight.

This was going to be so much fun, she thought, and could almost taste wet flesh.

'Trident formation!' she called out and, with her on the left prong, Panzicosta on the right and a horde of the most manic Cirratus in the centre, they charged.

They rushed through the empty farms, past headless corpses and battle-scarred landscapes, through the rambling huts, to a broken metal wall. Battle raged within: fires; smoke; explosions; laser fire. Praahs took it all in. This wasn't just a battle craze created by the Tathon hormones; there was a battle for supremacy raging here.

'Do not choose a side!' Praahs yelled as they stomped over a flattened barricade and the bodies of Ascent guards. 'They are *all* our enemy!'

Around her, the Cirratus sped forward and washed over the enemy: a tsunami of armoured cuttlefish, spearing with their metal-hard tentacles and leaping on fleeing soldiers, wrestling them to the ground.

Praahs' claws lengthened and her lips peeled back as she focussed on a bulky, white-headed soldier firing a blaster-cannon at a fast-moving group of bipeds riding quadrupeds. Noticing her army, the guard turned and fired at her. She dodged with ease and leaped in to clamp his torso between her dagger-tooth jaws, crunching through his toughened bones, feeling the life squeezed out of him. The Tathon didn't need this one, Praahs told herself, as she felt the creature's blood ooze down her throat.

Euryleia gripped her tocka tight with her thighs, feet and hands as they cut a tight corner. Her bow primed in her second pair of arms, she released her explosive arrow as the block of Ascent soldiers came into view. This bulk of enslaved soldiers the Ascent had mustered from the workhouses and night guard had been marched out of the Ascent leaders' inner sanctum nearest the tower's base to protect the last gateway. Heads and torsos nearby told Euryleia all she needed to know about the Ascent's rule of law.

She could feel that her tocka wanted to leap in to attack the phalanx of slave soldiers, but Euryleia guided it away, knowing the riders behind her would follow suit. As ever, Lavalle had other plans and had split his cohort to neutralise the Lutamek.

'We need more troops,' Euryleia told Cheng as they reached safety behind a long building, 'or we won't be able to get into the Ascent stronghold.'

'No news from Delta-Six?' Cheng asked.

Euryleia shook her head and felt that their grasp on the battle was slipping. The Ascent had been taken by surprise but were proving more resourceful than predicted.

'We need to get the pin mirrors to the slaves,' Sancha said as he peered around the corner.

'They won't let us get near enough,' Cheng replied.

'Then we need to go where we can get near,' Euryleia said and pointed to a tall building across an open plaza, where explosions suggested a battle was raging.

'Yes,' Sancha said. 'I see humans and Sorean. We just need to get across safely without–'

'Shit!' Cheng gasped. 'The Lutamek are back.'

Euryleia felt her pocket vibrate and remembered the device Delta-Six had given her. She saw several large bulks moving out of the Lutamek site. Had Lavalle stirred the hornets' nest?

'Quick, with me!' Euryleia ordered.

'Wait!' Sancha shouted.

Two seconds later, a wave of bizarre, shelled creatures like nothing Euryleia had seen before swept in from the farmland and smashed into the pockets of Ascent guards manning the

Ascent gateway. Among them she caught a glimpse of a long, serpentine beast and a Brakari-like soldier with a red rather than blue shell.

'They must be a rival faction,' Euryleia said, feeling her courage lift. 'Which means the Ascent are losing. Can you see any more coming?'

'No,' Sancha replied.

'Then we move! Guang, build me a light shield and let's go!'

Euryleia dug her heels in and her tocka leaped forward, followed by the rest. Streams of light swept past her as they rushed across the open stretch of ground, the tower and the newcomers on her right, their exit to the farms and desert on their left.

Halfway across the plaza and still invisible, Cheng shouted, 'What the hell are they?'

'Don't slow down!' Euryleia yelled back but allowed herself a quick glimpse back. Out towards the fields she saw a horde of new soldiers advancing in neat rows, ahead of a procession of three huge, shimmering blobs walking on thick tentacles. Their colours fluttered and flowed as they seemed to flicker in and out of view. Euryleia gasped for breath. No battle had ever been so disorientating. She forced herself to look ahead, where the group of humans Sancha had seen was taking up position around the building's entrance.

'Do not let the chemicals control you!' a robotic voice blasted from Euryleia's right, where the Lutamek strode out of their centre to form a protective semicircle. 'Resist your urge to fight unless absolutely necessary!'

'What do they mean?' Guang asked as they closed in on their allies by the scorched building.

'Mind games,' Cheng replied.

Euryleia recognised some of the humans in the pack ahead, so slung her bow over her shoulder and raised her arms in a peaceful pose. More soldiers were pouring out of the building – there had to be more than fifty and some had tocka. Among them, she saw a glowing figure floating several feet above the ground, flanked by two small Lutamek. Squinting, she recognised the samurai.

'You have come,' Isao said.

'We needed strength before attacking,' Euryleia explained.

'Your timing has coincided well with another advance,' Isao continued, the distant look in his eyes as disturbing as the way he floated. 'I felt their presence and they moved fast. But I do not know what course we should follow.'

'We need to fight!' Cheng said, turning his tocka around to face the battle between the new, shelled soldiers and the Ascent.

'Or we let them weaken each other?' Gal-qadan, the Mongol, said, standing almost naked. 'And fight the victors at the end?'

Euryleia gave him a look and realised some of the soldiers hadn't changed at all.

'I agree,' Olan, the Viking, said. 'We must regroup – find a fortification and wait.'

'But whoever wins will come for us next,' Sancha said. 'And I don't like the look of this new army.'

As he spoke, the bulky procession of huge creatures pushed into the main square, taking fire from groups of Ascent warriors who had come in from the opposite flank. Even the Lutamek opened fire on the new army, but the lines of soldiers in the vanguard – a myriad strange aliens, some of which Euryleia recognised from the dome – didn't return fire. Each shot was absorbed by an unseen force, which sparked around the advancing army as it pushed through single-storey buildings like an immense multicoloured slug devouring everything in its path.

'They are the Tathon,' Isao said, his eyes turning dark. 'From our dome. Hyper-evolved. Enemy or salvation, I can't tell.'

Euryleia watched in horror as tentacles from the three huge Tathon picked up dying soldiers from the battlefield and threw them into vats of steaming liquid, to then be dragged out by a set of tall, bony creatures and strapped into large grey machines pushed by a set of bulky beasts similar to the one Belsang had ridden during their battle.

'They revive and enhance new soldiers for their army,' Isao said.

'So none of us are safe?' Euryleia said, feeling the fear like never before.

John clutched his gun and paced around the cave entrance. He desperately wanted to fight but he was overwhelmed by the battle raging before him, across the Ascent city. The fighting rose and fell like a rough sea, with new groups of soldiers joining the melee, making it impossible to tell who was fighting who. An instinct made him reach for his gas-mask bag but his metal hand found nothing; his organic fingers found the tin soldier at his neck though.

Peronicus-Rax had returned and was ready to fight. 'Follow me to join the Lutamek,' he said.

'You obviously weren't with us in the desert,' Crossley replied, nodding at the metal behemoths, who were forming a defensive line around their encampment. 'We're not going anywhere near those bastards!'

'But we must fight!' a Korax said.

'They are our best fighters,' Yarcha added.

With a long sword in one hand and the battle rage in her eyes, John thought she looked like a different woman.

'But–' he started.

'You can't protect everyone, John,' Yarcha said, gripping his arm. 'Fight with us or fight here, we must survive.'

'Yes, but…' John looked back down into the dark chambers of the mine.

Yarcha released his arm and the group of fighters left with Peronicus-Rax for the Lutamek enclosure. A rush of movement made John turn as Lavalle rode up on his tocka, his coal-black armour scorched with white battle scars.

'We have spare tocka for you to join us,' Lavalle shouted to the crowd, who remained with John. 'We must mount an attack on the leaders before they re-strengthen!'

A dozen alien soldiers and the remaining Sorean stepped forward and leaped onto vacant tocka, unclipping weapons from their sides. John moved backwards into the crowd, avoiding Lavalle's eyes. Although his body told him to fight, John's mind was still questioning why. He turned to run, wanting only some peace from the battle, and found Crossley staring at him.

'You thinking what I'm thinking?'

'Err… yep,' John said with a nod.

'Damn right!' the American replied and slapped John on the shoulder. 'Come on, let's go and get some.' He ushered John along. 'Don't worry, the guards are all dead. I figured we could easily set up a mortar and use the entrance for protection.'

'Yeah,' John said, happy to go along with any plan that involved being sheltered.

He wanted to get somewhere safe, even if it meant walking back into what had been his prison.

'But who will we fire at?' John asked, checking the gun was still in his belt.

'Anyone we see our guys fighting against, I guess.'

The lights were still working in the cave, which was littered with the bodies of guards and miners who had lost their lives in the escape. Crossley stepped over them, searching for weapons as he passed, but John only had eyes for the dead. Back in this fetid air, his thoughts seemed clearer, if less positive.

'What are we fighting for?' he asked when they passed Falen's deconstructed body. Limbs lay like forgotten bones around her glass-eyed head.

'The same as before,' Crossley answered without stopping. 'We fight for our allies and to stay alive.'

John closed his eyes and saw little Joe. He remembered Rosie's smile and felt his eyes water.

'I've hardly thought about them,' he said.

'What?'

'I've hardly thought about them,' he said, swallowing. 'You know, my family... Rosie and Joe... they were my reason to survive, during my war.'

'That's hardly surprising,' Crossley replied. 'Come on.' He beckoned John down a shaft he hadn't been down before. 'It's different now you found out they're long gone, right?'

John remembered his conversation with Li and everything she had told him about Joe, who had grown up an orphan and fought in Crossley's war. He'd survived, had children and died at a ripe old age.

'Yes, but Rosie's always been gone, I–'

'They were linked to you,' Crossley said as he pulled open a rusted metal door to reveal a set of shelves cut into the rock, each filled with explosive charges, 'and to each other,' he continued. 'You fought for Joe so you could fight for Rosie, right?'

He handed John charges, loading them up in his arms.

'But now they've both definitely gone and you can't get home. You can't fight for any of them, can you?'

'No, I suppose I can fight for vengeance, but...' John remembered what had powered his anger during the battle against the Brakari. His knees felt weak. 'But it's too much. How can we find out the truth here? How can we find who brought us here when all these battles for power are kicking off?'

'If they destroy the tower we're really screwed,' Crossley said, and flicked his head for them to start walking back to the main cavern.

John followed and thought about his time at the tower and with the lock. The darkened glass and the obelisk within. They were walking through a cave he recognised, weaving round the scattered shaft pits dug into the ground.

'That's it!' John said. 'Enter to complete your path of ascendancy... that's what it said on the obelisk inside the tower.'

'Yeah, sure,' Crossley said, walking ahead. 'But how does that help?'

'We need to protect the tower!' John said as they passed through the section he used to mine. 'Are these safe if you drop them?' he asked.

'Yeah, they're not primed so... shit, no!'

John stopped by his old shaft and let his hoard of tubular-shaped explosives tumble down. He listened to them rattle and thump their way down the spiral staircase that Yam-mit, the Korax, had built for their first escape attempt.

'We needed those!' Crossley shouted.

'We'll be more use defending the tower, believe me!' John said and waited for Crossley to follow suit. 'We need to grab more weapons.'

'Jeez, you Limeys are crazy,' Crossley said and shook his head as his armful of explosives dropped down the hole. 'This better be a good plan,' he muttered as he thrust a rocket launcher into John's arms.

'We need to protect the tower, right?' John said as they

descended the spiral stairs and emerged into the chambers below, where the failed escape had taken place. It all looked the same, apart from some cracks John could have sworn weren't there before.

'I get it,' Crossley replied, keeping up with John. 'You know a way out that leads to the tower.'

'Well, sort of,' John said. 'The guards had a way in here somewhere and they're–'

'Shh.' Crossley raised his hand, turning to point. 'Someone's coming,' he whispered.

'No, someone's already here!' a voice boomed behind them.

John dropped his rocket launcher, sending a clattering crash echoing around the caves.

'Das and Pod?' Crossley said and smiled at the tiny, scaly mammals. 'Good to see you guys! How did you survive? You were with Gal-qadan's troops, right?'

'Looks like you had the same idea as us,' Das said. 'Cut round the back?'

'No,' John said, 'we're trying to get out. To protect the tower.'

'What do you mean "round the back"?' Crossley asked. 'We're not Ascent. Who are you fighting for?'

A group of soldiers John didn't recognise appeared behind Das and Pod.

'Where next, masters?' a strange, three-eyed amphibian asked.

Das pointed towards where John and Crossley had come from and the troops tramped off in single file.

'You.' Pod selected a soldier, then another. 'Take these prisoners – action one, five, six.'

'Yes, master,' a fox-like soldier in a long white robe replied and moved towards John and Crossley.

'Listen,' Crossley said as the Firstborn soldier checked him for weapons. 'We haven't picked sides… we were prisoners of the Ascent. We're just defending the tower.'

'We should *all* be defending the tower!' John said. 'A new army's here and we must join forces.'

Das scampered over to John. In any other circumstances, John would have considered him cute.

'Listen, human,' Das said, 'your meddling has brought this upon us. We allowed your questions and gave you the chance to fulfil your ancestors' inquisitive nature by climbing to your dome cap, but in doing so you have risked every life on the disc. This new army, these Tathon, were created by you!'

'Das, we don't have time for this,' Pod said, as a shudder shook the cave, shaking dust and flakes of stone from the ceiling.

Crossley was softly coughing as the last soldiers climbed up the steps, leaving the last two with them.

'Yes, very little time,' Das replied and pointed to the cave where Samas had died. 'Action one, five, six,' he ordered and scampered down a different passageway, with Pod behind him.

'Where are they going?' Crossley asked as the two soldiers advanced on them.

John felt cold sweat under his armpits and his cheeks burned. He stepped back and slipped on one of the explosive cartridges but kept his footing. Crossley did the same, sending the tube rolling to the wall, then kicked another to join it.

'You can't just kill us, okay?' Crossley said to the grimacing soldiers, who raised their shoulder rifles.

'Against the wall,' the second soldier, a rotund toad of a creature, growled and pressed buttons on its weapon.

John reached for an explosive on the floor but Crossley shook his head.

'It's okay,' he whispered.

They backed towards the wall that Samas, Yam-mit and

Rar-kin had been entombed in. John felt his heels scrape the wall behind them and, to his surprise, he felt a wave of relief.

It was over.

Finally, he could rest. He could join Rosie and Joe. He felt his shoulders relax and pictured Rosie with young Joe as he remembered the boy. It had never happened in real life of course – she had barely seen the baby before she died – but that was how John liked to remember them: together; waiting for him.

The soldiers aimed their weapons. John breathed in. Crossley coughed and the cave disappeared in a deafening explosion of smoke and pure white light.

Chapter 22

In the shadow of the arena, Euryleia spotted a crowd of soldiers at the mouth of a cave, staring around like lost children. A group of tocka had just left them and now skirted the edge of the open ground towards the Lutamek's encampment. Lavalle's obsidian armour stood out on the lead tocka and she felt drawn to him. She felt the urge to protect him, to talk to him.

'They've opened up the Ascent's inner wall,' Olan said with a shake of his head.

'And they're absorbing everyone in their path,' Sancha added.

Euryleia saw the pattern in the Tathon army's attack: the spearhead; the strongest troops on the wing taking out any resistance; the weaker soldiers mopping up the injured. It was like the shield walls Olan had mentioned where the young and old walked behind, despatching injured enemies. Only here, the injured soldiers were captured and processed through various machines and liquids.

'They'll be after us next,' Cheng said.

'What happens to the soldiers they take?' Euryleia asked Sancha, trusting his keen eyes.

'They're still alive… but different,' he said, squinting.

'The Tathon are making them their own,' Gal-qadan said with what Euryleia recognised as a look of admiration.

'Which is a trap I don't intend to fall into,' Euryleia said. 'It looks like we have a simple choice,' the men looked to her, 'we either fight now,' she aimed her bow tip at the Tathon leaders, 'or unite with stronger forces.' Her bow swung to Lavalle and the Lutamek, who stood in a protective semicircle around their compound.

'Not those bastards,' Olan said.

'They only did what we would have done,' Gal-qadan replied.

'You, maybe,' Olan replied, 'but I don't turn on my allies.'

'Even for your own family?' Cheng asked.

Olan looked away. 'That's not a decision I'm likely to make here.'

'All they have here is family,' Isao said, still floating above the soldiers in an orange haze, with the young Lutamek.

'Is that what your new friends told you?' Cheng asked with a long glare.

'Yes,' Isao replied calmly, 'but they recently changed their priorities.'

'How so?' Sancha asked.

'I changed their thought patterns,' Isao said.

Euryleia looked at the young Lutamek, then at Lavalle. She turned her tocka towards him. 'I will always choose family,' she said, then shouted to her men, 'Follow me or fight: you choose.'

She took off without looking back. The silent hooves of her tocka threw up clouds of dust as she cut the corner of the plaza. She caught a glimpse of movement in her peripheral vision and instinctively armed and aimed both bows. A group of shelled creatures were rolling towards her like a landslide. Whoever they were, they were enemy. She wheeled the tocka round to

face them and fired: an explosive arrow at the centre; two of
Bowman's wild arrows into the sky; three metal dart tips at
the front-runners. Each hit its mark. In twenty fast seconds,
Euryleia had slowed their advance and was wheeling around
for another attack when a bolt of white light ripped from the
sky, tearing a scar in the ground. Euryleia's group had joined
her, with Isao and the Lutamek floating overhead.

'Cross this line and you shall die,' Isao bellowed, catching the
attention of two of the larger soldiers fighting in the distance.

One shelled creature scrambled to the scar in the dirt and
Euryleia fired an arrow into its shell. Seemingly uninjured,
it paused before leaping forward, then exploded in the air,
sending shattered shell and gizzards across the ground. Euryleia
didn't have time for this, so turned her tocka and continued
towards Lavalle and the Lutamek, her platoon following her.
Even Isao had followed her, suggesting his line in the sand
would hold.

'We need to regroup!' Euryleia shouted as she approached
the long line of huge robots defending the compound.

'Agreed,' a Lutamek in the guard wall replied.

'But if you betray us again, I will personally tear you apart
and burn your organs.'

'Strong words for a human,' Ten-ten said, walking through
the defensive line.

A blue light flashed.

'You have no right to scan me!' she shouted as Lavalle rode
over to her.

'Your biochemistry has changed,' Ten-ten said, 'along with
your morphology.'

'Let them in,' Lavalle said, rushing forward. 'We need
everyone behind the Lutamek.'

'Yes,' Ten-ten said as Isao floated to the ground, flanked by

the two young Lutamek. 'We need to look after our offspring.'
The Lutamek turned to Lavalle. 'As do you.'

'What?' Lavalle said, confused. His head snapped to Euryleia.
'You're...?'

Euryleia sat up straight and glared back. She hadn't wanted
to do this in public, but she could use it to their advantage.

'It gives us more reason to survive this battle,' she said,
resisting the urge to place a protective palm on her belly. 'Now
tell me what you've got planned – are we going to attack the
leaders or wait here for them to attack us?'

'Neither,' Ten-ten replied, gesturing to the battle.

Euryleia turned to see the smoke and more explosions as
the battle raged on. The Tathon soldiers had moved ahead,
sweeping away all Ascent and Firstborn resistance and
absorbing attacks from Dakaniha's platoon on the other flank.
As they cleared a path, the three giant Tathon leaders glided
through unmolested.

'They're heading for the tower,' Olan said.

'And they've stopped selecting soldiers,' Sancha added.

'The tower is the centre of the disc,' Ten-ten said. 'It's the
natural destination for all victors.'

'And they will try to unlock it,' Isao said as a tremor shook
the ground.

Euryleia's tocka sidestepped to keep its balance, taking her
closer to Lavalle, who glanced at her. She looked away, not
wanting to talk about the baby, concentrating on Ten-ten's
conversation with Isao instead.

'There are changes in the alternate-matter reservoir,' Ten-
ten said. 'What do you sense?'

'The Tathon are drawing energy from it,' Isao replied. 'It
will restabilise if given time but, if it doesn't, the tidal strength
will increase.'

'What does that mean?' Euryleia asked.

'We need to stop them if we are to survive on this world,' a Lutamek answered.

'Then we must pool our resources and attack!' Lavalle said.

'Interesting,' Ten-ten said. 'When you entered our compound, you were all sprayed with an agent to counteract the Tathon's pheromone attack, yet you still wish to fight despite the odds.'

'What pheromones?' Cheng asked.

'The Tathon sent a cocktail of chemical triggers ahead of their attack, designed to disturb the army's thought processes and encourage them to fight.'

'But that doesn't mean we shouldn't fight,' Euryleia said. 'We can still trust our instincts.'

A series of deep thuds made the group turn to where the three Tathon leaders had breached the final Ascent barrier. A hairy alien was wrapped in one of the Tathon's long tentacles, while another had absorbed a stick-like creature into its jelly-like body.

'They have the Ascent leaders. Time is short,' Ten-ten said. 'We must decide whether to fight or escape.'

'How can we escape?' Euryleia asked.

'We have ships–' Ten-ten started.

'I don't think we have a choice,' Gal-qadan said, pointing to Isao's line in the ground, where two large creatures now joined the waiting shelled army.

'General Panzicosta,' Euryleia said, recognising the Brakari despite his colour change.

She thought of John and the pain this creature had caused him, and reached for her bow.

'And he's dragged up something from the ocean,' Sancha added.

Euryleia looked up at Isao and to the Lutamek guards, but

they did nothing as the two large beasts strode across Isao's line, bringing the small, shelled Tathon with them.

John came to, lying on the chalky floor of the mine, covered in dust and fist-sized lumps of rock. He sat up, sending debris rolling off him. He was alone, his ears were ringing and he was covered in lumps of some sticky substance. He probed the goo with his robotic forefinger and an odd sensation ran down his back. John chewed the saliva in his mouth – he could *taste* blood. That's what it was – iron-rich alien blood. Not his own.

John took a deep breath and pushed up onto his feet. A pile of stones nearby moved and he saw Crossley's bloodied hand.

'Crossley!' John tried to speak but heard nothing as he stumbled forward to help his friend out. 'What happened?' he asked when their eyes met, his ears still ringing.

Touching a cut on his forehead, Crossley mouthed something: *more hour fool than I ought?*

'What?'

Movement made John turn but there was nothing there. Just his jumpy nerves. He could hear strange scratching, tapping sounds now.

John had to concentrate on Crossley's lips, but he could just about make him out now. 'I said, more powerful than I thought.'

Alien blood was spread across the rock walls and there was no sign of the Firstborn guards.

The penny dropped.

'You didn't?' John asked.

His hearing was coming back as a rumble shook more stones from the roof and walls.

Crossley looked sheepish. 'I thought I'd trigger the

explosives remotely,' he said with a smile. 'Had to prime them first, obviously.'

'Obviously,' John replied as flakes of stone crumbled off the wall beside them. 'We have to get out of here,' he said. 'Get the weapons and explosives and defend the tower.'

He could hear more rocks falling behind them. Looking for a way out as he helped Crossley up, he squinted at a series of holes in the lava wall, bodies lying in the rubble.

'Oh my…' John said and grabbed Crossley, turning him around.

'How the fu–'

'Just like the tocka,' John said. 'The blood must have brought them back.'

'Water,' one of the shapes croaked and John rushed forward. Samas looked up at him, covered in dust.

Isao floated higher to get a better view of the ever-expanding gathering of soldiers seeking shelter in the Lutamek compound. They came from various warring sides, all avoiding the Tathon onslaught. Dakaniha had brought his cavalry to safety as well as Millok, with her Scion of Brakari, who told stories of how the Tathon had broken free of the dome and consumed everything in their path. Beside them, Firstborn and Ascent stood side by side for the first time in an age. All leaderless and facing a singular threat.

Isao had always been able to detach his thoughts from his emotions but, since his immersion in the shadow matter beneath the tower, he had felt less emotional. Since healing the young Lutamek, he'd made changes to the robots with a cold eye, knowing it was for everyone's benefit, making them less isolationist. He had tried the same trick on the Tathon leaders, but their subterranean fungal links to the shadow matter created a form of barrier he couldn't break.

Isao focussed on the turmoil tearing through the Ascent city and on the waves he felt rushing through the deep shadow matter, creating tremors across the disc. He focussed on the three Tathon leaders and phased between worlds, observing the true nature of their bodies. Their main oversized jellyfish–octopus bodies projected masses of translucent hyphae in every direction, wafting in the air, releasing potent chemicals, grabbing soldiers and delving deep into the ground, where they stirred the shadow matter. Some strings broke away to delve independently. Many fizzled out but some returned to their host body. This was how they'd undermined the dome shell before shattering it.

Isao felt a sense of weakness wash over him as the shadow matter that powered him ebbed away. The Tathon leaders were pooling and diverting around the tower. One had fixed itself to the base of the tower and pulsed a rainbow of flowing colours. The other two took a flank and absorbed attacks from the factions on the other side of the tower. When one Tathon reached the Platae flatworms, it absorbed them in a thick protrusion, then spat them out renewed and recharged. Now the Platae hurled themselves at the tower with greater fury than before, tarnishing the tower surface with acid.

A tickling sensation ran through Isao as Panzicosta and his small army crossed the mark in the ground.

'Now it's our turn to draw the line,' Panzicosta growled, flicking his shelled head at an equally large and vicious-looking creature beside him.

'Cirratus, form wall,' the serpentine beast hissed and the shelled octopi that had attacked Euryleia rolled and hopped to create a curved line between the Lutamek front line and the tower. Behind, myriad soldiers who'd been turned by the

Tathon lined up in defensive positions. They were defending the Tathon leaders.

'Defend all you like, but you've missed some of our army!' Lavalle shouted at Panzicosta with a hearty laugh.

Panzicosta and his companion twisted sharply, searching for enemy soldiers, their gazes locking on a distant shape.

'Is that a Lutamek?' Olan asked.

'Negative,' Ten-ten replied.

'But it looks like one,' Sancha said.

'They call him Troy,' Millok said as the huge armour-plated humanoid jogged into the Ascent city, towards the Tathon army's rear, leaving a trail of grey smoke in its wake. Nearby, Isao saw a flash of movement and recognised Althorn.

'I didn't mean that one,' Lavalle's deep voice cut through the chatter, 'I meant him.'

Isao followed the knight's armoured finger to where the gnarled and giant tree shape of Mata leaped from an Ascent building, onto the back of one of the Tathon leaders.

Isao moved forward and, through his shadow eyes, studied the Brakari and his large ally and saw energy blockages much like those he'd fixed in the Lutamek, only these were blue and had a vibrating frequency linking them to the Tathon.

'I can help you both,' Isao said, hovering above Panzicosta.

'Are you telling me I don't have to fight, human?' Panzicosta spoke sharply and clacked his shell.

Isao felt another wave surge through the shadow matter beneath the ground. Time was short.

'No,' Isao said. 'I'm offering you the same thing I offered the young Lutamek.'

'We won't accept your peace,' Panzicosta said, rising up on his back legs. 'I've promised Praahs the sweet taste of human flesh, and I never break my promises.'

'I do offer you peace,' Isao replied, dodging a barbed dart

fired in his direction. 'Peace of mind and freedom from your constraints.'

Isao switched more of his body to the shadow world and reached out with delicate tendrils into both creatures, to untie the blue knots, but a jolt of energy flashed through them, sending Isao reeling back.

What do you want with our subjects? a hollow voice echoed around Isao's mind.

They deserve freedom, Isao replied, turning to the three Tathon leaders, whose hive mind talked to him.

They are ours. We made them.

Isao reached out to the Tathon this time, stretching across the remaining section of the destroyed city to the tower base, where they pulsed and writhed. He sought patches of energy he could divert, something he could manipulate to stop these single-minded creatures from destroying their world.

Destruction is inevitable, came the voice again, reading Isao's thoughts. *We are untouchable and death inescapable.*

All true, Isao replied. *So why not release those who have served you well?*

While he waited for a response, Isao hoped his plan would work. Surely these two would turn on their former masters if released?

So be it, came the reply. *Our work is nearly done. We have no use for them. But they will always be in our debt.*

Isao closed the communication down and returned fully to the normal world. The whole conversation had taken less than a second.

'You are released,' the samurai said and watched as the blue patches within the large warriors stopped pulsing and faded away.

'What is this trickery?' Praahs said, looking at Panzicosta.

'Not to be trusted,' Panzicosta replied, keeping various eyes fixed on Isao. 'There is always a price, is there not?'

'You are no longer needed,' Isao said. 'But you now owe the Tathon a debt.'

'What?' the red Brakari roared. 'We owe a freedom debt to those who enslaved us?'

'Of course,' Isao replied, sensing a boost to Panzicosta's emotions – he *had* been freed. Just one push and he would turn on the Tathon. 'But you will never owe a debt to the dead.'

'Yes, we should kill them,' Praahs said, turning to the tower and the three large Tathon.

'Clear the debt now?' Panzicosta replied. 'No, we wait until they are weak…'

Isao left them to it and returned to the Lutamek compound.

'They will not fight us,' Isao told the waiting army.

'Well done,' Euryleia replied.

Isao watched a Lutamek in the distance he hadn't seen before. 'Who is that?' he asked the two young Lutamek.

'It is Alpha,' Ten-ten replied for them.

Isao felt a flood of annoyance wash over the young Lutamek and sent a wave of energy to soothe them.

'Alpha requires assistance,' Isao said and floated towards the strange Lutamek, whose energy signals mimicked a mishmash of the other robots'. It was weaker, with a full set of inhibitors distributed across its conduits. 'What has been done to it?'

'It's our ancestor,' a white Lutamek with blue stripes said.

'He won't understand, Nine-four,' Ten-ten said.

'I can fix it,' Isao said.

'Alpha was organic. It will take time to adapt to its transformation.'

Isao saw a flash of yellow within Alpha and recognised it. 'Alpha was the Velluta?' he asked, remembering the creature that had been in the cell next to him after Ten-ten had captured him. 'You didn't sacrifice it?'

'We honour the Velluta with our bodies,' Ten-ten replied. 'We gave it immortality and strength.'

'Or an eternal life of torture,' Isao said and floated over to push a wave of energy through Alpha to wash away its pain.

'Don't disrupt the programming!' Nine-four shouted and fired its arm-laser at Isao.

The pulse passed through Isao and he tilted his head to study Nine-four, then sent a wave of shadow matter back to cleanse its priority matrix. At the same time, another tremor shook the world.

Isao concentrated on the swirling mass beneath the bedrock. The shadow-energy container had been breached and was leaking. It was too late. The Tathon had won.

John scrambled up a bank of fallen rocks lit a ghostly blue by a bubble Yam-mit had formed with his antennae.

'Are you sure they went this way?' John asked, picturing Das and Pod scrambling down the tunnel.

'I can smell them,' Yam-mit replied, holding an insectoid claw out for John to grip.

'Thanks.'

'We should have brought more explosives,' Crossley said, looking down the narrow tunnel.

'Let's concentrate on water,' Samas replied as he climbed over the rise. 'My head is aching.'

'And mine,' Rar-kin said. 'But the chances of finding a natural aquifer are—'

'Yes, thank you,' Samas replied.

'If Das and Pod went this way there must be a way out,' John said. 'So let's keep moving.'

Further down the cave, the rough edges were replaced by smooth walls.

'They look machine-drilled,' Rar-kin said.

Crossley coughed and said, 'It seems old.'

'And they went this way,' Yam-mit said, pointing right before anyone asked.

'But there was light down the other tunnel,' John said, squinting at what he was sure was the exit.

'This way!' Samas ordered.

John sighed and followed as their tunnel descended to a set of neatly cut steps and, at their base, a metal-lined room.

'What on Earth?' John said, staring in wonder.

It reminded him of the buildings in the dome cap, but much smaller, with five doors, giving each soldier a thick window to peer through.

Crossley was coughing.

'What do you see?' Samas asked.

'The rooms on the other side are metal boxes,' Crossley replied, 'completely encased in the living rock.'

'Your thoughts, Rar-kin?' Samas asked.

'A place of safety,' Rar-kin replied.

'And we can't get in,' Crossley said.

John saw a flash of brown scales through his window and gasped, 'They're in here!'

He pressed buttons on the door but they flashed impotently and set off new lights on the other side of the door.

'Give me a go,' Crossley said, pushing in.

A crackle came from the ceiling, then a voice spoke.

'I'm not sure how you survived... any of you, but it's too late.' It was Das.

Crossley stopped what he was doing.

'The units are all occupied,' Das continued. 'So if you want to live I suggest you find one of the sample ships and strap in.'

John could hear Pod chatting in the background. 'We're finally getting off this place,' he said. 'Come on, brother!'

'Good luck,' Das said and the voice cut out.

'That's it?' Crossley said and thumped the window. 'That's all you've got, you pair of bloody armadillos? Seriously?'

'Maybe they're correct?' Rar-kin said.

'We should find shelter,' Yam-mit said.

'And water,' Samas said and led them back out.

'But we need to protect the tower!' John shouted, from the back of the group.

'Listen,' Crossley stopped and spoke softly, 'if those guys are sitting in a bunker, something big is about to happen, right?'

'Yes, but…' John looked away. They had to do something other than run.

'Let's just get somewhere safe,' Crossley said as another tremor shook the cave.

John wanted to say how they could fight together – how they were stronger together – but he saved his breath as they toured back up through the caves to the branching tunnel where John had seen the light. The air felt fresh as they climbed back up towards the sound of battle.

'We're nearly there!' Samas shouted as they scrambled up.

John saw orange lights ahead as the tunnel narrowed and twisted until they squeezed into a small room that felt like a tiny church.

'I'll have these!' Crossley said, grabbing weapons from an altar-like rock.

John stared at a sculpture of Das and Pod, with the sign 'Revere the Firstborn' carved above it, and shook his head.

'Come on!' Samas shouted, beckoning from some steps, where he barged a metal door open with his shoulder, flooding the room with light.

Pistol gripped in his metal hand, John held his good arm over his eyes as they crept forward, until his eyes adjusted to a view he recognised instantly.

'We're in no-man's-land,' he said, remembering the shock he'd received when he was rejected by the lock in the tower.

'And we aren't the only ones,' Crossley said.

Three huge, octopus-like creatures pulsed with colours as they pummelled and squeezed the tower base, surrounded by a white glow which shimmered with explosions from missiles attacking them from the other side of the tower. Something about how they moved reminded John of a species he'd seen before but he couldn't place it.

'These are a new enemy. Not the Ascent,' Yam-mit said.

John shook his head. 'Are they who Das and Pod called the Tathon?'

'Wait,' Crossley said, 'weren't they the guys who were brought into our dome when we were in the cap? Delta-Six did something, didn't he?'

John remembered the aliens on the live video screens and Delta-Six cutting the mission short, the panic in his eyes.

'That arrogant bastard created these monsters?' Crossley asked.

'It's not possible,' Samas said. 'These,' he pointed at the immense blobs of fading and pulsating colour, 'were created by whoever brought us here, not by us.'

John nodded and watched the group of Platae, who were working at twice the rate he'd seen when he was at the lock, and the nearest Tathon, whose probing tentacles scoured the glass tower, leaving liquid trails in its wake.

'Look!' Crossley shouted.

John turned to the city and caught a glimpse of green on a rooftop. Mata, swollen and covered in thick bark, ran and jumped at the Tathon.

'We should stop him!' Rar-kin said, taking a step forward. 'The odds are—'

'I don't care what the odds are,' Crossley replied. 'Nobody's stopping him.'

The five stood and watched in awe as Mata leaped at the Tathon farthest from them. His leaves and branches fluttered as he glided through the air and smashed straight into one of the Tathon leaders.

'Woah!' Crossley shouted as Mata sunk straight into the Tathon's body.

Spikes struck out from Mata's body, holding him in the centre of the jellied mass, and vines lashed out from his back, tearing at the tentacles, cutting them or prising them off the tower.

'He won't survive,' Rar-kin said.

'He has to,' Samas replied. 'And we must help him.'

'How?' Crossley replied.

'Follow me,' Samas said and jogged out into no-man's-land.

John ran, watching the ground for pitfalls, and spotted a shape on the ground, twenty steps ahead. A broken human body. The shade of grey of the suit told him all he needed to know.

'Delta-Six?' he whispered.

Samas rushed to their fallen comrade's body and checked him for signs of life. John kept back, staring at the broken body in disbelief, until Samas looked up and shook his head.

'He's dead.'

'Must have taken a few enemy with him,' John said, staring at his scorched suit.

'I take back what I said,' Crossley said, laying a hand on Delta-Six's shoulder. 'You were a mean bastard, my friend.'

Rar-kin said, 'We need to attack now.'

Samas picked up Delta-Six's rifle and shouted, 'With me!'

He fired at the Tathon struggling with Mata, and John joined in, firing his brown laser pistol. Pulses of energy peppered and cut the Tathon. Yam-mit sent a ball of energy at the nearest tentacle, shocking it and loosening its grip. Then an earthquake shook, sending foot-wide cracks splintering out from the tower's base.

'Keep firing!' John shouted.

'If this tower collapses, we need to get clear,' Samas shouted over the weapon fire.

'You think?' Crossley stared at the Babylonian. 'If that thing falls we need to be twenty clicks away!'

'I calculate fourteen of your Earth miles would be sufficient,' Rar-kin said, before firing its weapon with a look of manic glee.

Crossley laughed and ruffled the Sorean's shoulder hair.

John fired again, picking off the tentacles that were bending back to attack Mata. He imagined the corkscrew bullets he used to fire with his gun-arm and the blunt-headed smashers. He missed having that connection with his weapon.

With a piercing scream, the Tathon slowly peeled off the tower and fell to the ground, smothering Mata, who fought on with wild vines and roots that drained the Tathon of liquid.

'Now we need shelter,' Samas said, scouring the nearest buildings.

'Over there,' Yam-mit said, pointing to the Lutamek compound.

John saw the line of Lutamek soldiers facing off against a horde of giant shellfish and the rest of the Tathon's army. Behind the robots, a swathe of warriors milled about, some on tocka.

'Are the Lutamek protecting them?' John asked.

'I wouldn't trust them as far as I could throw them,' Crossley said.

'But it's safer than being here,' Samas said.

'We have little choice,' Yam-mit added.

Crossley was coughing and turning circles. Finally he looked up and said, 'Listen, guys, I think we need to move. I'm seeing some strange stuff down there.'

Another tremor backed him up.

'Let's go,' Samas said, leading them away from the tower.

'Better the devil you know, hey?' Crossley said.

John gave a nod and looked back to where the dead jellied mass of the Tathon leader sat, with Mata crouched in the centre. The Maori stood up, liquid pouring off his trunk and branches as he bellowed a primal victory roar.

'And what of our adaptations?' Gal-qadan asked the Lutamek. 'Were they natural?'

He didn't really want to know, but wanted to distract the metal giants. Unlike the rest of the human army, he had nothing against them – it was Das and Pod who had betrayed him.

'No, not natural,' the Lutamek replied. 'From what One-eight-seven tells us of the dome cap, the Synchronisers created a genetic malleability in each of us, so adaptations would arise when stimulated, whereas the Tathon are able to *choose* the physical change required.'

Gal-qadan sneered and looked back to where the Lutamek's stash of starships sat in neat rows, then at the Lutamek. Both were similar – empty metal hulks that could help him escape this hellhole.

'We could defeat them,' Olan said to Ten-ten, 'now Panzicosta won't fight.'

'But the tiny Tathon still hold the line,' Millok, the Brakari, said.

Gal-qadan eyed the shelled beasts and the two large alien warriors behind them. From what Isao had said, they were free of their Tathon masters and weighing up their revenge, but Gal-qadan knew it was too late for that. Proving him right, another tremor shook the world, sending the immense tower swaying and forming hairline fractures in the rocky ground.

Gal-qadan made his mind up: it was time to leave.

'Stay where you are!' Ten-ten yelled as Gal-qadan walked over to Panzicosta.

'Hey, old Brakari!' Gal-qadan yelled. 'Our time here is limited.'

Panzicosta and the serpentine warrior swished round to face him.

'Just enough time for one last fight,' Gal-qadan continued. 'To prove your worth.'

'You come to fight *us*, human?' Panzicosta growled. 'Because Praahs would swallow you whole, you metal mouthful, and shit you out the other end.'

'My teeth are stronger than you think,' Praahs replied, revealing several rows of knife-like incisors.

Gal-qadan felt the ground shake beneath his feet again and kept his eyes fixed on the alien warriors. The shelled creatures in between them were brainless foot soldiers, but he didn't want to get too close.

'I have come with an offer,' Gal-qadan replied, lowering his voice. 'I will let you join me.'

'Ha!' Panzicosta replied and his red shell pieces clacked like thunder. 'Your army must be weak if this is all you can offer us.'

'No,' Gal-qadan replied, 'I speak for myself. You and your companion can join *me*.'

'Why would we do that?' Praahs replied.

361

Gal-qadan nodded towards the starships the Lutamek had hidden away.

'Do we not have a debt to settle first?' Panzicosta said and started to turn.

'Not today,' Gal-qadan replied. 'Today we survive. Then we form a new army – one which will spring from the ashes of this world.'

He pointed to where Mata stood in the destroyed body of the Tathon leader. 'Victory will come.'

'To those who are patient,' Praahs added.

The creature's response surprised Gal-qadan and an equally shocking idea came to him. Strange, he thought, but these two could be his equals. Combined, they could achieve great things.

'Shall we fight or will you walk away now?' Panzicosta asked. 'Your noise is getting annoying.'

Gal-qadan laughed and glanced back at the Lutamek, then checked the starships in the distance. Praahs was on his side and Panzicosta would follow, but first Gal-qadan needed one more thing.

'The disc has started to break apart,' Isao told the group of leaders, who stood in a circle outside the doors to the Lutamek laboratory and prison.

John wondered what had happened to the samurai to give him such amazing powers and stared at his glowing body, floating several feet off the ground.

'And the disc's gravity?' a Lutamek asked.

'It is reducing,' Isao replied. 'The shadow matter is leaking through the disc's underside into the vacuum beyond, dissipating its power.'

'How do you even know that, I mean–' Crossley was

stopped by a flash of white light from Isao's fingertips. He looked down and coughed, then stumbled back. 'Woah, the whole structure is crumbling.'

'It reminds me of what Li told me of my country's future,' Samas said. 'Of the Macedonian, Alexander, and how he solved the riddle of the Gordian Knot of Phrygia.'

'We all know that story,' Crossley said. 'But what's that got to do with giant aliens destroying a whole world?'

John touched the American's shoulder to quieten him. 'Go on,' he said to Samas.

'This tower,' Samas continued, 'this land,' he stretched an arm out, 'is the knot. Whoever works out the solution has the power to rule, like Alexander did.'

'And the answer,' Ten-ten asked, 'to how this Alexander untied the knot?'

'He chopped it in half,' Crossley said with a smirk.

Samas nodded. 'Rather than solve the problem, he destroyed it.'

'If this world is destroyed what becomes of us?' Lavalle asked, with a glance at Euryleia.

'We have ships,' Ten-ten said. 'Recovered from the nearest domes and adapted for our use.'

'You were planning on leaving?' Samas asked.

'Not before we discovered a way to breach the security system which keeps the circling ships from entering.'

John looked into the clear sky and saw one of the lights he'd often spotted zipping across.

'But just in case, hey?' Crossley said.

Ten-ten ignored him. 'Each ship requires a Lutamek pilot.'

'Convenient,' Crossley said, raising an eyebrow at John.

'The ships have integrated communications systems and can be loaded with food for each species,' Ten-ten said as three Lutamek strode off, following an unheard order.

John saw other Lutamek inside their compound, disconnecting devices and packing large metal crates with bottles and boxes.

'Then we should make good our escape,' Samas said.

John tiptoed to get a better view of the distant grey hulks and could see humanoid shapes already at the ships, along with a small Lutamek and two large creatures he recognised instantly.

'Shit! Panzicosta!' he shouted. 'Look – they're stealing a ship.'

Seeing the Brakari who had tortured and fought him sent panic rising in John's chest.

'They won't get far without a Lutamek,' Lavalle replied.

'One-eight-seven is with them,' Sancha said, 'and a host of other soldiers.'

John was shocked. How had Gal-qadan managed to get One-eight-seven on his side?

'Not the shelled guard though,' Euryleia said and John turned to where the line of smaller Tathon still held strong.

'It is inconsequential,' Ten-ten said. 'There are plenty of ships remaining.'

A deep, booming sound like a distant barrage of artillery made John turn to the tower in time to see a giant crack split the rock it was imbedded in. White lines cracked across the glass of the tower, like shattered ice. Everyone backed away and some were already running for the ships.

'Split into groups!' Samas shouted.

John looked for Crossley and they jogged away together.

'Those bastards on the tocka will get there first,' Crossley said.

'We've just got to get somewhere safe,' John said. 'Get into the sky and away from the tower.'

'Sure,' Crossley replied. 'But I still don't trust the Lutamek. Where's Isao?'

John searched for the samurai and found his glowing colour, floating away from the ships. 'He's with the two young Lutamek.'

'Okay,' Crossley said, 'we need a robot, so our best bet is that new one – Alpha. Hopefully they've set a ship up for it to fly.'

'Right,' John replied, searching for the smaller Lutamek, but all he could see was the mob of panicking warriors racing to get to the ships.

Those reaching them first were fighting to get in, waiting for the assigned Lutamek to open the rear doors. Lutamek voices bellowed and laser shots ricocheted as tempers rose. Meanwhile, the world was crumbling around them, great cracks opening up in the dry ground.

A boom sounded, followed by a cloud of dust that covered the ships, as Panzicosta and Gal-qadan's vessel took off, sending the nearest soldiers running for shelter.

John spotted Alpha, and they skirted the nearest ships where Lavalle and Euryleia were coaxing their tocka on-board. John's lungs burned as he jogged, but he kept going, past a host of Korax climbing aboard another ship, one that he hoped Yammit had made it to okay.

'Alpha!' Crossley shouted but the robot didn't turn.

John and Crossley stumbled as another tremor shook the ground. The earthquakes were coming faster now and John didn't want to look back to see what was happening to the tower. Alpha was standing at an open panel by the back door of a ship, staring at the buttons and screen. As they reached it and caught their breath, they were joined by Samas, Rar-kin and a number of other stragglers.

'Come on!' Crossley shouted between breaths. 'Get it open.'

'Maybe it doesn't know how?' Samas asked as Alpha remained motionless.

'I know how,' a rasping half-robot voice came from Alpha. 'I'm not sure why.'

'Why?' Crossley shouted. 'To get us off this bloody death trap, that's why!'

'Just open it,' Samas ordered. 'We must get airborne immediately!'

John looked back at the tower. Mata was fighting the host of Platae while the remaining two Tathon leaders continued their attack on the tower, which was lined with more cracks. Giant shards of glass were fracturing and some had fallen inside, smashing on the giant obelisk, whose tip John could see through the gaps. At the tower's base, large cracks snaked through the bedrock away from the tower, swallowing soldiers and buildings.

'We have to ascend!' John shouted.

'I don't think it was meant as—' Crossley started.

'Yes,' Alpha said and twitched into action. 'Ascension. Rise above. An individual now. Chart our own course.'

'What did those guys do to him?' Crossley whispered.

'Advancement,' Alpha replied as the door swished open. 'Isao, the human, opened my mind to possibilities. Free thought.'

'That's great,' Crossley said and patted the Lutamek on the arm as he rushed into the starship.

John let Alpha in and was followed by a long line of impatient soldiers.

'It's the same as our ship,' John said as he walked down the white-walled corridor, remembering the chilling moment he'd found his own stasis pod.

'But built for bigger aliens,' Crossley shouted back.

John nodded, staring at the larger pods, as Samas pushed past, straight for Alpha.

'Can you get this ship flying?' he asked.

'Yes,' Alpha replied. 'We must leave now.'

'If we leave now we have a 40 per cent chance of survival,' Rar-kin said.

'As opposed to what exactly?' Crossley asked.

'Zero,' Rar-kin replied calmly and climbed into a pod.

'Well I'm not getting back into one of those things, whatever the odds,' Crossley said.

A swishing and clicking sound made John turn, followed by banging on the rear door.

'We have reached capacity,' Alpha said, stepping onto a platform that had lowered in the centre of the chamber. 'Now we shall lift off. Current gravity maintained.'

John watched the robot link its arms into a console. A series of large white rectangles flickered into life on the wall, each one snapping to what John presumed was a view of outside. The other ships were launching, some with scores of soldiers scrambling onto their sides.

'But there aren't any windows,' John said, sitting down on a pod edge.

Numbers and images flashed up on the screen near Alpha, reminding John of the devices in the dome cap. Then new rectangles appeared, showing images of individual Lutamek, which John guessed were live images of the pilots inside the other ships.

'I need to know what's going on,' Samas said. 'What are they saying?'

Alpha twitched and a series of voices broke into the long metal room.

'Not all at once!' Samas shouted, covering his ears.

'Audible contact for biological species assistance,' Alpha replied.

John couldn't take his eyes off the images of the ground below, which moved away as they rose. New cracks were spreading fast from the tower, with some leading as far as the nearest domes.

'There aren't many domes at the centre of the disc,' Rar-kin said, 'which must mean–'

'Not now, Rar-kin,' Samas said. 'What about the shield in the sky?' he asked Alpha.

'Still in place,' Alpha replied. 'We are to flock and wait.'

Screens flickered in the ceiling and floor, sending a wave of vertigo through John's head and stomach. It was like the whole ship was made of glass. Beneath, the remaining ships were taking off with a characteristic dust-ring cloud, but John could see plenty of soldiers still waiting to board.

'What the hell?' Crossley shouted and pointed to where a shadow of movement rolled across the ground. 'It must be those shelled bastards.'

'Oh…' John watched in horror as the army of specks washed over a ship as it tried to take off, overwhelming it and pulling it back to the ground. An explosion blotted the ship out, and John looked up to see one of the tiny screens in front of Alpha flash and disappear. He stared outside the window at the array of domes scattered across the disc world. The nearest domes had started to subside.

'Watch the tower,' Samas said and John moved to get a better view.

They were as high as the tower now. The glass was shattering and falling, bouncing off two white bubbles, which John guessed were the Tathon leaders' shields. What about Mata? he thought. And everyone who hadn't made it to the ships? As they ascended further, John imagined the horror of what was taking place on the ground. Then, with a flash, a white halo burned around the tower base and sent concentric rings blossoming away, across the disc.

'Shield disengaged,' Alpha said as the myriad voices on the screens picked up in volume and speed.

A shudder ran through the ship and the view outside instantly switched from powder blue to pitch black as they passed through where the force field had been. John rubbed his eyes. It took him a few seconds to register the change. They were in space, surrounded by stars and the shapes of new spaceships as varied as the soldiers he'd seen on the disc.

Below, the disc was splitting into a thousand chunks as it tore itself apart.

'What the hell are we gonna do now?' Crossley murmured.

'There are approximately 3,500 space-going vessels in our visual range,' Alpha said.

'All from the disc?' Samas asked.

'No,' Alpha replied. 'Many are scanning us and the other survivor vessels.'

'Where are they from?' John asked.

'Unknown,' Alpha replied.

'Can we speak with them?' Samas asked.

'Lutamek Command are deciding,' Alpha replied.

'Screw Lutamek Command!' Crossley shouted. 'Let's get talking – find out who can help us and who the hell brought us here!'

'Lutamek protocol–'

'Fuck the protocol,' Crossley snapped back. 'You're an individual now, you said it yourself.'

Alpha turned to Crossley, then back to the screen, and said, 'Scanning for known languages.'

The whole crew stared at the myriad rectangles popping up on Alpha's window. John saw various alien races appear and vanish; some he recognised but most were bizarre creatures to him.

Then a human appeared.

'Can you hear me, over?'

Samas, Crossley and John gasped in unison.

'Delta–Six?' John said and felt a cold chill run down his back. He'd seen Delta–Six's dead body, yet here he was on the screen. The shock and jubilation mixed in John's veins, sending his heart thumping.

'Enlarge the screen!' Samas ordered and Delta–Six's face appeared life-size on the window.

'Can we talk back?' Crossley asked.

'Yes,' Alpha replied and a screen of the occupants of John's ship appeared next to Delta–Six's face.

'We can hear you, Delta–Six,' Samas said.

Delta–Six's face lit up. 'Communication established,' he replied. 'Can you confirm you are human soldiers from planet Earth?'

'Yes,' Samas replied.

'Yes!' Crossley shouted and John followed suit.

'What are you doing up here, Delta–Six?' John shouted. 'We thought you were dead.'

'I don't know any Delta–Six,' the man replied. 'Is that a ship sign? I'll have station look into it. May be historical. We're having trouble communicating with the rest of your fleet. Can you–'

'No,' John replied. '*You* are Delta–Six. From Earth. From our future.'

'I can confirm I am from Earth, but my name is Captain Dunia Toa of the Earth Ship Gilgamesh. It's paramount that I ascertain the full contingent of human soldiers in your fleet.'

John breathed in deeply and felt his good hand sweat. What on Earth was going on here?

A flash to the left made him cover his eyes and the false windows dimmed to black.

'What was that?' Samas asked.

'I am scanning the energy source,' Alpha replied. 'A new vessel has arrived.'

'I can confirm that,' Captain Dunia Toa said, who was still in audio contact, 'and it's what we feared. Put up your shields and move away as fast as you can. We will retrieve you in good time.'

'We'll do what we can,' Samas replied.

John could see the panic on the other soldiers' faces.

'We have a new incoming transmission,' Alpha said as a new black screen appeared.

John squinted as white letters appeared. They were in the same script as the writing on the obelisks, which the fungus in his brain translated into English.

Congratulations on your ascension.

'And we have images of the new ship,' Alpha added as the windows flashed back into life.

John could see the same ships as before, but a portion of space behind them had changed.

'Where is it?' Crossley asked.

The image zoomed in, dots of light streaming past, until the patch of grey gained shape to form an immense, writhing mass of metal floating in the pitch black of space.

'That's a spaceship?' John asked, freaked out by the way sections moved like snakes. 'It's huge!'

'And it's our enemy,' Captain Dunia Toa's voice returned and his face appeared onscreen again. He looked grave when he said, 'Welcome to the war.'

THE END

Extract from Origin Wars

Find out what happens next by reading this extract from
Origin Wars **(Book Three of the Origin Trilogy)**

'Draw in!' Olan ordered. 'To me.' He raised his arm. 'Circle formation. Weapons ready.'

Olan counted his troops – twenty-two in total. Similar to the number he used to command on his longboat, he thought, but it felt too few for a mission in unknown territory. He'd asked Dunia Toa for backup but the captain had just made vague promises.

'Now form two circles,' Olan said from the centre. 'Team A kneeling, team B standing behind.'

The ring of soldiers split and reformed into two new circles surrounding him.

Still no sign of movement anywhere. Wouldn't his bloody chest plate help him? Olan wondered. All this time stuck inside the bizarre thing... he'd got used to it and knew its worth but there were times when he wanted to ask for a way to surgically remove it.

'Movement at three o'clock,' Sancha said.

John Greene swivelled round, holding his sensor at arm's length, and Olan copied him.

'I'm picking up something big,' John said. 'No, wait a minute... it's hundreds of readings. Tiny. Moving fast.'

'More incoming at nine o'clock,' Sancha said.

'Keep in position!' Cheng shouted, taking Olan by surprise.

Sancha shuffled back to his original place. Some of the old hierarchy was still in place, Olan realised, but chose to ignore it. Cheng was right after all.

'John, what have we got at nine o'clock?' Olan asked.

After a pause, John replied, 'The same, coming in fast.'

'I can see them!' Yarcha said.

'And movement in the sky,' Euryleia said, pointing south above their trail of footprints.

A dark cloud was building and swarming, swaying left and right like a creature sniffing a trail. What in Odin's name was happening? Olan gripped his rifle tightly and wished he was carrying his trusty axe. They were surrounded but the last thing Olan wanted to do was to contact the ESG and ask for help. This was their test. Were they worthy?

'Er, Olan?' Crossley said.

'What now?' Olan shouted back.

'There's something happening near the Thermo-line... underground.'

Olan looked back and, although he couldn't see anything new, he felt a change in the thin air. His chest plate tingled across his skin as feelings of hunger and thirst pulled at his stomach. His heart was racing, sending fight-or-flight chemicals around his body as it reacted to what he couldn't deny: they were being hunted. Rounded up to be consumed.

But they were here on a peaceful mission, Olan reminded himself. They had come to find life and interact with it – to trade and offer the products of the Alliance's knowledge. He slowed his breathing to keep calm and followed his protocols, pressing two buttons on his suit's sleeve to emit a message in all directions.

'We are peaceful.' The message started and Olan recognised the voice. 'We, the Alliance, mean you no harm. We are strong and wish to be your allies.'

Olan turned a circle, keeping an eye on each incoming threat. To his left, he could see the ground swarm of what looked like a low red mist – the same to the right – and the cloud to the south was blocking most of the light now.

'Something's coming up!' Crossley said. 'Twenty feet to the north.'

Olan spun around to see dark cracks spreading across the white floor like anti-lightning.

'They look like ants,' Sancha said. 'Skipping over the sand.'

Olan sent a silent prayer to Thor and switched his rifle on.

'I'm scanning inside the cloud,' John said, 'and see thousands of floating creatures… like dandelion seeds.'

It was too much for Olan. He switched his external message onto direct control.

'Do you hear us?' he broadcast. 'We come in peace. We come as allies.'

The ground shook as a deep, rumbling voice replied as clear as any voice on Olan's radio.

We have no need for you here, Alliance betrayers. But we accept your gift of food.

'Prepare to fire!' Olan shouted. 'Shoot at will, shoot to kill.'

'Aye,' came several replies as lasers ripped the dry sky into hot lines, radiating out from their two circles of defence.

A second later, scores of dark shapes erupted from the ground to the north of them in a cloud of white powder, sending salt rain pelting down on Olan's soldiers.

Now, Olan realised the real reason why they, and not the robotic soldiers, had been sent here.

They were the bait.

Pledge now at https://rebrand.ly/origintrilogy
to support Origin Wars

Acknowledgements

A massive thank you to Team Darwin for having faith in me and for your great taste in books! This novel wouldn't exist without your support, which means the world to me.

The team at Unbound have been brilliant as ever and I am proud to be published by such a forward-thinking publisher, who continually punch above their weight.

Survival Machines was edited through the 2020 lockdown and, as with *Darwin's Soldiers*, Hal Duncan and Derek Collett have worked their magic once again: chiselling, sanding and varnishing the original manuscript, transforming it into a smoother, more enjoyable read.

A huge thank you to my parents, Sheryll and Malcolm, for their continued support throughout my writing career.

And to Cath, Harry and Oscar: you continue to inspire and entertain me on a daily basis, and I'm incredibly proud of you all.

Unbound is the world's first crowdfunding publisher, established in 2011.

We believe that wonderful things can happen when you clear a path for people who share a passion. That's why we've built a platform that brings together readers and authors to crowdfund books they believe in – and give fresh ideas that don't fit the traditional mould the chance they deserve.

This book is in your hands because readers made it possible. Everyone who pledged their support is listed at the front of the book and below. Join them by visiting unbound.com and supporting a book today.

David Allington
Eli Allison
Ian Baker
Stephanie Bretherton
Victoria Chaplin
Mark Ciccone
Jason Cobley
Steve Davis
Simon Deacon
Ian Farrell

Adam Ferjani
Steve Fraser
G.E. Gallas
Faye Goodey
Steve Harris
Maximilian Hawker
Michael Hoey
Vicki Holland
Alex Ince
Richard Irving

Oli Jacobs
Mike James
Dan Kieran
Vaughan Knight
Claire Longhurst
Wayne Longhurst
Gary Mack
Marnie & Phill
John (the loon) Mason
Alice McVeigh
John Mitchinson
Rhel ná DecVandé
Carlo Navato
Sonya O'Reilly
Val Oakes
Ian Orchard
Luke Perry
Justin Pollard

Alvin Rindlisbacher
Michael J. Ritchie
Steve Routledge
Malcolm Sharp
Sandy Slade
Gary Smith
Jacob Smith
Paul Swales
Richard Taylor
Chris Tollworthy
Valerie Wallis
Julie Warren
John Wedge
Paul Weekes
Suzie Wilde
Lee Wilson
Amanda Witham